LORD OF THE ISLES

'So – you were right in this also!' Cathula commented. 'You must have a Norse mind, I think, to so well judge what they will do. I shall be warned!'

'I misjudged Ivar Blacktooth. And would be a dead man now, but for you, Cathula Maclan.' Somerland answered, deep-voiced. 'I thank you.'

'It was but one debt paid' she said, levelly.

'Nevertheless *my* debt is the greater – for my life. I shall not forget.'

'Others have paid more.'

'Aye – but that is war. We have suffered but lightly, however. Less than I had looked for, thank God. The enemy likewise, indeed. For they are defeated and gone but have left only small numbers of dead and dying behind. Cheap victory, cheap defeat. And what have we gained? Moidart largely cleared – like North Mull. The threat to Morven lifted. Six more longships. Much booty and gear. And best of all, repute. Repute for defeating Norsemen. Repute to rouse the spirit of our own down-trodden folk on all this seaboard, in all Argyll and Lochaber. That is what I seek – that *I* shall not have to do all the work of clearing and cleansing this land of the invader.'

'The Vikings will not always tamely dance to your fiddle, Lord Sorley,' she said. 'They will gather their wits and their hardihood and strike back. You cannot win always by guile and trickery.'

'I know it. But I have made a start, see you . . .'

Also by the same author,
and available in Coronet Books:

Lord of the Isles

Nigel Tranter

CORONET BOOKS
Hodder and Stoughton

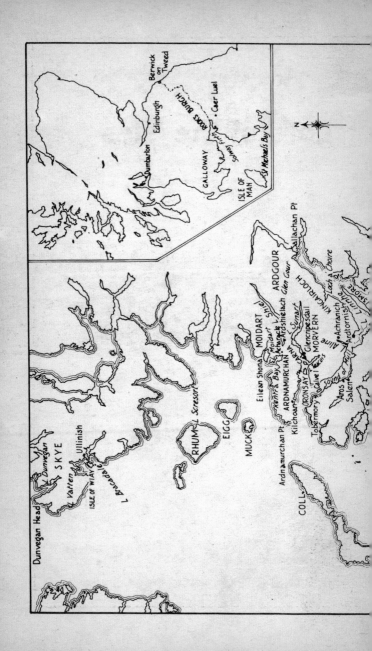

Berwick on Tweed
Edinburgh
Dumbarton
ROCKS BURGH
Caer Luel
GALLOWAY
Solway Firth
St Michael's Bay
ISLE OF MAN

N

Dunvegan Head
Dunvegan
SKYE
L Vatten
Ullinish
ISLE OF WIAY
L Bracadale
L Scresort
RHUM
EIGG
MUCK

Eilean Shona
Kentra Bay
Moidart L
MOIDART
Shiel
ARDNAMURCHAN
Ardshielach
Glen Gour
ARDGOUR
Loch à Choire
Callachan Pt
KINGAIRLOCH
Kilchoan
Ardnamurchan Pt
CRONSAY
Glencripesdail
Clive Kens
Tobermory
Sound of Mull
Achranich
Ardtornish
Salen
Aros
Aline
MORVERN
L LINNHE
SHORE
Sunart

COLL

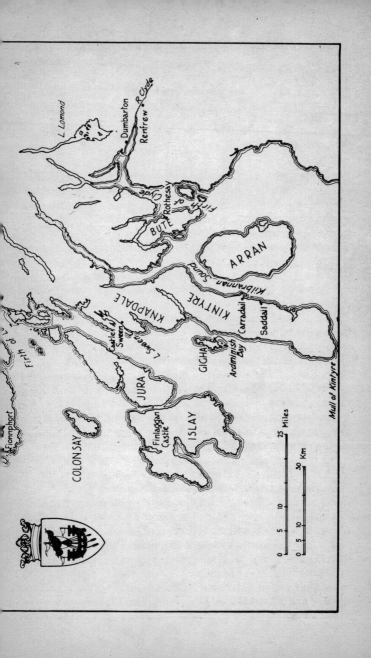

Principal Characters

In Order of Appearance

SOMERLED MAC GILLEBRIDE MACFERGUS: Son of the exiled Thane of Argyll.

CONN IRONHAND MACMAHON: Irish gallowglass captain and shipmaster.

SAOR MACNEIL: Foster-brother of Somerled.

DERMOT FLATNOSE MAGUIRE: Irish gallowglass captain and shipmaster.

CATHULA MACIAN: Young Morvern woman of spirit.

MACIAN OF ULADAIL: Morvern chieftain, half-brother of Cathula.

GILLEBRIDE MACFERGUS: Thane of Argyll.

MALCOLM MACETH, EARL OF ROSS: Brother-in-law to Somerled.

THORKELL FORKBEARD SVENSSON: Viking leader.

EWAN MACSWEEN: Titular King of Argyll and the Isles.

SIR MALCOLM MACGREGOR OF GLENORCHY: Chief of that clan.

FARQUHAR MACFERDOCH: Hereditary Abbot of Glendochart.

HERVEY DE WARENNE OF KEITH: Knight Marischal of Scotland.

DAVID THE FIRST: King of Scots, son of Malcolm Canmore and Margaret.

HUGO DE MORVILLE: High Constable of Scotland.

WALTER FITZ ALAN: High Steward of Scotland.

RAGNHILDE OLAFSDOTTER: Princess, daughter of the King of Man.

AFFRICA, QUEEN OF MAN: Daughter of Fergus of Galloway.

OLAF GODFREYSSON, THE MORSEL: King of Man.

MALACHY O'MOORE: Bishop of Armagh and Papal Legate.

WIMUND: Bishop of Man.

FERGUS, EARL OF GALLOWAY: Great noble.

ELIZABETH, COUNTESS OF ROSS: Somerled's sister.

GILLECOLM MAC SOMERLED MACFERGUS: Son of Somerled.
DONALD MACETH: Nephew of Somerled, later Earl of Moray.
ARCHBISHOP THURSTAN OF YORK: English prelate.
RAOUL D'AVRANCHES: Bishop of Durham.
THORFINN OTTARSSON: Manx chieftain.
DOUGAL MAC SOMERLED MACFERGUS: Somerled's second son. Ancestor of Clan MacDougall.
AUGUSTINE: Abbot of Iona.

Copyright © 1983 by Nigel Tranter

First published in Great Britain 1983 by
Hodder and Stoughton Ltd

Coronet edition 1985

British Library C.I.P.

Tranter, Nigel
    Lord of the Isles.
    I. Title
    823'.912[F]   PR6070.R34

    ISBN 0–340–36836–5

Printed and bound in Great Britain for
Hodder and Stoughton Paperbacks, a
division of Hodder and Stoughton Ltd.,
Mill Road, Dunton Green, Sevenoaks,
Kent (Editorial Office: 47 Bedford
Square, London, WC1 3DP) by
Cox & Wyman Ltd., Reading

PART ONE

CHAPTER 1

It made a peaceful scene in the warm May afternoon. The sea, in the wide loch-mouth, was almost mirror-calm so that the slap-slap of the wavelets against the longship's timbers was so gentle that it did not drown out the sleepy crooning of the eiders from the skerries. Even the haunting calling of the cuckoos drifted across the quarter-mile of blue-green water which separated them from the nearest island. Only the rhythmic snoring of one of the oarsmen, sprawled over his sweep, disturbed—that and the stench of sweat from near one-hundred male torsoes after long and strenuous exertion.

The young man who sat alone on the high prow-platform beneath the fierce dragon-head, chin on fist, elbow on bent bare knee, may have appeared to be in somnolent tune with it all, but was not. His mind was busy assessing, calculating, seeking to judge chances and distances, times and numbers, and probable odds; and every now and again his keen glance lifted to scan the long fretted coastline of Ardnamurchan to north and west, its features and contours, and then to swing still further westwards across the glittering waters of the Hebridean Sea, empty of sail if not of isle and skerry—and pray it to continue empty meantime. If all the beauty of that colourful seascape was scarcely in the front of his mind, it was not wholly lost on him, despite presently being impervious to the peace of it all.

For that matter there was little enough that spoke of peace about that ship, from the rearing red-painted dragon-prow and shield-hung sides, to the stacked arms at the high stern-platform, with swords, throwing-spears and battle-axes at the ready. Nor were the men pacific in appearance, any of them, most naked to the waist, in ragged saffron kilts, with shaggy hair and thin down-turning, long moustaches, Irish gallowglasses almost to a man. Few would look for peace and quiet from that crew.

11

The young man in the bows, so thoughtful, was distinct in almost every respect. He was fair-haired, for one thing, where the others were dark, hint of the Norse in his ancestry. He was clean-shaven, and though strong enough as to feature, it was a sculptured strength which spoke of a very different breeding. He wore the saffron kilt also but of finer quality, with a silken shirt reasonably clean and a long calf-skin waistcoat on which were sewn small metal scales to form a protective half-armour, pliable and light but effective. His great bulls'-horned helmet, silver-chased, the curling horns tipped with gold, lay on the deck at his side and the shoulder sword-belt gleamed golden also. Somerled MacGillebride MacGilladamnan MacFergus looked what he was, a Celtic princeling of part-Norse extraction. It was perhaps aptly amusing that his father, the exiled Thane Gillebride, should have given him, at his Norse mother's behest, the Christian name of Somerled, which in her tongue meant the peaceful-sounding Summer Voyager

He turned his speculative attention to the two smallish islands so close together on the south, off which they lay, in the very jaws of the long and fair sea-loch of Sunart. The islands, a bare half-mile apart, were extraordinarily dissimilar to be so close, the seaward one, Oronsay, jagged, rocky, strangely M-shaped, cleft into many small headlands yet nowhere much higher than one-hundred feet above the waves; whilst its neighbour, Carna, was smooth and green and lofty, no more than a mile-long grassy whaleback rising to a peaked central ridge five times as high as Oronsay. It was the former which held the man's attention.

A shout from the stern turned all waking heads towards where the helmsman, Big Conn of the Ironhand, pointed away north-westwards towards the far Ardnamurchan shore beyond the point of Ardslignish. At first it was difficult to distinguish anything in the hazy sunlight other than the frowning cliffs, ironbound shore and shadow-slashed corries of Beinn Hiant. But after a moment or two the keen-eyed were able to discern what appeared to be a small low white cloud, down at sea-level, a moving cloud which seemed to roll over the face of the water towards them. Presently to even the untutored eye it became apparent that most of the cloud was in fact spray, but rising out of it was a single square sail.

Until it was within half-a-mile or so, the hull of the oncoming craft could only be glimpsed occasionally amidst the spume set up by the double banks of long oars on each side, forty-eight all told, which lashed the sea in a disciplined frenzy, each pulled by two men, and with the sail's aid drove the slender, low-set galley at a scarcely believable speed in calm conditions. Evolved out of the Viking long-ship and the Celtic birlinn, the Hebridean galley represented by far the fastest craft on any water, greyhound of the seas indeed—although some would call them wolves, rather. They held their own grace, even beauty, but few saw them as beautiful.

The newcomer swept up in fine style, scarcely slackening speed until almost alongside and then pulling up in a few lengths with back-watering sweeps in masterly precision and timing, great sail crashing down at the exact moment and the helmsman bearing on his long steering-oar to swing the craft round on to the other stationary ship only a few yards from its prow, all in a flourish of dramatic seamanship. Saor Sleat MacNeil was like that.

A shout, part bark, part crow, part laugh, spanned the water-gap. "No shipping, no Norsemen, Somerled! Only a few fishing-cobles at Mingary and Kilchoan. And some dotards and old wives. We have it all to ourselves, man."

The fair-headed young man had risen. "That is well," he called back. "But why, then, half-slay your crew? In your return? I need these men for better work than as playthings for your vanity, Saor MacNeil! Mind it!"

"Yes, lord," the other acknowledged, grinning.

"Take heed, Saor—or you will find it difficult to laugh, hereafter! Even you." That was quietly said but with a sibilant hiss in the Highland voice.

Considering those actual few words, the impact of them was rather extraordinary, quite transforming the scene. Where all had been relaxed, all but somnolent, in tune with the warm May afternoon, abruptly in those ships there was a tension. Men sat upright on the rowing-benches. Saor MacNeil himself stood stiff, grin gone. The quiet sounds of lapping water and crooning eiders seemed suddenly

13

loud. Somerled MacGillebride MacGilladmnan MacFergus, roused, could frighten other men strangely, possessed of a violent shattering force supremely at odds with both his years and normal pleasing appearance and habit. That none knew just what could be expected to rouse him, was part of the difficulty.

For long moments this pause lasted. Then Somerled jerked a beckoning hand. "Come you aboard," he commanded, but mildly enough now.

Saor MacNeil wasted no time. He flung an order to his oarsmen on the starboard side, who dipped in their sweeps in a single controlled motion which slewed the galley's fierce prow round to leeward through a ninety-degree arc, to close the gap with the other vessel, whilst he himself leapt down from the stern-platform, ran lightly along the narrow gangway between the two sets of rowing-benches, sprang up onto the bow-platform and so was in position to jump the yard or two of space as the two prows came together, an agile, exactly-timed performance, like so much of what that man essayed—for he liked to impress.

Somerled smiled, less than impressed. And as the dark man leapt, so, as exactly timed, the fair man's fist flashed out, to take the leaper on the shoulder and spin him round and backwards. Balance gone, agile precision likewise, arms waving wildly, MacNeil toppled and fell, outboard. He hit the water with a splash and shouted curse.

A howl of mirth rose from the packed benches on both craft.

Stooping unhurriedly, Somerled picked up a rope and tossed it over to the flailing swimmer, to draw him up and aid his streaming person back and over the side. Then, as MacNeil panted and glared and spewed out salt water, the other clapped him on the wet shoulder with a blow which almost felled him, and burst into a shout of laughter.

"Ardour cooled?" he demanded.

For a second or two the dark man's eyes flashed dangerously; but meeting the amused but cool and piercing gaze of the other, he swallowed and shrugged and the grin reappeared in some fashion on his dripping, trim-bearded features. After all, Somerled was his foster-brother.

"Yes, lord," he said again, but in a different tone from last time.

"Yes, then—so be it." The Lord Somerled waved forward two others to the prow-platform, Conn Ironhand MacMahon, the steersman, and Dermot Flatnose Maguire, captain of gallowglasses, both Irishmen from Fermanagh, as were all save the pair already forward. When these came up, he at once reverted to the quietly businesslike, turning to face the south and the islands. He pointed. "This is the back-door to Morvern. Our rear, we hear, is safe from Ardnamurchan meantime. And we are hidden from Mull. No sail is in sight. God willing, this will serve. We beach the galleys behind this Oronsay, eat, and then march. March by night."

"March?" Dermot Flatnose said. "My lads are seamen, see you—not bog-trotters!" He spoke with the Erse brogue, so different from the lilting soft Hebridean tongue of Somerled which was so genial and so deceptive.

"They will march, nevertheless, my friend—march far and fast. And as like as not fight at the end of it. Or I will know the reason why!"

Maguire held his tongue.

"There may be as many as ten miles to cover, at a guess. I have not been here since I was a lad, mind. Up yonder glen, by Loch Teacuis and through the hills beyond to the Aline River, then down to Kinlochaline. The clachan there is where we make for, the principal place of this Morvern, where my father used to have a house. And where the Norse are like to be. For whosoever holds Loch Aline, if they have ships, holds the Sound of Mull and the key to the Firth of Lorn."

"Why march by night, lord?" Conn Ironhand asked. "If the men must march and fight, will they not be fighting better rested and in God's good daylight?"

"Perhaps. But the only way we may succeed here is by surprise. We have less than two hundred men, leaving some few with the ships. Even if they are all heroes, two hundred will not take Morvern from a thousand Vikings and more. There must be no warning. The local folk, these MacInneses, are much cowed, we know, lack spirit after all these years under the Norsemen's heavy hand. We cannot rely on them for help. And some might even warn of our presence in their hills. We march by night."

"The gallowglasses will not like it."

"I do not ask them to like it—only to march."

Saor MacNeil hooted. "And Mary Mother of God help them!" he said. He had stripped off his hide jerkin, ragged shirt and kilt and was wringing them out, standing naked and by no means ashamed or hiding himself.

The two Irishmen exchanged glances.

"See you to it, then," Somerled told them. "We row in behind this Oronsay. The passage is narrow and opens only towards the west. At the east it shallows and dries out at low-water. In there is a creek where we hide the galleys. Back to your ship, Saor, and follow me in. To your helm, Conn."

Gathering up his clothes in his arms and laughing, MacNeil the exhibitionist beckoned his own galley's bows closer and, naked as he was, leapt the gap once more, already shouting orders to his crew, who commented in frankest fashion. Somerled, watching, smiled. He was fond of that odd character, but well recognised the need to keep him in some control.

Quickly the two galleys were on the move again, wheeling about, first westwards then south round that promontory of Oronsay and in eastwards thereafter between the island and the mainland of Morvern by a channel little more than two hundred yards wide, and shallow—but not too much so for the shallow-draught galleys, provided that they kept to the centre, although they could see the waving weeds of the rocky bottom in the clear water below them. It was half-tide. Half-a-mile of narrows and the channel widened out to an almost landlocked lagoon a mile long and half that in width. The south or Morvern shore was open woodland sloping upwards; but to the north Oronsay itself was cut up here, like the rest, with narrow probing inlets. Into the central of these Somerled manoeuvred his galley, and cautiously, for there was barely space for the long oars to work, to beach his craft almost half-a-mile deep into the rocky isle, MacNeil close behind. A more secret and secure hidingplace would have been hard to find on all the intricate thousand-mile coastline of Argyll—but no place to get out of in a hurry.

"A death-trap!" Conn MacMahon called, critically, and a growl of assent rose from the rowing-benches.

"Just that," Somerled agreed. "If we are for dying, hereafter, as well here as anywhere! But matters will be in a bad way, whatever, if we need to fight our way out of here."

Unconvinced to say the least, the galley crews shipped their oars, gathered their gear and arms and made their way ashore.

There was wood about the place, a little scrub-oak and birch, also dry driftwood above the tidemark, and the Irish were for lighting fires and boiling a porridge of oats and roasting the venison, brought from the Isle of Rhum where they had left Thane Gillebride, Somerled's father, and the other half of the expedition. But Somerled would not allow it, however welcome would have been a cooked meal as against raw venison or old smoked beef and oatmeal mixed with cold water, shipboard diet. He had not gone to all this trouble to hide their arrival in Morvern, to give their presence away by the smoke of camp-fires. But, since they had time enough, and it was necessary to keep these Irishry in as good a temper as was possible, he offered them a diversion. No doubt they all had seen a number of wild-goats on the small cliffs of Oronsay, as they waited? Those who felt so inclined could go goat-hunting for an hour or two and stretch their legs after the constriction of the galleys—provided always that they kept to the north side of the island where they would not be seen from the mainland. Not that Morvern was populous—indeed it was the least populated area of all Argyll and this north-western corner in especial had always been empty, but there could be cattle-herders out at the start of the summer shieling season or egg-gatherers on the mainland cliffs. Young goat's flesh was sweet enough; and the warm fresh blood mixed with the oatmeal was better than water. Some small sport would do no harm.

So they awaited the evening. Somerled did not announce to the gallowglasses just how far they had to march. He was only too well aware of the problems of his situation, as to men as well as to task. These Irishmen were not his own, nor even his father's, only lent to them by the MacMahon, chief of Clann Cholla, at the behest of the High King of

Ireland—approximately four hundred men and four galleys. MacMahon was Somerled's father-in-law and it was probably as much for his late daughter's sake as in sympathy with the former Thane of Argyll that he agreed to provide these gallowglasses for an attempt to win back at least some part of Gillebride's lordship, wrested from him more than a dozen years before by the all-conquering Norsemen, who now controlled all the Hebrides as well as much of the West Highland mainland of Scotland as they did Man, Dublin and some of the east of Ireland. It was all Somerled's idea and project, his father less than hopeful—but then, the Lord Gillebride had never been an optimist and having waited a dozen years was quite prepared to wait longer. After sailing from Donegal Bay they had voyaged to the little-inhabited Isle of Rhum in the Inner Hebrides, where Somerled had left his father, unenthusiastic, with half the force, to make an attempt on the islands of Tiree, Islay and Jura, whilst the son essayed this hardly hopeful assault on mainland Morvern with his handful of doubtful Ulstermen, bonny fighters no doubt but here lacking involvement and conviction. He was going to require all his powers of leadership and control.

In due course the hunters straggled back, with three goats, none of them young and tender but made much of as symbols of prowess. Thereafter, Somerled informed all that they were going walking and by night, for their own safety. They would move as soon as the dusk came down.

There were grumblings and questionings but nothing sufficiently serious for drastic measures.

An hour after sundown they started off, leaving a dozen of the older men with the galleys, enough to get them afloat again at high-water if absolutely necessary. It was low-water now and they were able to cross to the mainland on wet sand and shingle at the east end of the island—Oronsay meaning half-tide island—and thereafter to turn away south-eastwards into the shadowy hills.

For the first four miles or so their route followed the boggy south shore of Loch Teacuis, a long and narrow arm of the sea, its mouth all but stoppered by the lumpish Isle of Carna. The gallowglasses were scarcely nimble walkers and it took two hours to get that far, with resentment beginning to become all too vocal. Somerled coaxed and jollied them on for another mile or more, then recognised that something more was required if he was to get his company the remaining four or five miles to Kinlochaline. There were many complainers, but one in especial, a heavy-built surly oaf whom his companions called Cathal Frog, was loudest, announcing that he was an oarsman and sword-fighter not a landloper or a night-prowler, and he had blisters on his feet. With others making a chorus of it, Somerled called a halt, but quite genially, and strolled back to the chief vocalist.

"Your feet, friend, pain you—as your voice pains me!" he said. "Let me see them."

"Eh . . .?" Cathal Frog blinked.

"These feet, man. That pain you. Show me."

The man drew back, doubtfully.

"Saor—I wish to consider these painful feet. See to it."

Grinning, MacNeil acted swiftly. He slipped behind Cathal Frog, flung an arm around his neck and with an expert explosion of strength heaved him backwards off his feet. As the man sprawled, Somerled stepped forward, stooped and jerked off first one filthy rawhide brogan, then the other, and tossed them to Conn MacMahon, then grabbed up both ankles high so that the gallowglass, for all his burly weight, hung like a sagging hammock between the two Scots. "So—feet of a sort, yes! Faugh—how they stink!" He peered close, in the half-light. "I see corns, the dirt of ages, scabs—but no blisters. Still, far be it from me to disbelieve an honest man. This sufferer shall ride. Lest he should hold up men with better feet. Saor—on my back with him. Up, I say!" And he dropped the legs and turned round, arms wide.

MacNeil promptly hoisted the protesting man to his feet, stamped on the bare toes by way of warning, and heaved. Somehow he got him on to the other's back, and Somerled reached round to grasp the legs firmly, and then started forward.

"Come!" he shouted, into the noisy laughter of the company. "Now we shall make the better time."

Cathal Frog struggled, of course, causing his lordly bearer to stagger. But the grip on him was strong. Moreover, Saor MacNeil's drawn dirk was a potent reminder of realities.

The march resumed.

Cathal Frog clearly was at a loss, however much of a fool he felt. He probably could have freed himself, at the cost perhaps of a few pricks of that dirk-point. But without his brogans he would have been able only to hobble along feebly, and look as ridiculous as he did now. And he was well aware of his companions' change of attitude, all suffering from a warped sense of humour.

Somerled kept it up for the best part of a mile, despite the rough going and poor light, before, breathing heavily and stumbling frequently, he set his burden down.

"I swear your feet are better than mine, now!" he asserted. "Soon you will have to be carrying *me*, Cathal man! Conn—give him his brogans."

After that, and the cheers of the gallowglasses, he had no more trouble with reluctant marchers.

There were two more lochs after Teacuis, one small, one larger, and then a short and winding little pass, not high, before the main central north-south glen of Morvern was reached, that of the Aline River, more than half-way down. Here they had to go more cautiously, for little-populated as this Morvern was, it was in this valley and along the southern shore that most of the folk lived. Indeed, within a mile or so of their entry was the main village of the great peninsula, the clachan of Aline—which they must avoid. The folk would probably be friendly enough, for they were Somerled's father's own people; but they would be terrified of the occupying and all-conquering Norsemen, and not without cause. The word was that the Vikings themselves did not use the village, save for the supply of women and food, preferring, as always, to remain close to their longships, at Kinlochaline, the head of the three-miles-long sea-loch. Norsemen were never happy far from their piratical ships.

It was not difficult to skirt the clachan, for most of it was on the other side of the river. Dogs scenting them and barking were a risk, but in the prevailing circumstances, nobody was likely to come to investigate, in the middle of the night, what could well be a prowling Viking. Nevertheless, Somerled took a route which contoured amongst wooded slopes fairly high, the gut of the valley a well of shadow beneath.

There was a narrow throat or wooded defile of over a

mile between clachan and loch-head and it was possible that the Norsemen might have a watching-guard therein. So, awkward as it was, they still kept to the steep high ground, amongst fallen pines and outcropping rock—although keeping quiet the progress of two hundred men on such terrain was not easy. Whether there were sentries below they had no means of telling, but they gained no impression of alarm roused.

At length they could sense rather than perceive the wide opening of Loch Aline. Somerled called a welcome halt whilst he considered the situation. It was all guesswork, to be sure—but informed guesswork. Part-Norse himself, he knew how Norsemen thought, acted and reacted. Kinlochaline, down there, all agreed was their headquarters for Morvern, central, and enabling them to dominate the important Sound of Mull, key to the Inner Isles, and much of the Firth of Lorn also. They might be away, of course, hosting—or some of them; but not all, for a presence here would remain. If he could destroy that presence, it would be a major step in his purpose.

How to find them in this light, or lack of it? No fires or even embers glowed. Almost certainly they would be near the loch-head, where their longships could be beached most effectively with the tides. Which side of the river? The far side, probably, the same as the clachan for convenience, there being no bridges. He would require to ford the river, therefore.

The main question was—to wait for daylight to discover the Norse position, or to risk going down now and trying to find it in the dark? There were probably more than two hours left before dawn. Was there any alternative to these courses? It was many years since he had been here, as a boy, years of exile, but he thought that he could recollect two or three huts, salmon-fishermen's huts, where the river entered the loch and their nets could trap the fish at their runs up and down. If these were still there, the fishermen might tell where the Vikings were.

He decided to chance it. He ordered a silent descent of the hill.

Silence was only approximate, but they reached the river at length where it began to shallow to salt-water. There they picked their way across without too much difficulty, if with muttered cursing at the slippery stones underfoot and the chill of the water. Leaving the company there in Saor MacNeil's charge, Somerled went onward, southwards, alone, following the river-bank, carefully.

It was further to the estuary than he had calculated. Then he stumbled over the stakes of salmon-nets, stubbing his toes. These stakes were not old, with netting still attached; so at least it looked as though the fishermen were still active. He came to the first hut soon thereafter, but found it broken down and abandoned. There was another, however, close enough for him to hear a dog growling. He decided that it would be wiser not to creep and crawl. He made for the sound, walking normally—but he drew his dirk.

At the black gape of an open doorway where a rough, old blanket hung, with the growling rising menacingly, he thumped on the hut timbers.

"God save all here," he called, quite strongly. "A friend calls—no Norseman. A friend, I say."

There was a pause and then some whispering. A distinctly hesitant voice spoke. "What friend? At this hour? Who speaks?"

"A friend in your need perhaps. Quieten your dog."

The authority in that command may have had its effect, for another voice spoke, and the dog sank its rumbling a little. "What do you want?" this other said.

"I mislike Norsemen and would know where they are, friend."

"You will have no difficulty in finding Norsemen, to my sorrow! They are everywhere."

"Yet—you sell them your salmon?"

"They *take* our salmon, God's curse on them!"

"Good! Then you will help me teach them to pay! Where are they, these robbers of honest Scots? The nearest?"

"Who are you, who comes in the night?"

"My name is Somerled. Somerled MacGillebride MacGilladamnan MacFergus. Is that sufficient for you?"

"MacGillebride? And MacFergus? Not, not . . .?"

"But, yes. Son of Gillebride himself, rightful lord here. Rightful lord of all Argyll."

There was silence then as his unseen hearers, simple men,

digested that. Then two of them materialised out of the gloom.

"Where, then?" Somerled insisted.

"Not far, lord," the more vocal of the pair said. "A half-mile, no more. There is a lesser river comes in from the east—the Ranich. A bit of a bay is formed. They are there, at Achranich."

"This side of the river, or that?"

"The far side, lord. But it is not deep. What do you intend?"

"Slaughter!" he answered simply.

"Ha! You, you have men?"

"Some two hundred. Enough? How many of the Norse?"

"Twice that. Or there were. They come and go."

"Fair enough odds, given surprise. Will you guide us?"

"Surely. When?"

"Now. Before daylight. Or when I have fetched my people. Wait for me."

Somerled hastened back, to bring his company along, the Irish all eagerness now that they scented action. The fishermen were ready, elderly men, their lurcher dog tied up. They carried their clubs for stunning the salmon—which was encouraging.

Skirting the mud, shingle and seaweed of the loch-head strand, they moved round to the eastern shore. Presently they came to the second river-mouth, smaller but productive of a little bay at an angle to the loch, hidden. And therein they could just make out the dark shapes of the beached longships, four or five of them so far as they could discern.

"Are these guarded? And where is their camp?" Somerled asked.

"They encamp just across the river. Beyond the trees—you can just see the trees, there. As to the ships, I know not."

The other fisherman spoke. "I cannot think that they will guard their ships. Not now. They are so sure of themselves, Satan burn them! Men may sleep aboard them . . ."

"Aye. Then we shall make them the less sure! Conn—take forty men. Half-a-dozen to each ship. Each with flint and tinder. I want those vessels ablaze. Even if it is only their upper works. Nothing will so upset Vikings as to see their

23

longships in trouble! But—give us time to surround their camp. If you are caught, and have to fight, see that some light the fires, any sort of fires. At all costs. You have it?"

"Aye, lord. How shall we know when you are ready?"

"A small fire of our own. Our friend here says that there is woodland. A few sticks and dead brackens. When you see it. But, Conn—*your* fires. Not too fierce, see you—unless you must. For we could use those longships. Gear, shrouds, cordage—anything which will burn . . ."

They parted company and the fishermen led the main party down to the river, to wade across near the mouth. Oddly enough, although smaller and narrower than the Aline, the Ranich was deeper here, though still it did not come above men's waists. Beyond, they were quickly into scattered oak-scrub woodland, on rising ground.

"Their camp is on a flat just after the last trees," their guide informed.

"Hutments, or in the open?"

"They sleep under spread sails, spare sails. On posts."

"And guards here?"

"I know not. We keep our distance. But . . . there will be women, from the clachan."

"Aye—always that! Well, then—here it is. We surround the camp. When I wheeple like a curlew, we move in slowly, all together. If we are discovered, we rush in. I see no possibility of stratagems. And no quarter! *They* offer none. Donal, and you, Cathal Frog—see you to a signal-fire for Conn. When I wheeple. You all have it?"

Swords and dirks were being drawn now. No questions were asked.

Saor MacNeil took half of the remaining one-hundred-and-fifty or so, to work around to the far side of the unseen encampment, with one fisherman, whilst Somerled marshalled the rest into a semi-circle. They had no need to insist on the necessary silence now.

Somerled was wondering whether the others would be in position and awaiting his signal, when a scarlet gout of flame shot into the air behind them, casting an eerie, flickering glow. He cursed. That only could be one of the longships, tarred cordage and sail-cloth no doubt, fired prematurely, possibly the attackers discovered. There were

24

cries, shouts, thin but clear on the still night. Unless these Norsemen were all heavy sleepers indeed, some must hear that.

He whistled, high and trilling, the yittering call of the curlew, thrice repeated. Then he waved on the men flanking him, right and left, to set the curving line in motion—although already some were creeping forward.

It made a strange, grim advance, silent, menacing, if less even and regular than the leaders would have wished. They did not see their target at first, for the night is darker before the dawn and there were whin-bushes and small birch here and there to confuse in the half-light. In fact, they heard the Norsemen before they saw their camp—and realised that they were not quite on the right line. Somerled tried to swing his wavering crescent further to the right.

The noise was of individual cries at first, merging into a confusion of shouting. It was hard to tell how far ahead, anything from two to four hundred yards perhaps. Somerled frowned—surprise was going to be no more than partial, it seemed. Time to hasten, to run. He raised his short stabbing-sword high and broke into a trot.

They saw the first figures now—and it was the growing conflagration behind at the ships which highlighted them in a ruddy glow. Possibly the same glow would outline themselves, the attackers?

At the sight of actual men, enemies, stumbling out from the shadows of what were presumably the sail-cloth awnings, the gallowglasses threw discipline and silence to the winds, Somerled's control abandoned. Dashing, leaping, yelling fiercely, they surged forward, weapons gleaming evilly in the firelight.

As an assault what followed was a shambles in every sense. Somerled had said that he saw little opportunity for stratagem; but he had scarcely visualised such chaos, blind fury and ungovernable savagery. There was no order, no method, nothing but blood-lust let loose—and certainly no mercy. Somerled was scarcely proud of this first blow struck for his inheritance—although he had little time to dwell on the matter.

Yet it was successful enough, if success was to be assessed in dead men. The Norse were amongst the fiercest fighters in the world, but here they had no least chance. Surprised, drugged with sleep and probably drink, they were able to put up no coherent defence, little defence of any sort. Individuals died fighting, but mainly with their bare hands, for few could reach their weapons. Those who got outside the shelters were overwhelmed in the rush, some pushed back inside, no doubt for swords and battle-axes and clubs, thereby cannoning into others seeking to get out and causing hopeless confusion in confined space, struggling bodies jammed close. Many smiting, stabbing Irishmen followed them in, of course to little purpose, for inside they were as tight-wedged and constricted as their would-be victims, sword-arms as though pinioned in the crush. The screams and shrieks, the thud of blows, the smell of blood and ordure, all in the flickering red glare of the flaming ships, made a fair representation of hell.

Somerled, seeking to exert some influence, direction and leadership over the appalling situation, tripped over a tie-rope supporting the upright poles on which the great sails were suspended—and perceived the opportunity. Slashing down with his sword, he hacked until the cordage was severed.

"The ropes!" he shouted. "Cut the ropes. Bring all down. The ropes, I say!"

Some heard his call and saw the point. They started slashing, with him. In only a few moments the poles were reeling, the sail-cloth sagging, and down came the first shelter atop all within, Norsemen and attackers alike. The outcry from beneath was beyond all description.

The rope-cutters ran to the next one. There proved to be five of these awnings and they brought them all down. Saor MacNeil's party had now come up with them and, coming later, were less crazed with excitement and the more amenable. Somerled ordered them to ring round each of the collapsed and heaving shelters, to deal with the Norsemen as they struggled out—and warning them that there were many of their own companions in there also.

So the real slaughter began. It was no battle, nothing but a massacre. After the first wild onslaught, indeed it became a wearisome killing—for hundreds of men take a considerable time to slay, when they are emerging in ones and twos under collapsed sail-cloth. It is to be feared that more than one of the Irish died also, not within the canvas or at Norse hands but as they too struggled out, assailed by their own over-enthusiastic fellows before they could identify themselves. One woman also was killed and another injured—for it was difficult in the half-light to distinguish between long-haired persons crawling on hands and knees, and all the Vikings were not bearded.

At last it was done—or at least no further victims emerged from the awnings—and it but remained for the canvas covers, now liberally splashed with blood, to be dragged aside and such faint-hearted or inert folk as were then revealed to be despatched and the women, in various stages of undress, rescued. If not a few of these were immediately raped once more by their rescuers, this was perhaps inevitable in the circumstances—even though Somerled and MacNeil loudly commanded otherwise and went about beating back determined lechers with the flats of their swords. But there was, of course, much turmoil and excitement and much else to attend to, and due order was scarcely possible.

Somerled was concerned about the ships position. There was plenty of flame visible to the north but it was impossible to tell from the camp site whether all the vessels were afire or captured or what. Conn might need help. Leaving MacNeil in charge of the chaotic devastation, he took about half of the gallowglasses and hurried back through the woodland to the hidden bay.

Beyond the trees they could see fairly clearly, what with flame and the fact that it was lightening towards dawn now. There were only four ships in the bay, three blazing. The three on fire were beached in the shallows, the fourth lying a little way out. There was no sound nor sign of fighting.

They hastened down to the shore and round it. A knot of men beside one of the beached longships produced Conn Ironhand.

"Is all well?" Somerled demanded. "No trouble?"

"One got away," MacMahon said. "And one fire died out. Was it enough? And you—what of the camp?"

"All over, there. We took them before they could make any stand. But—what do you mean? One got away?"

"One longship. There were five. Two lying off. We

27

boarded these ashore, easily enough. There were four men on one, asleep. We dirked them. Then waded out to the nearest other—yonder craft. There were three aboard it. They heard us coming. Then some fool fired one of these behind us—before your signal. It gave them warning on the fourth ship. They tried to fight us off, keep us from boarding. When they could not, they jumped and swam over to the fifth ship, further out. Then we saw your flame. We turned back, to light up the two remaining craft. The fifth raised anchor and sailed off. Or rowed. We could do nothing to stop them."

"A plague on it! So they escaped? To tell!"

"We could not help it, lord. She lay too far out. We would have had to swim. And they were warned. There was no chance for us. And your command was to light the fires . . ."

"Yes, yes. You have done well, Conn. I am not blaming you. There must have been more men aboard this other, if they could row off."

"We could not tell, in the dark. And we were busy with the fires, see you . . ."

"Aye, the fires. We must douse them. Is it the ships burning, or just gear, tarred ropes, oars, shrouds . . .?"

"Gear, yes. Anything that we could find that would burn. Some of the timbers may have caught, by now . . ."

"Then we must have them out. At once. These vessels are valuable to us—the more so now that one has escaped to tell. Come—wet sand, weed, shingle, anything which will douse the flames . . ."

With many hands it was not difficult to extinguish the fires. They found only one of the ships badly damaged, and that only to its upper works, which would not make it unseaworthy in summer seas. Leaving a guard to set matters to rights aboard, Somerled took the rest back to the encampment site.

There they were greeted by much celebration and noise, singing, women skirling, Saor with his hands full. He reported three-hundred-and-twenty-four Norsemen dead and none wounded nor prisoner, eighteen women retrieved, some subdued, some hysterical, and considerable provisioning and liquor—as would be apparent. The gallowglasses were for cutting off all the Norsemen's heads and hanging them up by the hair on trees, but he had held them back, to know Somerled's wishes—although some heads might already be off.

Somerled said no. He accepted that it was normal Viking custom—indeed the Norsemen went to quite elaborate lengths in the matter, washing the blood and dirt out of their victims' hair and combing it and their beards and moustaches before hanging the heads in neat rows, in batches of a score at a time, for easy assessment. Few Hebridean communities had not experienced such a display. But, although it might be poetic justice—and Somerled prided himself on being a poet in the heroic tradition—he felt that it was here unsuitable. Moreover it could well have an ill effect on his Irishry, who were wild and ungovernable enough as it was. Besides, it would all cause delay and he had more important matters to attend to. So, no decapitation. He would tell them so.

Much blowing of his bull's horn and eventually he succeeded in getting most of his roystering crew together, although some were already too drunk to pay heed. Somerled addressed them.

"You have done well," he said. "You have cleaned up this nest of adders. I thank you. Your reward you shall have, never fear. But the task is only half-done. One of the longships has escaped us, sailed. We know not where, as yet. But there are many more Norse raiding-bands around these coasts, some just across the Sound of Mull no doubt. We know that, at least. And nothing is more sure than that the escaped craft will make straight for one of these, probably the nearest, with the news. They will not know fully what has happened but they will know enough to bring down their friends upon us. You have it?"

He paused, to let that sink in. There was an uneasy muttering.

"So we are not finished yet, my friends! We may have to do some fighting! But you are fighting-men, are you not? And you have done no fighting yet. So now we need to know . . ."

He was interrupted. Two reeling individuals came bawling hoarsely behind him, one carrying a severed head,

29

by the hair, in one hand and a leathern wine-flagon in the other, his companion bearing two more heads. They were singing soulful songs of Ireland, not each the same song.

"Quiet, you!" Somerled barked.

They paid no heed, holding up their grisly trophies triumphantly. It was light enough now for all to see the sightless eyes and dripping, torn necks. Still more affecting for the others was to see that the two singers' bare arms were almost entirely hidden beneath gold bracelets, the broad bangle-like ornaments which the Vikings wore as honourable marks of courage and endurance.

"God in His Heaven!" Somerled swore. "Here are a pair requiring a lesson, indeed! And by the Powers they shall have it!" He strode over to the bibulous pair, snatched the dangling head from the one with the bottle and, swinging it in an arc, brought the gory thing smashing against the man's brow, who went down as though pole-axed. Then he rounded on the other repeating the blow and adding a return swipe which toppled the fellow headlong. Kicking them where they lay, he tossed the grinning trophy on top of one and called for Saor MacNeil to come and strip the bracelets from the miscreants' arms. All spoils were to be divided equally amongst the entire company, he had said. He repeated that loudly. The message was important. Keeping a hold over these Irish was difficult and called for constant exercise of judgement. They were not his own men, only loaned to him. A firm hand was necessary, essential—but they might well resent this treatment of their two drunken comrades by what they might name a foreigner. So the sharing of the loot amongst all was emphasised as counteraction.

The growling sank away and Somerled went on. "We need to know where that longship would go. Whom it will warn first. It will be able to go but slowly, for it will have only a few men aboard, I think, only enough to man a few of the oars. We must be after it. But where? Do our fishermen know?"

"No, lord," one of them answered. "How should we know that?"

"Did they never speak of other Norse bands, outposts, settlements? There must be many. This was a large encampment. It would have outposts, for sure, around

30

these coasts. The chances are that this longship would head for the nearest of these."

No-one ventured a suggestion.

"Unfortunately you have slain all the Norsemen here, or we might have won something out of a prisoner! But what of the women? Have any of them heard anything to aid us?"

Silence, save for the groaning drunks.

"Come, you—do not tell me that near a score of women have not heard something in their traffic with these Vikings, something which we could use. Speak up. Have you all lost your tongues as well as your maidenhood?"

There was some ribaldry at that. Then one female voice was raised.

"They spoke often of Kingairloch, lord. Of Loch a' Choire, with Kingairloch at its head. They were sent there at times. Two or three crews would go. They would be gone for some days, then back. They misliked it there. There was no, no . . ."

"No women, heh? At Kingairloch? That is on the east coast of this Morvern? A score of miles? Looking across to Lismore Isle? That would be an excellent place for commanding the narrows of Loch Linnhe and the Linn of Morvern. Just the place for an outpost. So—they could be going there. Any other? Mull is nearer—or parts of it."

Another woman's voice spoke, but indistinctly.

"Louder—let us hear you."

"Eric Half-Priest did not love Harald Oarbreaker, lord. I think that they would not go to Aros."

"Aros? That is on Mull, is it not?"

"Yes. Across the Sound from the mouth of our loch, of Aline. Vikings are there, under this Harald. But they are unfriends of Eric here."

"Ah. Eric was leader here? And he was at odds with this Harald at Aros? Now we are learning. I know that there is often bad blood between the various Norsemen. Would you also say Kingairloch, then?"

"Yes, lord."

"What of Lismore? The island across the Linn? It would be a fairer place to dwell than at Kingairloch."

"But less safe, lord. Less hidden. Less easy to defend."

"Ha—there speaks a woman of some wits! Then, since

31

we have no better scent to follow, we shall make for Kingairloch on Loch a' Choire. With all speed. There are four longships in the bay. We shall take three. They are but little damaged by fire, Conn says. There is no time to be lost if we are to prevent all the Viking coasts being roused against us. Before we are ready. So hasten. Down to the bay. Leave all here until we come back—although take the gold if you will. For sharing. The women to find their way back to the clachan. The fishermen to come with us . . ."

There was the inevitable grumbling, but no real trouble, although getting the men away from that encampment and down to the bay took longer than Somerled would have wished. And quite a lot more than gold bracelets and the like was carried along—together with the incapable drunks.

It was broad daylight before they reached the ships. They found that Conn's people had cleaned up the vessels fairly well, and the fire-damage was indeed only superficial. The great sail of one of the craft proved to be badly burned however, so there was no question as to which ship to leave behind. Dividing up the company into three groups of between sixty and seventy, Somerled gave Saor and Conn each a command and took the largest vessel himself. It did not require long to make them ready for sea, all oars and sails being to hand. None had a full crew of oarsmen, of course, but there were enough to man sixteen-a-side, two men per sweep. Without delay, Somerled beat the great gong which furnished each stern-platform, first in a re-sounding tattoo to signal a start, then in the regular rhythmic beat to time each oar-stroke, a beat which would increase in tempo as men got into the swing of it, muscles were tuned up and the speed rose.

The dawn breeze was south-west; and once out of the little bay of Achranich their course down-loch was south-west, so there was no point in hoisting sails. Gongs booming, they raced each other for open water.

CHAPTER 2

The Sound of Mull lies approximately north-west and south-east, for some twenty miles, between that great island and the mainland peninsula of Morvern, averaging perhaps one-and-a-half miles in width, major artery for all that complicated seaboard, since it gives access to Lorne, Appin and Lochaber. Loch Aline opens near the bottom end, through a narrow strait in which the tide runs strongly. As the tide was now making, the oarsmen had to row hard to win progress. It took half-an-hour to negotiate that half-mile, which was galling—save in recognition that it would no doubt have taken the undermanned Norse craft considerably longer.

In the open Sound beyond, as his leading vessel swung eastwards, Somerled scanned the waterway keenly for shipping. All he saw in the bright morning sunlight were a few small fishing-boats. It was early yet.

They could hoist sail now, with the wind favourable, but Somerled still kept his oarsmen hard at it, so that they drove down-Sound at a spanking pace. Almost at once, after leaving the loch-mouth, they passed a headland on the left where the ruins of a large hallhouse rose on a shelf above the cliff, like fangs. That man eyed it sombrely. As well he might, for this was Ardtornish, his old home, from which the Norsemen had driven his father, mother and self all those years ago, the last of the Thane of Argyll's houses left him by the invaders. One day, he would build up Ardtornish again, he promised himself.

Five miles down the Sound, keeping fairly close to the north or Morvern shore, they approached a much wider water, seeming almost an inland sea so landlocked did it appear, bordered by the mountainous bounds of Lorne and Appin, Mull, Lochaber and Morvern, blue slashed with shadow in the morning sunlight. Perhaps ten miles across, this vast basin, the Firth of Lorne, represented a veritable hub of seaways, for into it, like the spokes of a wheel, entered the Sound of Mull, the Sound of Kerrera and the large sea-lochs of Etive and Creran and Linnhe, as well as lesser ones. Like a spearhead thrusting down into this from the north was the long narrow island of Lismore, the Great Garden, green, fertile and low-lying, here dividing the mouth of Loch Linnhe into two channels, the Linns of Morvern and Lorne. Northwards into the first, Somerled turned his longships.

He was all vigilance, for this was, as it were, the main highway of the southern Inner Hebrides, or Sudreys as the Norse called them, as well as of much of the fretted mainland coast, the most favoured and sheltered navigation route through a sea notorious for its hazards equally with its beauty, of sudden storms and cross-winds, of overfalls and whirlpools, littered with a myriad of skerries, islets and reefs. It had been busy indeed before the Vikings came; but their devastations and massacres had depopulated the land and driven peaceful shipping from the sea-lanes. Nevertheless, the Norse themselves would use these waters inevitably, to a great extent, and it behoved wise men to sail warily—although, to be sure the sails of all three ships bore the black spread-winged raven device of the Norse and so would not be assumed to be dangerous.

Only two or three more fishing-boats dotted the sparkling waters.

A little less speedily, for the wind was now abeam not behind them, they beat up the long eastern coast of Morvern, close inshore to be the less conspicuous. They could see all of ten miles ahead here, but there was no sign of the escaped vessel. Somerled grew anxious that they had guessed amiss. He had hoped to have seen it in the distance. But to turn back now would be profitless; for if the escaper had in fact made for Mull, to Aros or one of the other havens therein, by now it would be too late, the Mull Norsemen would be roused, and they might find themselves confronted and outnumbered. They had to go on.

Past the northern tip of the eleven-mile-long Lismore they still had some four miles to go, the fishermen told them, before Loch a' Choire opened. The Morvern shore was steep, bare and fairly featureless here, so that the loch-mouth should have been evident—but was not. Apparently it was round a small headland which itself was not obvious. The loch was not large, they were informed, more like an elongated bay one-and-a-half miles deep, with Kingairloch at its head.

Despite this warning, they were surprised when they came on the loch-mouth, a bare quarter-mile across and hidden until the last moment. But more than that surprised them. For as they approached it, out of the jaws of it sailed a single longship, directly before them, its sail showing the same black raven as their own.

"Save us—who is this?" Somerled exclaimed. "One. Alone. A Norseman. Could it be . . .?"

"Undermanned!" his helmsman, Dermot Maguire, pointed out. "Look—only four oars each side . . ."

"Aye—it is, by all that's wonderful! Our escaper, coming out! And alone. Then—the chances are, the ones he came to warn are not here. At Kingairloch. Flown the nest! So we are not endangered . . ."

"This Viking is!" Maguire declared grimly.

That was clear to all but the newcomer, who recognised his late companion-craft and came on.

"He obliges us! Let us take him—and increase our knowledge." Somerled, from his stern-platform, waved his other two craft into an encircling movement.

Perhaps it was the beginnings of that movement to surround him that aroused the Norseman's suspicions. Perhaps he was keen-sighted enough to see that the crews of these ships were nearly all dark-haired and dark-bearded. At any rate he took fright, swung his vessel round almost in its own length, and set course northwards.

He had no chance, of course, with only four oars on either side against the other's sixteen each. Hand-over-hand the three made up on him.

"Heave to!" Somerled hailed, in Norn—his mother's tongue—as they came close. "Heave to, I say! Or I cut down your oars." That was a dire threat, one of the worst fates which could befall a longship or galley—to have its oars at one side sheered off by the prow of an attacker, splintering the shafts and making bloody havoc of the oarsmen. The

35

only escape, for the slower vessel, was to raise its long sweeps high, upright with consequent failure of propulsion. That the Norseman did, with little choice.

As Saor MacNeil came close on the other side, Somerled, sword in hand, leapt lightly from one craft to the other, followed by a stream of his Irish. He had seen that there were only about a score of men aboard, sixteen at the oars.

"Yield you!" he shouted. "I have ten times your numbers. Yield, and your lives will be spared. Resist and you are all dead men!"

The squat, bull-necked, villainous-looking individual with a cast in one eye, standing beside the steersman, scowled, shrugged, and then threw down his sword and took off his pinion-decked helmet, as token of submission. He uttered no word. His crew, one by one, tossed aside their weapons.

"You are men of some sense," Somerled commended. "Dermot—you will take over this ship," he shouted. "A dozen men from each of the other craft." He turned back to the surrendered shipmaster. "Your name, Norseman?"

"Ketil. Ketil Svensson."

"Then, Ketil Svensson, I am Somerled MacGillebride MacFergus. And I require information. Where were you heading just now? Are your people gone from Kingairloch? And where is the nearest Norse settlement of size?"

The other eyed him levelly from one eye and kept his mouth shut.

"Ha—so that is the way of it! I require an answer, Ketil Svensson—and will have it. I promised you your lives and I am a man of my word. I shall not take them. But you could lose other cherished faculties. Your nose, now, is bent anyway—so you would scarce miss that. But your ears? An eye, now, or even two? Your tongue—which you seem little to value, anyway! Or even lower down—can you spare these?" That was all said loudly, for all to hear, the Norse crewmen in especial.

Silence still from the shipmaster, although Somerled's own people made ample comment and suggestion.

He sheathed his sword but drew his dirk, and turned to the watching oarsmen. "My offer applies to you, each and all. We shall start with this Ketil. But come to the rest of you, until we gain our information. Simple questions to which you will all know the answers. Are your friends gone from Kingairloch? Where were you going? And where is the nearest Norse settlement of size? It would be best for all if one of you answered now, would it not?"

When there was still no response, verbal at any rate, Somerled turned to MacNeil, who had joined him on the ship.

"Saor—see you that pimpled youth there? Who scratches and mouths. You start with him, whilst I deal with this Ketil. Two at a time will be quicker . . ."

"No, lord—no!" the youngest member of the crew cried, little more than a boy. "Not that! I . . . I . . . it is Ardgour. The place they call the Sallachan of Ardgour. Where we go. Where are many men and ships. We sail there."

"You do? How do I know that this is true? Ketil Svensson—is this so?"

But although that man maintained his glowering silence, others of his men, now that responsibility was not theirs, nodded confirmation.

Raising voice, Somerled shouted in the Gaelic back to his own craft, asking their fishermen of this Ardgour—Sallachan of Ardgour.

"Yes, lord," the answer came. "It is to the north. Some dozen more miles. Where Loch Linnhe narrows to the Corran kyle. A township and haven. Of fishers. We have heard that there are Norse there."

"Good! Then we know our course. Dermot—if any of these bold Vikings will, for keep and feed, serve you as oarsmen, so use them, kindly. If not, put them ashore somewhere uncomfortable—and unarmed. Then follow us northwards towards this Ardgour. You have it?"

Somerled returned to his own vessel, ordered sail to be hoisted again but the oars to be shipped meantime. There was no great haste now and his men deserved and required rest. Also he had to have time to consider and plan. Twelve miles or so, and he must have his decisions made, in some sort.

As they tacked their less speedy way up great Loch Linnhe, he consulted the two fishermen. They were able to tell him something about the Ardgour area, if little as to the Norse strength therein—although they thought that there might indeed be many of them, for Ardgour commanded the very strategic and constricted Kyle of Corran, where Linnhe abruptly and dramatically narrowed in from nearly three miles of width to a bare quarter-mile, before opening again for another ten miles northwards, probing into the fertile heart of populous Lochaber. So Ardgour was the key to Lochaber, waterwise, where there would be fine pickings for Viking raiders. The district itself was mountainous and little populated. But Sallachan Point, just before the narrows, formed a shallow bay with low-lying shores and some level land, where shipping could be drawn up and where people could live. There would be the Norse base.

Somerled could be bold, but he was not foolhardy. Without a deal more information than this he could not risk any headlong confrontation, however much aided by possible surprise. He had four longships, but all under-manned. Until he knew approximately how many ships and men he might be facing, and in what conditions, he must go warily.

So, as they sailed northwards, he was all eyes, ready for swiftest action, possible flight. Particularly he eyed the nearby Morvern coast, which they hugged, looking for some break in the rugged, steep and ironbound shoreline which would provide the cover and hiding-place he required. But, mile after mile, the hillsides continued to rise almost sheer from the water, with neither coves nor beaches nor offshore islets to break the front, only cliffs, boiling skerries and the white aprons of waterfalls.

He was getting seriously worried, with the low dark line of what must be Sallachan Point beginning to be evident ahead three or four miles, and was contemplating a dash across the loch to the east shore, where a large bay opened on the Appin side—only, that would carry its own risk of his ships being very obvious from Sallachan as they crossed the open water—when one of the fishermen touched his arm and pointed.

"I had forgotten, lord. That peaked hill reminds me. There is a strange narrow bay below it, this side, the outfall of the Sanda River. Inversanda. There is not much of it, but it winds in. Enough to hide these four ships."

"You say so? How far from Sallachan?"

"Three miles, no more."

"That must serve, then. As well you remembered, friend. I do not see it."

"It is this side of the hill. Behind yonder small headland, I think."

Heading in and round a rocky spur, sure enough there opened the winding estuary of a modest river which seemed to issue out of a deep divide of the mountains, hitherto unseen. It was small, narrow and S-shaped—and could turn into a trap indeed. But beggars could not be choosers on this coast and Somerled decided that if they were to backwater, to move in stern-first, all four ships could just hide themselves therein. Getting out in a hurry would be the problem. He ordered the others in before him, so that his vessel might be first out.

Once round behind the first bend, he took stock of the situation. The great steep-sided valley, which the fishermen called Glen Tarbert and which they said divided Morvern proper from the Ardgour area, stretched away westwards. To the north was just rocky hillside, the flank of the peaked hill which had acted as landmark. Behind that could be glimpsed part of another hill, higher, which must bring them almost to Sallachan.

Leaving MacNeil to post a guard and then let the others sleep, he took only the younger fisherman, named Murdoch, jumped down into the shallows, waded to the shingle and made for the foot of that peaked hill. They were going to flex their muscles.

Tired as he was from lack of sleep, Somerled was glad enough of the exercise. Of a restless nature, he found the constrictions of shipboard cramping. And he liked hill-climbing.

He set a strong pace, lifting himself with an easy-seeming regular motion, slightly bent forward, using the sides of his feet to grip the slope, and with an instinctive eye for the surest route. Soon he had the fisherman panting. But steadily the little estuary and the ships dwindled below them. They did not make for the top of the hill, which turned out to be a long and narrow ridge of which the peak was only the eastern scarp, but traversed the seaward shoulder, to find a steep valley on the other side, before the second mountain. There was nothing for it but to descend and climb again. It was high noon now and warm, and that second climb was a trial and weariness. Nevertheless, when at length they reached the crest, Somerled had no doubts that it was worth the effort. For spread before them now was a vast panorama of hill and loch, river and valley, seemingly to all infinity. But it was not infinity which they considered, only the foreground thereto.

Directly below them to the north lay a wide bay, almost a mile across, created by a curving headland shaped like a sickle, and backed by a level plain containing a small fresh-water loch and dotted with cothouses and the poles for drying nets. And at the root of the headland itself was another of the sail-cloth tented encampments, but much larger than that at Achranich, fully a dozen of the shelters. As though there was one per vessel, twelve longships lay in the curve of the bay.

Somerled let out his breath in a soundless whistle. "So-o-o! Our young Viking was right about Ardgour. But—so many! There could be a thousand men there."

"Aye, lord. Too many!"

"M'mm." The other gazed, eyes narrowed.

Long they stood there, surveying the farflung scene—and the longer they stood the further sank the man Murdoch's heart. For most clearly his companion did not see it all as he did, was most evidently assessing and calculating, obviously planning to do something quite other than to flee the scene, as merest sanity demanded. This Somerled MacGillebride MacFergus was surely less than sane unfortunately—and his madness was of the sort which could cost blood, much blood.

The other spoke only once during that survey. "Lochan. Wood. Marsh. Cattle." And he jabbed a pointing finger as he enunciated each word. Then he nodded and turned to consider the wider scene, to west and south-west, the mountains and valleys there. At length he said "Come!" and turned to retrace his steps.

By the time that they got back to the ships, Somerled had made up his mind. There had been no alarms, and save for the sentries, all were sleeping. He summoned Saor, Conn and Dermot to a council-of-war—although there was little of council about it.

"There are twelve longships there," he told them. "As many as one thousand men, therefore. Too many to take by surprise at night, with our numbers. We might slay some, but the rest would be roused and able to overwhelm us. So it must be otherwise."

They waited, expressions varied.

"We must make the land fight for us. And it is good land for it. There is woodland, a lochan, bog and a slender hook of headland. Aye, and cattle. Enough to serve us, I say."

"Against a thousand?" Conn wondered.

"Used aright, the land could be worth many hundreds. The difficulty will be to get our two hundred to where the land is our ally. These gallowglasses will never cross these steep hills, as I have done, and be in a state to fight after. And there is no way round the shore. So they must be taken in the ships."

"Which means by night," MacNeil declared.

"Yes. There is no way that we can win past this Sallachan in daylight without being challenged. As we need. But a night attack will not do, this time. Dawn, it will have to be. They must see, be able to *see*, what is against them."

The others stared.

"I tell you, the land will fight for us—and must be seen to do so. But—more of that later. Meantime we wait here. I am tired and must sleep. We shall sail at the darkest, between midnight and dawn. Keep you watch . . ."

✱   ✱   ✱

So, fed and rested, a move was made by the company at about three in the morning. It was certainly dark enough for their requirements, so dark that getting the longships out by that narrow, twisting channel was no easy task, involving much cursing by oarsmen. But at length they were all in open water and sailing well out into the pale glimmer of Loch Linnhe.

They had to judge when they had gone some four miles, for the land offered no detail, only a darker line in the prevailing mirk. In fact, they calculated fairly accurately, for when they turned in again to the western shore, they made their landfall just beyond the far side of the Sallachan headland, which they were able to distinguish looming on their left.

Running their ships' prows up on to the shingle here, they disembarked, with strict orders for silence, since Somerled reckoned that they were less than a mile from the Norse encampment. Then he called the men to gather round a little marram-grass mound, from which he addressed them, keeping his voice low but distinct.

"This time, we are going to have to fight, my friends, not just slay!" he told them. "And not in darkness. Such night as is left, we shall use to get into position—*our* chosen positions. But we need light to defeat these people as they must be defeated. To do that, we must use our wits as well as our swords and dirks. And use the land. For there are many more here than at the last camp. But we shall have them, never fear."

He allowed that to sink in, as men muttered and questioned.

"Here is how we shall do it. We must split up their numbers. Which means that we must also divide ourselves. But heedfully. Our four ships must play their part. Each with only a very few men—we can spare no more than ten to each. These will make a seeming attack on the Norse craft beached in the bay behind yonder headland. A dozen of them, there are. Damage some if it can be done—but that is not the main intention. It is to draw some fair number of the Vikings away. This will have to be done with care. You cannot outsail the Norsemen, with their full crews. So you cannot go far before they would catch up. The wind is south-west, so you must sail off north-eastwards, up through the Kyle of Corran narrows and beyond that, quickly head for the east shore of Loch Linnhe, the Lochaber shore, beach your craft and bolt inland. The Norse will not follow you far on land, that I swear. They will recapture the four ships, but that is not important. We shall have plenty of shipping in the end—or else be dead men! You have it? The task of these forty men is to lure away four hundred, for long enough for us to defeat the rest. I foresee no fighting for these."

As he had anticipated, that produced a deal of talk and

squabble, which he allowed to continue for a while—although he commanded that voices be kept low. Some saw that no-fighting role as to their taste, most the reverse; some saw themselves as missing the main excitement and loot, as mere decoys, others well content.

"We shall decide who goes where hereafter," Somerled went on. "Another small party will light fires. Ten will serve. Behind the Norse camp is woodland and a small loch. Not far. That wood is to be lit. The south-west wind will drive the smoke and heat down on the camp. Rouse them. They will see our ships assailing theirs. Then our main force will make a flourish, a noise, on the flank, on two flanks. There is marsh as well as this lochan. We choose our ground. They will be much confused and confined, wasting their numbers on profitless sallies. We shall use the bog and loch and fire—and we shall smite them. Is it understood?"

Dermot Maguire spoke. "It is still one-hundred-and-forty men against many times that number, lord. They will see it, in time. Even in the smoke and confusion."

"Perhaps. But I have a device or two which we may use. Cattle. There are many cattle grazing beyond the loch. Also there are the folk here, in the township. They must be used, if only to make a noise, a show. Now—we have two hours, no more. Until daylight. And much to do. Does any wish to speak?"

"Who takes the ships?" Conn Ironhand asked.

"Not you. Nor Dermot. Nor Saor. I need you here. Choose four men, to lead. And nine others, for each craft. From those who prefer to sail. Little rowing will be possible, with these few. When they see the fires, they are to stand in and make some assault on the Norse shipping. But to be off again when the enemy come down to the shore. The Vikings will never let their longships be damaged, if they can help it. But—enough talk. To work, my friends . . ."

*   *   *

Two hours later, with the sky beginning to lighten beyond the mainland mountains across Loch Linnhe, men were wiping their bloodstained dirks and hands on the grass and moving down from the trees to the edge of the lochan to wash themselves and slake their thirst. Rounding-up and

43

killing can be thirsty work, as well as messy. It was not, however, Norse blood which they were disposing of but that of cattle. More than fifty beasts lay dead there just within the cover of the trees, all the township's precious stock which the Vikings had left to them. Somerled regretted this; but it could be assessed as the price the local people had to pay for their release from bondage. The knot of cottagers, rudely roused, who had been forced to help in the process, stood nearby in agitation and looked unappreciative.

The meat would no doubt be very useful hereafter, for a celebratory feast—assuming that there were sufficient of them left alive to do justice to it all. It was not for their meat that those beasts had died, however, but for their hides. All had been flayed, not always expertly, and the skins cut in halves. These now lay piled in smelly heaps, eyed rather askance by all.

Somerled was straining his eyes to see if there was any sign of their four ships. But in the half-light it was impossible to disinguish anything beyond the vague collection of hulls and masts which represented the mass of the Norse craft. It was a dull and cloudy dawn. He reckoned that there would have to be at least another half-hour before it would be light enough for action.

He ordered the half-hides to be laid out in neat rows for easy availability. He went to speak to the villagers. He checked that his leaders knew exactly what to do—at least in the early stages. He sent men to gather dry tinder, wood, dead branches and the like, to aid the fire-raisers, but also other material less combustible but more liable to smoke, old leaves, bracken fronds and broom foliage, separately. Then he could only wait.

At last he gave the signal for the fires to be lit. Quickly along the eastern half of the wood the flames sprang up and began to run together into a blazing wall, fanned by the quite strong morning breeze. Soon a great pall of smoke, luridly tinged with red, went rolling down across part of the lochan and marshland and pasture towards the Norse encampment.

After that, reaction was swift. Half-a-mile away, figures could be seen emerging from the sailcloth awnings, to stare. Shouting could be heard, growing in intensity. Within a

44

minute or two, sails of their own ships began to appear around the spur of the point.

Somerled had to restrain his people who would have rushed down, there and then, using the smoke as screen, crossed the marshy levels below the lochan and hurled themselves upon the sleep-bemused and disorganised enemy. He did allow them to shout, however—and a mighty and sustained din they made, which could not fail to be heard at the camp.

The alarm and indecision there was very evident, men milling about. But priorities and discipline were not long in beginning to assert themselves—especially when new smoke began to arise from two of their beached longships. Crews began to stream away down to the shore.

"More! More!" Somerled exclaimed, through the hubbub.

"They see only the four attacking craft," MacNeil pointed out.

"But cannot know how thinly they are manned. I had hoped . . . ah, there are more going. That is better. And more—another crew. Five crews. Or six. Now you see why I would have no revealing of numbers here, yet. I want as many away after our craft as may be—not all holding back here to face us. We wait awhile longer."

Their four decoys did not linger. Well before the first Norse crewmen were pushing out and boarding their vessels, the attackers had turned tail and were tacking out of the bay—but not before the gallowglasses had tossed many of the enemy oars into the water and rent furled sails with their dirks, to give them a fair start.

It was a little while, in the circumstances, before the Vikings were able to get their ships ready and off in pursuit, six of them, half the total, and in much of a straggle. Restraining his own impatience now, Somerled let them round Sallachan Point and out-of-sight, before at last he gave the orders that his men awaited and ran to put himself at their head.

He had said that the land must fight for them. A small, low spur of the same high hill, Beinn Leamhain the local folk called it, from whose crest he had viewed all the day before, projected in a broom-clad knoll at the end of their

45

wood. Behind this, away from the flame and smoke, Somerled took his one-hundred-and-forty, plus some of the local men, out-of-sight of the camp. Rounding the far side, they did come into view again, although even at this side the smoke formed a thin screen. Taking half the men, he led them, leaping and brandishing swords and battleaxes, along the front or northern flank of the knoll, amongst the broom-bushes, a yelling horde which the enemy could not fail to see. When they reached the wood again, and cover, each man grabbed up one of the half cattle-hides and went racing back round the far side of the hillock once more—whilst meantime the second section performed the same manoeuvre. Back at the starting-point, they slung the slimy hides, hair out, like cloaks over their shoulders and went bounding along the front of the knoll again, shouting louder than ever, their comrades repeating the crazy spectacle. A third time they all went through the exercise, on this occasion with the hides turned hair inwards. Finally, panting, they did it once more, hides discarded, before sinking down exhausted in the shelter of the trees, feeling fools but hopeful that the Norse would have seen, at half-mile range, no fewer than eight companies of over seventy each, all differently clad, hurrying from that hillside to the cover of the woodland, the part which was not burning.

How would this affect the enemy tactics? Gasping for breath, Somerled watched.

The Norsemen took their time, evidently somewhat at a loss. But presently they made a move. Two columns issued from the encampment, each of perhaps two hundred men, heading somewhat warily towards the smoking woodland, one round the east side of the loch, one round the west.

Somerled heaved a sigh of relief and thankfulness. "We have them!" he declared, "Or else we are poor fighters! We have them well divided. Those west of the lochan will be here first—for the ground is firm above the water, with only the burn to cross. But below it is marshy, soft and will take them time. We attack on the west first. Saor, Conn—ready your men. Dermot—make smoke, much more smoke. All the leaves and brackens we have gathered. We have to fight in it—but at least *we* are prepared. Let them well into the trees before we strike. When I blow the horn,

46

leave off, to turn on the others. Do no delaying, then. You understand? Break off, whatever. So—God be with us!"

The fight in the woodland was a horror, by any standards, a ghastly mêlée in smoke and gloom and chaos. There could be no front, no line nor any unified direction or control, on either side, amongst trees and bushes and shadows, nothing but innumerable individual encounters or duels battled out over a wide area. Yet duels would give a wrong impression, since it might imply an equality and there was little equality here. For though the Norsemen were as fierce fighters and expert swordsmen as the Irish, they were at a grievous disadvantage from the first. Somerled's tactics were for his gallowglasses to fight in pairs, to strive to make the clashes two-to-one where it was possible—and since the Vikings entered the wood just as they reached it, raggedly and in no order, this device was the more effective. Also one side knew the approximate numbers of the enemy and the other did not—always a great advantage. Again, the Irish, even though their eyes streamed and smarted, were by now more inured to the smoke. Moreover they had chosen the battleground, were prepared for its problems and likewise advantages and were not suffering from the shock of being rudely awakened from sleep and hurled into battle on empty stomachs. All of which told.

Somerled himself fought vehemently, almost joyfully, yet his attention was not wholly on what he was doing— which was dangerous. Part of his mind was busy in calculating how far the other wing of the Norse assault would have reached, across the marshland beyond the lochan. Deliberately he had had the dead leaves and bracken fires lit at this western end of the main blaze so that the denser clouds of brown smoke would billow down between this first battle and the rest, preventing the latter from seeing what went on here—but equally of course, *he* could not see in the other direction, and in the prevailing noise could not hear either. He had to guess at timing and to judge what the others would do when they reached the trees. They would presumably not plunge into the fiercely blazing woodland itself, so must swerve left or right. The chances were that they would swing right, to link up with their fellows. That must not be allowed to happen. When, having felled his third Norseman and, slow in withdrawing his sword from the man's rib-cage, he was assailed by another, with a battleaxe, and only saved by the swift intervention of one of his Irish, he recognised that this would not do and that his duty was otherwise. Extricating himself from the struggle he made his way over to his right, towards the smoke-fires—but was able to aid a hard-pressed gallowglass in the by-going. On the whole this battle appeared to be going well, he decided.

Penetrating the denser smoke, he pushed on above the lochan, choking, blinking, seeking for some thinning of the pall where he might observe. But the screen he had conjured up was all too effective.

When at length he gained some hazy visibility, it was to discover that the foremost of the enemy was almost up with the woodland near the loch-foot. Admittedly many others seemed to be much scattered and strung out, plowtering and stumbling and making deviations in the bog. But it would not be long before these reassembled, to become a menace. It was time for a diversion.

Hurrying back, he found his way, with some difficulty, to where he had left the group of local men, herders, fishers and the like, standing in alarm behind the line of fire and listening to the sounds of battle.

"You men," he called hoarsely, "show your worth! Aid us to defeat these pirates who oppress you. I do not ask you to fight. But run you down to the edge of the lochan, there, shouting your loudest. A company of Norse are making for here, across the bog. Give them pause. No need for blows. Just show yourselves, in all the smoke, with much noise—then back here into the trees. No danger—but it will give us more time."

The men looked doubtful but could scarcely refuse. He left them to it.

Back in the area of the main battle, he blew on the bull's horn which hung at his side. Long and loud he blew, the signal to break off this struggle and rally for the next.

It was not so easy, of course, to break off at a summons when one was fighting for one's life. That was why Somerled, aware of it, needed time. He had to blow two or three times before he got any large proportion of his warriors assembled, a reproachful, disgruntled, battered lot, not a few of them wounded, all weary. He told them that he was sorry but this was necessary, one last push and then it should be as good as over. The Norsemen here, he reckoned, would have had enough. They were unlikely to rally and attack again meantime, although they might not be totally defeated. They could be left, for the moment.

Shouting from the other end of the woodland seemed to indicate that the Sallachan men were carrying out instructions. Somerled took his reluctant Irish through the smoke and trees in that direction.

They met the others coming running back, declaring that they were being close followed. This was what Somerled had hoped for. Telling his men to hide themselves as best they could—it was not difficult amongst woodland and smoke—hardly had he flung himself to the ground than the first Norsemen loomed up, in coughing, stumbling pursuit. They let these past, some way, to encourage the others, then set upon their successors as they appeared.

At this stage it was almost too easy, picking off the enemy in twos and threes as they came hurrying. The Irishmen became careless, laughing and joking at the grim business and pushing one another aside in order to get their due share of the killing. But when the oncoming Vikings began to trip over the growing numbers of their fallen, they became more wary, and presently leadership asserted itself and they fell back to regroup.

This Somerled sought not to allow. Shouting, the gallowglasses went over to the assault, hurling themselves after the retiring foe.

Once again forethought and planning gave them much advantage. The Norse had already suffered reverse and losses here, and found themselves on the defensive against unknown and confident numbers. They fought in denser smoke and heat than had the others—and they must have wondered what had happened to their fellows. So, although individuals fought bravely enough, they were not in a winning state and were gradually pressed back towards the lochan-foot and marsh.

Somerled grabbed a pair of gallowglasses. "Back to those villagers," he ordered. "Find them and bring them.

Shouting and yelling again. Round from the right, the east. No need to fight, just noise. A seeming new attack from that side. That should aid us. Off with you."

The pair must have found the locals not far behind, for, more speedily than Somerled could have expected, there was a great outcry on their right and, armed with sticks and stones and the weapons of fallen Vikings, the Sallachan men came charging in from the east, cheering.

That was sufficient for the disheartened Norsemen. Almost with one accord they turned and sought to bolt back into the bog.

Although Somerled had indicated that this would be the last of his demands on his men meantime, he was not quite finished.

"The ships!" he shouted. "They must not reach their ships. Cut them off. Quickly—east-about. Round the bog. Down to the bay-shore. Follow me!" And he went leaping off.

The fleeing Norse had the shorter distance to cover, but they had gone, as they had come, through the soft marsh-land. It might give them a sense of security but it slowed them down notably. By skirting round on firmer ground, Somerled's people were able to run where the others plodded and jumped and circled, to reach the salt-water shore, half-a-mile from the longships. But once on the hard shingle they were able to race directly for the beaching area, with only the shallow outfall of the Water of Gour to splash across.

The enemy could not fail to see it and to recognise who would reach the ships first. They began to swing away northwards, the only direction which offered any escape. And there, ahead of them, were the survivors of their first company, also streaming off from the burning woodland in the same direction. Not unnaturally they headed to join them.

It was a strange situation, with Somerled the clear victor and left in possession of the field, and more than that, the precious ships, yet the enemy still outnumbering them heavily—although they clearly did not know it. To be sure there were the other six ships, somewhere up Loch Linnhe chasing decoys, still to be reckoned with.

Reaching the vessels, Somerled sought to review the position and decide upon priorities. He had been prepared to get the vessels afloat, then board and if necessary defend them, ready to fight the other six when they returned. But it seemed that such a programme was not called for meantime, for the dispirited Norsemen were continuing to hurry off north-westwards into the hills, a straggling horde. So what was best now? The thought of trying to wage a sea-battle at this stage, with his exhausted force in six sorely under-manned ships, was less than appealing. It occurred to him that this might not be advisable now anyway. What would most upset these returning Vikings—a sea-battle against an inferior force, which they might so well win? Or to find their other ships burned and destroyed, their camp wrecked and their comrades gone, obviously defeated? He knew what would impress *himself* most.

So he issued new orders. These ships were to be fired, thoroughly, burned out. Then they would go up to the camp, eat and rest themselves briefly—provisioning would be there—then destroy the place and follow after the retreating foe, to keep them on the run and prevent any junction with the ship-borne group.

So more flame and smoke was added to that Sallachan conflagration and thereafter refreshment, if not much in the way of rest, was the order of the day. Celebration too, for amazingly they had not lost a single man dead, although there were not a few wounded, some seriously. These were roughly aided and then handed over to the Sallachan folk to be cared for—who also were charged with burying the Norse dead.

Before they left the camp—most of them extremely un-willingly—to follow the fleeing enemy into the hills, Somerled consulted the township men as to where the Norsemen would be likely to head in these circumstances. All agreed that they would almost certainly make through these Ardgour mountains, up Glen Gour and over the Sunart watershed for the great sea-loch of Shiel in Moidart, which lay some twenty difficult miles north-westwards and reached another score of miles inland from the ocean. The Vikings were known to have a base on Loch Shiel, from which they dominated Moidart and Sunart. These defeated would almost certainly seek to join their fellow-countrymen there.

Twenty miles. Somerled calculated. These sea-pirates were not likely to be good hillmen and, dejected and with their wounded, they would not cover that distance quickly through rough country. But his own people were desperately tired also and in no state for further fighting meantime. Besides, he had achieved his immediate objectives. There was no need actually to catch up with these fleeing men, so long as they saw them off these Argyll territories and prevented any reunion with their shipping. He would follow on slowly, therefore, and allow the enemy to know that they were being pursued.

He left behind a couple of men, and Murdoch the Achranich fisherman, to keep hidden watch for the returning longships and to bring him word as to what they did. He also warned the Sallachan folk to be ready to retire from their township meantime, with his wounded, for the returning Norse crews might well seek to work off their wrath on the local population, although in the circumstances he thought that they would be more likely to fear further attack and be concerned with leaving the neighbourhood. Somerled assured the people that he and his men would be back before long. Also their four decoy ships, from the Lochaber side, might well turn up in due course and should be instructed to await him here.

This all arranged, the company set off unhurriedly in the wake of the Norsemen, up Glen Gour and into the empty hills. It was nearly noonday.

*   *   *

No need to detail that long tramp across the hills of Ardgour and Sunart. It was not enjoyable for weary men, but on the other hand it was not any ordeal, with no great pressures upon anyone and the tensions of the last days slackened. Now and again they caught glimpses of the Norsemen in the distance—and it was desirable that they themselves should be seen to be following—but in the main, each party was out-of-sight of the other in that wild, upheaved country.

Glen Gour ran for some five miles north-westwards

through increasingly high and rugged mountains and then petered out amidst a chaos of soaring peaks which formed the watershed and through which a lofty, steep and narrow pass penetrated. Two or three stony miles of this and Somerled decided that he had asked enough of his Irishmen. It was an inhospitable spot in which to spend the night but he reckoned that his people were sufficiently tired not to care. They had brought beef with them and though there was no woodland here now, there were plenty of whitened bog-pine roots for fires. That the Norsemen ahead might see these fires or their reflections and realise that their pursuers had halted, did not matter; probably they would be relieved and call a halt likewise. He posted sentries, however, well ahead in the defile. For the rest, full bellies and sleep, at last.

There were no alarms. Morning brought reports from the sentries that about a mile further the ground began to drop steadily, and that the lower ground beyond could be seen to be much wooded, with in the distance a large loch, no doubt Shiel. The Vikings could be seen, well down towards the woods, and still moving westwards.

Fairly soon after this the man Murdoch turned up from Sallachan, having been walking since dawn. He brought word that the six enemy ships had indeed returned in mid-afternoon, had not been long in assessing the situation and, without descending upon the township, had hurriedly de-parted down Loch Linnhe as though making for the Sound of Mull. There was no sign, as yet, of their own four craft.

Somerled was satisfied. The fleeing Norsemen to the west would surely not come back, now, over these harsh mountains, but would proceed on to Loch Shiel to join their fellow-countrymen in Moidart—and that represented a challenge, but for the future, not today. Those in the ships were presumably bound for Mull or Nether Lorne—or even for Kinlochaline, where they would get another shock. The chances of any counter-attack meantime were small. He would get back to Sallachan, then, and hope that their decoys would arrive there fairly speedily. If they did not, there would be nothing for it but to return over these mountains again, making across-country for Oronsay and Carna at the mouth of Loch Sunart, where they had left their original two vessels. It was a pity that they had had to burn those ships at Sallachan . . .

So far as he could tell now master of Morvern, Somerled gave the order to retrace their steps.

Their four decoy-ships they found awaiting them at the township bay.

CHAPTER 3

The din was beyond description and Somerled cupped his ear. "Speak up, man," he shouted. "I can hear only a word in three!"

"Then quieten your Irish savages!" the other exclaimed. "This is beyond bearing!"

"My Irish savages have bought your freedom and welfare, MacInnes. And you did nothing to earn it. Mind it! They deserve their amusement."

The older man frowned. "Living under the Vikings is hard . . . I say, living under Vikings is hard, desperate," MacInnes of Killundine declared. "If you have not been after suffering it you cannot understand. There was nothing that I could do . . ."

"So say all here. Yet if all had united, or most, and taken your courage in your own hands, you could have driven out these Norsemen. For you much outnumber them."

"It is not so easy . . ."

"*I* did it, in three days. With two hundred Irish. How many men are there able to bear sword, in Morvern? Fifteen hundred? Two thousand?"

"But they are not at one—not at one, I say. MacCormick and MacIan are enemies of MacInnes, see you. The clans do not make common cause, MacFergus. I cannot . . ."

"Then they *will* do so, hereafter, by God! Or I will hang a few MacCormicks and MacIans and MacInneses and see if that will unite them—if only against myself!" Somerled cried, jumping up from his bench, transformed in an instant, as he could be, on occasion. "And call me lord, man. I am Lord of Morvern now and will be Lord of Lorne and of Mull and of Kintyre, aye of all Argyll, one day. So lord me, MacInnes—so that you get used to it!"

"Yes, lord . . ."

They were carrying on this difficult conversation in what

had been the courtyard of the ruined hallhouse of Ardtornish, near the mouth of Loch Aline overlooking the Sound of Mull, and which was the ancient *duthus* or capital messuage of the entire lordship of Morvern. Learning from the Norse, they had spread captured Viking sails, erected on poles, as awnings over the yard and against the broken walling, to give some illusion of cover from the elements; and beneath this, celebratory feasting—by no means the first—was proceeding, with the gallowglasses in highest spirits and voice. There were local people there also, but these were considerably less vocal, more restrained in their merrymaking. Music of a sort, produced by bagpipers, added to the uproar, in the interests of dancing—although the dancers in the main seemed to prefer their own bawled and breathless singing, which evidently gave spice to the jigs and reels, the wording to be suitably emphasised to the women and girls present in case they missed the allusions. Captured Norse ale and spirits, and the Scots *uisge beatha* or whisky, flowed freely, and whole bullocks roasting over fires outside provided an ongoing sustenance for those who still had any capacity left to stomach it.

The occasion was an especial one, a summons to all the native chieftains and landholders, or tacksmen, of Morvern, to come and greet the son of their hereditary and undoubted lord, the Thane Gillebride MacFergus. Most had come, in the main somewhat doubtfully although there were one or two enthusiasts. But there was precious little goodwill and converse between them, however respectful they might seem towards Somerled himself.

It was nine days after the Sallachan affair and there had been no further encounters with the Norse invaders meantime. They had seen the occasional Viking longship, but these had kept their distance, usually clinging close to the Mull shoreline. Presumably the word had gone round that a large and powerful force had taken over Morvern and, until the Norse had gained fuller information and gathered their own strength, they were unwilling to try conclusions. It was a help that these pirate bands were themselves apt to be far from united and often in acrimonious competition for territories and prizes; indeed they were by no means all truly Norsemen, although all of Scandinavian extraction, including Danes, Icelanders, Orkneymen, Manxmen and groups from Dublin and the Norse colonies in Ireland.

Somerled, who had been sitting at a laden trestle-table on a roughly-made dais, or slightly-raised platform, made of decking from damaged shipping, left the MacInnes chieftain and jumped down, to push through the riotous dancers. He had had his eye for some time on a young woman who stood out from the others there like a swan amongst geese, but a lively and far from decorous swan, a tall, well-built, big-breasted creature with a loose mane of tawny hair which she kept tossing back as she cavorted. Most of the women present, from the townships and fishing villages, were distinctly shy, embarrassed, co-operating with the dancing and demanding Irishmen with at least token protest and coy reluctance, their menfolk scarcely approving. Not so this female, who was clearly enjoying herself. Or had been. Now she was being squabbled over by three drunken gallowglasses, who had knocked down the last individual dancing with her and were now in process of pulling her this way and that between them. Slapping one of them hard for his attentions, she had been grabbed from behind by another and in the tussle her tight-fitting bodice had been wrenched half-off, releasing one full and shapely breast which jigged to and fro in lively fashion as she struggled—to the cheering appreciation of much of the company. This did not seem greatly to worry her, for she seemed more concerned with kneeing a third man in the groin and kicking backwards at the shins of the character behind with her heels.

Somerled came up, smiling. Reaching out, he grasped the slapped individual—who was beginning to bore in again, truculent now—by one shoulder, whirled him round and with a violent thrust threw him bodily over into a group of his vociferous colleagues, where he, and one of them, crashed to the ground. Then turning on the remaining two, he lifted the one in front, in a bear's hug, completely off his feet and tossed him headlong on top of the pair scrabbling on the floor. Stretching then across the young woman, he took the third gallowglass by the hair of his head and jerked him sideways. The fellow yelled in pain and indignation but unfortunately he clung on to the girl's upper parts as he toppled, thereby further tearing her bodice. With his other fist he made a wild swipe at his tormentor, who parried it easily with a stiff forearm and then spun the sufferer round, still by the hair and, in a notable irruption of muscular strength, flung him to join the others. Standing there, hands on hips now, he looked down at them, and roared great laughter. He kept on laughing, too, until all around, suddenly tense features relaxed and general mirth joined his own—and a potentially ugly situation was deflated. Stooping, he picked up one of the floored gallowglasses, to shake him lightly, genially, then bent to the second.

"You drank too much whisky, my friends," he cried. "For dancing, for women or for sport! Try again when you are sober!"

He turned back to the young woman and bowed. "Your pardon, lady, if you have been incommoded. These others meant well, admiring you too much. But they have imbibed freely. Our Scots spirits are stronger than the Irish sort, I vow! But I, now, am sober enough. Will you dance with me?"

She eyed him wonderingly, hands seeking to cover her bosom now. "If it is your wish, lord."

"It is." He went to her and solicitously helped her to tuck in her breasts within the torn bodice again—with only partial success and advice from all around. Then waving to the two instrumentalists, who had taken the opportunity to rest from their blowings, to resume, he stepped out with her into the skipping, jouncing rhythm of a Fermanagh jig, which soon had her bust bouncing free again. They let it stay that way.

"Your name?" he enquired.

"Cathula, lord."

"Cathula what? It is a good name. And we can do without the lord, I think."

"Cathula MacIan, sir."

"You are good to look at and good to hold, Cathula MacIan! Wasted on the likes of these! Perhaps this hand will help? I can scarce spare two! What MacIans are you of?"

"Uladail, sir. MacIan of Uladail was my father—only he failed to wed my mother . . . having a wife already!" She panted that somewhat, for the exercise was less than gentle.

"Ha! That way? I thought that I saw quality. Uladail? Was I not speaking with MacIan of Uladail just now?"

"My half-brother, Neil. But . . . he prefers not to acknowledge me."

"I see. Then I think the less of his judgement! *I* would. Although I am glad that you are not *my* sister! Who else do you have, besides a brother lacking judgement?"

"None, sir—none now. My mother is dead. I live . . . free."

"Free? Free . . . for all?"

"No. Free, for my own self."

"So—then I congratulate you, Cathula MacIan."

They danced for a little and then Somerled took her back to his dais-table and offered her refreshment. Her breathing recovered, she sipped wine and hummed softly the basic melody behind the present piping.

"You sing?" he asked, although he could barely hear her.

"I sing—after my fashion."

"Sing better than these? These Irish jigs? Sing songs of our own isles?"

"Some, yes. On occasion."

"This is an occasion. Sing for me, Cathula. Sing me a song of my own people, such as I have not heard for long. Other than these wild Irish I have had to dwell for too long in Ireland. Too long. I have longed for my own land and its songs."

"Ireland, yes. Is that where you lingered, Somerled MacFergus, all these long years whilst the Norsemen slew and ravaged and burned? We, your folk, could have done with your company before this!"

He eyed her doubtfully. "Your freedom extends to your tongue, I see, Cathula MacIan!" he said. "But, yes—I would have been here ere this, had I had my way. But my father fled to Ireland when I was a mere boy, dispossessed. We had nothing, lived wholly on the charity of MacMahon of Fermanagh. I grew up to fight in MacMahon's wars, not our own. In time, I married MacMahon's daughter. Who died, giving me a son. Only then, when he had a grandson to inherit Argyll, would the MacMahon consider lending us his men. I have had to wait, God knows—wait! But now the waiting is over, and I intend to win back all Argyll. Does that content you, woman?"

She was searching his face. "I will tell you that . . . later," she said.

"Ah! Then meantime sing me a song of Argyll and the Isles, girl. Yours and mine."

"In this noise, sir? You would hear nothing. Here is no place for such singing."

"I will gain you quiet, never fear. Indeed, I desire quiet for a while So, sing you." He rose, and taking an ale-tankard, beat on the table with it. When that had little effect he banged it more resoundingly, on and on. When still the din continued, he took a full tankard and went to toss its contents directly over the two pipers who blew so lustily just below the dais. The piping promptly expired in a cacophony of groans and squeals and bubblings.

That had its effect and when reinforced by more bangings, gradually an approximate hush was achieved.

"Quiet, you!" he shouted. "Cathula MacIan here will sing for us. A song of these parts. I will listen—and so will you! All of you. Or I will sing my own song, to a different tune that few will enjoy!" He took the girl's arm to raise her. "Sing, woman of this land," he said.

She was neither hesitant nor brazen. She gave them the ancient lays of Fionn MacCumhaill and Ossian the Fawn, his son, of Deirdre and the Sons of Uisneach and the heroes, lovely lilting things of passion and heartache, of sorrow and parting, sung in a clear and tuneful voice, strong but expressive. The themes touched a chord in the Irish, and there was applause and shouts for more.

She followed with one of the milking songs which the women sang when they crooned to the cows to yield, a gentle repetitive melody which soon had the gallowglasses joining in. Before all this got noisy again, Somerled touched her arm and held up his hand.

"That was good for us, and we thank you, Cathula MacIan. Now—I have something to say. In especial to those who have come here from other parts of this Morvern. Heed well. We have driven the Norsemen away meanwhile. But they will be back. You know that as well as I do. And I understand how it makes some of you doubtful, less than eager to take any part with me. But I tell you, *I* will be here also. I will not go away. So you will be wise to join me. I am

60

here to stay. It is the Norsemen who will go, not I. For I am Lord of Morvern, both by right and by the sword, and will remain so. And more than Morvern. So consider well."

He paused and stared round at the company.

"Consider this also. My father Gillebride is lord of you all. You owe him duty and service for your lands. It has not been paid for long, for you have allowed Norse masters to take what was his, these many years. But those years are over. Now you will return to your due allegiance. I am here to see that you do."

Again the silence. Even the most brash gallowglass held his tongue now. "What you have paid the Vikings, I do not know. But I do know what you owe my father. You owe him in goods and gear, in provender and the service of armed men. Each his own due tribute, depending on his lands and state. It will be paid to me forthwith—in especial the last, the men. I require these men, armed and ready. They will be used to drive the last Norsemen from Argyll. I shall accept no excuse. You each know your required number, with one to lead them, yourself or other. Aid me in your leal duty, in my father's name, and you will be the gainers, I promise you. Fail me, and your lands are forfeit! I give you one week to muster and equip your men and have them here at Ardtornish. After that, I come for them, with my Irish! It is understood? You can be my friends and gain and grow strong, with me. Or you can be your own enemies, and suffer. That is all."

There was some cheering but little of it amongst the Morvern folk.

Later, Somerled took the young woman's arm. "You are a free woman, you say, Cathula MacIan," he remarked. "How free, this night?"

"Free to choose, lord."

"The name is Somerled, sometimes called Sorley. You would choose me?"

"I could. Or other. Or none."

"To be sure. I would not force you."

"I would not be forced, Somerled or Sorley MacFergus. See you." And reaching in within a slit at the side of her homespun skirt, she drew out a small, slender *sgian dubh* or dagger, in its leather sheath, so narrow of blade as to be

61

almost a stiletto, which gleamed evilly in the light of the torches, now lit.

"Ah, yes. I see. A women of spirit, as I thought! I admire spirit. I see that I need not have rescued you from those Irishry!"

"I was glad that you did."

"Good. Then make me glad, tonight."

"Would my body make you glad? So easy a thing as that?"

"The body—but the spirit also. I have not been with a woman for long."

"I grieve for you! And for your wife, at home!"

"I have no wife. Not now. I had, but she died. Giving birth to our son. Three years back."

She nodded. "The price some pay. I had a husband once. The Vikings slew him. And raped me. Now I carry a *sgian dubh*. I will pass this night with you, Sorley MacFergus."

"I thank you. I have a chamber of a sort in the ruin here. Which I have made fit to sleep in. It is the chamber in which I was born, twenty-eight years ago . . ."

★   ★   ★

The response to Somerled's demand for men from the Morvern chieftains and communities was less than over-whelming. Those nearest at hand, at Acharn and Arienas, at Uladail and Kinloch and Savary, produced a quota, with the Irishry too close for comfort—but even these were in minimal numbers, along with a variety of explanations. But those further off delayed, including some of those most able to contribute, such as MacInnes of Killundine himself, Fiunary, Drimnin and Glencripesdail. Somerled perceived that some persuasion was going to be necessary.

He had decided on a showing-the-flag gesture, by sea—since nearly all the townships and communities were on the coast—when a messenger arrived from the last-named, the north-coast area of Glencripesdail, with the news that there had been a Norse raid thereon, from Moidart, with the usual slaughter and rapine. The Vikings had come in strength, in eight ships, and were still there. Who could tell who would be next?

Somerled had no doubts that this almost certainly was a

retaliation for Sallachan, and required to be dealt with promptly, from every point of view. These would be the Norse from Loch Shiel, in Moidart, where the Sallachan men had fled. Although Moidart was not in Argyll, this mattered nothing to the Vikings. Sunart was the next sea-loch below Shiel, around the mighty headland of Ardnamurchan, which divided the Nordreys from the Sudreys, the Northern Hebrides from the Southern—and Glencripesdail was on the north shore of Loch Sunart. If this move was not countered speedily, it would be but the start of a Norse bid to reoccupy Morvern; and it would effectively prevent any further recruitment of clansmen here, nothing surer.

He had seven ships now—the two originals, brought round from Sunart, the four former decoys, and one of the burned vessels from the first attack at Achranich, patched up and made approximately seaworthy. As well as these, MacInnes of Kinloch and MacIan of Uladail had birlinns, chieftains' small galleys. And he could muster some four hundred men—which, although twice his earlier force, was nothing like what he required. The longships, fully manned, as the Norse ones would be, with two men to an oar, called for ninety-six rowers each, apart from other hands; and sixty of his new men were to be used up in the two birlinns, which their owners insisted on retaining in their own hands. So undermanning was again the rule, with only some fifty men per longship, therefore with half the oars unused—which meant that sea-battles and stern-chases would have to be foregone, except under very special circumstances. Somerled's disappointment with the Morvern chieftains therefore was pronounced—but this was scarcely the time to display it.

One aspect of the manning situation did surprise him. Cathula MacIan, who had been spending the nights with him at Ardtornish, when commands went out for men to drop everything and board ship, came to Somerled with the urgent request that she be allowed to go along. She declared that every extra pair of hands would help, and while admitting that she might not be as good as a man at pulling a great sweep, she could work sail, steer, beat the timing-gong, act look-out or serve water or ale, and so on. She was used to boats and often went out with the fishermen—her husband had been a fisher. Somerled was doubtful, but she was pressing and persuasive—and reminded him that she had a reckoning to settle with the Vikings. When, weakening, Somerled suggested that she had better go in her half-brother's birlinn then, she hotly declared that that was the last thing that she would do. Against his better judgement he allowed her aboard his own craft—amidst uninhibited comments from his crew.

He did not just dash off into the blue in headlong fashion, for Glencripesdail. The courier reached him in the late afternoon and he made quite elaborate plans that evening and night, whilst assembling his force. There were a number of factors to be taken into account. The great island of Mull, across the Sound, larger even than the Morvern peninsula, was an important Norse domain, on which they were known to have a number of footholds, for it was very strategically-placed for the control of the Hebridean seas. The principal base was midway down the west or seaward side, on Loch na Keal; and the next largest at Fionnphort on the Sound of Iona, near the southern tip. Here, on the northern shore, on the Sound of Mull itself, they had but two known settlements, at Aros, not far from opposite Loch Aline; and at Tobermory, the Well of Mary, about ten miles further north-west, where there was an excellent anchorage and harbour, this last to guard the seawards mouth of the Sound. All accounts put the Viking strength at Aros at only three or four longships—which was why, no doubt, there had been no attack from there as yet. But Tobermory was said to have double that number and represented danger in this situation.

So, with his nine craft—which at least looked like an impressive squadron, from any distance, they set sail at first light, directly across the Sound, westwards, tacking into a south-westerly breeze. Somerled made no attempt at stealth but bore down, as straight as the wind would allow, on the Aros area. They had a bare six miles to go, most of it within sight of the Aros headland, if not the shallow bay beyond. Unless the Norse were fools—which was seldom the case—they would have look-outs posted on that headland. These would surely warn of the presence of a nine-ship

64

flotilla in the Sound, even though they would not be certain whose; and when they perceived that it was probably making for Aros, there would be alarm and action. But they would not be sure of that until fairly late in the approach, for the Sound here was barely two miles wide and all shipping proceeding up-Sound, particularly when having to tack, must pass fairly close.

So Somerled, Cathula at his side on the steering-platform, watched heedfully, counting every minute.

He expected to see reaction before he did. It was still early morning, of course, no more than sunrise. They were a bare mile from Rudha Mor, the headland which guarded the double-bay of Salen and Aros, when they saw the mast and raven-sail of a longship emerging from Aros Bay. Eagerly they watched, as their gongs beat fast for maximum speed, to count how many vessels came out. As yet there was only this one.

They raced in, the fully-manned birlinns managing to keep up with the under-manned longships. The single Norse craft, clear of the bay, turned westwards, up-Sound. This was anticipated—but scarcely that it would be alone. Somerled let it go without attempt at interception.

They had crossed Salen Bay and were nearing the mouth of Aros Bay, really only the narrow estuary of the Aros River, when they saw three other vessels coming out, one behind another—and no doubt themselves were seen by the Norse at the same moment. What had delayed these they could only guess; perhaps only the one craft and crew was always kept on emergency duty.

For moments the two flotillas approached each other, three against nine. Then the Vikings evidently came to a swift decision that the odds were altogether too great, and the narrow river-channel through the mud too restricted, for any effective manoeuvre. All three sails were lowered, in a rush, and the oarsmen began to back-water.

Stern-first the Norsemen moved back whence they had come. Somerled's ship led on after them, a mere six hundred yards behind.

The enemy could not go far. Round a bend in the river, screened by a wooded bluff, there opened a shallow basin, quite wide, with fishermen's cabins on its bank and the usual Norse tentage nearby; whereafter the channel became too narrow to navigate. By the time that Somerled's craft had rounded the bluff and this could be perceived, the three enemy ships had been run up on the muddy shore and the crews had leapt to land and were hurrying off, up the riverside.

It was all better than Somerled could have hoped for— and with not a blow struck. He beached his own ship, but shouted orders for the others not to do so. He did not wish the numbers of his men, or the lack of them, to become evident to watching eyes. He called for all captains and leaders, however, to join him on the shingle. Meantime he sent up crewmen to examine the Norse quarters and cabins in case any remained there, and to bring in any local fishermen they found.

When, with that basin packed indeed with shipping, he had his leaders assembled, he told them what was now required, unpopular as it was bound to be, especially with the shipmasters and the two chieftains. He wanted the already direly reduced crews cut by no less than half. Skeleton crews must be provided for the three new longships which he was now adding to his fleet. And Saor MacNeil was to take the remainder of the men thus creamed off—say one-hundred-and-twenty of them—and follow up these retiring Norsemen. Almost certainly they would be heading for Tobermory, through the hills—where, no doubt the escaped longship was already bound. No need to catch up with the enemy—who presumably would be not much less than three times that number—but to show themselves occasionally and to keep them on the move, as after the Sallachan incident. They should light a few large fires, too, as they went, to make a lot of smoke and to look as though they were burning cabins and townships as they advanced—also to help inform himself as to progress, out on the Sound. The fires would be seen from Tobermory. Saor had better take mainly Morvern men, as more practised walkers and hillman—the birlinns would have to manage with reduced crews, like the rest. There was no time, nor occasion, for argument.

Grumbling did not matter. But finding leadership for the three new vessels did, in their over-stretched circumstances.

Oarsmen presented no problem, save in their insufficient numbers; but shipmasters and steersmen did, for few of the crewmen knew anything but their rowing, and the most responsible were already promoted. Somerled reluctantly dispensed with his own shipmaster and helmsman, to take on the duties himself, when Cathula MacIan asserted her readiness and ability to manage his steering-oar herself. It was not brute-strength but judgement and some knowledge which was required, she declared. In their pressing need, Somerled doubtfully acceded. He would always be there to keep an eye on her. It certainly made swift and unlikely promotion.

So they saw Saor's contingent on their way on the ten-mile trudge to Tobermory—assuming that was where the Norse were heading, and there was little choice for them—and then, with the three abandoned longships, in prime condition, manned after a fashion, they reformed line and pulled out to the open Sound, Somerled insisting on taking the steering-oar of his own craft for this delicate initial proceeding.

The entire incident had taken little more than an hour.

The next hour was spent beating up the Sound of Mull. It lay more north than west and the prevailing breeze forced them to considerable tacking, especially with such feeble oar-propulsion; so the ten miles was extended to over twenty, and an hour saw them still some distance from Tobermory Bay, but with Calve Island, which sheltered its anchorage, in view. Cathula was handling her long steering-oar perfectly adequately, and the advice and quips from her oarsmen had died away. The flotilla had become somewhat strung-out, covering quite a lot of sea; but there was no harm in that, meantime—it would all look the more impressive from a distance.

In their slow progress a succession of pillars of smoke, ascending in the morning air, could be seen above the cliffs and hills of the coastline on their left, indicating that Saor was busy. But it also indicated how far behind the ships, slow as they were, came the marching men. Somerled realised that a deal more patience was called for.

By the time that they were within a mile or so of Calve Island, it was clear that deliberate delay was necessary.

MacNeil's people—and presumably the Norsemen they were trailing—had to be allowed to make headway, or these would have no impact on their Tobermory associates. Some marshalling and parading of his fleet now seemed to be called for—although this would have to be carefully judged, lest it push the Tobermory Norse in the wrong direction, panic them unprofitably.

Somerled passed orders from ship to ship to halt all forward movement, to wheel and beat to and fro, even to turn back, some way. It would seem, from the land, as though they were waiting, presumably for reinforcements.

So they filled in another hour or so—with Cathula MacIan at least proving her competence in manoeuvring her craft, to Somerled's orders, and exercising her own initiative now and again. The man recognised that he could probably leave her to it, if necessary.

The furthest ahead column of smoke was now in the region of an isolated small hill which Cathula called Guallan Dubh, the Dark Shoulder, about three miles from Tobermory; which ought to mean that the pursued Norse should be perhaps a mile nearer. Their Tobermory friends should be well warned by now, both by the escaped ship and the smoke of the advancing fires. Surely the overland party would have sent runners ahead to inform of their plight and danger?

If Somerled could have risked going forward, beyond Calve Island, he could have seen into Tobermory Bay, to observe what went on there. But that would seem to imply the blocking of the bay's entrance with his fleet—which was the last thing he wanted. He had to restrain his impatience, and hope. He had done all that he could, he considered—recollecting that this was all merely a precautionary prelude to his main purpose today.

It was almost noon before he saw what he had been waiting for, almost praying for—for undoubtedly many lives were at risk in this matter. A mast-tip and part of a great sail appeared over the low profile of Calve Island. And then another and another. Clearly these vessels were not close behind the island either, but far over towards the northern horn of the bay. It looked good.

A fourth and fifth sail appeared—by which time the first

ship could be seen fully, clear of the island and half-a-mile over, hugging the other shore, the others following the same line. It could hardly be more evident that they were seeking to keep as far away from the Scots flotilla as was possible. Two more longships' masts appeared, after a pause, then no more. Seven in all.

"Aye," Somerled breathed out. "In a few minutes we shall know whether I calculated aright. Seven ships against twelve."

"You do not think that they will turn and fight?" Cathula asked.

"Who knows? But they are keeping well over, as though to get out of the bay and north-abouts round the tip of Mull, as quickly as possible. Once out, they *could* turn back, to be sure, to face us . . ."

But the first, second and third Norsemen certainly did no such thing, as yet. Oars flashing vigorously in the midday sun, they swept on even more into the north, out into the open water—and kept on that course, the others following. Soon the leaders disappeared behind Rudha nan Gall, the Strangers' Point, and out of the Sound into the Hebridean Sea proper.

"So—you judged truly! They make for Loch na Keal and their friends at Ulva," the young woman said. "I would have thought the fierce Norsemen bolder!"

"They are bold enough. We would be fools to doubt their courage. Wiser to consider how their minds work. I had a Norse mother, mind you. They are pirates, these ones, robbers, raiders. They care nothing for lands, territories, as do we. They fight for booty, food, women, gear, not for places or notions of race or pride or glory. In their own country it would be different. But here they do what is expedient. Why fight a superior force—as they will think us—risking defeat and death, for a mere toehold on a coast where there are hundreds of miles of other toeholds as good? These have already lost Aros to us. Why battle for Tobermory when they can reinforce themselves at Loch na Keal?"

Whether or not Somerled rightly assessed the Norse reaction, the last of the seven ships disappeared round Rudha nan Gall. To make sure, however, that they did not rally and form up for battle, screened thus, he sent the two birlinns after them, to observe, and to be seen. Then he gave the order for his fleet to move into Tobermory Bay.

Rounding the tip of Calve Island, it was as he anticipated. A few fishing craft were drawn up at the boat-strand beside the township. No Norse presence remained at Tobermory, only a litter of their belongings hastily abandoned. The local people too, prudently, seemed to have disappeared. The head of Saor MacNeil's column could be seen descending the wooded hillside to the south, about a mile away.

If it was all another anti-climax for the hot bloods, it was satisfaction for Somerled MacFergus—since it was all as he had planned it and better. The north and east of Mull no longer represented a threat to him—meantime at least—and he could sail on northwards for Sunart and Moidart without fear that all he had gained thus far might be lost behind him.

*   *   *

Once out of the Sound, the flotilla could make better time, with the wind consistently half-astern as they sped northwards. If most of his people expected them to do better still, as they turned eastwards into Loch Sunart, however, they were surprised, for Somerled's leading craft headed on northwards, even a point or two into the west, clearly to round the great Ardnamurchan headland, the most westerly point of the mainland of Scotland. So it was for Moidart that they made.

Less than three hours after leaving Tobermory they were off the wide mouth of outer Loch Moidart and not another vessel in sight. They turned in.

The physical lay-out of land and water here was complicated. It was the outfall of the twenty-miles-long Loch Shiel; but Shiel was not a sea-loch at all, its waters reaching the sea by the twists and coils of a two-miles-long Shiel River. As well as this there was the Moidart River to the north, which entered the loch by inner Loch Moidart, having itself two channels, north and south, round the quite large island of Shona. In addition there was the almost landlocked major bay of Kentra with its narrow entry, besides innumerable other smaller bays and coves and creeks. None of the Morvern people knew its intricacies really well.

The question was, where in all this was the Norsemen's lair? The base of the force which had raided Glencripesdail? It was certainly not obvious from seawards and could be anywhere, hidden away amongst any of the creeks and inlets. Eilean Shona, almost blocking inner Loch Moidart, might well provide a good hidden anchorage, behind. But they could scarcely just sail round, to see. Although already, no doubt, their own presence would have been observed and reported.

There was nothing for it but to send out scouts to explore this network whilst they waited in the outer loch. Somerled despatched the two birlinns and one of the larger ships to seek out the enemy. For the rest, a well-earned respite. They had been active for eleven hours, now.

Somerled held a conference of his leaders, and sought especially the help of the fisherman Murdoch MacCormick, from Achranich.

"You, Murdoch, heard the Sallachan men say that when the Norse there fled inland they would make for their friends at Loch Shiel. You also agreed that it would be Loch Shiel. Why did you say Shiel and not Loch Moidart? Since, it seems, this Loch Shiel does not itself reach the sea?"

"The talk is, lord, that there is a strong force of the pirates in Loch Shiel. I have never been there, nor here. But it is Shiel, not Loch Moidart that is spoken of."

"I have heard the same," Cathula confirmed. "The Norse on Loch Shiel. They terrorise all of Moidart from Loch Shiel, it is said. Shiel is a score of miles long, and much of the land of Moidart can be reached from it."

"But how do they get their ships into Loch Shiel? This Shiel River, you say, is small and winding. Shallow. They cannot get longships up that?"

"I know not, lord," Murdoch said. "But somehow they must get in. There is an island, see you, part-way up the loch, a holy isle named for the Blessed Finnan. And that the Norsemen sacked. They crucified the good monks. Two or three years ago. They must have had ships, to reach that isle."

"I remember that evil deed," the young woman agreed. "I have heard that they sail right to the head of the loch, at Glenfinnan."

"Then, in all this tangle of bays and lochs and kyles, there must be some way in from the sea. For sea-going craft. We must find it . . ."

"Does it matter?" Saor asked. "Are we not concerned with assailing the Norse who have attacked Glencripesdail, back in Morvern? Not in seeking to conquer this Moidart, which is not even in Argyll?"

There was a murmur of agreement at that.

"We are told that they descended on Glencripesdail in strength. Eight longships. If fully-manned, that could mean near one thousand men. And alert, in mood for battle. It is a reprisal raid. Likely they will be moving south from Glencripesdail, making for Loch Aline, possibly Ardgour. Would you have this indifferent company go bareheaded at such a force?"

None answered.

"We shall do this my way, then . . ."

A shout interrupted him, and a look-out gestured. A single longship had shot out of one of the creeks to the south, indeed the southernmost, that from Kentra Bay, oars lashing the water in clouds of spray. It was well over a mile from where they lay off Eilean Shona, but it did not require keen sight to perceive that this was not one of their scouting vessels. All its forty-eight oars were fully manned and being worked in tremendous style, as it headed north-westwards, seawards.

As some of the shipmasters yelled about going in chase, Somerled said no. Let them go. Anyway, they would never catch them, not under-oared as they were. The Norse could only flee southwards, which meant that they must either make for their Glencripesdail friends, or go on to Loch na Keal in Mull—the former, almost certainly. Which was what he wanted.

They waited there a little longer, until the Norsemen disappeared round the coast, and in case any more appeared. When none did, they turned about to reach and enter the channel from which the other had appeared, and so into Kentra Bay.

This proved to be a large, oblong expanse of fairly shallow water, hidden from seawards, well over a mile deep and almost another wide, with shores low-lying and open on the north and east sides, steeper and wooded to the south. There were signs of habitation all along the northern shores, cabins and cot-houses and hutments—but no canvas awnings to be seen. About half-way along there was a concentration of cabins, a village of sorts, a largish hallhouse, a number of fishing craft drawn up, and amidst these one longship beached well clear of the water. Peat-smoke rose from some of the houses.

"So—this is where they came from. Kentra. That ship, it seems, is not manned," Somerled said. "And only the one."

"In *this* bay," Cathula added.

They rowed to the boat-strand, heedfully eyeing the hinterland all around for signs of enemy. Running their prows ashore, and landing, the newcomers could see why this longship had been left behind. It was being repaired, much of its timbering in course of renewal.

No welcoming villagers came to greet them, but they could see that they were being watched, warily, from one or two of the cabin-doors. Somerled sent men to fetch him someone whom he could question.

An elderly lame man was brought, with a keen eye, who gave his name as Calum MacGilchrist. He admitted that most of the able-bodied folk had fled, at word of their ships' appearance. They had learned to flee from almost everything, these last years. The Norse often fought amongst themselves, parties raiding each other from different areas—and the local people suffered. They were here, the Norse, in great numbers; it was their greatest base between Mull and Skye. They were very fierce. But their main force had sailed off three days back, for Loch Sunart it was said—all except the one ship here and the three in Loch Shiel. Ivar Blacktooth commanded, a terrible man. He occupied the hallhouse now. He had slain MacRaith of Kentra and put out his wife's eyes, using her for sport.

"You say that there are three longships still in Loch Shiel?" Somerled interrupted. "How do they get them there?"

"On rollers, just, lord—pulled on rollers."

He stared. "What? Rollers . . .?"

"They draw them overland. Many men, pulling on ropes, and pushing. Using smooth, round tree-trunks as rollers."

"Save us! How can they do that? Great ships . . .?"

"None so difficult, lord—with many men. And level land. See—there. And there. They have cleared roads for their rollers. Bedded with pebbles and sand from the beach. There are two of these roads, over the flats here. A mile, less, to the foot of Shiel. Another to Ardtoe Bay."

"So that is it! Rollers. I salute them for that, at least! I never heard the like. These three ships on Loch Shiel? Where are they? Near at hand?"

"Usually they lie at Ardshielach, near the loch-foot. Three miles."

"How many men? Full crews?"

"No, lord, I think not. Most came over to join the Sunart attempt."

"Ha! So only a few will be left with the ships? Saor, my friend—do you hear that? Three ships and only a few men, at this place. At the foot of Loch Shiel, three miles. Take one hundred men and off with you! They would not be warned? By these Norse who have just left?"

"I think not, no. When these were told of your ships come into the outer loch, they delayed nothing. They were up and off, before you blocked the escape. For Sunart . . ."

"Aye. Then you have it, Saor? Go secretly. Surprise them, at the ships. It should not be difficult. And we win three more vessels . . ."

Nothing loth, MacNeil called for volunteers. Surprisingly, Cathula MacIan asked if she could go with them. She wanted to see Vikings *slain*, she declared—not just fleeing off like kicked curs! She had come with a score to settle, and so far had settled nothing.

The men eyed her warily but did not deny her.

When they were gone Somerled asked the man MacGilchrist whether there were any other Norse bases in the area, to be told that there was only the one small encampment behind Eilean Shona, at Doirlinn. But its people had likewise been brought in to join the Sunart force. Nevertheless, Dermot Maguire and some fifty men were despatched to this Dorlinn, to deal with anyone left there, and to destroy the place as a base.

The remainder of his people Somerled then set to fire-raising. All Norse installations and belongings were to be burned; but the main objective was to create a show—and a show which would be visible from major distances. He wanted it to look as though all this centre of Moidart was being set alight. Great smoke-clouds. On the other hand, he did not want the local people's interests seriously to suffer. So their cot-houses and byres and hay were not to be fired. But elsewhere, conflagration—old heather, dead bracken, scrub-woodland, beach-wrack, whins, broom and thorn. The smoke must be very great and widespread, demanding attention, from right across Loch Sunart in Morvern. As the crow flew, it was less than ten miles to Glencripesdail although nearly forty miles by sea, round Ardnamurchan Point. He wanted those Norse to be in no doubt but that their Moidart headquarters was in serious trouble. But wait an hour, to give MacNeil and Maguire time to surprise their quarry—then see to it.

Burning other folk's property is always a heartening process. There was no lack of enthusiasm for this task.

By the evening, central Moidart seemed to be ablaze. If the vast, billowing smoke-clouds, towering high as thunderheads, made it early dark, the angry red glow in the sky compensated with its own ominous light. Saor and Cathula returned, the former cheerfully complacent, the young woman notably quiet and withdrawn. There had been only two dozen Vikings left with the ships, none of whom were now alive. The vessels were in good order and there was useful booty. MacNeil mentioned privately that the MacIan woman had been bold enough to start with, but despite her assertions, once the real bloodshed began she changed her tune and retired to vomit.

Somerled let her find her own couch, that night.

He warned his people that they had better not sit up drinking captured ale and admiring Norse loot—which was considerable—for they were all to be up and busy well before dawn.

It was late, however, before he himself slept, mind active, planning, guessing, assessing.

★   ★   ★

Sun-up saw Somerled drawing a plan, with a stick on smooth sand, of the intricate area round about. They had

75

persuaded many of the local folk that they were in no danger, and won a certain amount of co-operation. MacGilchrist and others helped him with his map, with information as to depth and width of channels and bays, links and passes between, hiding-places and the like. He was possibly going to need every scrap of information that he could glean.

Timing was a major problem. He was assuming that the fires and the news would bring Ivar Blacktooth's force back from Glencripesdail in haste. But if they had proceeded on beyond that glen, southwards towards Arienas and Aline, then it would take the longer for them to get back. He reassured himself however that these Norsemen all hated marching, preferring never to be far from their ships—so the chances were that if they intended descent on the centre of Morvern, they would be more apt to essay it by sea, however much of a detour, rather than march miles across empty mountains. If this was so, to be sure, timing could be still more difficult, since they might have been on their way when alarm was raised, and so could be here the sooner. So he had to be ready for almost anything.

Certain basic reckonings he allowed himself. The master of perhaps a thousand men would not be likely to be over-cautious, especially in territory which he had ruled for some time. And he would be angry. He would have nine long-ships, presumably—a formidable force, which his own could nowise challenge at sea. But in this narrow network of waterways, the marshalling and controlling of nine ships could be difficult . . .

Somerled already had most of his men out, reinforced by some of the locals. His ships were all hidden away in coves and creeks, for the last thing he wanted was to have them possibly bottled up in this Kentra Bay. The chop-chop of tree-felling sounded on the chill morning air. A certain amount of smoke still blanketed the hills and blurred all outlines, and its smell was acrid, choking.

He had some final words with his leaders and then scuffed out his sandmap with his foot. They had judged and debated as far as they were able. The rest must lie with God and His saints.

He sent Saor left-about round Kentra Bay, to the far side and beyond, up the south flank of the narrow entrance channel, where beneath the steep wooded slopes the tree-felling was in progress. Conn Ironhand he left with the main bulk of their men, at Kentra township meantime. Himself he took a hundred or so and went down the north side of the entrance channel, opposite Saor and the lumbermen, there to prospect the ground and pick out hiding-places. Cathula went with him.

That entrance channel was over a mile long and for half its extent no more than two hundred yards wide—an admirable gateway for a secret base, so long as it was held by the right hands. But it was a gate which could be shut. They made what preparations they could and Somerled established his look-outs and line of runners behind, local men. Then all that he could do was to wait.

They waited for long and most men slept. Doubts were expressed as to the worth of all this, as time went on; and even Somerled himself began to wonder whether he had been perhaps just too clever?

It was almost midday before the first signal reached them, a man waving a plaid, from the top of a nearby hillock with a view. He went on waving, up and down. That meant that ships, many ships, had come into sight, presumably round Ardnamurchan Point. It was not long before another signal, circular, indicated that the vessels had indeed turned into outer Loch Moidart.

Now all was activity in the narrows, messages being sent, final positions taken up, men covering themselves in greenery. But there were still doubts. So much depended on what the Norse leader did now.

Signals continued to be received. The oncoming fleet was keeping to this south side of the loch. It was not dispersing or lying-to. It was approaching the Kentra entrance.

The excitement grew as men crouched, hidden. Somerled had difficulty in keeping himself from getting caught up in it, especially with that young woman beside him no help. He had to be ready to use the most exact and careful judgement presently. All might stand or fall by one swift decision—*his* decision, for once the enemy entered Kentra channel, decision for the time-being was no longer theirs.

The final signal from the hillock came—the first ship had entered.

From his stance of vantage behind a rock outcrop Somerled watched. Soon the first longship came into view, alone. In these tidal narrows, ships had to go in single file anyway; but no second craft appeared. And this, he was certain, was not Ivar's own ship; there were no special markings, on sail or prow, to distinguish the leader. So this was but a scout, to spy out conditions ahead. Ivar was being careful, after all.

Somerled gave no sign, therefore, though biting his lip.

The time factor was now, of course, more urgent than ever. Half-a-mile further and this vessel would be into Kentra Bay proper, and fairly soon after that would be able to see the township and Conn's company massed there. Then, presumably, it would turn back, or otherwise seek to warn the others—which must not happen. Yet to intercept it now would give away this ambush.

The ship rowed on, in mid-channel, and past.

Then the agonising further waiting, every moment counting. Would the Norse leadership hold back out there until they got a signal from their scout? Or would they be satisfied that it had got through these dangerous narrows without trouble? In Ivar's place, what would *he* do? With a thousand men to play with? He would come on, he thought . . .

The scout-ship disappeared into the bay.

A man, further along this bank than himself, held up a hand, presumably indicating action. Then, almost at once, a prow rounded one of the bends in the channel—and this was a prow indeed, an arrogant, towering dragon-head, painted red-and-black. The vessel behind was half as large again as the ordinary longship, with sixty-four oars, not forty-eight, a full-sized dragon-ship, most certainly Ivar's own. A few lengths behind it came another craft, this one of normal size, then another behind that.

So this was it—the moments for judgement, decision, at last.

Holding himself in—and hoping that his men would do so likewise—Somerled calculated, assessing distances. Every yard could tell. He snapped a curse at Cathula when she whispered. He let the dragon-ship pass. A fourth vessel was now in view and a fifth appearing round the bend—too close behind to please him. With a muttered exclamation, part-prayer, part-imprecation, he raised his horn and blew two blasts.

Men had been waiting anxiously for this, and there was no delay now. Between the dragon-ship and the next craft, narrow as the gap was, there was an explosion of activity. Out from the farther, west side, men raced, straight into the water, many men, dragging behind them a boom, a succession of tree-trunks bound together and linked close with ropes. Pushing and pulling, they splashed and swam out with this, whilst from this east side others emerged from hiding to plunge in and swim to join them across the mere two hundred yards of channel. At the same time, arrows began to shower down upon the ships from both sides. Archery was not greatly advanced amongst the Celtic peoples, any more than with the Norse, as a weapon of war—it was the Normans who had developed this arm— but Somerled had recognised its advantages and had gathered a number of bows and arrows—of the hunting variety necessarily—and this was an easy target.

When he saw the first boom well under way, and the confusion aboard the vessels, he blew another three blasts on the horn, and set off another similar manoeuvre between the second and third ships.

The Vikings were not idle, meantime, however surprised. But strung out as they were, there was no coherent action. Those facing the booms hastily backed-water with their oars, and in consequence bunching developed. Clearly a third boom was going to be difficult to get across—although the archery was having effect amongst the oarsmen.

It was the dragon-ship which demanded most of Somerled's attention. It had no boom in front of it. When the trouble erupted astern, it slowed, uncertainly, then also began to back-water to the aid of the ships behind. There was much shouting and sword- and battleaxe-brandishing.

A single long blowing of the horn was the signal for Saor to have another log boom run out, the most southerly, in front of the dragon-ship. Almost immediately after this, a succession of short blasts initiated a new stage in the attack.

This inevitably took more time to mount, for it entailed flint-and-tinder work, lighting resin-soaked rags attached to arrows, to shoot down into the ships. This was slow work, at first, but it was certainly effective in causing maximum confusion amongst the packed rowing-benches and setting canvas, shrouds and gear alight.

Somerled sent racing messengers to Conn and to Dermot, the one to bring on the rest of their men, making much noise about it, the other to mount a display, a distraction, in the outer loch with some of their longships.

There was a brief hiatus in this peculiar encounter. The Norse, the first four ships at least, found themselves bottled up individually, unable to move more than a few yards one way or the other. Apart from the arrow-shooting, Somerled's people could do little in attack, since any assault by swimmers on the shield-hung sides of the stationary longships would be suicidal; and they had no javelins for throwing. Given a little time the enemy would undoubtedly rally and evolve some coherent strategy, but for the moment there was confusion and indecision.

More horn-blowing therefore, ushered in the second phase of Somerled's plan. Fire again, this time localised and over on the far side, where piles of dead timber, brushwood and the branches of the felled trees were lit along that western hillside, for the smoke to pour down, on the pre-vailing south-westerly breeze of that seaboard, into the channel-valley, enfolding ships and men ashore alike in its murky, throat-catching shroud. Just before it became really thick, however, Conn's men came baying round at the run, scattered, and in the haze looking more numerous than they were.

Somerled, eyes running, moved down to meet Conn as near to the dragon-ship as he could get. He was going to concentrate on Ivar Blacktooth.

It must have been a strange situation for the Viking chief to find himself so divorced from initiative, and with so few options open to him. He could either sit still in his ship and do nothing, under the falling fire arrows. Or he could order his men over the side to try to come to grips with the enemy, or to seek to remove those booms and free his vessels. There was not much doubt, of course, as to which the savage sea-rover would choose.

With much splashing of long oars, and considerable chaos

on the rowing-benches, the dragon-ship began to swing its tall prow round, to turn in on the eastern shore, where at least the smoke was not in Norse faces. Only a few yards were involved. There were perhaps one-hundred-and-sixty men aboard.

After all the tactics and artifices, it came down to sheer bloody hand-to-hand fighting in the end, of course. But at least Somerled had evened the odds very considerably. The Norse thousand was split up and detached from the leader-ship, unsure of what was happening, or of what numbers were against them, initiative lost, amidst conditions bad for unified action, smoke hiding everything more than fifty or so yards away.

With Conn's men, Somerled had some two hundred at this point, surely sufficient to deal with Ivar and his dragon-ship's crew. In time, no doubt others would come to aid their leader. It was Saor's task to delay this for as long as possible.

There was no mistaking Ivar Blacktooth, smoke or none, as he stood on his forward platform, in leather-scaled armour and great horned helmet, a thick massive man of early middle years, battleaxe in hand. He looked formidable.

As the dragon-ship's prow ran aground, the Norsemen began to leap down into the water, with swords and axes and their round, painted shields, to be faced at once by the eager gallowglasses. The advantage was with the latter, for the others had of course to jump down individually, recover themselves in the shallows and wade ashore into a solid phalanx of their enemies. Quickly this was proved to be an expensive procedure and they began to mass at the ship's side before wading to land in groups. This was more effect-ive but they were still much outnumbered.

Somerled refrained from joining in the hacking, stabbing, shouting mêlée. From streaming eyes he was watching the man Ivar, who was trying to direct his people's assault from his platform.

A messenger arrived from MacIan of Uladail to say that the last three enemy ships were backing out of the channel. If they then turned to land their men on this shore, three hundred at least, he with his mere sixty could do little to prevent them coming to join their chief. What should he do?

Somerled hoped that Dermot Maguire's display of their

81

ships in the outer loch might inhibit any such move, but he could not rely on it—and three hundred newcomers arriving could change the picture here drastically, especially as there were four other ships' crews in the narrows who might also break out. He told the runner that Uladail should demonstrate along the shore, if a landing seemed to be contemplated, to discourage it, disguising his lack of numbers as best he could; but to send word at once if they got ashore and to retire here before them, making suitable noise opposite the other trapped ships.

Cathula was tugging at his arm. Ivar Blacktooth had evidently decided that he was losing this immediate battle by letting his crew trickle ashore in groups. He had jumped into the water himself and was gathering all his remaining men into a tight formation around him, leaving only a few in the ship. With this, behind a solid defensive ring of shields, he made for the shore.

Almost with a sigh of relief, now that he could give in to his urge for personal combat, as distinct from detached generalship, Somerled hurried down into the fray.

He pushed his way through the struggling, smiting throng to where Conn Ironhand was seeking to maintain some sort of direction in the confused conflict, his helmet gone and with a bleeding scalp wound.

"Ivar comes! With some eighty men," he shouted. "Solid. Behind shields. We must open. Encircle him. Part your gallowglasses."

That was more easily ordered than done and there was chaos before anything like an encirclement was achieved. However, the turmoil likewise affected the enemy, with the Norse who were already engaged faced with their colleagues' ring of shields and negating their impact. Their absorption into Ivar's tight company in fact much loosened it.

Somerled and Conn saw their opportunity and bored in, hacking and thrusting mightily, ably supported. They were almost two-to-one, to be sure, and morale high. Once broken, the circle, which could have been very effective, did not fully reform.

Somerled sought to cleave his way directly to Ivar him-self and not to be inveigled into lesser contests, difficult as this was. He had necessarily to exchange many a blow with others and indeed suffered a glancing blow on his left shoulder from the axe of an opponent for whom he had shown insufficient respect. In the excitement he scarcely felt this, and pressed on.

At length he won through to the Viking chief. He was younger and taller and armed with a short stabbing sword against the other's battleaxe and dirk. The sword was more manageable, lighter, but the axe could decide the issue with one well-placed blow. He was wary, therefore.

Ivar was nothing loth and no doubt recognising the quality of this assailant by his gold belt, if nothing else, hurled himself upon him without pause. With a curious sideways swipe to the neck, he could have finished the matter there and then, for Somerled was unready for so unorthodox a stroke and only managed to jerk himself aside with a mere inch or so to spare.

Admittedly such wielding of a heavy axe required some recovery. Unfortunately Somerled's hasty avoiding action threw him a little off-balance and he was unable to take advantage of the other's very brief vulnerability, especially as Ivar's dirk, in his left hand, contrived a lightning-quick thrust which the other had to avoid by a further contortion. He did achieve a jab with his sword but it was less than truly aimed and without full force. The steel struck only an oblique blow and by no means penetrated the Norseman's leather.

They circled. Other men left them to it.

Somerled drew his own dirk. As the other's eyes flickered towards it, he lunged, low. But even as Ivar slashed down with his axe and took a pace backwards, the sword changed direction, swept up, and as its owner leapt forward, stabbed at the throat.

It was a near thing. But Somerled's footwork on the pebbly strand flung him off-true and his sword-tip only grazed the other's jaw, scoring a gash but nowise disabling him. The Norse dirk nearly caught him, also, as he teetered close.

He danced back, panting. He recognised that he must retain the initiative, the advantage of his speed. Barely giving time for the other to raise the axe again, he flung his dirk in Ivar's face. The man, surprised, dodged and staggered; and darting in again, both hands on his sword-hilt now, with all his might Somerled slashed down his blade on the unprotected axe-arm. Bone snapped and blood spurted.

But the effort carried the Scot onwards, to cannon right into the wounded Viking. And Ivar Blacktooth was not finished yet, although grievously wounded. He still had another arm, and a dirk in its hand. He staggered and all but fell, with the dire shock, but raised that arm desperately, to plunge in his steel, before his opponent could pull himself free. The hand came down, the blow fell—but the dagger slipped harmlessly from nerveless fingers. At the Norseman's back, Cathula MacIan withdrew her *sgian dubh*, gleaming blade now brightly red. Ivar slumped to the ground.

Somerled and the young woman stared at each other as the battle raged around them. Neither spoke.

Presently the man turned to rejoin the fray—but the fire had gone out of him and now his shoulder hurt grievously.

Their leader fallen, and out-numbered, the dragon-ship's crew lost heart. They by no means broke and bolted, but their fury flagged and soon almost all were seeking opportunity to break off. Some splashed back to the ship, some sought to reach the other vessels, others ran off inland.

Jadedly now, Somerled turned his attention to the remaining boom-bound smoke-shrouded craft. He found that the first required no attention—Saor and his people, their other duties completed, were dealing with it, adequately it seemed. The smoke made it impossible to see what was happening with the others.

Pressing on, he discovered that the second ship's crew had disembarked, in the main, but on the farther side, presumably having heard all the noise of battle on this eastern shore and deciding that they would be better off elsewhere. They would have to be left meantime. The third and fourth captains had recognised different priorities. They had a large proportion of their men over the side and hacking at ropes and timber with their axes, seeking to clear the two booms away behind them, no doubt so that they could follow the other three ships out to the open loch again, sternwards—these assailed in only token fashion by small numbers of MacInnes of Kinloch's men, who were spread only very thinly along this shore. Somerled urged his people down to the attack here, although, being into the water, it was difficult and inevitably less than effective—this, of course, applying equally to the defence.

For a while thereafter, then, the entire struggle took on a strangely vague and almost subdued character, diffuse, dispersed, to which smoke, lack of enemy leadership and communications, plus sheer physical problems contributed. Indeed, for much of the time at least some proportion of the opposing forces were merely glaring at each other, through running eyes, across water, from various distances, an inglorious state of affairs.

Yet Somerled was not upset nor distracted—for these circumstances inevitably worked in his favour. The longer this continued the less likely were the Norse to rally and form any coherent front, their morale sinking.

He had to think of possible developments from the ships which had got away. Also the single vessel isolated in Kentra Bay. The latter probably would not represent much danger, in the circumstances; but the three in the outer loch might. Presumably they had not, as yet, sought to land men at the mouth of these narrows, or MacInnes would have sent word.

In fact, no contingency tactics were necessary. The fighting along the channel just gradually petered out. The surviving Norsemen—which was most of them, to be sure—appeared to come to the conclusion that nothing was to be gained by continuing with this scattered struggle against opponents unknown as to identity and numbers but who must seem to be everywhere, and had successfully carved up their fleet and disposed of their renowned chief. The smoke from the fires of the west bank was thinning away now and it became evident that there were comparatively few of Somerled's force on that side. So thither the Vikings began to drift, into the cover of the smoke-curtained woodland, abandoning their confined ships. And soon the drift became a flood as the confused and leaderless Norse went streaming off.

"What now?" the wounded MacMahon demanded, panting. "How shall we take them now? Weary as we are."

85

"We shall not have to, friend Conn. Or so I hope. Let them go. They can retire westwards along that coast for many empty miles, at no danger to us. And when they are some way along the shore of the outer loch, they will seek to be picked up by the three ships which went back there. Is it not what *you* would do? They will signal the ships, to come for them. And the shipmasters, I say, will be glad enough to see them and to go for them, seeking information. For they will know nothing of what is done here, how the others have fared—but they will fear ill. And they will feel guilt, I swear! For having cut free when the others could not. So—they will take these aboard. But I do not think that they will turn back to the attack. Indeed, I am sure that they will not. How think you?"

The older man nodded a bloody head. "That makes fair sense, yes. You believe that they will sail away, then? Leave all here?"

"I do. None will be in any heart to take up the battle again, against unknown numbers in a burning land, after what will seem to them a sore defeat. They will have been told that we have ten ships but not know that we are but four hundred men. With only the three overcrowded craft, will they challenge us again? They will go, I say—and we can leave them to do so—for we are in no state to seek more fighting, our own selves."

"And what of that one ship which won into the bay?" Cathula asked.

"That we must now go to find out . . ."

It did not take them long to discover the situation of the scout vessel. They could see it, presently, drawn up on the shingle at the head of Kentra Bay, apparently deserted. And when the lame MacGilchrist met them from the township, he informed that its crew had beached it there and hurried off overland in the direction of Loch Shiel. There they would find their dead comrades and three empty longships, at Ardshielach. What they would do then was any man's guess.

"My guess is that they will sail off, in one of the ships, up Loch Shiel and hope to escape us in some fashion. Or else go on overland, by Acharacle and Salen to Loch Sunart," Somerled said. "Certainly they will not return here."

That was accepted. But a small party was sent to ascertain.

With his tired, battered and somewhat bemused people trickling back in twos and threes and small groups, many well endowed now with Norse booty and golden armlets, to compensate for wounds and bruises, a messenger arrived from Dermot Maguire to report that the three vessels in the outer loch had moved into the western shore and taken off many men there. He, Dermot, had made a display of his own craft, but had not felt strong enough to venture close. The enemy had then sailed off seawards and were still going, heading north-westwards, not south, presumably for Knoydart or Skye.

"So—you were right in this also!" Cathula commented. "You must have a Norse mind, I think, to so well judge what they will do. I shall be warned!"

"I misjudged Ivar Blacktooth. And would be a dead man now, but for you, Cathula MacIan." Somerled answered, deep-voiced. "I thank you."

"It was but one debt paid," she said, levelly.

"Nevertheless *my* debt is the greater—for my life. I shall not forget."

"Your shoulder hurts? Let me see it. I shall find something to rub on it . . ."

"It is nothing. It will be stiff for a couple of days, that is all. A small price to pay for what is gained."

"Others have paid more."

"Aye—but that is war. We have suffered but lightly, however. Less than I had looked for, thank God. The enemy likewise, indeed. For they are defeated and gone but have left only small numbers of dead and dying behind. I have not counted them but cannot think that there can be one hundred bodies. Out of a thousand. Cheap victory, cheap defeat! And what have we gained? Moidart largely cleared—like North Mull. The threat to Morvern lifted. Six more longships, in good order, won—nine, if these on Shiel are counted. Much booty and gear. And best of all, repute. Repute for defeating Norsemen. Repute to rouse the spirit of our own down-trodden folk on all this seaboard, in all Argyll and Lochaber. That is what I seek—that *I* shall not have to do all the work of clearing and cleansing this land of the invader. That, lass, that is the gain that I seek."

"The Vikings will not always tamely dance to your fiddle, Lord Sorley," she said. "They will gather their wits and their hardihood and strike back. You cannot win always by guile and trickery."

"I know it. But I have made a start, see you . . ."

CHAPTER 4

The dragon-ship thrust its proud prow steadily north-westwards through the colourful but quite rough waters of the Hebridean Sea, Cathula MacIan beating the gong with rhythmic precision to maintain a regular speed. The great vessel was by no means being driven flat-out, with a new crew not yet entirely used to the feel of its length and weight and sixty-four oars. Besides, there was no hurry. The two escorting longships, although undermanned, were quite able to keep up. The oarsmen sang to the pulsing beat of it, a gasping, repetitive refrain almost coughed out on each deep breath, a strangely dramatic, even barbaric sound.

Somerled paced the high stern-platform, between the girl and the helmsman, humming the simple but almost hypnotic cadence, eyes on the jagged blue outline of the shadow-slashed mountains of Rhum ahead, each with its remarkable halo of parasitic cloud above. He frowned thoughtfully as he hummed, judging, assessing. He was a great assessor, that young man. He would wait to call for maximum effort and increased speed until they were well up the east coast of Rhum, for they would not be seen from inside Loch Scresort there before that, however soon they were spotted by look-outs, and there was no point in wasting energy and effort for no purpose. Meantime he would sail close enough past the islands of Muck and Eigg, on the way, to consider their usefulness or otherwise, for the future. Eigg, he was told, had considerable good tillable land, unusual in the Hebrides, which might serve well as a granary in a properly exploited lordship.

The Cuillin mountains of Skye, named after Cuchullin, a semi-legendary ancestor of his own, were piercing the

89

horizon far ahead with their purple fangs, when he decided that it was worth demonstrating his new style and status for the benefit of beholders on Rhum—assuming that they were still there and not off on some venture of their own. Almost half-way up the dramatic island's cliff-girt east coast, Somerled nodded to the young woman.

"Now! Show them the worth of us!" he called.

Her tawny hair blowing in the wind, Cathula brought down her club on the gong with a mighty clang which shattered the rhythm of the pulling and chanting, and jerked up all the oarsmen's heads. Then she recommenced her beating but now with an increased pace, slight at first but building up, as the long, heavy sweeps were forced by urgent muscles into the changed pulse of the gong, ever quickening. The singing died into mere regimented gasps and grunts as men bent and strained and cursed, and the dragon-ship's speed increased and went on increasing. Spray began to rise like mist, both from the surging prow and the flashing oars, so that soon only those on the high bow and stern platforms could see beyond the curtains of their own making. In the stern, the smell of male sweat grew strong, pungent.

It was not all just simple gong-beating for Cathula MacIan. She had to watch the helmsman all the time, for as well as the normal idiosyncrasies of the Hebridean Sea, he had to contend with the down-draughts and swirling winds coming off the fierce and lofty mountains of Rhum, Askival, Hallival, Trollaval, Alival and the rest, which could play havoc with the steering, the sail-work and even the rowing. The sail-handlers had to be considered also, and Somerled likewise, who was acting as his own shipmaster. But the girl appeared to have an instinctive flare for it all, and clearly the crew now had confidence in her judgement.

So in spectacular fashion the great ship swept round the jutting southern headland of Loch Scresort, which was really just a deep U-shaped bay, and which provided the only reasonably sheltered haven of an island nine miles long by six wide. Their escorts were lagging behind now. Somerled stared eagerly ahead.

The bay was over a mile deep, and at its head was

the usual township and hallhouse. Four longships and some smaller craft lay there—amidst obviously urgent activity.

"Four!" he exclaimed. "Only four—I had thought to see better than that! Others may be off on some ploy. But . . ."

"They make ready to receive us," the helmsman commented. "Busy, they are!"

"Aye—belatedly. Enemies, we could have surprised them. This is not as it ought to be."

"Your fine flourish wasted!" Cathula said. She had much slowed down the beat of her gong.

Somerled had been unable, as yet, to change the emblems on the sails of his newly-acquired vessels. The galley was the device of his house of Argyll, and in due course all his ships would sail under that symbol. But for the moment he had had to content himself with painting a great red cross over the black raven device of the Norsemen, in the hope that this would stand out with sufficient significance.

Whether or not the people at Kinloch-Scresort perceived or understood this, they could not tell. But obviously they did realise that the one dragon-ship, and two ordinary longships trailing a fair way behind, coming openly into the loch, were unlikely to represent any threat. Men could be seen, on anchored ships and on shore, watching, many men.

As they drew near, Somerled peered, to scan those waiting ranks keenly, searchingly—but was disappointed. The young woman watched him consideringly, as she slowed down the oarsmen.

As their stem ran up on to the weed-strewn shingle and sixty-four oars were raised vertically in impressive style, well rehearsed, Somerled leapt down on to the beach, to shouts, as the watchers recognised him.

"Ha—Manus!" he called. "Greetings—greetings to you all! My father—he is here?"

"I salute you, Lord Somerled," Manus O'Ryan answered. "It is good to see you. Your father is here, yes—but he is sick. Sorry I am, but he is sorely sick."

"Sick! Sorely, you say? Dear God—how sick? How long, man? What is this?"

"These ten days and more, lord. None know what it is. He lies, silent. Eats nothing, day after day. In the hallhouse, yonder."

"I shall go to him. And the Earl Malcolm?"

"He hunts deer, lord. He is the great hunter! And this isle is full of deer. He goes . . ." The man's voice tailed away as his attention was distracted, seeing Cathula MacIan climbing down from the ship, much white leg inevitably if briefly on view. "Och yes, then," he ended. "Well, now."

Somerled called to her, without explanation, and set off long-strided for the hallhouse.

In an upper room thereof he found Gillebride MacGilladamnan MacFergus, one-time Thane of Argyll—and was shocked at what he saw, scarcely recognising the gaunt, haggard figure, lying on the couch of old deerskins, as his father. Gillebride, in his sixties now, had never been robust, any more than he was a warrior; but this grey, shrunken man, lying limp and staring with great lack-lustre eyes, was the merest shadow of his former self. Yet it was barely three weeks since they had parted.

"Father!" Somerled went to the couch and knelt, taking a nerveless hand. "Here's a sorry plight. You are sick, ill? I did not know. You should have sent me word. What ails you? I am sorry, sorry."

The other was slow in answering, his voice little more than a whisper. "I am far gone, Sorley—far gone. All strength melted away. There is a curse on me, I swear—has been, all my days. I, I have achieved nothing. Now any strength I had has gone and I rot here . . ."

"Are you in pain?"

"Pain, yes. Some pain. But it is in my heart that the grievous pain is, lad—the ache of the heart and soul. That all is wasted away, lost. I am but a winnowed husk . . ."

"All is *not* lost, Father. You will be lord of all Argyll again. I have won back Morvern. And have driven the Norsemen back from much of Moidart and Mull also. When you are recovered, you will go back to what is your own, I promise you. Do not speak now of all being lost."

Gillebride did not seem to hear him. "Nothing that I have

touched has come aright," he muttered. "God's hand has always been heavy on me. While your mother lived, I was able to do more. She was strong, strong. Now, all is dust and ashes. I needed her, Sorley, always. I am lost . . ."

"No!" That was almost a bark. "You will recover from this sickness and then take your true place in Scotland again. I tell you, I am winning Argyll back for you . . ." Somerled's voice died away as his father's eyes closed and remained so. Biting his lip he stared down. They had never been very close, these two, of such different temperament and spirit. Now as the young man gazed at his defeated sire, he shook his head—and blamed himself the while that the emotion he felt was largely irritation, impatience, disappointment rather than pity and concern for this loser in life's battles who was his progenitor.

When Gillebride opened his eyes again, his regard went past his son. "There is a woman," he said. "Who?"

Somerled turned, and rose to his feet. Cathula stood in the doorway, watching.

"That is Cathula. Of the Morvern MacIans. She has . . . aided me."

His father made no comment.

She came forward. "Can I help?" she asked. "I have some small skills in healing, as I told you, taught me by a wise woman. Perhaps I can at the least make my lord more comfortable?"

"Yes. Do that. This place stinks . . .!"

With the older man's eyes closing again, Somerled left the young woman to it and went in search of enlightenment as to the general situation.

He found Manus O'Ryan again, one of his father's loaned shipmasters, and questioned him about the state of affairs here on Rhum and what had been achieved since he left them twenty days before. He was shaken to discover that, in fact, little or nothing had been gained. The neighbouring islands of Eigg and Muck and Canna had been taken over, and that of Coll rather further off. But that was all, apparently—and these practically unopposed. His father's illness and his brother-in-law Malcolm MacEth, Earl of Ross's lack of enthusiasm and fondness for hunting, seemed to have precluded all agressive enterprise by the main part

93

of the expedition. It had been left to the junior detachment, Somerled's own, to make all the running.

O'Ryan was apologetic, even shame-faced. He had urged some activity, he declared, but had no authority to act independently. Anyway, he was no Islesman, no Scot, only *lent* to the Lord Gillebride by the MacMahon. It was not for an Irishman to take the lead here . . .

Somerled, seething, went back to his own people.

Later, when Malcolm MacEth and his party returned from the chase, well-pleased with their prowess, Somerled was perhaps less affable, not to say respectful, than he ought to have been towards an earl of Scotland and member of the royal house. Malcolm, a year older, and wed to Somerled's sister, was a pleasant young man but no fire-eater. He had indeed come on this venture less than eagerly, conceiving it to be really no concern of his own—although if successful it might provide a useful stepping-stone towards what *was* his concern, or his family's, the throne of Scotland. He was the second son of Ethelred, himself second son of Malcolm the Third, Canmore, and his Queen Margaret the Saint. Ethelred had been debarred from succeeding to the throne when his father and elder brother were slain together, on account of his being in holy orders. He had been made Primate of the Columban Church as a youth, for political reasons. But that did not debar his lawful progeny, marriage being lawful for priests in the Celtic Church. Nevertheless David, youngest of the five brothers of Ethelred, or Eth, now sat on the throne; and Angus MacEth, Earl of Moray, Malcolm's brother and David's nephew, believed that he had the better right; also that he could rely upon most of the Highlands and Isles, and North of Scotland area, to support him; for David, although making a good monarch, was bringing in large numbers of his Norman friends from England and giving them high positions and lands. The Celtic north disapproved. And Malcolm, Earl of Ross, supported his elder brother.

"I trust that I see you well, Malcolm, and not wearying yourself with forays against the Norse!" Somerled greeted, with heavy sarcasm. "A pity if it was to interfere with your deer-slaying!"

"I fare well enough, Sorley," the other returned, easily.

"The Norse seem to be scarce around here—whereas the deer, now, are otherwise. I have never seen so many and such fine beasts as on this island, the stags with great heads. And large herds of them. Come and see what we have brought in, this day."

"I thank you—but I am content to leave the provisioning to others," his brother-in-law said stiffly. "Having more to do."

The other shrugged. "As you will. I see that you have acquired a great ship from somewhere?"

"That—and near a score of others! Whereas you, it appears, have still only the four craft I left with you. At least you do not seem to have lost any!"

"Oh, we have picked up a few small vessels. As I say, the Norsemen are few in these parts, and do not leave their longships lying around! Clearly you have been more fortunate. You have seen your father?"

"Yes. It is grievous. I could scarcely credit it—the change in him. He is sore stricken. How did it happen?"

"God knows! One day, when I returned, he had taken to his couch. And there he has lain since. I can get no sense out of him. Only moans and forebodings. What is amiss I do not know."

Malcolm MacEth was a darkly good-looking man, equable, almost casual, and popular. Somerled liked him well enough but recognised an essential weakness somewhere, which might hold its dangers for himself and for others. What sort of a King of Scots he would make, should he eventually reach the throne, his brother being unwed, was open to doubt.

Somerled was in a quandary. What he found here at Rhum inevitably must change all his plans. He dared not remain away from his newly-won territories for long, where he had left Saor MacNeil in charge at Ardtornish, Conn MacMahon at Moidart and Dermot Maguire at Tobermory of Mull, all dangerously scattered although to keep in touch. He had been going to transport his father in triumph to his old home of Ardtornish; but that was meantime out of the question. And he could by no means wait here for his father to recover. The old man clearly required skilled attention, which was not to be had on Rhum or anywhere nearby.

Best if he went back to Ireland, to the High King's court—but *he* could not take him, lest he lose all that he had gained for them both.

He had come here, also, to collect more men, the remainder of the expeditionary force from Fermanagh, about two-hundred-and-fifty strong. He needed these additional men—and they were being wasted here. Malcolm clearly was no great asset at this stage, although he might be later, to attract allies on the mainland. If he could be persuaded to take his father back to Ireland in one under-manned ship, leaving the rest, that would be the answer. But he, Somerled, was in no position to command a royal earl, even though married to his sister.

So that evening in the hallhouse, Somerled swallowed his ire and disappointment and went to work to gentle and manoeuvre—to the evident amusement of Cathula MacIan, who discovered a man different from the masterful character she had come to know. Fortunately the Earl Malcolm was not really hard to persuade. He was very much enamoured of his wife and small son Donald, back in Fermanagh, and had not left them for so long as a month previously. Although reluctant to abandon the so-fine hunting here, he was well enough content to leave the warfare to his brother-in-law, and after only token resistance agreed to escort the sick man back to Ireland and better care, and to return to the Hebridean seaboard later, with reinforcements if possible. The word of Somerled's successes should ensure that these would be forthcoming.

So the matter was settled, and next morning Somerled took a difficult, unsatisfactory farewell of his father, who registered scarcely any interest, and set off southwards again, with the three extra longships and almost two hundred more gallowglasses. He was particularly glad of these trained crews, for he was getting desperately short of experienced hands to man, and especially to skipper, his captured ships.

Before leaving, he handed over to Earl Malcolm a handsome armlet of wrought gold and jewels, taken from the slain Norse leader Ivar Blacktooth, for presentation to Somerled's five-year-old son Gillecolm, whose mother had died at his birth. Gillecolm, who had been left in the care of his aunt, the Countess, was something of a problem, which his father tended to push to the back of his mind. This trophy was a not very adequate gesture, indicative of the sense of guilt Somerled could not quite dismiss.

They were all relieved to get away from Rhum and its aura of unreality.

CHAPTER 5

The atmosphere at Ardtornish was eager, almost tense, as men waited. This day could mean much in the lives of almost all there, for good or ill. Somerled mac Gillebride was taking a great risk, and all were aware of it. He had been highly successful in his warfare and strategy hitherto, admittedly; but that was not to say that he would be equally effective in this other role as man of words, negotiator, bargainer—especially when he had in fact no great deal to bargain with.

At least they knew that the Norsemen were coming, were on their way—that word had been passed, by signal-fires, right down the Sound of Mull from Tobermory; but that could imply ill equally with good. One could not trust these pirates, and they might be coming to deceive and fight and slay just as easily as to confer. And they had the overwhelming numbers and strength still, if it came to blows.

For his part, Somerled assumed an air of quiet confidence. He had done all that he could, made arrangements to try to meet such developments as he could foresee, sought to keep open lines of retreat. The rest lay with fate—and quick wits.

At length the second signal, columns of smoke in pairs, appeared to the west, signifying that the visitors and escort were actually entering the Sound of Mull from the open sea. It should not be long before they saw them, now.

He cast a last glance over the serried ranks of his shipping, lined up in the bay below. Too late to try to better that now. Every vessel which he had been able to lay hands on, from far and near, was there, pressed into this demonstration, however old and unseaworthy; even the longship under repair at Kentra in Moidart, towed round. Carefully they were marshalled in neat rows, with the decrepit and useless in the centre, hopefully inconspicuous as such, the good longships at the outside, forty-three craft all told although made to look more by the erection of extra masts amongst them. Somerled had grudged having to detach the six long-ships under Saor sent to escort the Norsemen in, but he had judged that such a gesture was called for.

Presently the look-outs on the higher ground shouted that they could see the approaching ships coming down the Sound—and the excitement rose as they called down numbers. It was a great fleet which was bearing down on them, scores of ships. Even subtracting their own half-dozen escort vessels, there were more Norse craft than were supposed to be drawn up here at Ardtornish.

Somerled stroked his chin but made no comment. Thorkell Forkbeard did not have more than a dozen long-ships of his own at Inch Kenneth of Mull, it was reported. He must have raked around in a large way to raise this impressive assembly—especially as the Norse pirates were not in the habit of co-operating with each other, each group more or less self-contained and jealous of its own dominated territory. Therefore this presumed united front was very significant. It could represent a serious and new drawing together of enemy forces; but it also probably meant that he had the Norse much worried and apprehensive, if they were forced to these unusual measures. Which was worth now taking into account.

As the fleet drew near it could be seen to be led by a great dragon-ship similar to Somerled's own, flanked on either side by one of Saor's escorts, these longships identifiable from the rest by the prominent diagonal red crosses which barred their black raven device on the sails. Somerled strode down to the beach, followed by his available leaders and a few local chieftains, where a small boat waited to take them out to his own dragon-ship, anchored further out in the bay. He had chosen this as the venue rather than the hallhouse, for various reasons—the effect of having to talk terms on one of the Norsemen's own captured proudest vessels was worth emphasising; also the fact that this must limit the numbers who would accompany this Thorkell; and that from here, at deck-level, it would be not so apparent that many of the Ardtornish fleet were sham, in the centre.

Aboard, they waited.

As arranged beforehand, when the Norse leader's craft drew close, the two escorts suddenly shot ahead, to come and place themselves one on either side of Somerled's vessel, hulls touching. This meant that Thorkell could not board his enemy's ship direct but must step down on to one of the lower longships, cross it and then climb up on to the dragon-ship—all productive of effect.

This sequence duly developed, Saor MacNeil shouting that the Norsemen must be alarmed indeed to have come in such force. They all hoped that this was a true interpretation of the situation.

When Forkbeard duly appeared, admittedly he evinced little sign of alarm or despondency, a big, hot-eyed man, his long, thin and divided yellow beard notable, wearing a great raven-winged helmet, scale-armour, rusty but bare arms all but covered with gold bracelets. Backed by a fierce-looking group of warriors, armed to the teeth with battleaxes, maces, swords and daggers, he frowned down at MacNeil and his intervening craft, but recognising realities, gestured forward and jumped down on to the lesser vessel's stern-platform, stamped across it, ignoring Saor, and, brushing aside the helpful hands held out to him, hoisted himself up on to the dragon-ship. His supporters, very much hung about with their weapons, made heavier going of it.

"Greetings, Thorkell Svensson!" Somerled said, in the Norn. "I welcome you to Ardtornish, since you come in peace."

"I come prepared for war!" the other growled.

"Perhaps. But you come, nevertheless! Being, I am assured, a wise man. We have much to discuss."

"Have we, Scot? You must teach me, then. I am not accustomed to discussing, save with my sword-hand!"

"I will gladly teach you, this and aught else. But if you prefer swords, Norseman, I can pleasure you, as gladly. I can raise this whole country against you. But that is a slow and clumsy way to solve any differences between us. When we could do it here and now, in a few words. Do you not agree?"

The other did not commit himself, but turned to his lieutenants. "Do we require to talk to this man?" he asked.

He got his answer, of course, in vigorous negatives.

"I think that you do," Somerled went on, easily. "Or you would not be here. And with all these assembled, from so many coasts. You are come because, although you speak of the sword, you doubt whether you can meet me in war and can hope to win—as none of your fellow-Norse have been able to do. So you hope by this meeting to learn the style of me, to search out if I have any weaknesses, and perhaps to strike a bargain for your own advantage. Is it not so?"

The silent, glum row of faces was sufficient answer.

"I asked you to come because I might be willing to come to terms with you instead of fighting you. Not because I cannot outfight and beat you, as I have done the others, but because I have more to do with my time than merely fight. My father is rightful lord of this Argyll and I have to govern and rule it for him. You, now, neither govern nor rule, only pillage and destroy. So I would have you out of my Argyll. And I am willing to pay for you to go."

"Pay . . .?"

"Pay, yes. Not in gold or the like. But in freedom from my dispute and enmity. Leave my domains, leave Argyll— aye, and Moidart and Lochaber also. There is all the North for you—Knoydart, Skye, Kintail, Lochalsh, Torridon and the rest. Go there, and I shall not trouble you. Others may, but not I!"

"You said pay. That is not payment."

"I say that it is—excellent payment. You gain much. You no longer need fear my hostility—and none other on these coasts appears to be challenging you. What matters it to you whether you do your raiding from Knoydart or Skye instead of from Mull or Islay? The land matters nothing to you, only what you can steal from it! Go steal elsewhere, then—there is plenty of land on this seaboard, hundreds of miles washed by the Hebridean Sea, further north. Go steal there—with my blessing!"

Thorkell stared at him, hot eyes searching. "How do I know that you will do as you say?" he demanded. "That you will not come chasing after me where we may go?"

Somerled tried to keep the elation out of his voice. With those words spoken he knew that he had won Mull and Iona and possibly much besides.

"None have ever had to question the word of Somerled

MacFergus!" he declared. "I give it here, before all these. Go, and stay, north of Moidart, and I shall not trouble you. If the time should come, one day, when I too require to come north, I shall give you due warning. I cannot say fairer. Is it a bargain?"

There was silence for a little as the Vikings eyed each other. Then Thorkell said, "I can speak only for myself. I cannot give you all this Argyll. Others there are, on Jura and on Lorn and Kintyre . . ."

"I know it. But you will serve for a start! I would advise therefore, that you do not delay in your sailing north! For these others may follow you, hungry for new territory and spoil also."

That appeared to register. There was some muttering.

"Whilst you consider the matter, there is refreshment." And at a sign, whisky and ale, oat-cakes and honey, were brought to set before the visitors.

As they partook, arguing amongst themselves, Somerled scanned their fleet. It was lying hove-to in the outer part of the bay, with the remaining four of the Scots escort vessels patrolling back and forth to prevent any too close approach to the sham Ardtornish assembly.

Cathula came to speak low-voiced. "These Vikings, so bold and brave, but make believe, to save their faces, in this talking now. They will do as you say."

"So I think also."

"You are very agile with your tongue, my lord Sorley! As well as with other parts! But you have bought your peace at others' cost. Not these Norsemen's."

"How so?"

"The folk of Knoydart and Skye and the rest. Will they have cause to thank you for this day's fine talk? A prey to these pirates."

"I have nothing worsened their state. They have always been a prey. Think you that these robbers infest only Argyll? All this Hebridean coast is plagued with them. I have heard that Skye in especial is bad. So sending more Norse there will only cause them to fight each other, to squabble with the Norse already there over the pickings, like the black corbies they paint upon their sails! The Skiachs will suffer no more than they already do."

"You will convince yourself that you are their benefactor, next!"

"It may be, one day. When I have Argyll safe won. You would hear that I did not promise these Vikings that I would never come after them? Only, that if I did, I would give them due warning."

She eyed him curiously. "So—you intend to win more than Argyll before you are done, do you?"

"I did not say so," he returned shortly.

Presently Thorkell Forkbeard seemed to decide that appearances were adequately maintained. He beckoned to Somerled.

"I shall go to Skye," he announced abruptly. "We had thought of it, ourselves, in any case. We have had a sufficiency of Mull. But—who knows, we may return!"

"In that case, I shall be here to welcome you!" Somerled said pleasantly. "But meantime, we shall not tread on each other's heels. It is agreed?"

"Yes."

"That is well. It will save much trouble for us both, I think. And tell any of your Norse friends whom you may see, that I am ready to conclude a like agreement with them."

"I cannot speak for others."

"No. But you can warn them. Warn that I intend to restore all Argyll to my father's rule, at whatever cost. And thus that their trade would be more profitably pursued elsewhere!"

Thorkell glared, with sheer hatred in those pale eyes, but said nothing.

"How soon, my new-found friend, will you find it convenient to leave for Skye and the north? If I can aid you in any way, shipping, escort, you must call upon me . . ."

"A curse on you, Scot—I need no aid from such as you! I shall go when I am ready, and not before."

"To be sure. Then I must not delay you. I wish you good sailing. And may Skye treat you as kindly as you treat Skye!"

If that sounded like dismissal, the Norseman had little option but to accept it. Without another word he swung on his heel and strode off, to jump down on to MacNeil's

103

vessel and cross it to his own, his supporters in a scowling bunch behind him, all clanking and gleaming steel.

"Escort our friends out of our waters, back to the open see, Saor," Somerled called. "They are on their way, bless them!" That was in the Gaelic.

"You drive a notable bargain!" Cathula said. "I must remember, if I have occasion to make trade with you!"

"Ah, but I do not bargain with women. I am but as clay in their fair hands!"

"That we shall test, one day . . . ."

CHAPTER 6

"I would not wish to be coming here in war," Somerled said, gazing about him. "This Knapdale could be a sore trap, with all these shallows, dead-end lochs and tangle of islets. I can see why the MacSweens roost here undisturbed and even the Norsemen leave them alone. Why, in this back-water of the Sudreys they have sat secure for so long, feeble folk as they are."

"Until Somerled MacFergus came along!" Saor MacNeil said.

"I wish them no ill."

"Only desire what they have!"

"I seek the welfare and unity of this seaboard, man. You know that. Ewan MacSween represents weakness, a back-door into Argyll. Which I cannot afford to leave unlocked."

"Yet you have just said that Knapdale is secure," Cathula MacIan pointed out. "A trap that even the Norse leave untouched. How then is it a weakness to you?"

"Because, although this of Knapdale may be secure enough, what lies behind it is not. Across Loch Fyne." As he spoke, Somerled's eyes were busy, scanning those dangerous waters, ready to command the helmsman to changes of course. "Ewan is lord of Cowal as well as Knapdale, that great mainland domain. He does not control it, leaves it to riot and despoliation. But it remains *his*. And he acknowledges David, King of Scots, as monarch. I fear that David, a strong king it seems, once he is more settled on his new throne, will surely turn to put Cowal to rights. It is on the edge of his earldom of Lennox, a source of weakness to him, as it is to me. He must in time deal with it. And it is part of Argyll. I want it, first!"

"As I said," Saor nodded. "Somerled, the mighty Lord of Argyll, desires what Ewan MacSween has. And will have it! Was I wrong?"

Somerled's open hand jerked out, to clench and quiver only an inch or two from his foster-brother's too outspoken lips, in a gesture eloquent of simple threat at which the other recoiled, no word spoken. Then his eyes were back to scanning the dangerous waters.

MacNeil took a great breath and turned away, aware of somehow greater dangers than offered by mere waters.

Cathula MacIan, who could be outspoken also on occasion, and was by no means always the peacemaker, sought now to lower the tension.

"Is that not this Castle Sween which I see now?" she asked, pointing. "Yonder grey pile, a mile or more. On those rocks beneath that long scarp. I think . . . yes, I think that I can see the masts of shipping below. One Conn's longship, no doubt."

Somerled, effectively distracted from MacNeil at least, gave a quick glance, and nodded. "It can be none other. There is no similar Norman castle on all these coasts. Another reason why Ewan sits so secure. I am interested in that castle. I have long wished to examine one . . ."

The dragon-ship and two escorts had rounded the southern end of the Isle of Danna, the detached tip of the long, wooded peninsula of Knapdale, which itself was no more than the northern horn of the vastly greater peninsula of Kintyre, the longest in Scotland, reaching southwards seventy miles from Nether Lorne, to form the most southerly portion of the Hebrides, although no island. Somerled had never ventured thus far south previously. But with Lorne and Islay, Tiree and Jura now his, at least for the time-being, Knapdale, Kintyre and Cowal, the remaining portions of the huge province and thanedom of Argyll, beckoned. He was not the first conqueror to discover that once the conquering has started it can be difficult to halt the process and cry enough.

They were now in the shallow sea-loch of Sween or Suibhne, with all its tributary lochs and inlets, channels and sandbanks, a navigator's nightmare; so that man was more tense than usual, for to run his fine dragon-ship aground, on such a mission, and under the eyes of that castle, would be a humiliation indeed. He had no local pilot. The fact that Conn MacMahon, sent ahead the day previously as herald,

had presumably managed the approach, would make any mishap the more distressing.

So Somerled, acting his own shipmaster, had little opportunity to scan the great stone castle which loomed ever more prominently before them on its rocky knoll above the tide—although he could not prevent himself from ever taking quick glances at it from his watching for shoals and banks, skerries and reefs. Castle Sween had been built late in the previous century by Suibhne, son of Hugh Anradhan, brother of the King of Ulster, High King of Ireland, who had wed a princess of the house of Argyll, gaining Knapdale and Cowal with her, and then calling himself Regulus or sub-King of the Isles. It was not quite clear as to which High King he was sub, his Irish brother, the King of Scots, or even the King of Norway who also claimed overlordship of the Hebrides. Probably it was to the King of Scots, for he had erected this great stone castle, undoubtedly with Norman guidance which only that monarch could have supplied to him, the first and still the only such Norman-type stronghold in the West Highlands, and to all intents impregnable. Here his grandson Ewan MacSween still permitted himself the empty title of King of Argyll and the Isles, something that Somerled found hard to swallow, even though Ewan made no least attempt to enforce any major authority, semi-royal or otherwise.

As, crabwise, dodging the shoals of low-water, they won close enough to Castle Sween, on the east side of the loch, to perceive a clear channel into the haven, Somerled could relax and hand over to Cathula and the helmsman. He considered the massive building more carefully. It was simple enough as to plan, merely a great rectangle, externally perhaps ninety feet by seventy, with walls, obviously very thick, rising to some twenty-five feet, with squared buttresses at each angle, the whole cunningly grafted on to the living, uneven rock-base of the bluff as though growing out of it. Clearly there was a parapet-walk along the wallhead, for men could be seen pacing there; and no doubt there was a courtyard within. The walling was pierced with loopholes and narrow slit-windows. There was no keep nor tower. A single arched entrance opened at ground level on the south front, protected by a ditch cut in the rock and a drawbridge. Some cabins and hutments festooned the slope below the long, high escarpment behind.

"A stark, harsh place," he commented. "But strong. Well might the Norse leave it alone."

"To dwell there might be like to live in a prison," Saor said.

"Perhaps there is more of comfort within than appears from here."

They had both forgotten their spat of wrath.

In the haven, formed by a mere re-entrant of the cliff below, two birlinns and Conn's longship lay amongst a cluster of fishing-craft. A long flight of steps, cut in the rock, led down from the castle. At the head of this stair a group of men stood watching, Conn Ironhand's massive figure prominent amongst them.

Skilfully Cathula insinuated the dragon-ship through the clutter of boats, to draw up beside Conn's craft with as much flourish as the constriction permitted. Somerled had two pipers to play them ashore in suitable fashion, and led the way.

Regulating their pace to that of the blowing musicians, they mounted the steps. An elderly spare man, grey and of delicate features, stepped forward to greet them.

"Welcome to my poor house, Lord Thane of Argyll," he said carefully. "I have heard much of you."

"And I of you, Lord Ewan of Knapdale and Cowal." That was equally careful. It was important to try to establish attitudes towards styles and pretension right away. The other had been accurate enough in naming his visitor Thane of Argyll, although it was not a title he chose to use. His father had in fact died soon after his return to Ireland, so Somerled was now lawful head of his house. For himself, he was not going to acknowledge MacSween as any sort of king, since that would imply a superiority to himself.

The other did not press the matter. "I never knew your father, but was saddened by his misfortunes," he said. "He was younger than am I and his early death grieved me."

"You are kind, generous," Somerled admitted. "I thank you. These are Saor MacNeil of Oronsay, Dermot Maguire out of Fermanagh, MacInnes of Kinlochaline and Cathula MacIan, all friends of mine."

"Then may they be mine also. Come—my hall is yours for so long as you wish it."

They followed their courteous and rather sad-faced host, who seemed to be so at odds with his frowning stone fortalice, round the side of the castle, over the drawbridge and in at the sole entrance, by a narrow, dark pend through the tremendously thick walling, ten feet and more. Within, they found the expected courtyard open to the sky, cobbled and with a well in one corner. Lean-to buildings lined the internal walling, two-storeyed on the longer lateral north side, reaching up to parapet-level, single-storeyed to east and west. Armed men looked down upon them from the parapet-walk.

They were led across the yard to the main north range, where another narrow doorway admitted to a dark stone-vaulted basement, which held a distinct chill. A straight and constricted stairway in the thickness of the walling mounted on their right, and up this they were taken. It gave access to a large hall on the first floor and here a different atmosphere prevailed. It was comparatively bright, lit by three larger windows facing south across the yard, each provided with a stone seat in the ingoing. And it was warm, with a fire smouldering on a circular hearth in the centre of the stone-flagged floor, which was the upper side of the basement vaulting, the smoke rising to escape through a hole in the blackened rafters of the roofing. This hall, indeed, furnished with table and chests and benches, skins on the floor and wall-hangings, was not dissimilar from that of any large hallhouse of clay-coated timber.

Food and drink was laid out in plenty for the guests. There appeared to be no women about the establishment. Their host was very attentive. Somerled could have wished him less so, in view of the object of their visit.

Endeavouring not to show impatience at the required polite small talk, refreshment over, Somerled sought to come to the point, but as pleasantly as he was able.

"You, my lord, are aware of my position," he said. "You named me Thane of Argyll—which implies that I am lord of all Argyll, under the High King of Scots as liege lord. I myself prefer the Celtic usage of Toiseach. But no matter, in this of the lordship the implication is the same. Of *all* Argyll."

Ewan inclined his head gravely.

"Yes, then. But you, my lord, style yourself, I understand, Regulus or King of Argyll and the Isles. Forgive me if I am ignorant, but I do not perceive how there can be a sub-king in Argyll and also a thane or lord thereof. Responsible for it to the King of Scots."

"I understand your difficulty, Toiseach. But think that there need be no conflict in this matter. I am called Regulus or King merely because my father was so-called before me, and his father, Suibhne mac Hugh Anradhan. We are a royal line. But it is a style only. I seek no dominion over Argyll and have never done so."

"That is fair. So far as it goes. But it still holds problems. You are Lord of Knapdale and Cowal. Possibly could claim Kintyre also. And Knapdale, Cowal and Kintyre are the southern parts of Argyll. *I* am Lord of Argyll. The part cannot be as great as the whole. Therefore I must be your superior in this. Yet you are called king, and king cannot be inferior to thane or toiseach. You perceive my difficulty?"

"As Lord of Knapdale and Cowal I accept your superiority, my lord Thane. But as Regulus and King I can accept only the superiority of my High King, David mac Malcolm."

"And there's the rub! King David cannot have *two* lords responsible to him for the one lordship of Argyll. It must be one or the other."

"But I do not challenge your position or authority, my lord Somerled."

"Perhaps not. But it is implied. All Argyll is an entity, I cannot share it."

"But—forgive me if I point it out—you do not *hold* all Argyll, my lord. You have won back much—Morvern and Mull, Islay and Jura, Tiree and the other isles, Lorne and Appin and much more. Even part of Moidart and Lochaber, I am told, beyond Argyll. But you do not yet hold the south. So how can you be responsible for it to King David?" That was quite gently but firmly put. "Have you, indeed, yet made fealty to King David for Argyll? Any of it?"

Somerled smiled at this shrewd thrusting by the so civil MacSween. "I plan to go to David when I can present to him all Argyll recovered from Norse domination," he said. "I have not yet attempted the reconquest of the south parts.

I esteemed it right to come to see you first. Since you are lord here at Knapdale. And in name, in Cowal and Kintyre. Where you have not sought to expel the Norse. Or others."

So there they were, down to realities at length, cards as it were on the table.

"I am beholden to you for coming," Ewan acknowledged. "What do you want from me?"

"I want your goodwill, first," the younger man said, tactfully for him. "I want you to accept me as superior over the lands of Knapdale, Cowal and Kintyre. And I want you to resign the style and title of King and Regulus. In return, I shall clear the Norsemen out of Kintyre, restore good order and authority in Cowal, and sustain you here under my protection at Knapdale. That, and assure you of my friendship."

Ewan MacSween was silent for a few moments, the others watching his fine features. At length he spoke.

"The first two of your wishes, my lord Somerled, I grant, willingly. My goodwill and the superiority over the lordships. But this on the title of Regulus and King is a different matter. It is an inheritance, a rank and status inherent in my family. It is not something which I can, or may, discard like an old cloak. I *am* King and Regulus. Saying that I am not will change nothing. So your third request I cannot accept. I am sorry."

Somerled frowned and tapped the table-top with his finger-nails.

The older man spoke again, thoughtfully. "It comes to me, my young friend, that we need not come to disagreement over this—which would be a pity. I recognise your problem and sympathise with you. Also admire you for what you have done. Even though I cannot give up my style of King. *You* claim that you, as Thane or Toiseach, cannot be accepted as superior whilst I retain that style, king being above these. But if you also were Regulus and King, how then?"

"Eh . . .?"

"Why not? The style usually given me is King of Argyll and the Isles. Argyll it is which concerns you. How if I remain King, but King of the Isles only? Whilst you are King of Argyll?"

"But . . . but how could that be?" Somerled stared. "I am no king."

"You could be. In name, as I am. Who could stop it? It might serve you well, when dealing with others. My ancestor gave himself the style because he was of the royal blood. And married to a princess of the royal house of this Argyll. I believe that you, too, descend from that same royal house of Argyll. Moreover, if I mistake not, you have also the blood of the Irish royal house. Was not Conn of the Hundred Battles, High King, your remote ancestor? I am much interested in genealogies—an old man's concern. And your mother, I think, was of the Norse line of Ivar and Echmarcach, Kings of Dublin. So your blood is sufficiently royal. Name yourself King and Regulus of Argyll, my friend, instead of Thane. None may prevent it. And I shall be King of the Isles—which isles is no matter. There are scores in Knapdale alone! You will therefore be the more important king, whilst I keep the style I was born to."

"Lord!" Somerled exclaimed, and turned to gaze at his companions. They looked as dumbfounded as he by this proposal. "I . . . I do not know what to say." It was not often that Somerled MacFergus was at a loss for words.

"Would it not solve our problems, my lord? You are undoubted superior of all Argyll, you have my agreement that you take over Kintyre and Cowal. I retain Knapdale under your overlordship, and also the style of King of the Isles. I have no heir, as you will know. So when I die you can be King of the Isles also."

Somerled moved, to pace to and fro over the skin-strewn stone floor. "This is . . . something which I have never thought on," he said. "King of Argyll!" It was as though he savoured the phrase on his tongue. "And King David of Scots? What of him? What will *he* say to this new kingship?"

"It is not a new kingship. There have been Kings of Argyll for these three generations. What *can* he say? It is merely a new holder of the kingship. With the consent of the old. He cannot say you nay, so long as you pay fealty to him as High King."

"Is it not for him to create such titles? He is *Ard Righ*, High King. Lesser kings, *Ri*, stem from him, surely?"

"Not so. The *Ri* it was who chose the *Ard Righ*, elected

from members of the royal house. No High King has ever created a lesser king, to my knowledge. The *Ri* were mormaors, now earls. But they succeeded, were not created. The High King confirmed them only, in their mormaorships and earldoms. But you would not claim to be an earl, any more than do I. This style of Regulus or King is different. None who ever bore it were *created*. All assumed it or inherited it—Dalriada, Argyll, Dumbarton or Strathclyde, Fortrenn, Galloway, Man and the rest. None were so made by others. Why not yourself?"

"I must consider . . ."

"Do so, my friend. There is no haste. My house is yours."

"What is there to consider, then?" Saor MacNeil raised a half-mocking hand. "Hail, O King! Hail!"

CHAPTER 7

Somerled drew rein, to gaze down the long, fair vale of the Teviot, and behind him his party were thankful to pull up also, stiff and aching in their saddles. Islesmen and West Highlanders did not tend to be good horsemen, getting little practice; and this was their second day of riding. Not for the first time they cursed the King of Scots for choosing to spend most of his time at such a God-forsaken spot as Rook's Burgh Castle, where Teviot joined Tweed on the East March of the Borderland, so far from the sea, or at least their Western Sea. They had come as near to it as they could in the ships, to the head of the Firth of Solway at Eskmouth, and there hired these wretched horses. That was over forty miles back. They had passed the night at a monkish hospice of the new Romish Church which the late Margaret and her sons had imposed on mainland Scotland, dedicated oddly to St. Paul now, although formerly to the good Celtic St. Bride, right up on the watershed between the West and Middle Marches of this Lowland Scotland. Another twenty-odd miles, they were told, and downhill now following this Teviot, and they would reach journey's end. They had sent Saor MacNeil ahead, to announce their coming.

"It is a green and fertile land," Somerled commented. "But why does David dwell here, on the very edge of his realm? Northumbria is English now—it can be only a few miles to the south. It is strange."

"He loves the English—or at least the Normans. Perhaps he likes to be near them?" put in Sir Malcolm MacGregor of Glenorchy.

"They say that he does not trust his good-brother, King Henry of England, and fears that he might seek to take these southern parts from him. And so keeps watch here." That was Farquhar MacFerdoch, Hereditary Abbot of Glendochart.

114

"More like it that he does not love the people of the North and the Highlands, despite his father's blood, and chooses to live as far away from them as he can!" Fingan MacFingan of Dunara suggested. "Since he is no warrior and leaves the fighting to others!"

"David is no craven, from all that I have heard," Somerled said. "He brought Galloway to heel and ruled Cumbria strongly, for Henry. De Morville, his High Constable, won the Battle of Stracathro for him against Angus of Moray— but that was because Angus chose to march in his attempt on the throne, whilst David himself was away in London. He is not to be blamed for that."

Further back in the group Conn MacMahon said something about those who never did any fighting being ever loudest at condemning others for cowardice. Frowning, Somerled rode on.

He had been having difficulties with the two very different and distinct sections of his present party, from the start. He had felt it advisable, especially in view of his new style and status, to bring south with him some suitably chiefly supporters, however recent their adherence, since Hebridean shipmasters and Irish gallowglass captains, effective though they might be otherwise, scarcely enhanced the dignity of the King of Argyll appearing before the monarch of them all. Unfortunately the said fighting-men did not approve of the new lairdly ones, and *vice versa*.

Teviotdale widened notably beyond the town of Hawick and the Argyll party were the more impressed by the richness of the land, its fruitfulness, the size and numbers of its farmeries and granges, villages, mills and orchards, so very different from what they were accustomed to in the Highlands and Isles. It was harvest time here, mid-August—although it would not be so in Argyll for a full month yet—and everywhere folk were at work amongst the rigs of strip cultivation which clothed all the valley-floors and the gentle flanking slopes with their golden mantling; cutting, stooking, gleaning, leading-in on sleds. Notable was the number of monkish figures, by their habits, working the land; the Highlanders had heard that the Roman Church was strong on garnering the fruits of the land and turning it into wealth—which seemed to them a strange

115

preoccupation for the religious. But it certainly seemed to enhance the countryside and no doubt aided the people. Somerled promised himself that when he could ensure reasonable security and peace in his own domains on the Hebridean seaboard, he would seek to encourage a like industry and productivity insofar as that very different land would allow. There were parts, he believed, where corn and fruits would grow well, level areas such as Loch Etive-side, Loch Fyne-side, Appin, Lismore, the Ross of Mull and best of all the flat isle of Tiree and much of Islay. He must learn more about cultivation of the soil, seeds, drainage and the like, whilst he was here in the South.

They followed the south bank of Teviot, mile upon plenteous mile, having to ford the major incoming tributary waters of Rule, Jed and Kale, as well as a host of lesser streams. Near each ford there was a village or hamlet, with mills and usually a hospice of monks, for the shelter of travellers, for payment—never had these travellers seen the like, so many people, so much preoccupation with work, so much evidence of wealth, so many acquisitive churchmen. It was all very different from their anticipation.

Impressed as they were, it was nothing to the interest and even excitement with which they at length set eyes on Rook's Burgh, where their great Teviot eventually emptied itself into the greater Tweed. The last mile or so of land between the two converging rivers formed a narrowing peninsula, and this area was a remarkable sight indeed, wholly filled with buildings, cabins, houses, barns, sheds, pavilions, warehouses, churches, a vast jumble of roofs and gables, chimneys and spires, all in timber and clay and stone, more buildings huddled together than any of the visitors had ever before set eyes on. They had no towns in the West Highlands, only scattered townships; and although they had recently passed towns of a sort on their way here, Graitney at Esk-mouth, Langholm in Ewes-water and Hawick-on-Teviot, none of these compared in size and density of housing with this new Rook's Burgh, the smoke of whose myriad fires hung above the area in a blue cloud. Out of this cloud rose, above the town, the royal castle, on the thrusting spine of rock which formed the final apex of the peninsula and which came to a sharp point where the two rivers met, a notably strong position, protected by cliffs and water on two of its arrowhead-shaped sides. The royal emblem of the Boar of Scotland, blue on silver, flew from great banners along its frowning ramparts. It all made Castle Sween seem like a toy fortalice.

Seeking not to be too much affected by what they saw, the Highlanders rode on.

They were met and challenged on the outskirts of the town by a clanking troop of mounted men in plate-armour, with the boar painted on their breastplates, led by a young knight in glistening steel, crested helmet and colourful heraldry, obviously a Norman, who demanded haughtily to know who they were and what they wanted at His Grace's town of Rook's Burgh.

"I am Somerled, King of Argyll, come to see David, King of Scots," he was answered, just as haughtily. "Conduct me to his presence, sirrah."

The knight looked a little offput. "First . . . first we shall have to discover whether His Grace will receive you," he declared.

"He will receive me," Somerled assured. "Unless he is a fool, as well as a boor. Your liege lord is no fool, I take it?"

The other all but choked, glared, found no words, and reined round his magnificent charger, his troop following suit in well-trained fashion, amidst much clatter. Taking this to be sufficient invitation, the Argyll party trotted after.

They threaded the narrow streets and twisting wynds of the town, seeking to hold their breaths against the stench of it, the folk all drawing heedfully aside to give the crown of the causeway to the imperious horsemen. They passed no fewer than four establishments which they took to be monasteries, by the tonsured and habited guardians—a very holy town, despite the smells. But then David mac Malcolm was known to be a very holy man, and founder of abbeys and churches innumerable. It was to be hoped that he would prove to be as reasonable as he was religious— which was not always the case.

They jingled up a steep track above the houses, zigzagging to the ridge which bore the castle, but westwards of this. Along, eastwards they turned and came to a gap in the spine, high above the swirling Teviot, part-natural, part-artificial, sheer-sided and filled with water, being dammed at the ends. Across this a drawbridge was thrown, guarded by massive circular drum-towers and portcullis, lofty curtain-walls extending left and right. This was the only access to the fortress-palace.

They drummed across the bridge and through the gate-house-pend into a large forecourt beyond. Here their escort dismounted, the Highlanders stiffly did likewise, and as grooms came to take the horses, their knight disappeared. They were left, without further word, to kick their heels.

They had not long to wait, however. Presently the young Norman returned with Saor MacNeil, looking somewhat abashed, and an older man, good-looking and richly-dressed, in his early forties.

"I am Hervey de Warenne of Keith, Knight Marischal of this realm," the last announced. "I greet you, on behalf of the King. Which is the so-called King of Argyll?"

"I am Somerled MacGillebride MacGilladmnan MacFergus of Argyll, Norman. Of older royal blood than your master, who is grandson of the miller's daughter of Forteviot! Take me to him."

The Knight Marischal raised his brows. "You speak rashly, sir!"

"I speak truthfully. I have travelled a long way, by sea and land, to speak with David mac Malcolm. I sent MacNeil of Oronsay here, to inform him. Now—where is your King?"

"At this present, he is at his devotions." That was short.

"Devotions? At this hour! What do you mean? Is this a king or a monk?"

"Very much a king—as you will discover, sir!"

"It is but two hours past noon. Devotions?"

"His Grace is much troubled," de Warenne declared stiffly. "Since the Queen died, he is sore stricken. He is not . . ."

"The Queen? Matilda of Huntingdon. Dead . . .?"

"Yes. Have you not heard? Queen Matilda died near a month ago. They were close. His Grace spends much time in prayer."

"I did not know. I am sorry. No word of this had reached Argyll when we left. I would not have come at this time."

"No doubt, sir. But since you are here, we must make the best of it. You and yours will be weary, requiring sustenance. Come—I will conduct you to quarters . . ."

The Knight Marischal led them through two inner courtyards, to reach the main range of buildings. Erected along a spine of rock, this castle could have no conventional shape or plan, consisting of strung-out towers and blocks linked by lower subsidiary works and wings, so that the whole was many hundreds of feet in length. Through halls and great apartments and along corridors of stone-vaulting, all seeming to teem with folk, they went, their Highland garb and tartans stared at. Eventually, in a lesser hall, comfortable with wall-hangings, woven carpeting on the stone floor such as Somerled had never before seen, mural garderobes and a fire on a wide hearth, de Warenne deposited them.

"Bedchambers are above in the tower, sufficient for all," he said. "The wherewithal to cleanse yourselves is in the garderobes. Meats and wine will be before you shortly. And I shall inform His Grace of your presence when he comes from his chamber . . ."

"No need, Hervey—I am here," a voice declared, to turn all heads. In the further doorway a man stood, of noble but ravaged features, of middle years and middle height, slender, almost emaciated, dressed in nondescript fashion but with a far from nondescript carriage and expression. His eyes were large and fine, his countenance sensitive—but there was nothing weak about the mobile mouth and firm jawline.

"Sire!" De Warenne bowed deeply, and perforce so did the others.

"I heard the arrival of newcomers. Are these our friends from Argyll?"

"One naming himself *King* of Argyll, Your Grace." The Marischal distinctly emphasised the title.

"Ah—no doubt he has his reasons. I bid him, and you all, welcome to my house. Even though you find us in sore straits."

"I am sorry, my lord King. I grieve for you in your great loss. We did not know. I would have delayed. I am Somerled of Argyll. And these are chiefs and great men of that kingdom."

"I thank you." David came forward. "Do I take it, Lord Somerled, that you have come from Argyll of a purpose to visit me? Only that?"

"I have, my lord David. A long road."

"So I judged. Therefore, friend, you must have had good reason for making that journey. What, I wonder? Could it be that it concerns your good-brother's brother, Angus MacEth of Moray, my nephew, who has recently fallen in the field, in revolt against me?"

Somerled blinked. This sorrowing, noble-seeming devotionalist could still aim a shrewd thrust, it seemed.

"Not so," he declared. "I was much against that ill-conceived venture. As was my good-brother, Malcolm of Ross. My concern here is quite otherwise." The time did not appear to be propitious, at this stage, to divulge the true reason behind his visit.

"Ah—then I am the better pleased. No doubt we shall learn why we are thus honoured, then, in due course!"

"Is it not sufficient that I come to pay my respects? And to inform your Grace of what transpires on the north-western seaboard?"

"To be sure. I am suitably rebuked!" David inclined his head. "My good friend Hervey of Keith, the Marischal, is looking to your comfort. Any requirements or wishes he, or my Chamberlain, will attend to, on my behalf. You have but to ask. Refreshment will perhaps . . . inspirit you! Afterwards we shall talk further." Without formality, he turned and went whence he had come, de Warenne at least bowing deeply to his back.

The monarch gone, the Marischal turned almost hotly on Somerled. "I cannot congratulate you!" he exclaimed. "That was no way to behave before the King of Scots. His Grace was too patient! Hereafter, I charge you, be more respectful, sirrah!"

"Respectful, Norman? I respect David mac Malcolm very well. Did I not tell him that I came to pay respects? But I do not grovel! I am, thank God, my own man. And King of Argyll. By the same token, Sir Marischal, I could ask that you show more respect to *my* kingship!"

The other was spared having adequately to answer that by the arrival of a file of servitors with meats and wine.

In the stir and clatter of setting down this provision, he took his departure a deal more stiffly than his master had done.

When they were alone, some of Somerled's new chieftains turned on him, also of the opinion that his attitude to King David was too strong, and unlikely to forward their cause.

Mouth full, he shook his head. "I think not. I have given him warning that I am not easy to deal with—always good policy if you have a bargain to strike. That one will not fail to perceive my message. He knows what is important and what is not. Nor will he take offence at what does not injure him."

Certainly, later, when they were summoned to a private chamber in the King's own tower, they found David still courteous and unruffled. He could scarcely be called affable, but then he was a man in deep mourning for a wife deeply loved. He was seated at a table, with three other men, de Warenne again, another Norman whom he named Hugo de Morville, no doubt some relative of the High Constable who had won Stracathro, and a cleric introduced as John, Bishop of Glasgow, Chancellor of the realm. There were benches for Somerled and three of his group, opposite, the others having to stand behind.

"I trust that you are now rested and refreshed from your journeying, my friend," the monarch said. "I shall be interested to learn what are your intentions and desires. But first, my Lord Somerled, this of title and address. I hear that you are naming yourself King. Will you enlighten me?"

"To be sure, my Lord David. I am King and Regulus of Argyll, an ancient style and designation."

"H'mm. I know of the Lord Ewan, one of my vassals, who so styled himself. On what authority I am less than clear."

"Ewan MacSween, yes. We are kin, at some distance. He is now naming himself King of the Isles, only. I have taken over Argyll, and Ewan has resigned that style to myself."

"Ah. A private arrangement! Yet Argyll is part of *my* kingdom, friend Somerled."

"As is Man—yet there is a King of Man. And Argyll was wholly in the hands of the Norsemen, these many years. I have recovered it—or most of it."

"I have heard of your prowess," David nodded. "I congratulate you and admire. But conquering Norsemen scarcely makes you a king, does it? Your father formerly held the style of *Thane* of Argyll, I understand?"

"What makes a king, my lord? Other than being your father's son. A sharp sword and a strong arm. That, and the will. Nothing more, I say. My father is dead. He was content to be an exile, dispossessed. *Your* father was not. He took the sword and slew King MacBeth. And made himself a king. There is your answer."

Into the murmuring of his supporters, David spoke. "I see. But there is a difference, is there not? My father, Malcolm, was the son of King Duncan. Yours was but son of the previous Thane."

"He was lawfully born, at least!"

The scrape of de Warenne's bench on the stone floor was loud, as he half-rose to his feet. "Sire, this is intolerable!" he exclaimed. "This man's insolent tongue should be cut out!"

The monarch raised a monitory hand. "Quiet, Hervey. The Lord Somerled has come a long way to say this. No doubt for a purpose. We must let him say it. Besides, it is true. My grandsire, King Duncan, did omit to wed my father's mother. The omission seemed never to trouble Malcolm!" He turned back to Somerled. "So you claim, my friend, that a sword makes the king? That may be true also, sometimes. So long as another king with a longer and sharper sword does not dispute the issue!"

"That is so, Your Grace."

"Good. I am glad that you agree. You believe, therefore, that I should accept you and your kingship in my Argyll? Why?"

"Because it is in your interests to do so. Only so can you keep Argyll within the kingdom of Scotland."

"You mean that you might otherwise take it out of Scotland? What of the longer sword, then?"

"That longer sword might at the time be fully employed! And nearer here than Argyll and the isles. As it has been, but recently."

"Ah. So you consider that there might be another threat to my kingdom and throne? But . . . . Angus MacEth is dead."

"Malcolm, his brother, is not."

"I see. But you told me, earlier, that Malcolm was much against this recent rising? As were you."

"So I advised him, yes."

David nodded. "So, if you advised him differently again . . .?"

"I would not *wish* to do that, Your Grace."

"If Angus of Moray was beaten, with great loss, and slain, why not Malcolm of Ross?"

"Malcolm might have better allies."

There was silence for a little. The Chancellor-Bishop spoke. "The Earl of Ross is a vassal of the crown, my lord. And more than a vassal, one of the *Ri*, or Seven Earls of the King's Council. Have you considered that to urge or counsel such to rise in arms against the High King, even to suggest it, could be construed as highest treason?"

"In another vassal of the crown, perhaps, Sir Priest."

"And you are not that?"

"Not . . . yet."

"So—we come to it," David said. "At length. You do not consider yourself to be my vassal, although Argyll is in my realm of Scotland. But you *might* be. If I accepted your kingship and conquest of Argyll. Is that it? Is that what you have come here to say?"

"Only partly, my lord King."

For a moment the monarch seemed to lose his carefully nurtured patience and calm. His fists clenched and he leaned forward over the table. "There is more, then? What more? Out with it, man."

Somerled was the more assured, reasonable. "Bute and Arran, my lord King. These islands, although not part of Argyll, belong under its sway, by any true judgement. They are in the lee of Kintyre. Indeed, in wrong hands, they constitute a threat to all southern Argyll. The Norse now dominate them."

"So . . .?"

"If I free them of the Norse, I would wish them added to Argyll."

"You have a notable appetite for lands and territories, sir! Have you not already sufficient? These have a lord, as it is."

"Who does nothing. Like Ewan MacSween. Lord only in name. There is grave weakness along all those coasts,

123

amongst the Scots, a failure of the spirit. Has been for long. And for sufficient reason."

"You mean, because of the Norse invasions?"

"I mean, Lord David, because they have had no aid and support over the years from the King of Scots, their liege-lord!"

Not a few there drew quick breaths at that, on both sides of the table. De Warenne glared, stirring.

David, however, had recovered his calm. "You speak very plainly, my lord," he said.

"Would you have it otherwise? It is truth. Not your Grace to blame, to be sure—before your reign. But your royal father and brothers, in especial Edgar, abandoned all the Highland West and its folk. Malcolm even *gave* the Hebrides to King Magnus Barefoot of Norway. My father paid the price, losing Argyll. Others likewise. Now, I win it back. Without your aid."

"Then, no doubt, you will win back Bute and Arran also. Whether I grant them to you or no!"

"Perhaps. But I do not seek to win them for another lord. Who may continue to do little to hold them."

"These are great and extensive lands, Arran in especial. Held by my High Steward . . ."

"With all respect, my lord King—not held! Granted to, by charter—that is all. If the Steward *held* them, I would not now be seeking them. Who sits in Rothesay Castle? Not Walter fitz Alan, your Steward, but one MacRoderick, keeper for the King of Man! By passing the lordship to me, under your suzerainty, you will gain much, and your Steward will lose nothing which is not already lost to him. Is it not so?"

The monarch glanced round at his supporters, and shrugged. "All this will have to be considered," he said, after a moment. "I cannot give you any answers now. Enough for the moment. You will join me in the great hall presently, for repast and entertainment?" Clearly the audience was at an end.

The Highland party rose, bowed and left.

"How, think you, will David respond to all that?" Saor MacNeil asked, as they made for their own tower. "You did not spare him!"

"Nor did I injure him. All that I said was honest, and he will know it. He will do as I have asked."

"Are you so sure?" MacFerdoch, Abbot of Glendochart, demanded. "After such mauling, he will hardly love you."

"I do not ask that he loves me—although I would not be sorry if he did. I ask only that he faces the facts. And I judge that one will do so. For he is an honest man, I think. Indeed I hope that he will, for more than my own cause. I have a notion that he could be a man after my own heart, that David mac Malcolm, and I would be happy to call him my friend."

None saw fit to comment on that.

They certainly had no cause to complain over the quality of their royal host's hospitality and entertainment that night. A banquet was produced, remarkable for its variety as well as abundance, at such short notice, with Somerled in the place of honour at David's right hand; and this followed by excellent diversion, with singers and minstrels, dancers and jugglers, sennachies and storytellers or sagamen—who presumably were domiciled here in the town of Rook's Burgh. It made a lively and enjoyable evening, even if the monarch himself could scarcely have been in a mood to enjoy it to the full.

Next day a deer-hunt was arranged for the visitors, in the nearby Forest of Jedworth, part of the vast Ettrick Forest which covered so much of the Middle March. Despite his strictures towards Malcolm of Ross over a preoccupation with the deer, Somerled was very fond of hunting—when it did not interfere with more vital matters. He enjoyed the challenge of the chase; moreover, as a kind of token warfare, it helped in time of peace to maintain men's fitness for real action. David himself did not accompany them and the hunt was led by Hugo de Morville who, with de Warenne, appeared to be one of the High King's closest associates; fortunately he was less hot-tempered and more amiable than the Marischal. Somerled distinguished himself by spearing a fierce and massive boar—only to discover afterwards that in this royal forest the boar, the royal emblem, was reserved for slaying by the royal family only. Needless to say it was de Warenne who in due course pointed this out.

Tired after a long day's sport, no serious discussions were

initiated that night. Somerled was not concerned at such delay, although some of his people were. King David, for dignity's sake, required a certain amount of time to elapse before he could decently concede victory, he asserted.

In the morning, however, with no sign of the monarch and no summons to his presence nor any recreation or pastime organised for the visitors, they became distinctly uneasy and Somerled began to wonder, even though he endeavoured not to reveal his doubts. They were brought meals in their own tower but otherwise left severely alone. But in mid-afternoon there was some commotion in the courtyards, obviously the arrival of a quite large party; and about an hour later they received the awaited call to the same plain royal chamber as before.

They found David flanked by his three aides as previously but with another, a tall, stooping hawklike man of middle years, whose great beak of a nose and tight lips were in part belied by great liquid dark eyes almost like a woman's.

"Greetings, my Lord Somerled," the monarch said. "I hope that you have not wearied in my house? Here is my friend, Walter fitz Alan, High Steward of this my realm."

So that was the reason for the delay, the summoning of the Steward from wherever he roosted. No doubt it was significant—but could bear more than the one interpretation.

Somerled inclined his head but made no comment.

"I have told the Lord Walter of your . . . contentions, sir. But come, sit, and we shall discuss further."

"I believed that discussion was finished, my lord King, and the time come for decisions," Somerled said levelly. But he and his party seated themselves.

"Allow me to state again your proposals, my lord—and correct me if I mistake," David went on easily. "You wish that I should accept your occupation of Argyll and the other lands which you have taken from the Norsemen; to acknowledge you as Regulus and sub-King of Argyll; and you desire me to permit you to recapture the islands of Bute and Arran and thereafter, if successful, to add them to your lordship of Argyll—although these already belong to the High Steward. These are your . . . requirements?"

"Yes. Save that I do not ask to be *permitted* to recapture Bute and Arran. I intend to do so. For the rest, it is correct."

"I see. Tell me, then, why do you ask my agreement first, if you intend to take these islands anyway?"

"I do not ask your agreement, Sir King. I ask only for a *grant* of these lands in my name, a mere paper, a charter—if I can take them. If not, and the Norse retain them, neither you nor the Steward have lost anything."

"But why these? You asked no grant nor charter for the rest!"

"Because these islands lie close to your Lowland shores, within sight and striking distance of your Ayr and Renfrew coasts. None other of my lands do so. You could, or your Steward could, seek to take them back from me after I had ousted the Norsemen. I would not wish to be for ever defending them against you. So I would have a charter, bearing your royal signature—which I believe you would adhere to."

"Thank you!" That was curt. Then David mustered a faint smile and turned to the tall man. "You hear that, Walter? How you are esteemed! Does it alter your decision?"

The Steward shook his head, wordless.

"Very well. The Lord Walter has agreed to resign to me Arran and Bute in exchange for new lands to be transferred to him in Galloway and Dundonald of Kyle. My Lord Somerled, in return for my acceptance of all this, you are prepared to become my leal vassal, to take me as your liege lord and to accord to me your full and strong support at all times, as honest vassal should?"

"I am, my lord David. And more than that."

"More . . .?"

"I would take you for my friend," the younger man said simply.

Gasps and exclamations from all the company, astonishment, alarm, even outrage, writ large on faces. But not on David of Scotland's face. He sat staring at Somerled for a few moments, expression strange, then rose and leaning across the table, held out his hand—clearly not for any ritual gesture of fealty which would have required a different attitude and would have been difficult above that board, but to be shaken by the speaker.

"Well said, Somerled my friend, King of Argyll!" he exclaimed.

For once Somerled MacFergus found no words.

They stood thus for a little, and all others must stand likewise, holding each other not only in the normal hand-shake but each leaning to grasp the other's forearm with the left hand. Then, as their grips relaxed, Somerled stepped back, eyes still on David's, to stride round the table-end to behind the High King's chair, sank down on one knee.

Again David held out his hand, this time differently, palm vertical, and the other took it between his own two, in the age-old token of homage and allegiance.

"I, Somerled, take you, David, to be my liege lord," he intoned. "I swear by Almighty God to be your man, for the lands I hold of you in this your realm. And I vow to support you, with all my powers, from this day forward, in your royal and right causes and endeavours. Before these as witness, I, Somerled MacGillebride MacFergus, have spoken it."

"And I, David of Scotland, take you, Somerled, to be my man, of heart and hand and military service, to trust and sustain you at all times. Be faithful, as shall I. Arise, King of Argyll."

So it was done. The watchers looked with varying expressions at the two men who stood together smiling, so suddenly in evident harmony and accord after all the warfare of words. Enthusiasm seemed to be confined to the two principals. It was going to stick in many throats to call Somerled king. But the High King was doing so, and his subjects could do no less.

The Highland party left Rook's Burgh the next day for Esk-mouth and their ships. David and Somerled parted firm friends.

CHAPTER 8

"This place would not be difficult to defend, at least," Somerled said grimly, gazing shorewards. "Perhaps they rely on all these cliffs and rock and reefs? Or are they all asleep? Or drunken? I had thought that we would have had fifty longships or galleys sniffing around us by now."

"They must know that we are here," Cathula MacIan said. "Therefore they conceive themselves to be in no danger from us. The King of Argyll's emblem on our sails is sufficient to reassure all!" That verged on the disrespectful.

"Perhaps Olaf Morsel has shrunk away still further, until he has become invisible!" Saor MacNeil suggested. "They say that he grows smaller every year."

Somerled ignored this further example of humour. "He may yet surprise us. I am not prepared to be fooled, even if you are. You, Conn, have been here before, you say. It is your notion that the Manx fleet is like to be at this south end of the island?"

"Aye, lord. There is a deep and fair haven, in a notable bottle of a bay. It is not to be seen, behind St. Michael's Isle. It is large enough and secure enough, facing almost due north, to be sheltering a hundred ships and more. There will be Olaf's fleet—for his castle of Rushen is nearby, they told me. There is another bay beyond, on which the castle stands, but it is shallow, tidal. Venture into this St. Michael's Bay unbidden and you would be trapped."

They were sailing in formation, eight ships, a mile or so off the eastern shore of the Isle of Man, with its long and dire rampart of cliffs and stacks and screes, against the feet of which the seas boiled whitely. Somerled had been careful as to the number of vessels he had brought, leaving almost forty others in Rothesay Bay of Bute, over one hundred miles to the north. He calculated that eight was approximately right, enough to establish his dignity but not enough to seem to pose any real threat to the King of Man. At Rothesay, the Bute capital, he had not had to fight for possession, as he had been prepared to do; but he had learned that before he could take over his new-granted territories of Bute and Arran he would have to settle with Olaf of Man who, although himself a vassal of David of Scotland, apparently exercised dominion over these islands, belonging to the High Steward or not. Such was the state of the western seaboard of Scotland. Somerled was bold and could be rash; but he was not prepared to challenge the power of Man. Not just yet, at any rate.

They were nearing the southern end of the thirty-three-miles-long island when they saw the first of the Manxmen, two longships a couple of miles ahead, their sails bearing the curious three-legged emblem. These kept their distance, obviously sent out to watch and shadow.

Well past a prominent headland which Conn named as St. Sanctan's Head—Man appeared to be a great place for saints—MacMahon, peering half-right, declared that he thought that was St. Michael's Isle almost directly ahead. It did not look like an island from here, being fairly close inshore. But that long low line of small cliffs beyond it must be the southernmost peninsula of Man, Langness. If so, the hidden bay he had spoken of would be just west of St. Michael's. They should turn in shortly.

If the others tended to doubt Conn's memory, for there was no sign of any sizeable bay, at least there were a scattering of houses to be seen now above the cliffs and coves, inlets and reefs—although still nothing to suggest that this Man was the densely populated and prominent little kingdom which it was known to be. So far, in the thirty-odd miles they had seen little evidence that it was any more populous and important a place than was, for instance, the Isle of Jura in their own Argyll.

It was not until they were almost up with St. Michael's Isle, fearsomely ringed with skerries, that they began to perceive that what had seemed to be merely a small bay of that island was in fact the opening to something much larger, this impression added to by a jutting point at the other side, which proved to be on the mainland of Man. Steering further over, westwards, to avoid approaching this gap directly, suddenly they saw within—and all was abruptly, astonishingly, transformed.

A deep, round basin appeared, almost a mile deep, probably, and after this narrow opening, widening to almost as much, all backed by gentler green slopes and woodland, the first they had seen, this rising ground dotted plentifully with houses and cabins of stone and timber. But it was the bay itself which constrained the attention, being so full of shipping that scarcely any water was visible from outside—longships, galleys, birlinns but also heavier trading vessels, barks, carracks and fishing-craft, all neatly drawn up in ranks and groupings. At a guess there must have been at least one hundred vessels there, a concentration larger than any Somerled had ever seen, the more extraordinary after the empty waters they had sailed through.

He was impressed, although he did not say so. Although it was quite a decision to take, he ordered the dragon-ship to turn and sail directly in.

He led his squadron into the crowded bay, all alert for the first sign of trouble or assault, Somerled wondering whether there was going to be room for his eight ships. But proceeding down a narrow central channel, watched by silent men on some of the flanking craft, they came presently to an area left open at the head of the bay, not visible from the sea. Here a stone jetty thrust out. Only one vessel was berthed at this, a great dragon-ship even larger than Somerled's.

Manoeuvring his own ship to the other side of this jetty, and leaving his other craft to look after themselves, he disembarked, his party after him, not waiting for any guidance or permission. No hostile moves were apparent around them, only a wary watching—although it was to be seen, now, that the central channel had been closed behind their last vessel by the two longships which had shadowed them.

On land, quite large numbers of folk had appeared, to eye the newcomers. But nobody came forward to greet them. There was a notable lack of welcome, but no real atmosphere of tension.

Somerled turned to MacNeil. "Tell them," he said.

Saor stepped forward, hand high. "Greetings to all here," he called. "I, MacNeil of Oronsay, announce that the great

131

and potent Somerled the Mighty, King of Argyll, comes to visit the good King Olaf of Man. Let all rejoice!" If that held mockery as well as flourish, few there would perceive it.

No response was apparent amongst the onlookers.

"An unmannerly folk," Somerled commented. He raised his voice. "Who is chiefest here?" he demanded.

Although men amongst the crowd facing them looked at each other, none made any move, nor spoke. They were a mixed lot, villagers, seamen, fisher-folk and not a few who looked as though they might be Norsemen.

"Very well." Somerled waved the others forward and started off, up towards the waiting throng.

The crowd parted before them. Ignoring them now, as though they did not exist, he marched on and through, men close enough to touch on either side. Behind him Saor and Cathula led half-a-dozen others, including MacIan of Uladail, the young woman's half-brother. Dermot Maguire remained with the ship. The unforthcoming crowd turned and followed on, at a distance.

Stalking ahead, Somerled made for a stone building, part-way up the hill, unlike any of the others there, warehouses, sheds, cabins or typical Viking-houses, in that it was much longer, single-storeyed, with roundheaded windows. He guessed it to be a church, a Romish kirk. He had seen two or three of these on his visit to Scotland to see King David. The Celtic Columban Church did not go in for such buildings, preferring open-air worship, and using modest beehive-shaped cells and huts for their cashels and shelters for portable altars, fonts and the like. But Man would adhere to the Roman rite, at least as far as its Norse aristocracy was concerned. At the east end of this long building, the gable was surmounted by a cross; but at the other end, a smoking chimney.

Somerled was spared the indignity of having to knock and wait at the west-end door, presumably to the presbytery-house, for a priest in a brown girdled habit, head tonsured on the crown, appeared therein as they approached.

"Sir Monk—I am Somerled of Argyll. I come to speak with Olaf Godfreysson of Man. None here appear to have any wits or courtesy. Have you? Can you direct me where to go to find the King?"

"To be sure, my lord. I . . . I greet you . . . in the name of God." That last sounded doubtful.

"I thank you. Where do we go, then? Likewise in the name of God!"

"I will take you, my son," the priest said, presumably enheartened by this sign of piety. "It is not far. Scarce two miles, if we go over the hill and by the shore. To Rushen, the King's house."

"Two miles! Lord—do all his guests have to walk two miles to see Olaf Buttered-Bread?"

"If they are known to be coming, he usually sends horses, my son."

"The Lord Somerled is usually called King rather than son, Sir Priest!" Saor said grinning. He turned to his foster-brother. "Do we wait for horses then, my lord King?"

"I prefer to stretch my legs than endure such company, man! Come."

"Permit that I get my staff, Sire . . ."

The priest leading, they set off, amidst grumbling from some of the party. The crowd behind made no attempt to follow now. At first they followed a well-defined road westwards, flanked by warehouses, barns and the like, which appeared to lead to a low pass in the gentle hillsides here. But soon they turned off, to the left, to climb rather more steeply into woodland, but still by a path. Conn declared that they were here crossing the neck of the long Langness peninsula, which extended for almost three miles southwards.

The change from populated country to scrub woodland and heath and small rocky outcrops was sudden and dramatic. Their track probed and wound, sometimes in open glades and brackeny slopes but more often in dense greenwood. It seemed an odd way to go seeking the King of Man. "Does this lead to your castle?" Somerled demanded of the priest. "Surely there is a better way than this."

"It is the shorter way," he was told. "Since Your Highness seemed loth to walk. The road, the other road, takes a longer route, for carts and the carriage of goods. To the Castle Haven of Rushen. This cuts off a corner."

It was whilst crossing one of the glades, green and open, with the less energetic of the company already complaining that surely they had covered more than any two miles, that there was an interruption, an eruption. A trampling, crashing sound, and the sudden baying of hounds, in the woodland to their half-left, turned all heads. Out from the thickets there bounded a tall, heavy-antlered stag, shaggy-maned and mud-coated from wallowing, which dashed across the grassy glade at an angle, apparently scarcely perceiving the walkers. As it leapt on into the further trees, an arrow could be seen to be projecting from its rump.

"A hunt! And a fine beast!" Somerled exclaimed. "A score of stones, at the least."

"Yes—this Langness is the King's hunting-forest, lord."

"If it holds beasts like that then Olaf is to be congratu-lated . . ."

But this appreciation from a keen sportsman was short-lived. Preceded by bounding, long-legged, shaggy deer-hounds, a scatter of horsemen burst out from the woodland on the same line as the stag but spread over quite a wide front. Shouting and beating at their animals' flanks, they thundered across the open glade, perhaps a dozen of them, colourfully-clad. Three were much in the lead, young men these, all with reddish-yellow hair streaming, and astride fine mounts. Because of their placing as they emerged from the trees, two of these, to follow the disappearing stag's route, found the walkers on the road directly in their line. Without pause or the least drawing aside of their beasts to take avoiding action, these spurred on straight for the Scots party.

"Save us—they are going to ride us down!" Saor cried, as it became clear that the huntsmen were not going to swerve. "Fiend seize them . . .!"

Somerled, swiftly judging which direction to move to avoid being struck, began to jump, then remembered Cathula at his back, and jerking round, grabbed her bodily and all in the same movement flung himself and her aside. Only just in time. A grinning horseman pounded past within a yard of them, as they stumbled and fell, the young woman undermost, and the ground shook to the beat of the horse's hooves as they collapsed on it. At the other side, Farquhar MacFerdoch, Abbot of Glendochart, was spun round by the second laughing huntsman and cannoned into

134

MacIan of Uladail so that both lost their balance and fell also.

"Precious soul of God . . .!" Somerled gasped in an explosion of wrath—before solicitude for the woman beneath him overcame even that elemental fury and he picked himself up, to raise her in some concern. She was winded, her bosom heaving, but otherwise apparently unhurt, although she could not find her voice at first.

A female voice did speak, however, to lift the man's head. Another of the hunters was there beside them, had reined up, a young woman, a mere girl in fact, who was looking down at them a trifle anxiously.

"You are not hurt?" she was asking. "That was not well done. I am sorry."

"By all the Powers—it was *not* well done!" Somerled burst out. "A God's name—what oafs are these? What way is that to behave? Ridden down like dumb cattle . . .!"

"I am sorry. It was unfortunate, yes. I . . . ."

"Unfortunate!" Somerled found that he was almost shaking Cathula in his ire. He swallowed and sought to restrain himself, aided undoubtedly by the fact that he was glaring up into a very lovely, piquant young face of delicately-chiselled features, fine greenish-grey eyes and flaming red hair. Moreover the expression was disarmingly sympathetic. "This, this lady might have been sorely injured," he ended, rather feebly.

The girl's eyebrows rose. Clearly she had not perceived that Cathula was a woman and no mere youth—after all, her hair was no longer than that of most of the men and she was dressed as they were, in saffron kilt and shirt with long, calfskin, sleeveless jerkin, wearing belt and dirk. Admittedly her breasts were prominent and shapely, far from masculine, but Somerled had his arms round her, largely masking them.

"Lady . . .! I did not see it. I am the more sorry. They, they would not know . . ."

"Does that excuse them, the ruffians?"

"It is no matter—I am well enough," Cathula got out. "And it was no fault of this girl."

"No. But . . ." He shrugged. "Who are these people? I do not intend to forget them!"

135

"They are my brothers—my *half*-brothers. I make apology for them. They are too . . . spirited. And the hunt further rouses them. I am Ragnhilde. If you require aid, remedy, succour, name my name at Rushen. Ragnhilde. I bid you good-day. And to you, lady." Nodding her red head, the horsewoman heeled her mount onwards after the disappeared hunt. Two attendants, who had halted with her, spurred on behind.

"Lord—a piece, that one! Not more than seventeen years, I swear—yet sure of herself. Ragnhilde, she said—a Norse name."

"She is the Lady Ragnhilde Olafsdotter, the King's favourite child," their priest informed, in some agitation. "This was . . . unfortunate."

"Unfortunate again! Save us—I would call it otherwise!" But Somerled's tone was more thoughtful than angry now. "Olaf's own daughter? Then, the others—half-brothers, she said?"

"Yes, lord—natural sons of the King. Three. The Lords Logmann, Ranald and Harald."

"So! And mannerless churls all! Is this the style of Olaf, then? Uncouth, ill-bred indeed, inhospitable. Is that the Kingdom of Man?"

"No, lord—King Olaf is not so. He is mannerly, fair-spoken. Of good Christian quality . . ."

"But spawns ill-natured bastards, it seems!"

Their guide shrugged and sighed over the lapses of princes. "These are . . . unfortunate," he conceded. "Those lawfully begotten are otherwise. His true son, Godfrey. And the Lady Ragnhilde. The King was long sick, unable to control these young lords. They run wild . . ."

"Then they will not run wild again, with me!" Somerled turned to MacIan and MacFerdoch who were dusting themselves down in frowning offence, apparently unhurt but muddied from a puddle. "You are none the worse? Save in your feelings? Keep your wrath for later, then! Now—how much further to this Rushen Castle, Sir Priest?"

"A mile, no more, Sire . . ."

"Do I thank you for knocking me down and near flattening my person, my lord King?" Cathula asked, as they moved on. "I take it that it was kindly meant?"

136

"Better than being trampled by hooves," he asserted. "You are not hurt, in truth?"

"My breasts may be a mite tender. For kissing! That is all. If such still interests your Highness—after feasting your royal eyes on the Lady Ragnhilde!"

"What do you mean—feasting my eyes!"

"I saw how you looked at that chit of a girl, Sorley MacFergus! You will know her again next time you meet, I have no doubt. Her eyes, her hair, her face, her person! You missed nothing of that one!"

"You have an ill tongue in your head, Cathula MacIan—as I have remarked before!"

"I also have good eyes—even if they are not green! And I have learned about men, to my cost."

"But not when to hold your peace, woman!"

"That one will not hold her peace either, I think! But then, she is a king's daughter and I am a king's harlot!"

He frowned and increased his pace.

They emerged from the forest and scrub presently and came to cultivated land above another bay, a vastly larger bay than St. Michael's, fully a couple of miles wide and the same in depth, but clearly shallow this, littered with rocks and shoals making it unfit for navigation save by small craft. All the far side of this bay was dotted with houses, a large township at the mouth of a fair-sized stream. And standing apart from the town on the near side of the river, and quite close to the tide's-edge, rose a peculiar long straggle of buildings, of various sorts, some stone, some plastered with clay, some painted timber, high and towering or low and squat. Had all not been surrounded by a ditch and rampart of earth, this last topped by a high wall, irregular in outline, it could have been taken for another village or detached suburb of the town, rather than what the priest declared was the castle of Rushen. The Norse, of course, had never been true castle-makers, nor indeed greatly interested in the art of building—save shipbuilding, at which they were the acknowledged experts. Man had been Norse now for over two centuries—at least as far as the overlordship was concerned, although the folk were still of Celtic stock.

To reach this strange castle, which clearly covered many acres of land, they did not have to go as far as the town—

which the priest said they would have to have done had they taken the cart-road. Here, having pointed out to them a gatehouse of sorts and gap in the glacis, he asked to be excused further attendance. In lordly fashion Somerled presented him with a silver coin.

There appeared to be no guards at this gatehouse and the newcomers wandered inside, accosted by none. Nothing could have been more unlike King David's fortress-palace at Rook's Burgh. There were people about, but although these stared at the visitors, none enquired their business or even spoke.

"These are strange folk," Saor MacNeil declared. "They make us as welcome as a visitation of the plague—yet none challenges us either. All those ships, these townships, yet we walk in here with none asking what we do or who we are."

"It is a kingdom mismanaged, I think, by all the signs," Somerled said. "It could be ripe for taking over."

"Ha! Do you have designs on Man, then? As well as Arran and Bute?"

"Do not be a fool, man! This is a sub-kingdom of Scotland now. Olaf pays fealty to David—as do I. Unless David himself gave me Man, I could not take it. It is others who might esteem it worth trying for—England perhaps. Or the Irish Norse. Or Sigurd of Norway himself."

Still unchallenged they had come to an inner space—it would be absurd to call it a courtyard, more like a small village-green, with grass growing amongst the outcropping rock of a low ridge where three cows were tethered and poultry pecked around. A woman with a milking-stool was making for the cows, and her Somerled hailed.

"Can you tell us, friend, where in this rabbit-warren I will find King Olaf?"

"Och, he will be in his bed, just." This was no Norse maiden.

"Ah! His bed? Is he sick, then?"

She shrugged. "Who knows? He likes his bed."

"I see. And where do we find this royal bed?"

"The tall house, yonder." She pointed with her stool.

The building indicated seemed little different from others they had seen, if somewhat larger, a fairly typical Norse hallhouse, clay-covered, with a high-roofed hall in the centre and a double-storey wing at each end. Entering this, they found nobody about the spacious, untidy hall with its rush-strewn floor, long tables and smoke-blackened timbers. They could smell cookery however, and following their noses to a kitchen in one of the wings, they enquired of the King from half-a-dozen scullions busy therein. They were told curtly that the Lord Olaf was asleep and was not to be disturbed.

Somewhat at a loss, the visitors debated. Saor declared roundly that they should go wake the old man there and then—it was mid-afternoon, was it not? MacFerdoch the Abbot agreed; but Cathula pointed out that few men she had known were at their best and kindest when rudely awoken from sleep—and they had come to bargain, she understood? Her half-brother for once agreed with her, suggesting that they should seek out whoever was in charge of this ramshackle establishment, as was only civil, even if civility seemed to be little regarded here.

Somerled nodded. Addressing one of the cooks, he asked whom they should see meantime? Was there a chamberlain? Or a steward?

The man looked blank at such titles, but announced that it was a hunting day and therefore there was nobody about the place. No, he had no idea when the hunters would return.

Swallowing his hot temper, Somerled recollected the young huntswoman's parting words. "The Lady Ragnhilde said that we should seek refreshment and solace here. In her name. It would seem hard to come by!"

"The Lady Ragnhilde? You have seen her?"

"Yes. Less than an hour back. Hunting."

It was extraordinary the difference that name made, in this situation. It was like a key to open the door of attention and service. The scullions were changed folk. If the good lords were friends of the Lady Ragnhilde they must come through to the hall. There they would eat and drink their fill, whatever they would have. Come, come . . .

They found themselves almost fêted instead of ignored, ushered to table, handsomely fed and wined, more servitors appearing all the while and nothing too much trouble.

"This Ragnhilde appears to be queen here," Saor observed, belching approvingly. "But did I not hear that Olaf had married again? So there should be a Queen of Man other than this girl?"

Somerled nodded. "My father heard, just before we left Ireland, that Olaf was wed again. To Affrica, daughter of Fergus of Galloway. Fergus himself cannot be much more than forty years. So this Affrica must be a young wife for Olaf, who is past sixty. Perhaps that is why he keeps to his bed of an afternoon!"

Sage heads nodded at that, with leering glances at Cathula. She was otherwise concerned.

"Who, then, was the former queen? The mother of this girl?"

"She was Ingebiorg, daughter of Earl Hakon of Orkney. Who was himself grandson of Thorfinn Raven-Feeder the Mighty, King MacBeth's half-brother."

"So—she is wholly Norse, then. I could have guessed it!"

Somerled eyed her thoughtfully. They were still at the table, well-satisfied and pique forgotten on the whole, when the young woman in question arrived in the hall, still in her hunting clothes, glorious hair windblown, and another woman with her, not greatly older apparently. They came over to the table.

"I heard that you had come," Ragnhilde said. "You are being well cared for? Are suitably refreshed?"

Somerled had risen, as perforce had the others, save for Cathula. "I thank you, yes, lady. Your name worked the miracle! From lepers, we became as honoured guests!"

"Lepers . . .?" She stared, then shrugged. "If you will tell me your names I will present you to the Queen—Queen Affrica, here."

"Ah, yes. We shall be honoured indeed." He bowed, but scarcely low. "This is Cathula MacIan from Kinlochaline. Her brother MacIan of Uladail. Saor MacNeil of Oronsay. The titular Abbot of Glendochart. And Conn MacMahon from Fermanagh. Myself, I am Somerled of Argyll."

The quick intake of breath at the last was eloquent, as the girl blinked, glanced quickly at her companion, and then back.

"Somerled? You, you . . .?" She swallowed. "You tell

me, you say that you are the great Somerled? He who, who . . .?"

"I am the King of Argyll, yes. Although great is scarcely the word to use, lady, I think."

"But—why did you not say so? Why did you not tell us? Back there . . ."

"I was otherwise engaged, you will recollect? Concerned with more vital matters. Picking up myself and my friend here. Regaining breath. You must forgive me if I was remiss!"

She wagged her head helplessly. Then remembered the required formalities. "My lord King, here is Queen Affrica, wife of my father. Madam—the King of Argyll."

Somerled smiled and bowed again, slightly more deeply. "I congratulate King Olaf to be so blest in his ladies!"

The other young woman had not spoken hitherto, but her eyes had been busy, bold, calculating eyes. She inclined her head.

"I have heard much of the Lord Somerled," she said. "Seeing him, I think that I may not be disappointed."

"I seek never to disappoint, Madam—in especial, ladies!"

"Then we should fare very well." This Affrica was a very different creature from her step-daughter, obviously. Fairly plain-featured, dark, lean of build, she had an almost hungry look to her. She might have reached her twentieth year but looked a deal older than that in experience. Somerled's congratulations to Olaf were less than honest as regards the Queen.

"My friends . . ." he said, and they all bowed, Cathula on her feet now.

"You come to Man to see my father, my lord?" Ragnhilde asked.

"Yes, lady. It appears that he sleeps!"

There was a brief tinkle of laughter from Affrica.

"He has been unwell, has suffered much ill-health," the younger woman said. "But he will be happy to see you, I am sure."

"I hope so. When he awakes."

"You have come far, King Somerled?" the Queen asked.

"Far enough. But more than rewarded by my reception! So . . . heartening!"

Ragnhilde cleared her throat. "I shall go to prepare suitable lodging for Your Highness. You will be weary from journeying."

"And I to change clothing," the Queen said. "No doubt I stink of horse and sweat!"

"Impossible, Madam . . .!"

The ladies left. But in a few moments Ragnhilde was back, alone.

"My lord," she said, urgently, low-voiced. "I would beseech you, of your kindness, to spare my father. He has had much of trouble, sickness and . . . disappointment. If you would forbear to complain to him of my half-brothers' behaviour? It would much distress him. He has enough to bear. It is much to ask—but I would be grateful."

"Why, yes—since *you* ask it. But I would wish a word with those young men."

"To be sure. I have already spoken with them. No doubt they will express their regrets. They are headstrong, grieve our father. Today they were much in wine. Because the Saint was here it was an especial hunt. It was much delayed, because of him—and waiting, they drank."

It was Somerled's turn to blink. "Forgive me if I am stupid. But . . . saint? Drank? I fear that I do not take you . . .?"

"It is St. Malachy O'Moore. You will surely have heard of him? My lord Bishop of Armagh. The great healer and seer. He has been to Rome, and is on his way home to Ireland. As Papal Legate, no less. He dearly loves the hunt, strangely. He is a strange man—but very holy, to be sure."

"Aye? I have heard of Malachy O'Moore. Who has not? He is here, on Man?"

"Yes. He had been at King David's court, in Scotland. Curing the Prince Henry of sickness. He returns to Ireland, but calls here with a message for my father from Pope Innocent. The hunt was arranged for him—but he delayed long. Perhaps at his devotions. My brothers were impatient and, waiting, drank deeply. So . . ."

"I see. Did the saintly huntsman get his stag?"

"Yes. He was in another part of the forest. With the Queen and our Bishop Wimund." She sighed a little. "It is

142

all . . . difficult. But, I thank you, my lord King, for your forbearance. I will now see to your quarters. And inform you when my father will see you . . ."

"That young woman appears to have too much on her mind for her years," Somerled observed, when she had gone. "She it is who orders this house, it seems, not the Queen. She who comes back, concerned for Olaf, not that Affrica. She who will bring us to her father."

"The priest said that she was old Olaf's favourite," Saor pointed out.

"She will do nothing which she does not choose to do, that one," Cathula asserted.

Presently they were conducted, by a servitor, to another house within that wall, not dissimilar to this one, which appeared to be wholly at their disposal—although it was no palace. And there, later, Ragnhilde herself came to escort them to her father's presence in his chamber in one of the wings flanking the hall. She was dressed now in a simple blue linen gown which went well with her colouring and did no injustice to her burgeoning figure.

They found Olaf still in bed, but sitting up and not obviously ailing, a cherubic-featured little man, almost beardless, red hair turning grey, but bright-eyed, not at all the sad-faced invalid Somerled had pictured. He was not alone, two companions sitting one on either side of the great bed: a small, wizened gnome of a man, elderly with a face like a monkey and a birdlike manner, dressed all in rusty black; and a smooth, plumpish cleric with pale protruberant eyes and an expressionless face, richly robed, youthful-seeming to be a prince of the Church.

Olaf waved genially. "You are Somerled, Gillebride's son?" he greeted. "Welcome to my house and kingdom. We have heard much of you, some of it to your credit! I once had words with your father. They tell me that you are a very different man."

"As is Olaf Godfreysson!" That was promptly returned, equally smiling. King Godfrey Crovan the Pale had been a great warrior and catholic in his slayings.

"Ah yes, yes." The little eyes twinkled. "To be sure. Come closer, friend—come closer. This is the new Papal Legate to Ireland, the Lord Bishop of Armagh, who honours

143

my house meantime. And here is our Bishop of Man, the Lord Wimund, an Englishman."

"I fear that I am less holy, my Lord Olaf. I can only offer you the Abbot of Glendochart—and he only inherited that title from his father! But I greet these bishops with due respect, although I am no Roman. These are my friends . . ."

Presentations over, Olaf was not dilatory in coming to the point—only, he addressed the little gnome of a man. "And what can the King of Argyll want with the King of Man, think you, St. Malachy? Which of our territories does this young man covet, do you suppose? He has a great appetite for lands, I hear."

Somewhat taken aback by such bluntness, however genially expressed, Somerled had to quickly revise his own approach. The Irish oddity gave him opportunity.

"Ha—this one comes to bargain, my friend. He brings only eight galleys when he could have brought a hundred! He does not be announcing his coming, whatever—and brings no gifts, it seems. So he thinks to outwit you as he tried to outwit David Margaretson. Och, it is a fine young man—just fine!" All this bubbling out in a wheezing chuckle, with the Papal Legate ending by slapping his black-robed thigh.

More wary than ever, Somerled sought to adjust to this new dimension. Clearly he was not going to pull any wool over these two pairs of elderly eyes. He glanced at Ragnhilde, who had not left the room but had taken up her stance near the door.

"I would not dream of trying to outwit the noble Olaf— even if I could. Nor yet your good self, my lord Bishop. My poor wits are insufficiently sharp for such trade. I but come with some honest proposals to put before Your Highness."

"Well said, young man. My daughter said that she esteemed you honest—after a fashion. Too rare a virtue— eh, Bishop Wimund?"

That very different prelate inclined his head but did not commit himself.

"I thank the Lady Ragnhilde. You must judge my honesty by my proposals."

"We shall, friend—we shall."

"Who could say fairer, at all?" the Legate nodded, rubbing his hands. "A young man to heed, to cherish!"

"You desire to hear my suggestions *now*, King Olaf? At this time? In this . . . company?"

"When better, friend? The company is good."

"Yes. As you will. I come to speak of Arran and Bute."

"To be sure. Where you left your fleet, in Rothesay Bay."

"M'mm. You are well informed, my lord. Yes, where I left my fleet. I spoke there with the Keeper of Rothesay Castle, one MacRoderick—*your* keeper, he declared!"

"Ah, yes the good MacRoderick. He would not trouble you, with your one hundred longships!"

"No. But he told me that *you* were his lord, not the High Steward of Scotland. That Man ruled Bute and Arran."

"Does this trouble you, friend Somerled?"

"A little, yes. For King David of Scots has granted *me* Arran and Bute, in place of the Steward."

"So many seeking to possess these poor islands. But I *hold* them."

"That is why I am here. We believed that the Norse held them—as they had held so much. But found that it was yourself. I was prepared to drive out the Norsemen. But . . . you are different."

"You fear that you could not drive me out, young man?" That was interested.

"I could, I think. But I would not wish to do so. You and I are both vassals of King David. It would be unsuitable that we should fight. And over a grant of our liege-lord David."

"Is not the King of Argyll considerate?" Olaf observed, beaming.

"Och, he is a lesson to us, just," St. Malachy asserted. "God be praised for the likes o' him!"

Somerled bit his lip, frowning.

"Heed him, father." That was Ragnhilde from the doorway.

"I do so, my dear—I do so. I but wait to hear King Somerled's proposals, which he has come to put before me."

"My proposals are simple. Friendship."

It was the old man's turn to look at a loss. "Friendship . . .?" he repeated, sitting forward.

"Friendship, yes. No more, no less. Is it not sufficient?"

Olaf wagged his head. "This is no proposal, young man."

"Is it not? Many, I think, would wish to have me their friend. And few, on this seaboard, their enemy! Ask your fellow-Norsemen."

"Are you threatening me, Somerled MacGillebride?"

"How can you ask that? When I am offering you my friendship."

"In exchange for Arran and Bute!"

"Also, *your* friendship for me, in return."

"I thought that you came to bargain, young man?"

"I did. Consider. You require a friend such as Somerled of Argyll. This kingdom of Man is vulnerable. You must know that sufficiently well. Anyone can see it. And if anyone, then the Norsemen, the Irish Norse in especial. Or the English—these Normans are ever seeking new conquests. Or even Sigurd of Norway, who is said to be considering binding all the lands and territories held by Norsemen into one Norse empire under his sway—Canute's dream. That is partly why I entered into firm friendship with King David—in case Sigurd thinks to try to take *my* lands back, and I can be assured of David's aid. Can you? Are you more secure, on Man? As I sailed round your coasts, I could not judge it so."

The other fiddled with his bed-clothes. "I have no fears of Sigurd. My son Godfrey is in Norway even now, at Sigurd's court."

"Sent for good reason, no doubt! Because you had heard this of Sigurd's empire? But, other than Sigurd, you are vulnerable. If such as I could consider an attempt on Man, so could others. I say that friendship with me would serve you well. You are now wed to Fergus of Galloway's daughter—again no doubt for good reason. Arran and Bute start where Fergus's territories end. Then my lands of Kintyre, Cowal, Lorne, Moidart and the isles extend. Your entire eastern flank would be protected, since David I think would not let Cumbria be used against you—unless you displeased him!"

"You are very concerned for me, King Somerled!"

"I want Arran and Bute."

"Why? So greatly."

"Because they represent a weakness to *my* kingdom, a danger. If not in the strongest and most sure of hands. They are the postern-door to Argyll. Takeable from the sea, yet lying between Kintyre and Cowal. *You* do not greatly value them—or you would have left a large fleet protecting them and a more notable governor than this MacRoderick."

"So you would enter into a treaty of friendship with Man. How think you of this, St. Malachy? You, a seer."

"Och, och, my eyes are growing dim, alas—years upon years! But still I can see a little. Eight ships brought, just, when these might have been a hundred. A choice young man, whom your lass deems to be honest. And no gifts—myself, I am a sad doubter when gifts are brought, a very Thomas! How much do these islands he speaks of mean to you, my friend?"

Olaf shrugged. "My sons took them from the Norse pirates."

"But your sons do not themselves occupy them?"

"No. Would God that they did!"

The Legate spread his hands, chuckled and said no more.

"And you, Lord Wimund? You are Bishop and have pastoral care of these isles. How say you?"

"I say, Lord King, that these islands must remain in the nurture and care of Holy Church, with no return to the Columban heresy. That assured, I see no great ill in this. Not that I fear this King's ill will, but rather King David's. It would be unwise to risk David's ire—if he has indeed granted these islands to King Somerled."

"So-o-o! It seems, my young friend, that I am advised towards discretion. I shall give you my answer later. But first, tell me—what of this of Holy Church? Of Rome and the Columban Church. I am sure that this will also interest the Papal Legate here."

Somerled spread his hands. "I am no churchman. If the folk of Arran and Bute now worship according to the Roman rite, I for one would not seek to change it. Myself, I worship otherwise—but that is of no matter. All men should worship as they will."

"As I say, a choice young man!" Malachy O'Moore nodded. "We live and learn, just."

"So—we shall see you later, Somerled MacGillebride MacFergus—if you will honour my table below. Hilde—escort our friends . . ."

The interview over, Ragnhilde took them back to their quarters.

"Thank you for saying nothing to my father about my brothers' behaviour," she said quietly, to Somerled. "I think that you will find that your journey here has not been fruitless."

"It could not be that, in any event, since I have met you here, lady!" he said gallantly.

Cathula snorted.

★   ★   ★

In the evening they were summoned to the same hall in which they had eaten previously—although now it seemed a different place, packed with folk, torches lit, a great fire blazing on the central hearth, tables groaning with meats and drink. There was little ceremony, indeed almost pandemonium prevailed, men shouting and laughing, women skirling, hounds barking, musicians playing, servitors hurrying hither and thither. The fact that King Olaf was present in person appeared to make no difference—but then the Norse had odd ideas about kingship.

There was no raised dais in this hall, but a top table stretched at right angles to the others at one end, and in the centre of this Somerled was ushered into a place between Olaf and Queen Affrica. He would have preferred to have been on the other, left, side of the King, where the little Legate sat next to Ragnhilde, even though the less honourable position. The three bastard sons sat together further left still, in a noisy group, carefully not looking as the Scots party was shown in. Cathula was disposed near them, with Saor and her brother—but she would have little difficulty in looking after herself.

Seen on his feet, Olaf Morsel was even tinier than he had seemed in bed, with very short legs, making even Bishop Malachy look sizeable, his clothing now a curious mixture of bed and day wear. His wife wore the lowest-cut gown Somerled could recollect having seen at table, although her figure scarcely justified it.

The provender proved to be hearty rather than imaginative, salmon, wildfowl, venison and beef, washed down with vast quantities of ale, wine, aquavit and whisky.

The noise increased as the meal went on, conversation difficult.

Somerled was surprised at how much food and drink Olaf managed to put away—he had that other by-name of Olaf Buttered-Bread, to be sure—although Affrica only toyed with her share. At one stage of the repast, his host, pressing more wine upon him, further shouted—but without any evident significance—that friendship was an admirable exchange for islands. No more appeared to be forthcoming. It was as simple as that.

Presently, after much yawning and belching, Olaf announced that he was tired and was going to his bed. Without more ado, he rose and tottered off to the door and out, nobody appearing to pay the least attention. Somerled was the only one to rise—although, when they perceived it, his own party followed suit.

However, despite all this lack of formality and seeming respect, it became apparent that the King of Man's presence had in fact had more influence on the company than it might have appeared. For quickly thereafter the tone and tenor of the proceedings commenced to change noticeably. Noise redoubled, although this had scarcely seemed possible. Horseplay began, scuffling broke out, the King's three bastards very much the ringleaders. The Queen appeared far from censorious, approving rather—indeed she moved along the bench closer to Somerled, in frank appreciation, to fill up his goblet, actually rubbing herself against him. Evidently intent on speech, she had to come closer still, to be heard, so that he was looking down the front of her gown, with no great delight, her lips almost at his ear.

"The woman you have with you—is she your concubine?" she screeched.

Frowning, Somerled chose his words. "Cathula MacIan is shipmaster of my dragon-ship."

She smiled disbelievingly and patted his arm. "How . . . convenient! When seafaring. A man of good appetite. A man after my own heart, I think."

He drew away, in noticeable fashion, but said nothing.

She followed him. "Your wife died, did she not?"

"Sadly, yes." He looked along the table and saw Ragnhilde

149

watching, beyond the Legate, who was sitting back with his eyes closed. "Your father, Madam—I heard that he was at odds with King David?"

"Oh, some small matter." She offered him her own goblet to drink from, since he neglected his.

"I have had sufficient, I thank you . . ."

Bishop Wimund aided him by rising, bowing stiffly in the direction of the Queen and himself, more deeply to the unseeing Legate, and stalked off.

Somerled took the opportunity to rise also, disengaging with difficulty, so close was the Queen. "With your permission, Madam, I also will retire. It has been a long day. It is long since I slept."

"Come, Somerled—they call you the Mighty, do they not? Do not tell me that you are so weary that you must seek bed to *sleep* in! I esteemed you more lusty than that!"

It went against the grain for that man to reject any lady's so frankly offered favours, but in present circumstances he felt that he could do no other.

"I regret to disappoint. But as your lord's guest, I feel . . . constrained." Misliking the sound of that himself, he did not wonder at the sudden constriction of brows and lips, until he perceived that the Queen was looking past his shoulder. He turned, to find Ragnhilde at his back.

"Do you wish to withdraw, my lord?" she asked. "I fear that the further entertainment may not please, perhaps." She looked from Affrica, expressionless, back to where one of her half-brothers was now standing amongst the debris of the table-top and hauling up one of the serving-wenches, her clothing already in disarray.

"Yes. I thank you. I was telling the Queen that my couch beckons. I have dined all too well . . ."

"Then I will conduct Your Highness . . ."

"I am sure that King Somerled and I can find our own way back to our chamber unaided!" That was Cathula, who had come to join them.

"No doubt. But it is my duty to accompany His Highness, in my father's house," the younger woman said quietly.

"Perhaps it is *mine*!" Affrica put in.

Somerled looked from one to the other of the three women. It was to Cathula that he spoke. "Tell Saor that he and the others should stay, if so they wish." To the Queen he bowed. But he took Ragnhilde's arm. "I am honoured," he said. "Come, then . . ."

The Papal Legate appeared to be asleep.

"You obtained what you came for, my lord King?" the girl asked, as they stepped out into the night air.

"I did. Thanks perhaps, in some measure, to yourself?"

"I could say only a word. But I am glad. You will perceive something of my father's problems."

"I perceive also that he has a notable daughter, whatever his sons may be!"

"I do what I can. And my true brother, Godfrey, is very different . . ." At the door of his quarters she paused. "I wish you a good night, my lord. For how long do you stay with us?"

"I must leave in the morning. I left my eight ships at your St. Michael's Haven. And my fleet awaits me at Rothesay Bay, in Bute."

"So short a visit. I am sorry."

"So am I. But . . . now that your father and I are in friendship and league, there will be other meetings . . ."

Cathula came, with MacFerdoch. "The others wait," she reported. "More fools them! We are better in our bed, my lord, you and I!"

Without another word, Ragnhilde turned and left them.

"A plague on you, Cathula MacIan!" Somerled exclaimed. "You . . . you find your own bed this night!" And he stamped into the house.

In the morning they did not have to walk the miles to St. Michael's Haven, Ragnhilde providing horses and accompanying them herself. They took leave of Olaf, genial in his bed, and got a cheerful farewell and some sort of benediction from St. Malachy, who seemed to find life unfailingly amusing, and Old Satanicus, the Devil, a foe with whom it was a pleasure to deal. There was no sign of Olaf's bastards.

On the road back to the haven, Ragnhilde was quiet, reserved; but when they came to say goodbye at the quayside she seemed genuinely affected, although she kept glancing over at Cathula. For his part Somerled found the parting moving, and assured her he would be back. He was not usually concerned over the presence of others, but on this occasion he felt much inhibited, for some reason. The actual leave-taking was somewhat abrupt.

It was as the dragon-ship drew away from the jetty, with Cathula efficiently ordering the oarsmen in the quite complicated process, and Somerled staring back at the single slight figure who stood beside the horses watching them go, that Saor MacNeil made his comment.

"Given a year or two, that creature will be bed-worthy indeed! I swear the thought has not escaped you, Sorley MacFergus!"

He should have known better, been prepared to dodge, at least. His foster-brother's fist caught him on the side of the head and he was spun round against the helmsman almost toppling them both, to the danger, momentarily, of the ship's steering.

Even Cathula MacIan held her tongue thereafter.

CHAPTER 9

Somerled paced out the uneven platform of greensward and stone for the third time, counting, calculating, frowning. "It will be a tight squeeze," he announced. "The shape will be uneven. But I think that it will serve. Just sufficiently large. I make it four-hundred-and-seventy-two paces around. One-hundred-and-forty paces in greatest length, north to south. Less wide at the north than this south end, forty as against one-hundred-and-ten—as much difference as that. With something of a bite out of it yonder, at the cliff. If we brought the stonework lower there, part way down the cliff, that would help. I do not think that the shape being irregular would greatly signify. It is much the best site."

The others, sprawling on the grass in the warm sunshine, made no comment, looking scarcely interested. This had been going on for an hour.

"It commands the head of this inner Loch Moidart, the mouths of both the rivers, Shiel and Moidart, as well as this shallow bay of Doirlinn," he went on. "Forby, there is this wet hollow here—if I mistake not, this is a spring welling up through the rock. Water we must have. And there is stone nearby, to quarry—over there on the mainland shore. This would ease the work. I think that we should have it here."

"As good as any," Saor said, yawning.

"Yes. We shall not find better on Loch Moidart. See—go down to the tideline and gather me driftwood. To drive in as stakes. To mark out the lines of it. Then we shall cut the turf. That the builders make no mistakes."

Saor passed on the command to the lounging oarsmen. He was much too great a man, Chamberlain of Argyll, to go gathering driftwood sticks.

"Where will you find masons, in Moidart?" Cathula

asked, toying with sea-pink flowers. "You cannot expect herders and fisherfolk to build you castles. It will be long before this one, or others, will be more than a dream, I think."

"Not so," he said. "These folk can hew and carry stone. Cut and fetch timber. Clear the site. Lay the foundations. Then, when my master-mason comes, they can work to his orders. He will go from site to site, showing them how. It will take time, yes—but greatly *less* time than if all was left to skilled masons . . ."

They were on the top of a mound, a knobbly knoll of grass and outcropping rock which rose like the stopper of a flagon in the centre of the tidal narrows at the head of Loch Moidart, the north-east head not the south-east at Kentra Bay. This was the place where the Norse of Ivar Blacktooth had had a small base, behind Eilean Shona, which Dermot Maguire had been sent to destroy, four years ago now, at the Battle of Moidart, if so it could be called. The mound, some one-hundred-and-twenty feet high, was in fact a tiny island, called Eilean Tioram, drying out at low-water, and with an excellent sheltered anchorage between it and Shona, where at least a score of longships could lie, although only Somerled's dragon-ship and one escort lay there now. Its base no more than a few acres, the summit narrowed to an uneven little plateau, part grass, part rock, of the measurements Somerled had called out. It was on the small side, admittedly, for a castle, and of distinctly unusual outline, for every inch of the ground would have to be utilised; but its other advantages were evident.

This was the furthest north of Somerled's ambitious scheme to bind together, encircle and protect his new kingdom with a chain of strongholds, not after the Celtic ramparted-fort style nor yet of the Norse stockaded hall-house type, but stone keeps within high curtain-walls after the Norman fashion, as at Castle Sween and David's Rook's Burgh, on a smaller scale. He had already chosen sites at Duart and Salen on Mull, Dunstaffnage in Lorne, Mingary on Sunart—and hereafter intended to prospect others in Islay, Jura and other islands, and in Kintyre and Cowal. His friends saw all this as a folly of grandeur, but he reckoned that these strongholds would well repay their cost and trouble in serving notice on marauders and raiders to keep out of his domains.

Somerled, who only acted the king when strangers were present, and not always then, was digging into the wet patch and gaining assurance that it was indeed a fortunately-placed spring, when a man came running across the wet sands from the south shore, calling. He was a local fisherman and when they could hear his shouts his message was that there was a large fleet beating up into the outer loch, apparently from the south.

Somerled was both astonished and at a loss. Who this could be he had no idea; and what the situation called for, from himself, was equally in doubt. The fisherman could tell him no more than that there were a great many ships, a mixed fleet of galleys, longships and transports or merchanters, with no identifiable markings.

Somerled had to see for himself. He ran down the side of the mound, to cross the tidal sands whence the man had come, to the Doirlinn shore, and there promptly to clamber up the quite steep hillside to a viewpoint high enough to see seawards beyond the intervening point. He had to climb quite some distance, panting, before he was rewarded with the panorama of the wide outer loch.

There was no exaggeration as to the size of the fleet, nor the fact that at least some of the ships were heading in towards them in the inner loch. He counted between eighty and ninety vessels.

"Who is this? And what do they here?" he demanded. "Could they be Manxmen? Or Irishry? This is no Norse raid . . ."

"They are sending ships in to seek out what is here," Saor pointed out.

"They will not see our two craft from out there."

"Four ships only. And they sail in openly. This is no invasion. Forby, why invade Moidart?"

Leaving a couple of men to keep watch, they hurried down to the shore again and signalled for the dragon-ship to come for them, judging that they would be better aboard. If, in fact, they were assailed, and by overwhelming numbers, they could row their two vessels behind Shona Beg, beach them on the north shore and take cover in the woodlands there, with an infinity of empty country behind them.

When the four strange galleys came sailing up the inner loch and round the point into view, however, they displayed no aspect of hostility. Perceiving Somerled's two craft lying there, the leading ship turned in towards them, leaving the other three lying off—clear enough indication that no assault was intended.

Eyeing the oncoming galley keenly, Somerled suddenly exclaimed. "On my soul—it is Malcolm MacEth, my good-brother! The Earl of Ross. There, in the stern. Save us—what brings him here? And with a fleet . . .?"

The galley drew alongside and the Earl Malcolm, waving, clambered over on to the dragon-ship's stern-platform.

"Sorley!" he cried, hand out. "At last, I run you to earth. I have been seeking you all over Argyll! My salutations! I have been at Ardtornish and Tobermory and Islay and Mingary. From there they sent me here . . ."

"If you had sent me word, man. But . . . it is good to see you, Malcolm. It must be three years? Four? Is all well? How is my sister? And my young son, Gillecolm? I have been thinking to send for him. Now that I have matters here in hand. It is time. He will be eight years . . ."

"Gillecolm is well. As is my wife. He and Donald, our son, are notable friends. He asks if he is prince now, to crow over Donald. Since you call yourself king!"

"That—that is little more than a device, Malcolm. It serves a purpose. But what do you do in these parts? And whose great fleet is that, out there?"

"It is mine, man—mine. And three thousand men. All mine."

"Sakes!" Somerled stared. "What is this? What are you at?"

"I am going to unseat David Margaretson—that is what I am at, Sorley! I am on my way to Morayland, there to rouse our folk. I am by rights Earl of Moray now—although David says that he has forfeited the earldom. But the folk will support me. All the North will. I have sure word. And more than the North—all Celtic Scotland."

'But . . . are you crazed, Malcolm? Your brother sought to do that, and failed. Died."

"Angus made his mistakes, chose the wrong time. And was unfortunate. Even so, had he not been struck down, in the battle, and his people lost heart, he would have been King today."

"That I doubt, man. But, for all that, he was more of a warrior than you will ever be, Malcolm! If he could not do it, why should you?"

"I tell you, had he not been slain at Stracathro . . ."

"What makes you attempt this now? You had no notion of it before. When last I saw you . . ."

"The time is ripe. David is much occupied with Northumbria. King Henry of England is sick, dying, they say. There is going to be great trouble in that land, since he leaves no son. David is pledged to support the succession of the Empress Maud, the daughter of Henry and of David's own sister. But Stephen of Blois, Henry's nephew, is also claiming the throne, as grandson of the Conqueror. There will be war. David has always claimed Northumbria, as part of his late wife's inheritance—her father was Earl there. He claims it for their son Henry. So, in this broil, he seeks to put himself in a good position to take Northumbria if this Stephen wins the day, as seems likely . . ."

"Yes, yes—I know all this. But think you that David will be so engaged in Northumbria that he will be unable to defend his own kingdom? I say that this is folly."

"Henry may die any day—and then David will move fast. Southwards. I have to be mustered and ready, in Moray, to move as fast as does he! I tell you it is a notable opportunity. Moreover, there is the Church—the chance to bring back our Celtic Church to power. Rome is in disarray—this scandal of the two Popes, Innocent and Anacletus. The Romish Church is at war with itself, some for Innocent, some for Anacletus, many not knowing where to turn. Scotland could have her own Columban Church again. Many abbots and bishops have urged me to move. I tell you all the North, hating the Margaretsons and their Normans, and disavowing the Roman Church, will rally to my banner, I am assured."

"Who so assures you? Who has urged you to all this, man? Beyond a few churchmen?"

"Many. Earl Colban of Buchan. Melmore of Atholl. Fergus of Galloway . . ."

"That snake! He has betrayed David more than once. Has married Henry of England's bastard daughter, now . . ."

"Perhaps so. But he could aid me on to the Scots throne."

"No man can trust Fergus."

"He could bring in Man. His daughter is now Olaf's queen . . ."

"Olaf will not rise against David—that I swear! He is bed-bound and seeks only peace and quiet."

"He has sons, of much spirit I am told. Fergus has influence with them. The Manx fleet is great . . ."

"These are all but dreams, Malcolm. Merest hopes. You will require more than these to win a kingdom . . ."

"You won one, with less! With *you* aiding me, Somerled, we shall win Scotland. And then . . ."

"Me! Ah, no—not so, Malcolm. This is not for me, at all . . ."

"But, Sorley—surely you will come in? Surely you, of all men, will not fail me? I have relied on you."

"I am sorry—but no. This is something that I cannot do, man. I have taken an oath of allegiance to David. I am his vassal, now. As are you, indeed! Forby, I esteem him my friend. I cannot take up arms against him."

"But . . . you are my wife's brother! I was relying on your fleet to assail the South-West and Clyde for me. David can mean but little to you."

"I cannot, will not, do it, Malcolm. An oath is an oath. And David is making a good king."

"When I am King, you will wish that you had aided me. See, Sorley—surely I can persuade you? What do you want? I will give you anything, in reason, in my kingdom. You have but to ask it."

Somerled shook his head.

"I have come far seeking you. Much out of my way. With this great fleet of ships. I would not have believed that you, that you . . ." Malcolm also shook his head. "It is not like you. You, the fire-eater . . .!"

"I have eaten sufficient fire, and meantime digest it! But it is not only that. I have cast my lot with David. I shall not betray him. Whoever else does."

"*I* do not betray David. I am his elder brother's son. Also I am King Lulach's daughter's son—of the older line. By both tokens I should have the throne."

"Nevertheless, Malcolm, David has been accepted by your fellow *Ri*, the mormaors and earls, and crowned on the Stone of Destiny. He *is* the King. My duty is to him, not to you. Indeed, instead of joining you, it could be my duty to inform him of this danger!"

"You would not, by God!" The other stared. "I . . . I would not permit it. I tell you, you will *not* do that! I will stop you, I promise you. Silence even my wife's brother, if I must!"

"You would go so far, my deer-hunting good-brother? Have you it in you, I wonder? So great a change. You say that this is not like me. What of you? What has changed Malcolm MacEth into so fierce a warrior?"

"I but seek what is mine. And must avenge my brother. I will not allow you, or any, to stay me . . ."

"Never fear, man—I shall not send word to David. Even if I should. I wager that he can fight his own battles, that one. But I would counsel you to think well on this, Malcolm. For if you fail, as Angus failed, it will not be just a crown that you lose, but your life, your all."

"*You* talk like that—you, Somerled Norse-Slayer! Counselling caution, back-drawing in others—but never for yourself! No—all is in train. Moray and the North are being raised to my cause. Angus and the Mearns will join me. Thereafter all Scotland."

"As you will. I cannot wish you well in this, Malcolm. But I wish you a safe outcome . . ."

So, disappointed, disgruntled, the Earl of Ross took leave of his brother-in-law there behind Shona Beg and sailed back to his fleet.

"I doubt if that one will be Malcolm the Fourth!" Saor commented. "But, if so, you may have cost us dear, King Sorley!"

"What is cost, foster-brother . . .?"

CHAPTER 10

The summons from the High King reached Somerled on the island of Islay, scarcely convenient. It came by a weary messenger, a Clan Alpine Mac-an-Leister, who had had to travel thus far fast. King David requested the attendance of his friend and vassal, King Somerled of Argyll, at Rook's Burgh in the Middle March, with his fullest strength and at all possible speed—as simple as that.

Questioned, Mac-an-Leister said that it was to be invasion of England. King Henry dead, Stephen of Blois his nephew had usurped the English throne in place of the Empress Maud, Henry's daughter. David had vowed to support Maud, his own niece—as once indeed had Stephen himself—and so was going to march into England to encourage the English nobility to rise against the usurper. David was a man of peace, but was always prepared to put his promises into practice. Now that the abortive rising of the Earl of Ross was safely over and done with, the King could move south with an easy mind.

Somerled was by no means eager. It was early summer of 1138 and a busy time in the Highland year, with the hay to cut and dry. Not that he need concern himself with hay-making and the like, of course; but it was no convenient time to take away the bulk of his manpower, the winter feed for whose cattle depended on a good hay-crop. For himself, he was supervising the building of his new castle of Finlaggan, on an islet in the loch of that name, on Islay; and lacking his supervision the work would suffer. But he was not the man to fail the High King, at his first call. Especially with his unwise brother-in-law Malcolm a condemned prisoner in David's hands.

If his participation and contribution was to be of any use, there was no time to be lost. Men had to be summoned and collected from a vast area, to muster at a convenient centre.

Ardtornish, on the Sound of Mull, would be best. Even with the utmost speed it would take many days to assemble a major force from all of mainland and island Argyll—but presumably David Margaretson had thought of that.

So the couriers were sent out in all directions, as far north as Eigg and Rhum and Moidart, as far south as Kintyre and Bute and Arran, as far west as Tiree, whilst Somerled himself sailed back to Ardtornish, dropping off messengers to rouse Mull in the by-going, to assemble the necessary flotilla.

It was ten days later before he was able to depart, with twelve hundred men in eleven ships, with instructions left behind for the onward despatch of a further contingent when it should be assembled from the more distant territories and islands.

They sailed southwards down the coasts of Nether Lorne, Knapdale and long Kintyre, to turn the Mull thereof and cross the mouth of the Firth of Clyde making for that of Solway. Once again they made their landfall at Eskmouth, near where Galloway and Cumbria joined. It took them almost four days to march the twelve hundred across the watershed of Lowland Scotland, sixty-five miles, by Eskdale and Teviotdale to Rook's Burgh—for this force, of course, was not mounted.

Any fears that they might be too late were dispelled long before they got that far, by meeting many other groups and contingents of armed men, although none so large as themselves, all heading in the same direction. These tended to look askance at the fierce-seeming, dismounted Highlanders in their kilts and plaids and barbaric jewellery. Most of the other parties were Borderers, mounted on the hardy, long-maned horses for which these parts were famed, and would go to make up the light skirmishing cavalry of the King's host.

Rook's Burgh itself was one vast armed camp, the town swallowed up within a spreading tented and pavilioned city which spilled over both Tweed and Teviot and filled the haughlands beyond, endless rows of idling men and tethered horses, with the blue smoke from innumerable camp-fires rising everywhere.

The newcomers discovered that there had been dramatic

developments in the situation since David's messenger had brought them their summons. Before any large proportion of this present host had assembled, King Stephen himself had sought to settle the issue by invading Scotland. For surprise, he had brought his main English-French force by sea to Berwick-on-Tweed, Scotland's greatest port, no more than twenty-five miles east of Rook's Burgh, and from there marched up Tweed. David, caught without any large army, had devised and executed a masterly stroke, with great daring. With only a few hundred light horse, Normans and Borderers, he had made a night dash down the south bank of Tweed to Berwick, passing unseen the huge area lit by Stephen's camp-fires on the north side; and at the estuary-bay of Tweedmouth had put his men on many fishing-boats, to row out in the darkness to all the anchored English fleet, whose crews were in the main roistering in Berwick town. They had set every ship on fire, with little effective opposition. Then, riding back westwards along the north side of the river, they had descended upon and ridden down, stampeded Stephen's sleeping camp, in the Coldstream area, just before dawn, creating extraordinary panic and havoc—unconventional warfare and scarcely chivalrous by knightly standards, but exceedingly effective. The bewildered and sleep-heavy English had broken and run before the pounding, trampling cavalry, bolting at first for Berwick and their burning ships and then streaming away southwards into Northumberland, Stephen and his demoralised nobles well to the fore. The usurper was now thought to be somewhere in the Durham area.

They found the High King in the camp, conferring with his leaders. He greeted Somerled warmly, almost affectionately.

"So, my friend, you have answered my call. And speedily, as a friend should, despite Argyll being so far away. More speedily than many nearer, and owing greater service! And you have brought a notable array, I see—a potent addition to my host."

"Twelve hundred, Sire—with more to come, when they win in from the Isles. I hastened, fearing that you would have marched already."

"We march in two days' time. Many others, besides yours,

will have to follow on. I have forty thousand assembled here now—so you will perceive that the King of Argyll, with his twelve hundred, has served me better than have many of my lords." And David looked around his lieutenants, meaningfully.

"I have no horsed chivalry for Your Grace. But my broadswords and gallowglasses will fight where horse cannot go."

"That I well believe. And I shall need their aid, I think. For although we gave Stephen of Blois a sore head there at Coldstream those weeks back, I learn that he is gathering much strength at Durham and York, with too many of the English lords forswearing their allegiance to Maud. And Holy Church is supporting him—or, at least, the Archbishop of York is, shame on him! So I must needs strike a blow for the Empress, as none other seems to be eager to do. Ah—here now is your friend the High Steward, who yielded you Bute and Arran—at a price . . .!"

Walter Stewart came up, unsmiling. "So we are honoured by the presence of Malcolm MacEth's good-brother!" he commented, thinly.

"King Somerled has brought twelve hundred, Walter. Despite his foolish good-brother. That compares none so ill with *your* numbers, if I recollect?"

The other frowned but said nothing.

"I much regret Malcolm's folly and defection, Sire. What was his fate? I have not heard."

"His fate is to be ever near but not *on* the throne he sought to win!" David answered, smiling. "But he will become accustomed to it in time. Already he scowls less!"

"Near? Scowls less? I do not understand . . .?"

"His Grace is over tender of heart," the Steward declared. "When MacEth was captured, instead of execution for highest treason, he but made of him a perpetual prisoner in the royal house. Nursing a viper to his bosom, I say! Wherever the King goes, Malcolm goes. Living mighty well, when he should be under the sod!"

A growl from others standing by most evidently indicated approval of the Steward's sentiments.

"The Earl of Ross is one of the *Ri* of Scotland, and my own nephew," David pointed out, mildly. "There has been enough of death and vengeance in our royal house. He was misled—and now must suffer his uncle to lead him, always! Sufficiently galling for any man! If you seek word with him, Somerled, you will find him fishing in Teviot, from a window in my castle yonder. Or he was, when I left him . . ."

Astonished, Somerled withdrew from the royal presence, and went to see to the encampment of his men.

Later he found his way to Rook's Burgh Castle, in search of Malcolm, to find him, not fishing but playing chess with Prince Henry of Strathclyde, David's son, the good-looking but delicate young man whom St. Malachy O'Moore had so dramatically brought back from death's door. He and his cousin appeared to be on the best of terms.

When the prince left the brothers-in-law to their private conversation, they eyed each other doubtfully.

"You will spare me your complacency, Somerled, I hope. Likewise your commiserations," the Earl said. "I was betrayed, and so am here, thus. Those I trusted failed me. That is the beginning and the end of it. There is little more to be said."

"As you wish. I cannot in honesty say that I am sorry, Malcolm. At the outcome. But I am glad that you are no worse off than this your present state. I would scarcely have expected so, so congenial an outcome!"

"Do not be misled, man. I am a prisoner, no better. Wholly at David's mercy. And am to remain so, for God knows how long! I may seem to live well enough, but I live entirely in David's shadow. And at any time he may change his mind and have done with me. This is no life for any man . . ."

"Yet it *is* life, Malcolm—not death! When David's nobles, those Normans, are calling for your execution. And a tolerably comfortable life, it does seem. At least you are not immured in pit or dungeon. And David is a fair and honourable man. I say that you are scarcely ill done by."

"Had you said differently at Moidart, that time, I belike would not be a prisoner now!"

The other shrugged. "You fought no battles? I heard of none."

"I had no opportunity, man. I was betrayed, I tell you.

Before ever I could march south. The Moraymen turned craven, at David's threats. They lost all their spirit. They yielded me up. Whilst I was separated from my ships and host. Sent me captive to David's Constable de Morville, he who slew my brother. Lord—that I ever thought to trust my fellow-Scots . . .!"

Feeling unable to weep with or for his sister's husband, Somerled excused himself and made his way back to his troops.

In the two days before the great army made a move, he became acquainted with many of the commanders of the royal host, mainly Normans but with a number of the old Celtic nobility. With the former he could not feel on easy terms. They seemed to him stiff, arrogant and clearly conceived themselves to be a superior breed to the native Scots, the Highlanders in especial. None treated Somerled like any sort of monarch, none indeed so respectfully as did David himself. He elected to remain most of the time with his own Argyll men.

With some fifty thousand now assembled, it was too large a host to be manageable on the march as one entity. David decided to split it into four distinct armies and to invade England on the broadest front, in fact right across the country from the Norse to the Irish Sea. This made sense in more ways than one. Stephen's actual whereabouts at present was uncertain, and this broadly-based advance ought to ensure that he could not be in a position to outflank them. Cumbria on the west, of which David had been Earl and governor for King Henry of England before succeeding to the Scots throne, was of doubtful allegiance to either kingdom and should be shown to which side it would be profitable to adhere. David's long-term aim, beyond demonstrating his support for his niece, the Empress Maud, was to establish the Scots border across the land from the Tees to the Ribble, instead of Tweed and Solway, so that his realm would eventually include Cumbria, which had originally been part of Strathclyde, and also Northumbria, to which great earldom his late wife had been lawful heiress and which should now be vested in their son, Henry, Prince of Strathclyde. Also, and of very practical importance, with the Scots forces under their various lords tending to fight amongst themselves, Celt against Norman, North against South, Highland against Lowland, some judicious division was a wise precaution. So the Lord William of Allerdale, the King's Cumbrian cousin, son of the brief-reigning Duncan the Second, was given the extreme west wing, to move southwards through that province; the young Earl Cospatrick of Dunbar, commanding his own men of Lothian and the Merse with other Borderers, took the left or east flank, down through the Northumbrian coastal plain; and dividing the upland central front between these was the youthful Prince Henry supported by the veteran Malise, Earl of Strathearn, and Fergus, Lord of Galloway, newly promoted Earl thereof for reasons of diplomacy, he being a notably slippery and untrustworthy character but a strong fighter. These four each were allotted some ten thousand men. David himself, with the remainder and his tight bodyguard of two hundred Norman knights, brought up the rear, but behind Fergus of Galloway's host, he conceiving himself to be the only one who might exercise some control over that masterful individual. The High King asked Somerled to attach himself to the Galloway force, admitting privately that it might well prove a difficult and possibly trying assignment, Fergus being the man he was and the Galloway kerns probably the most ungovernable of all the Scots host; but he considered that the King of Argyll, a proven warrior and bearing a Celtic style and title superior to Fergus's own, might possibly have a good and restraining influence. Doubtful as Somerled was, he could scarcely refuse.

So a move was made, on the Eve of St. Fillan, on a front over ninety miles wide. Inevitably it was a somewhat ragged and unco-ordinated advance, however hard David sought to control it, with a corps of mounted messengers dashing back and forth between forces and parts of forces.

Somerled and his people found themselves to be given the east wing of Fergus's army, with an approximately four-mile front to cope with, initially crossing the Border in the Carter Fell and Redesdale area. Fergus himself he discovered to be amiable enough, in a sardonic, fleering way, a slightly-built, dark and quite handsome man in his late forties, who like David had been reared largely at the English-Norman court, more or less as a hostage, but who, unlike his monarch, neither loved nor admired the Normans—even though he was now married to one of the late King Henry's bastard daughters as second wife. He was, of course, the father of Affrica, Queen of Man, by the earlier marriage. Somerled did not like the man any more than he had done the daughter, but sought to co-operate and get on as well with him as was possible. Their mutual positions were from the start a little difficult, Fergus being the commander, with nine thousand men, six thousand of them being his own Gallowegians, while Somerled had only twelve hundred as yet, although nominally superior in rank, king as against earl, but considerably junior in age. There would require to be much give-and-take, it was evident.

Very quickly, even on the second day of the advance, something of the problems of the situation became all too apparent. They had not moved far into Northumbria before, in the Otterburn and Elishaw area of Redesdale, much smoke and flame began to appear on the Argyll contingent's right. At David's last conference of commanders he had emphasised strongly that there was to be no indiscriminate slaughter, no burning nor ravishment, that Northumbria and Cumbria in especial were to be treated as if already part of Scotland, their people encouraged to join forces with the Scots in this venture. Yet here was already widespread burning, seemingly. Somerled sent Saor MacNeil to investigate and if necessary halt any misbehaviour.

That man returned, after a while, with his report. There was complete and unbridled savagery going on over there, looting, raping, massacre, the Galloway kerns destroying all before them, as bad as any Norsemen. His protests had met with scorn and abuse, and the local commander, one MacKerrell, had shouted him down, declaring that the Earl Fergus was his master, and similarly engaged further west.

Somerled debated with himself as to what he ought to do, if anything. In one way it was no business of his; he was only a sub-commander here.

On the other hand, as well as being shameful and contrary to David's express orders, this sort of indiscipline could be catching and might well spread to his own people. Also it was bound to delay the advance and result in weakened, drunken and booty-laden troops, a danger to all concerned. He decided to go and have a word with Fergus.

Leaving his scattered force under the command of Conn Ironhand, Dermot Maguire and Sir Malcolm MacGregor—Cathula MacIan had been left discreetly behind with the ships at Esk-mouth—he and Saor rode off westwards over the rolling countryside where the Cheviot foothills sank to the high Northumberland moorlands. Once out of their own sector it was quickly evident that Saor had not exaggerated. It was sparsely populated territory, with few and isolated farmsteads and occasional small villages nestling in hidden, narrow valleys. Some of the farms had escaped, but none of the hamlets and village communities, so far as they could see. The first they came to, Plashetts on the North Tyne, was typical, a smouldering ruin of smoking thatch and blackened walls, dead bodies lying everywhere, men, women and children, the women usually naked, livestock indiscriminately butchered and left, barns and mills destroyed, corpses thrust down wells. Such few distracted survivors as they perceived fled at their approach.

The Islesmen, used to warfare and bloodshed as they might be, sickened at this wholesale and pointless slaughter. Grim-faced they rode on.

They passed half-a-dozen and more such desecrated and ravaged communities before they ran the Earl of Galloway to earth in the manorhouse of Falstone further down Tyne. They found Fergus relaxed in sated ease in the disordered hall, drinking deep and watching some of his officers make sport of four barely conscious and unclothed young women, one little more than a child. A bound and gagged man was sharing the high table with the Earl, no doubt the owner of the establishment. A priest lay, either dead or unconscious, on the floor.

"Ha—my friend of Argyll!" Fergus called, as they were ushered in. "Welcome! Welcome to Sir Ranulf d'Orsay's table and hospitality! *This* is Sir Ranulf. You will forgive him for being retarded in his speech, at the moment? Two of these wenches are his daughters, I believe—I mind not which. Their hospitality has been fair enough—at short notice, you will understand—but no doubt we can find you fresher fare."

"That will not be necessary, my lord Earl," Somerled returned. "I come only for urgent word with you and then must return. Since *my* force at least is advancing according to orders, if yours is not!"

"Ah, a pity. Such haste! But at the least you will have a flagon of Sir Ranulf's wine, whilst we talk? Sit, you."

"You wish that we talk *here*? In . . . this?"

"Why not? We are comfortable enough, are we not? And entertained the while. None will overhear, I think. Save Sir Ranulf here. And *he* will not disclose our converse here-after—for he hangs when I leave!"

"I would prefer, my lord, to be spared your entertain-ment!" Somerled gestured distastefully towards the ravishers and their victims.

"So! You are dainty in such matters, eh, King Somerled? You are not one of those who favour . . . others? I dare-say that we might still find a comely youth somewhere, unhanged." The Earl looked from Somerled to Saor. "Or two . . .?"

Seeking to swallow his hot temper, Somerled clenched his fists. "I desire but word with you. As to the behaviour of your men. Indeed, as to what I see here on every hand. Rapine, slaughter, sack, pillage. All contrary to King David's royal command."

Fergus stared. "And you? *You* find fault?"

"I do. As must any wise commander. Since it will delay the advance, make enemies of the entire country about, so endanger our rear, and spoil and unman our own people."

"All that, you tell me? This is war, man—war. Do not say that you and your Highlandmen cannot stomach simple warfare . . .?"

"This is not warfare, my lord, but savagery! We are here to fight King Stephen, not unarmed folk, women and bairns. People whom David would have his own subjects . . ."

"Islesman—I'd remind you to whom you speak! *I* command this host—remember it! I'll thank you not to try to teach me my business. I was commanding hosts when you were but a puling child!"

"Then, by this, you ought to know better, my lord."

"Christ God save us—enough of this! If you cannot speak

fairer, then speak no more. Back to your bareshanked caterans, and mind your own affairs, not mine!"

"This *is* my affair. You delay all, on a wide front. And therefore break the line and endanger me, and others. And your kerns' behaviour and riot could affect mine, cause trouble, discontent . . ."

"Nor would I blame them, with such a lily-livered lord! Get you back to them, then, before they start acting like full-blooded men. And spare me more of your whimperings!"

The younger man half-rose from the bench in crouching, trembling rage. For long moments he stared into the other's dark, scornful eyes, throat working convulsively. Greatly daring, Saor gripped his foster-brother's arm.

Gradually Somerled recovered his self-control, straightening up. Without another word he turned and strode for the door.

"That one might have had you bound and gagged, Sorley MacFergus, like that Norman knight," Saor pointed out reasonably, as they mounted their horses. "With but the two of us in it, wiser to have somewhat bridled your kingly tongue!"

"The man is a barbarian! An oaf and savage beneath the skin of gentility!"

"Och yes, indeed. But a savage who held us in the palm of his hand, just. I am thankful to get out of there with a whole skin, King and Chamberlain of Argyll or none."

Although Somerled did not say so, he rather wished that he had not come on this errand. For what was he to do about it? It had hopelessly soured relations between himself and Fergus, without in any way bettering the situation. He could scarcely go bleating to David—who anyway was held up some thirty miles back besieging Wark Castle, the only English Border strength which had failed to capitulate to the invaders and which was formidable enough to be a danger in their rear; otherwise the High King himself would no doubt have seen the smoke of the Galloway depredations and come forward to deal with it all. Somerled would have to slow his own force's advance so as not to lose touch with the rioting host on his right, whilst at the same time seeking to keep in some sort of line with the Earl Cospatrick on the left. It was a thoroughly bad and frustrating situation, looked at from any angle.

He decided that he was not cut out for subordinate leadership.

Back with his own men, he sent word to Cospatrick to slow the eastern advance as the centre was lagging.

So that strange invasion proceeded, by fits and starts, on a notably gapped and uneven front, with William of Allerdale pushing ahead fast through Cumbria, Cospatrick impatient in lower Northumbria, but the hilly centre hopelessly delayed and erratic—for which Somerled received a certain amount of blame. Fortunately there was no real opposition, only local skirmishing, with fords and passes briefly held against them at times. Undoubtedly the main armed man-power of the region was withdrawing before them discreetly, either to join Stephen or in doubt as to a final allegiance.

Progress did improve somewhat in the centre when, three days later, David came up, having reluctantly had to abandon his siege of Wark as too costly in time. He moved to reprove and control Fergus. Just what transpired between the two was not reported, but thereafter there was much less of pillage and delay on Somerled's right. It became rumoured throughout the army that the High King had threatened to send Fergus home to Galloway unless he mended his ways—even though that would have lost the host six thousand Gallowegians, who would undoubtedly have turned back with their lord.

The first real resistance materialised as the spearhead of the host neared Durham, where the Bishop, a Norman named Raoul, was a known fighter. His castle and cathedral together occupied a strong defensive position on a lofty and narrow spine of rock within a loop of the River Wear. Recognising the hopelessness of direct assault upon such a place, although he was able to occupy the town below without much difficulty, David instituted another starving-out siege, whilst he sent out probing horsed parties east, south and west to try to glean information as to Stephen's dispositions. He was all too well aware of the peculiar and vulnerable situation of his host, sitting there over one hundred miles deep into England, with so far no sign of any counter-stroke, only this bishop's castle glowering down on them.

At last reasonably firm news reached them as to the position to the south. Stephen himself had returned to London, leaving his army under the veteran Walter d'Espec, whilst calling on all the English barons to rally to his standard at York, and ordering the old Archishop Thurstan thereof to defend the entire North and more or less conduct a holy war against the invaders. This inglorious attitude drew scornful cheers and jeers from the Scots leadership. But David was less sure that it was good news, deeming that he would have preferred to have Stephen in charge and facing him than the renowned warrior d'Espec. The Archbishop as figurehead might not mean a lot militarily; but probably most of the northern lords would rally to his banner more readily than they would have done to Stephen's own usurping one.

Then a second item of news reached Durham. The Lord William, waiting for none, had pressed on to reach the Ribble, where he had fought a major battle against West Midland forces at Clitheroe and defeated them soundly. He was now advancing up the Ribble line north-eastwards, objective achieved, and called upon the High King to meet him at Tees, to be the new Scots Border.

This was heady stuff, of course, for the rest of the Scots army and the immediate demand was for a move to be made for Tees, for York itself, leaving this Durham to stew in its own juice. David, who was not a rash man, was doubtful as to the wisdom of this, strategically and politically. But he had also to consider other factors—the dangers of idleness in his heterogeneous host, the passage of time with the vital corn harvest at home beginning to preoccupy his troops, and the all but unanimous advice of his lieutenants.

He decided to leave a small force besieging Durham and to move his main army south by west towards Tees, and to link up with William of Allerdale. He did not commit himself, however, to go on as far as York.

*   *   *

Somerled stood unhappy—which was not like him on the eve of battle. The less so in that all around him men were

172

in highest spirits, eager, impatient. All except one or two, that is—David mac Malcolm himself, notably, who, unlike the great majority of his leaders, looked distinctly uneasy, not to say anxious.

They stood in a large group around the High King, the cream of Scotland's lords, Celtic and Norman, some eyeing their monarch askance, more gazing south-westwards across Cowton Moor towards the enemy, the foe that they had come so far to find and fight, brought to bay at last.

David was staring in that direction also, but not so much at the mass of gleaming steel which seemed to clothe a small hill which rose out of the comparatively level moorland and rough pasture half-a-mile away, as at the little group of three riders who rode midway between the two armies, under a white flag—and rode away from the Scots now. Two of these horsemen, had they not been riding under a flag of truce, would have been sporting very different banners, prestigious and Scots, the banners of Annandale and Cavers, in the West and Middle Marches of the Borders; for these were Scots lords—or at least Norman Scots— Robert de Brus, Lord of Annandale and Bernard de Baliol, Lord of Cavers in Teviotdale. Yet they were riding in the wrong direction, back to the English lines from which they had come. Leaving David set-faced.

These two, like sundry others of David's Norman friends and importations, had in time succeeded to manors and lands in England on the death of fathers or brothers. Brus and Baliol had, in fact, been visiting their English properties when this present invasion venture started. And today they had come to the King of Scots under that white flag, not to offer their swords to their sovereign-lord but to try to dissuade him from fighting, to urge him indeed to turn back and retire again to Scotland. They had been very insistent, despite the jeers and even threats of their fellow Scots lords, declaring that they were much exercised for the High King's and for Scotland's own good; that England needed a male and fighting king not a weakly woman like Maud, especially one domiciled abroad; that the host facing them was strong, determined, assured, Norman armed knights by the thousand; and most important, that it would fight under the authority and protection of Holy Church, with the

Archbishop Thurstan threatening excommunication, no less, on all who raised the sword against the Papal power. When David had told them that he would not, could not turn back weakly now, that they had come to the Tees-Ribble line in Scotland's own interests as well as the Empress Maud's, the visitors had turned in their saddles to point back at what the Scots were seeking to pit their strength—the Lord Christ Himself. Staring in astonishment, the King and his lieutenants had been informed that they were in fact facing not mere steel and armed might but the Most High Himself, for on the hill there the standard raised against them was a great mast on which the Archbishop had affixed the holy pyx, the consecrated host of the Body and Blood of the Lord Christ flanked by the sacred banners of St. Peter of York, St. John of Beverley and St. Wilfred of Ripon. If they drew sword, it would be against not only Holy Church but Holy Church's Master. Speechless, appalled and angry too, the Scots had gazed aghast. Oddly, it had been left to Fergus of Galloway to save the day, for he had cursed roundly and laughed at the same time, declaring that old Thurstan must be scared out of his tonsured pate to think of such a device; and this had to some extent broken the horrified spell of that terrible standard. Brus and Baliol had been dismissed empty-handed and had gone off, pursued by reproaches and cursing, evidently preferring to fight on the side of Norman might and Holy Church, if not Stephen the Usurper, than on that of their adopted country.

If it was his friends' defection and the dread of challenging this dire power of Holy Church, which was troubling King David, the sainted Margaret's son, it was otherwise with King Somerled. He, belonging to the Celtic Columban Church, had no concern for the Vatican or its minions or anathemas. It was the mass of the Norman armour on the hill which worried him, glistening and glittering in the sunlight, the serried ranks of steel-clad knights and men-at-arms drawn up under a host of colourful streaming banners. Seldom reluctant for a fight, he was nevertheless apprehensive as to the prospect of hurling his lightly-armed swordsmen and axemen unprotected save by leathern targes or round shields, against such iron-encased foe—especially as the Earl Fergus had been vociferously insisting on the age-old right of the Galloway men to lead the van in war, so that it looked as though his Argyll force would be in the forefront.

If David had any thoughts of postponing the attack or engaging in any sort of negotiations with the enemy, his lieutenants made it clear that nothing of the sort was to be contemplated. One and all they demanded immediate assault, what they had marched one-hundred-and-twenty miles into England to do. Strike now, before this wretched Archbishop and his turncoat crew were further reinforced. An army such as this, made up of the levies of individual lords and chiefs, had its weaknesses, the most basic of which was that its many leaders had all too great a say in the strategy and tactics applied, as against the wishes of the overall commander, since to fight at their best, even to fight at all in certain instances, each grouping had to be at least moderately satisfied and placated. When, as now, the consensus was wholly in favour of prompt action, the figure-head, be he monarch or general commanding, had little option but to agree, even if against his own better judgement. Otherwise there would be next to mutiny.

Fergus of Galloway forthwith demonstrated the truth of this in no uncertain fashion, demanding immediate attack and reiterating his claim to lead the van. When there were angry counter-claims from the Earls of Fife and Strathearn, who pointed out that they were of the *Ri*, the ancient Seven Earls of Scotland, not jumped-up newcomers, Fergus drew his sword and shouted that the Galloway host would lead or the High King's army would be six thousand men fewer there and then. Galloway would either have the van or march for home.

That there was not greater protest and outcry from the others, notably the Normans, possibly had something to do with that daunting hill of steel across the moor.

David bowed to the inevitable and ordered his leaders to place themselves at the head of their hosts, the Earl Fergus in the front, the Earl Cospatrick of Dunbar on the left, supported by, of all people, Malcolm MacEth, Earl of Ross, whom David had allowed to come along, William of Allerdale and the Earl of Strathearn, with the main mass of the foot, in the centre, and Prince Henry and the young Earl of Fife, with the cavalry, on the right. The High King himself, with the Knight Marischal, the High Constable, and the bodyguard of Norman knights and a reserve force, would remain in the rear meantime.

There were not much more than some twenty-five thousand men available, for quite sizeable numbers had been left behind to neutralise sundry castles and fortresses, notably Durham; there had been the inevitable casualties; and as always in such affairs, some parties had quietly turned about and gone home, with stolen gear and cattle. Here, on Cowton Moor, they were six miles beyond Tees, half-way between Durham and York and only a mile or two from Northallerton.

Somerled found himself allotted by Fergus the least honourable position on the left of the van and behind the Galloway front lines—but made no complaint. He for one had not agitated to lead the attack. Otherwise, Fergus divided his force into three sections, with only a small reserve behind the centre. The Galloway kerns, however savage and undisciplined, were nothing loth now, for, whatever else they were, they were born fighters. Impatient, they waited, actually inching forward in their eagerness.

On the left wing, it was all utterly foreign to Somerled's ideas of warfare. He was used to planning, surprise, device and artifice and making the land fight for him, usually with few against many. This head-on confrontation of scores of thousands in sheer battering mass appalled him, especially against ranked and embattled armour. He kept asking himself why he was here, a mere pawn in others' mismanaged game.

They had to wait for some time for the various detachments of the great army to get into position. At length, the trumpets blew from David's command group at the rear. And like a spring released, with a mighty roar of "Albani! Albani!" the ancient Pictish war-cry, the Galloway front surged forward immediately into a run, Fergus well in the lead under his blue-lion-on-white banner. Argyll followed on, however doubtfully.

The van had some five hundred yards to cover from its advanced stance to the foot of that hill, racing over the uneven moorland in yelling, screaming fury, brandishing swords, axes, maces and dirks, a fearsome sight. By contrast, the enemy massed on the rising ground seemed scarcely animate, utterly still, silent. About halfway across the gap, David's trumpets sounded again, signal for the rest of the host to start the general advance. As though afraid of being overtaken, the Gallowegians even increased their pace.

Despite their bounding haste, before they had covered most of the remaining open space they were indeed overtaken, on their far right, by the main cavalry wing under Prince Henry and the Earl of Fife, a gallant cohort under fluttering flags, riding at the gallop, lances levelled, the ground shaking under the thunder of thousands of hooves. It made a rousing sight, reassuring to Somerled at least, even though Fergus himself actually shook his fist at the horsemen, presumably wrathful that they were stealing pride of place.

Somerled's reassurance did not last for long. As the Galloway front reached to within about one hundred yards of the first rows of kneeling English spearmen, the leaping, yelling ranks suddenly seemed to wither and crumble and collapse, in extraordinary, apparently causeless disaster. One moment they were furious, shouting menace, the next they were shrieking, falling ruin, over which the following files stumbled in heaps. Soundlessly death rained down in a terrifying and unrelenting storm—arrows of course, the dread English archery, developed here as nowhere else in Christendom. Up on the top of the hill, behind the massed armour, the longbowmen were ranked in their hundreds, utterly unassailable. Once within range, the Galloway men were entirely at the mercy of those vicious clothyard shafts, shot into the air above the heads of the main English host, to descend in an unceasing hail on the close-packed Scots, their fall regulated only by the speed with which the marksmen could aim, loose and fit new arrows to their bows.

Yet the Galloway charge was not to be halted, even so. A mixture of sheer momentum, hate and elemental courage carried it on, the oncoming horde tripping and sprawling over the growing mounds of slain, but surging unevenly on like a driven tide on a broken shore. Wider and wider grew the belt of the screaming fallen, and nearer and nearer the survivors came to the crouching spearmen. Three times

Somerled saw the blue lion banner fall and be snatched up again to wave crazily over Fergus, who seemed to bear a charmed life—although, of course, he wore a chain-mail shirt which arrows could not penetrate.

Somerled had more than such observations on his mind. He and his men were almost within range of those deadly bowmen also, and it was not his intention to charge on regardless, like the others, squandering Argyll's manpower in useless gallantry. His mind working swiftly, assessingly, he reached for the bull's horn at his side, to blow three ululant blasts, and then waved his arm left, left, left, pointing with his sword. Thankfully, no doubt, his people perceived, and swung off in that direction.

Typically, Somerled was seeking to use the land to aid him. He had noted the configuration of that hill, how there was an outcropping knoll of bare rock shouldering the east summit, steeper than the rest, rising above the thickly-clustered English. Not unnaturally, none clung to that inhospitable rock. By swinging his men over some way to that side, he could put that knoll between them and most of the archers. They would still be in view of a few, he imagined, but at a very extreme angle of shot. So, making a major curve, he led his now somewhat bunched force round to the east, and then bored in again from that flank, comparatively protected, for the moment. One or two arrows, dropping shots, fell amongst them, but nothing to do much damage.

Now they had the spearmen to face, a long line of them, kneeling in front, standing behind, their eight-foot spears thrusting out in a fearsome frieze, a formidable barrier indeed. But at least, unlike the arrows, there was something the attackers could do to help nullify this, as the Highlandmen had learned against Norse spears. They were mostly wearing plaids across one shoulder, the tartan shawls which served as both coat and blanket. In the lead, Somerled and Saor snatched off their own plaids and, waving them, rushed on. It was a simple device but effective, for some hundreds of flapping plaids bearing down on only a limited front of spears can cause a deal of upset, confusing the wielders, entangling and muffling the spearheads and deflecting thrusts. It could not wholly neutralise that bristling array but it greatly lessened the menace and allowed swords and axes to beat and slash in amongst the staves and their holders. And now the crouching position of the front ranks, from being an added strength and protection for those behind, became a weakness, kneeling men being at a disadvantage as against close-range swordery; and when they sought to rise, they got in the way of those at their backs.

For hectic minutes, then, there was utter and bloody havoc and turmoil along that sector of the front, a smiting, swiping, hacking struggle for mastery. But, once a defensive barrier is breached, charging and attacking men usually have the edge over stationary, waiting men. The spearmen broke at a number of points, and once that happened the rest of the line speedily collapsed.

And now a further disadvantage of tight-packed defence was demonstrated. The broken spearmen had to go somewhere to escape the flailing broadswords, and of course they could only push blindly back amongst their own waiting ranks of men-at-arms in their desperation, disordering all, masking their weapons, creating a belt of major chaos along the lower slopes of the hill at this eastern end.

It was not to be expected, to be sure, that Somerled's people could remain an orderly and controlled unit in all this stramash; but at least they had the initiative, knew what they were doing, had more space to operate, and had effective leadership. Their impetus flagged, inevitably, nevertheless.

Somerled, recognising that further decision was required of him, and quickly, sought to disengage and draw back a little, to view and consider. This was all very well, but it could speedily develop into disaster. They could not press on into that mass for much longer, before they were swallowed up and annihilated. Admittedly some of Cospatrick's Lothian men were now coming up behind them. But once these got involved in the struggle, the chaos would be but the greater, all inextricably mixed. He would then have great difficulty in holding his men together as a unit—which he was determined to do. Better to try to withdraw now whilst they could.

He stared round, seeking to take in and assess the general scene. From this position he could not see all the battle area, the western sector being hidden. There was no sign of the cavalry now. In the centre the remnants of the Galloway force appeared to be withdrawing, after a fashion, and William's and Strathearn's foot taking over the assault. So far little impression seemed to have been made on the main enemy mass, and the ranked Norman knights higher were still not engaged. David and the Scots reserve remained where they had been.

Somerled had been doubtful from the start as to the probabilities of success in this attack, considering the strong defensive position of the English, their archers and their great weight of armour. Now he was convinced that the Scots could not win the day, not if the enemy remained solidly on this hill and did not risk a counter-attack. In other words, it was either defeat or stalemate for David, a most dire failure. Should he himself try to return and tell the High King so? Little point in that, when David himself was scarcely in control of his army. Anyway, *could* all be set in reverse now? Would these fire-eating lords heed any such command? His own concern must be to extricate his Argyll people at minimum cost.

He blew a long continuous note on his horn, the signal for disengagement. It was never easy for men involved in mortal struggle to break it all off and retire; but in this case it was likely to be less difficult than sometimes, for the disordered defenders looked to be only too eager to let their immediate attackers go. The English ranks further back, no doubt, would have desired to take a hand and punish these Scots whilst they were vulnerable; but so close-packed were they that they could not move forward without trampling down their own backward-pressing front rows, amongst the tangle of cast and broken eight-foot-long spears.

So, gradually the Highlandmen heeded that horn's note and withdrew, singly and in groups, most not having to actually fight their way out. Some they left behind, inevitably, fallen, and a few were wounded, although most of these were aided out by their colleagues. Many managed even to snatch up discarded plaids in the by-going. Fortunately no arrows were coming down on them, the bowmen no doubt having a superfluity of less difficult targets, with the main Scots assault in progress.

Before the last Argyll men were extricated, the Lothian ranks were pushing through and past them in their hundreds, thousands. This indeed was more difficult to cope with than the disengagement from the English, not to get caught up and swept forward again by the eager newcomers. There was much confusion for a while and Somerled saw his force almost utterly dispersed and swallowed up, an infuriating development. This was not his idea of warfare. He kept blowing and blowing on his horn and hoped that its message would get through all the yelling, bellowing frenzy.

In consequence, it was quite some while before the High-landers could reform, even after a fashion, to gather around their leaders in a dazed and bemused state, finding them-selves in a sort of no-man's-land eastwards behind the fierce battlefront. By which time the entire engagement had developed significantly. From back here it was possible to gain a fairly accurate overall picture—and it was not a cheering prospect. For one thing, the Scots cavalry, which had been supposed to curve in and support Fergus's assault on the right, had completely disappeared. Presumably, for some reason, it had ridden around the western side of the hill. At any rate, its task of riding down the tight ranks of the English men-at-arms, once the Gallowegians had dis-posed of the bristling menace of the spears, was not being effected, with dire result for the entire front. Everywhere the Scots foot was held up against that barrier, hacking and dying whilst the arrows rained down on them, most of the manpower on both sides frustratingly unable to get at each other in the dense press. Clearly little impact had been made on the English front, despite the heavy Scots casualties; and the knightly Norman host on the higher ground was still waiting motionless. With all the noise and shouting and blood being spilt, little or nothing was being achieved.

To Somerled's eyes, the position was in fact hopeless. He did not see how the Scots were going to improve on the situation. They would go on dying uselessly on the heaps of the already slain until they were exhausted—or, hopefully, until the archers ran out of arrows. Then, no doubt, the fresh and unbloodied Norman chivalry would at last sweep down upon them in their armoured might and it would become little more than a massacre, complete defeat. For the life of him he could see no strategy which might change this and give them any sort of victory.

Presumably a similar recognition had been dawning upon David and his lieutenants back at the Scots base. He had sent part of the reserve to reinforce certain sectors of the battle, but most evidently no major breakthrough was being effected. Even as Somerled sought to make up his mind as to whether there was anything that he could usefully do in a desperate effort—as perhaps race his men east-about round to the rear of this hill, in the hope that it might be more assailable from behind, and so a diversion might be created—the blare of David's trumpets rang out, sounding the recall. On and on the trumpeting shrilled, and for the first time a great roar rose from the English host, a triumphant shouting as they recognised the message.

As though the fog of war had not been sufficiently demonstrated already that day, the confusion which followed almost equalled what had gone before. Retiral was not achieved swiftly nor coherently. Not all, indeed, were prepared to retire, and were forced to do so only when they found themselves isolated and their flanks exposed by the retiral of others. Some, on the other hand, were only too glad to withdraw and did so in haste and disorder. Fortunately the actual configuration of the ground was a help in this, in that the enemy hill resembled an island, from which the tide could ebb away almost naturally.

That it was all not much worse, to be sure, was aided by the attitude of the English. The fear was that at this stage they would go over to the attack. But throughout, their strategy had been defensive, and successfully so. It would have taken strong and aggressive leadership to reverse that posture now, when thankfulness to have survived, and won the day, after a fashion, against superior numbers, undoubtedly would be the natural reaction. Moreover those mail-clad knights, the elite of the army, were used to fighting on horseback and were presently unmounted—and their heavy armour would in itself be a dissuasion from any chase. The English, then, stood firm, as they had done all along; they could well have anticipated that this was only a temporary withdrawal and regrouping, anyway, and that the attack would be resumed. The more responsible of the Scots leadership heaved sighs of relief.

Somerled, by the nature of things, was one of the first leaders to arrive back at the base. All around David were much too busy and preoccupied to indulge in debate, argument and blame over the débâcle, at this moment; but clearly one over-riding transgression was held to be largely accountable—and undoubtedly, to the High King's added sorrow and distress, it was his son's responsibility. The cavalry, under Prince Henry and the Earl of Fife, had failed hopelessly in their duty. Apparently, just when they should have swung in, on the right wing, to aid Fergus's Gallowegians, a horsed force of the enemy had appeared from behind the hill. Henry and Fife had turned, necessarily, to deal with this; but having indeed won this cavalry tussle and broken the English array, the two young men had made the grievous mistake of forgetting their obligations towards the Scots foot and gone chasing off after the fleeing enemy horse. Where they had gone none knew, but they still had not returned.

Censure and castigation however must wait. Meantime the Scots leadership was fully engaged in the difficult business of gathering and marshalling the retiring fighting-men, exhausted, dejected or unruly and protesting, getting them into columns of some sort and marching them off the field northwards. The wounded, and there were large numbers, had to be attended to in some degree and aided on their way, the dead and stricken inevitably had to be left where they had fallen. And all the time the English waited watchfully on their hill.

David himself would not quit that sorry scene until he was assured that all was in as fair order as was possible in the circumstances, and a strong rearguard organised—of which the Argyll contingent was a prominent part. When at length the High King allowed himself to leave, still with no sign of his son or the cavalry, it was to turn in his saddle and look back.

"God forgive me," he said, set-faced. "I drew the sword in vain. And leave behind those who had to pay the price. God in Heaven forgive me!"

These were the words of a caring and noble man. But in

a way, even these were ill-judged. For they were quickly repeated throughout the dispirited host and so helped to perpetuate the superstitious notion that Almighty God had been very much involved against them, that the disaster was a judgement on the Scots for having attacked Holy Church and the Consecrated Host borne aloft on that standard—in what became known as the Battle of the Standard. This constituted a grievous burden on morale, and came to affect almost all, from highest noble to humblest footman, out of all proportion to the military reverse. For after all, in fact it was no great defeat. The Scots army marched off the field intact and unpursued, and still greater in size and might than the enemy. They had merely failed to take, at considerable cost, a strongly-defended position. Nevertheless, the aura of fate against them was strong as the host faced the long march back to Scotland.

Somerled, for one, felt no such weight of divine wrath, having only the scantest respect for the authority of the Romish church. He had done his duty by David and was now concerned to get his people back to Argyll with all speed, to resume a life and reality to which all this was in the nature of an irrelevance. Fortunately he was no longer tied to Fergus. That man had survived the battle, although wounded, and with his force greatly depleted. He chose to return homewards through the west country and Cumbria detached from David's main army—no doubt, as most guessed, in order to spoil the Cumbrians *en route* and so to reach Galloway again at least much richer if lacking something in manpower. Somerled, whose Highlanders were much lighter of foot and quicker at covering ground than the generality of the Scots force, obtained David's permission to make his own way northwards at speed, since he had so much further to go.

It was scarcely a joyful parting; but if Somerled's respect for his High King's military prowess had suffered a declension, his regard for him as a man had not diminished. After all, David's reputation was not as a warrior-king but as an able monarch, lawgiver and man of peace. That would remain.

PART TWO

CHAPTER 11

It was a celebration. Aros, on the Isle of Mull across the Sound from Ardtornish, was the first of Somerled's new Norman-style castles to be completed. His great conception of protecting his Argyll kingdom against Norse and other attack, and at the same time to more firmly establish his own hold on these far-flung territories, by setting up this network of strongholds at strategic points, deserved and indeed required to be noised abroad. So the prominent from far and near were summoned to Aros, on its lofty promontory above the bay, this breezy day of May, to admire and take note. Feasting and jollification was the order of the day, on the face of it; but few present were in any doubts as to the serious purpose behind it all. The Lord of the Isles intended to be, and to remain, just that—for although he did call himself King of Argyll on occasion, more or less to keep that title valid, he, like others, thought of himself essentially as Lord of the Isles, a much more meaningful identification.

In mid-afternoon the proceedings were interrupted by the arrival in the bay of a strange ship. They had observed this vessel sailing down the Sound of Mull earlier in the day, noting it particularly in that it was of an unusual type for these waters, neither longship, birlinn nor galley, but a heavily-built merchanter of distinctly foreign aspect; in fact, Somerled had sent one of his captains after it, to enquire, since it was possible that it might be making for Ardtornish, across and further down the Sound, still the main seat of his lordship. Anyway, he made it his business to know what most of the traffic through his seaway was up to. Now his longship had returned with the stranger, into Aros Bay already crowded with shipping.

Somerled was applauding a wrestling-match on the grassy platform of the rock-summit before the castle drawbridge and gatehouse, when he perceived that two of the people being led up from the shore were women. As they came closer, it was also evident that of the others two were boys, or youths in their early teens, noticeable amongst the armed escort.

Suddenly Saor MacNeil, beside his foster-brother, gripped his arm, gazing towards the newcomers. Somerled stared, in turn, and then, drawing a quick breath, strode off in the direction of the oncoming party.

A few yards from him, the visitors, panting a little from their climb, halted, scanning his features keenly, almost tensely.

"Elizabeth!" he cried. "You—Bethoc!"

"Aye, Sorley—Bethoc, your sister," one of the women answered. "I rejoice that you still remember me! It has been so long."

There was undoubtedly criticism in that, but he went to embrace her. "My dear, long, yes. Too long. But here is joy! Surprise, indeed. Welcome to Argyll, at last! It is years . . ."

"Years, yes. Over many years, Sorley. You did not come. It is none so far to Fermanagh . . ."

"No. But I have been . . . occupied. So much to do here, Bethoc, to establish, to build. A whole kingdom to set up. I had hoped that *you* would come to me . . ."

"You had a son to visit—not only a sister!"

"Aye." He drew back a little, his expression set, strained a little. He turned, to look at the two boys—and was appalled to find himself looking from one to the other, for the moment wondering. Then, of course, the thing was clear—and the old stab at the heart was there again. They were both good-looking, well-built lads, but the one, fair-haired and blue-eyed where the other was dark, was the taller, broader and finer-featured, features not unlike Somerled's own. But there was a difference, something about the eyes and the set of the jaw, a vagueness of the one and a blurring of the other, an essential weakness which was not to be hid and was emphasised in this moment of emotion by a twitching at the corner of a slightly slack mouth.

"Gillecolm!" Somerled went to his son, to enfold him in his arms. "Laddie, laddie—the size of you! Save us—here's a marvel! Colm mac Sorley—almost a man grown!" As he exclaimed it, the pain at the heart grew the sharper—for Gillecolm mac Somerled MacFergus would never be fully a man. The boy had been born just slightly lacking in his mental faculties, the tragedy of his young father's life, responsible perhaps for much of what that man had become. Not a few had said that it was a pity that the child had not died with the MacMahon girl-mother who gave such difficult birth to him—although Somerled had steadfastly refused to admit to such a wish. Here was the answer to many a question.

Gillecolm gulped and mumbled something into his father's chest, embarrassed, unsure. Still holding him, Somerled looked at the other boy, his nephew, and reached out to clasp his shoulder.

"So, Donald—you too, twice the size I last saw you. A fine support for your mother, I warrant. Two brave heroes to be." He raised his eyes to their mother and aunt. "You have raised these warriors well, Bethoc."

"Pray God I have not raised them to be warriors and heroes! I have had sufficient of such in our family," the Countess of Ross and Moray said. "We are on our way, even now, to visit that other fallen hero, Donald's father, in his captivity."

"Ah—so that is it? You go to Malcolm."

"Yes. Since it seems that he cannot come to us. I am still his wife. David has sent for us. No doubt for his own purposes. But . . . I could not refuse. Malcolm left it to my choice. It was not easy—to go into perpetual captivity . . ."

"You mean—it is not just a visit, then? You intend to stay? With Malcolm."

"I am his wife. And Donald is his son. Perhaps it is Donald whom David wants, in truth? That there be no more attempts on his throne, by the MacEths."

"M'mm. It may be so. But David is a fair and honest man. There will be concern in it, too, for Malcolm and yourself, I think. He much loved his own wife. He would not wish you to be parted for all time."

"Does such concern enter into the thinking of kings?"

"This king is different, Bethoc—that I have found out. He can act the good-hearted man as well as the monarch. The very fact that he spared Malcolm's life shows that, when the others were clamouring for his death. And this of perpetual captivity is none so ill. Malcolm lives as one of David's close household—as his nephew, indeed. Even, he accompanied us on the invasion of England."

She shrugged. "We shall see . . ."

The celebratory proceedings continued and the new-comers were drawn in, in some measure, the two boys at least appreciative.

In the early evening they sailed back across the Sound to Ardtornish.

Later, relaxed, in the lesser hall there, the boys bedded down, brother and sister watched the sun sink behind the mountains of Mull, in the company of Somerled's close companions, Saor, Conn, Dermot and Cathula. Presently Somerled asked,

"What caused Malcolm to attempt to unseat David, Bethoc? I could not understand it. He was never a fighting man. He loved hunting and ease, not kingship. He could not win—I told him so . . ."

"It was the MacMahon, your goodsire, who persuaded him. At the behest of the High King, Muirchertach. They say that it was the English King Stephen's doing, behind it all. To cause trouble in Scotland, so that he himself might take and rule there. The Irish High King sorely requires Norman help against the Norse. This was part of the price."

"So that was it! I might have guessed."

"That Stephen is a craven, I say. He gets others to fight his battles for him," Saor commented. "The sorrow that it had to be the Earl Malcolm."

"I tried to dissuade him," the Countess said. "But he can be obstinate. And he owed much to the MacMahon, of course—who provided ships and men, as ever. Moreover, Malcolm wished to avenge his brother Angus. It was a sorry business—he was made a sacrifice, just. Can you wonder if I have no love for kings?"

"David you will find . . . different. You will fare none so ill at Rook's Burgh, Beth. It is a fair place in a fair land. In David's house, I swear, you will live better than at Enniskillen."

"Perhaps. I am not sorry to leave Fermanagh. Since our

190

father died, it has not been the same. And with Malcolm gone, I have been the less welcome there. I had even thought of coming to you, Sorley—although you did not ask me!"

Uncomfortably, he stirred. "I should have done, yes. There has been so much to do . . ."

"I would have thought that at least you would have sent for your son."

He spread his hands, wordless.

"I have carried the responsibility sufficiently long, Sorley. I love Colm—he is a gentle, amiable lad, warm of heart, but easily hurt. He says little but his wits are sharp enough in some matters. He and Donald are very close. But now that he is growing apace, he needs a man's guidance, his father's. So I have brought him to you. I shall miss him—but this is best, now. I cannot take *him* into this captivity."

From the moment they had arrived, Somerled had recognised that it must come to this. Yet even so, his reluctance could not be hid.

"Yes," he said.

She looked at him, as did Cathula. The men looked out at the sunset.

"Your son," the Countess added, deliberately.

"Yes. To be sure. He must stay."

"What else?" she asked. And when he did not further respond, went on. "You have put this off over-long, Sorley. The boy deserves better of you."

"Yes, yes. I know it. But you must understand, Bethoc—it will not be easy. Living as I do . . ."

"Easy? It has not been easy for me, either. Is it ease that you seek—Somerled the Mighty, Norse-Slayer, Lord of the Isles, King of Argyll? All this you have done, achieved—and you say that it will not be easy. To take your own son to you."

He rose abruptly and went over to the window, to stare out at the gathering night. "You make it sound so simple. It is not. Colm is not . . . as others. He requires much heeding, care. Which I will find it difficult to give him. I am but seldom here, at Ardtornish. I am a man with much on my mind. It is, in the main, a woman's work, is it not?"

"Perhaps you should find yourself another wife, then?"

He turned, partly at Cathula's sudden hoot of laughter,

and stared from one woman to the other. Saor came to his rescue.

"Sakes—there are some cures worse than the disease!" he observed, grinning.

"I . . . we shall make do," Somerled said shortly. He came back to the fireside circle. "When do you sail, Bethoc?"

"In a day or two. To Eskmouth, in Galloway. I must go. Already I am delayed . . ."

Before the Countess left, Somerled was in one respect less concerned over his son's arrival and in another, more so. He found himself to be more at ease and in sympathy with the boy than he had expected, more *close* to him. But that was also the trouble, the very closeness. Gillecolm, in fact, clung to him all too closely. Wherever he turned the lad was there, both lads until Donald left with his mother. Clearly Somerled was hero and paladin to his son as well as long-lost father, not to be let long out of his sight now that he had been found again. This was obviously going to create problems; but the man was loth indeed to seem to repulse the youngster in any way. The hope was that in time this too close dependence would lessen.

After the moving, indeed all but tearful parting with aunt and cousin, however, Gillecolm clung but the closer to his father, his only anchor in abruptly changed waters. The boy demonstrated a sort of dumb anxiety, like a dog which fears that it will be locked away. Somerled's friends sought to help, Cathula in especial; but the lad was only marginally responsive, seemingly suspicious. He was young for his years, of course, and his mental handicap almost certainly emphasised by this drastic change in his hitherto sheltered life. Somerled's forebodings grew, however much he felt for and cherished the son he had fathered.

In these circumstances he was more receptive, perhaps, than might otherwise have been the case, when a longship arrived at Ardtornish from the south, bearing a message from Olaf, King of Man. This was to the effect that his new abbey of Rushen, which he had built to the glory of God and in memory of his late wife Ingebiorg Hakonsdotter, was now completed and was to be consecrated by Archbishop Thurstan of York, on St. Barnabus' Eve, the tenth day of June. Olaf hoped that his ally and friend, the King of Argyll and the Isles, would honour the occasion with his presence. He suggested that it might be wise, as well as suitable, that he should do so, if possible; for he understood that the Archbishop, as well as consecrating, intended to use the occasion to advance Bishop Wimund to be Bishop of the Isles, in addition to Man, no doubt for his own purposes, and his friend Somerled might have his own ideas about this, being of a different faith. This invitation came in the form of a letter penned by Olaf. But the longship's master added a verbal message. The Princess Ragnhilde had asked him to say that she hoped very much that King Somerled would come.

Normally, to travel one-hundred-and-fifty miles and more to attend such an affair would scarcely have been considered. But this of Archbishop Thurstan and a new Romish bishopric of the Isles required some examination. Also, an excursion to Man might be helpful with regard to young Gillecolm, a distraction which could possibly widen the boy's outlook and loosen this utter dependence on his father's company. Somerled did not so much as admit to himself that the verbal message from Ragnhilde might be the true deciding factor. He agreed to go.

Cathula MacIan, however, although she was not informed about that postscript, was not to be misled about motives. When she heard that her lord actually proposed to sail all the way to Man for an abbey-opening, she was typically direct and scornful.

"You are not going there to see any archbishop, nor yet to talk about church matters, Sorley MacFergus!" she exclaimed. "You are going because of that chit of a girl, Ragnhilde. A child, young enough to be your daughter! I have not forgotten how you mooned over her, the great Somerled! I knew that you had not forgotten her either, and her whey-faced simperings. That is why you consider going to Man. You have been but looking for excuse."

"You talk nonsense," he said, but mildly enough.

"Do I, then? Do you think that I am a fool? Or blind? Can you say in honesty that when you have been lying with me of a night you have never wished it was that daughter of Norse pirates you had under you? I have seen you, felt you, watched your eyes . . ."

"You *are* a fool, Cat! If you believe that. In your bed, you are sufficiently potent to keep any man's wits from straying, I assure you! Besides, the Princess Ragnhilde is not to be considered so. She is . . . different."

"*Princess*—oh, yes! Different, indeed! No mere cot-woman nor ship-woman, but a female Viking, of a long line of cut-throat ravishers! Different . . .!"

He left her while still he had his temper under control.

They would sail in three days, calling on the way at Castle Sween in Knapdale, where old King Ewan MacSween was said to be sick, failing and wishful to see Somerled.

*   *   *

The Argyll flotilla reached St. Michael's Bay of Man the day before the consecration ceremony. So far the excursion had been a success. Young Colm was excited and happy—after all, aboard ship he had his father close at hand all the time; and the voyage down through the island-dotted and most colourful sea in the world, in fine weather, could scarcely fail to delight. Cathula, although subdued, had made no more outbursts. Somerled had said that she could remain behind at Ardtornish if she so disapproved of this Manx visit, but she had elected to play her accustomed role of master of the dragon-ship, at which she was notably proficient. The Castle Sween interlude had been moving, distressing after a fashion but eminently satisfactory after another. Ewan was obviously dying, well aware of it, and anxious that Somerled, in taking over his lands and nominal kingdom, should do so in trouble-free style and with full respect for his chieftains and people, as according to their compact of seven years before. They had parted with a good understanding, the old man reassured, Somerled confirmed in a large increase in his territories and influence, to which he had little doubt that David, as overlord, would agree.

Landing, as before, in the basin-like bay of St. Michael, again full of shipping, they were faced with the same problem of lack of transport to Rushen Castle. Olaf should surely establish some pool of horses here, available for visitors. Would old Archbishop Thurstan also have had to tramp the two miles? Not that it was a long nor taxing walk, but most surely it lacked suitablity.

194

Oddly, they had reached almost the same spot in the forest of Langness, in their progress, where they had been harried by the huntsmen, when again they were approached by a hard-riding company, with at least one of the personnel the same. It was Ragnhilde Olafsdotter come hastening, with a party of grooms and spare horses.

For long moments Somerled—and not only Somerled—stared at her as she drew up her snorting mount and sat looking down at them. It was almost three years since he had been here and in that time this daughter of Olaf's who, whatever his denials, had got between him and his sleep many a night, had changed from a girl into a woman. Flushed as she was with fast riding, red hair blown, breathing disturbed and disturbing, she nevertheless had exchanged her aspect of youthful charm and piquancy, tinged with a kind of permanent anxiety, for a serenity and poise which complemented her sculptured loveliness of feature and colouring. That her figure had burgeoned also did not go unnoticed.

"My lord King—greeting!" she smiled, panting a little. "I rejoice that you have come. When news was brought that your ships had been sighted, I made haste to meet you. Had you sent word, I would have been at the haven."

He found difficulty in answering her, just then. "No need," he got out. "You are very good, kind. And very fair. I too rejoice."

"Thank you." They eyed each other for moments and then, as she moved in her saddle to dismount, he strode forward, to lift her down—and in no haste to release her.

The others watched, with varying expressions.

When she stirred, he schooled himself to the civilities, turning.

"All here you know, I think—save this, my son. Here is Gillecolm. The Princess Ragnhilde, lad."

Wide-eyed she looked from man to boy and back again. "Son!" she said. "You did not tell me that you had a son. And, and . . ." She left the rest unsaid.

"Did I not?" he said flatly. "He was in Fermanagh. In care of my sister. Now he is with me. Come, Colm—your respects to the princess."

As the boy hesitated, shyly, she searched his face for a

moment, then stepped over to reach out for both his hands.

"Colm, is it? Colm Somerledsson, the well-favoured! We shall be friends, I think." She kissed his cheek, but with a laugh, to spare him embarrassment. "Myself, *I* favour handsome young men!"

He flushed, but those vague, unsure eyes took on a momentary sparkle. His father's gleamed also.

"Good!" Somerled exclaimed. And again, "Good. Colm is tall, for fourteen years. He will be a bigger man than I am, before long. You remember Saor? And Conn? And Sir Malcolm? Also this Cathula, who masters my ship?"

"Who could forget? I greet all kindly."

There were too few horses for all to ride singly, so some of the party mounted behind the grooms. Somerled was going to take Gillecolm up pillion on his beast when Ragnhilde beckoned the boy to ride with her.

"Will you ride front or shall I?" she asked.

He mumbled something, but eagerly climbed into the saddle first, to bend and help her up behind. He was used to horses.

As they rode on side-by-side, the girl said to Somerled, "I am glad that you came. And brought this one."

He did not usually lower his voice when he spoke. "I came because *you* asked me to." The others behind were not to hear that.

She eyed him quickly. "Then I am the more glad. But I hoped that you might come. Feared that you might not—the great Somerled to come to a churchmen's assembly, the consecration of an abbey! And one not of your own faith."

"It will be the first that I have attended," he admitted.

"Yes. But this is intended to be more than but a Church gathering—much more. I thought that you ought to be present."

"M'mm. Is that so?" The man sounded less than elated. He had hoped that her concern for his presence might have been more personal.

"King Stephen of England's hand is behind this," she went on. "It is aimed against King David. And you said that you were friend to David. My father is not sufficiently strong to withstand both England and Holy Church. And Earl Fergus of Galloway, also, the Queen's father . . ."

"Is that man here?"

"Yes, more's the pity. I do not trust him."

"Nor I. This is unfortunate. We are scarcely friendly! But—both he and your father are vassals of David of Scotland."

She nodded. "King David is perhaps less than fortunate in all his vassals! What is planned, I think, is for Bishop Wimund to be made Bishop of all the Isles. Under Archbishop Thurstan's sway from York, of course. When that is done the Archbishop will claim that he is spiritual overlord of Scotland, from Galloway to Orkney. He claims that already, to be sure, saying that there is no archbishop nor metropolitan north of York. But now he will have a diocese of Scotland to which he has appointed the bishop, right up to the Isles of Orkney—where already there is a Catholic bishop."

"I see, yes. So that is it! I see, too, lady, that *you* have wits and understanding, in this matter, much beyond mine. How is all this to aid Stephen and hurt David?"

"Do you not see it? The English kings have always sought to claim paramountcy over Scotland. If their archbishop, York, can show that he is spiritual overlord of Scotland, a way is cleared for his master, the King."

"Such claim would carry no weight, surely? David would but laugh at it. The Romish Church prevails in his realm, yes—thanks to his mother, Margaret. But his bishops are not appointed from England and pay no service to York or Canterbury. As for the Isles and the Hebrides, no Roman churchmen are there and the Columban Church prevails."

"But once Rome has a bishop there, it can claim spiritual authority, in name. And if that authority is resisted, York can appeal to the Pope in Rome. And if the Pope supports his archbishop—as he would be like to do—then all Roman Catholic monarchs and princes have a right and duty to support the Papal edict. By force of arms, if necessary."

"Lord . . .! You, you credit this?"

"It is what I have heard discussed in my father's hall. Or in his bedchamber!"

"But . . . if Stephen could not successfully invade Scotland before—as he could not, at Berwick-on-Tweed—how shall this advantage him? The fact that he has the Pope's blessing and command will not add to his armed strength."

"Surely you must see! Now it would not be Stephen alone. But others. Other Catholic princes would have excuse to invade, the excuse they may seek. Norway. Norway ever seeks to gain lands—I heard you tell my father so, when last you were here. Sigurd Half-Deacon is dead. But King Ingi Cripple his son is no less greedy . . ."

"The Norwegians would not think to take over Scotland!"

"No—that is for Stephen. But your Isles and Argyll—that could be Ingi's reward."

"Save us, lassie—all this, out of a new bishopric!"

"The bishopric would be but the start of it. And there is not only Norway and the Danes. The Norse-Irish of Dublin are Catholic too and would be glad of pickings. They ever seek to control Man itself—which is why my father considers taking a part in all this, to save his own small kingdom. King David could be faced with a great alliance—the more so since he fought against Holy Church at that battle in England, of the Standard."

Wonderingly, Somerled stared at her, behind his son. "So this is why you wanted me to come!"

"Partly, my lord King. Was I foolish?"

"A mercy—no! But—why? Why this concern for my island realm? And for King David? Against your own father's interest?"

"I believe that my father's true interests are not being served in this. That he is but being used as a mere cat's-paw, and will be cast off when he has served his turn. Then Man itself swallowed up. I believe that he is mistaken. Affrica and Fergus and Wimund have persuaded him. But they have not persuaded me."

"Aye," he said, nodding. "I perceive that you have grown into a woman indeed since I left here three years back, lady. God be praised that you chose *my* side in this matter!"

"I think that I chose my own side, Lord Somerled. You happened to be on it!"

Silenced, he rode on, thoughtful indeed.

When they came to Olaf's ramshackle castle, the Argyll party, coming late and unheralded, had to occupy only inferior quarters, with the place full to overflowing.

Ragnhilde apologised but said that she would try to find Somerled himself some better room. There were a lot of churchmen in evidence.

Olaf, never one for ceremony, came to their crowded lodging in person, presently, to receive his guests. He was affable but a trifle uneasy, presumably aware that he had a delicate path to tread.

"Welcome to Man again, my young friend," he greeted. "It is good that you could come. You have been to war, I hear, since last we saw you? Not your own warring, this time, but David's. A costly venture, I am told."

"War is generally costly, I fear. You, I think, Olaf Godfreysson, seldom go to war, if ever. Unlike Fergus, you did not go, nor send men, to David's venture into England!"

"I chose the wiser part, as was proved. I swear that Fergus now wishes that he could say the same! You also, perhaps?"

"I did not see it as a choice, man. I swore to be David's vassal. When he called, I had to answer. You felt otherwise?"

"I see my first duty to my own people, my friend. Do not you?"

"To be sure. But a ruler must look ahead. Further than this month or this year. If he can. There is the longer view, for small kingdoms—as I think you do not fail to perceive on occasion. And an oath is an oath."

"I took oath to cherish Man first! But—no doubt we shall speak of this further hereafter. Tonight we feast in my hall. And tomorrow we consecrate my abbey. There is duty to Almighty God also, is there not? David, the abbey-builder, would agree with that, at least!"

Guest and host eyed each other assessingly.

The banquet that evening got off to an awkward start, and the fault was undeniably Somerled's. An usher had been sent to their quarters to bring the Argyll party to the hall. When they arrived, it was to find Olaf, Ragnhilde, Wimund and two of the King's deplorable sons already seated at the top table—but sundry other seats vacant. Somerled was no stickler for ceremony and precedence, any more than was Olaf; but sojourn at David's court had taught him a little. He quickly counted the empty spaces near the centre of the King's table, and came to the conclusion that there were places left for a further six principal guests. Since none of his own party would so rank, apart from himself, that meant that there were five others still to come. These would no doubt include Queen Affrica presumably. But also Archbishop Thurstan and Fergus of Galloway. If he went and sat down now, it would mean waiting for the Archbishop and Fergus, possibly even having to stand when the former appeared, especially if he was with Affrica. Such would imply that he recognised some precedence and seniority—which the King of Argyll was by no means prepared to concede. Somerled stood just within the hall doorway, raising a hand to halt his companions. Any waiting they would do there.

Up at the head of the hall, Olaf beckoned them forward.

Somerled chose to misinterpret the gesture, bowed to his host, but stayed where he was.

Their usher agitatedly urged them on.

When Olaf's second wave produced no movement, Ragnhilde rose from her place and came down between the crowded tables in the body of the hall, to them. She was looking beautiful, all in simple white tonight. All watched.

"My father's greetings, my lord," she said. "Will you come to table? You are to sit beside myself."

"In that I rejoice, lady," he answered. "But, by your leave, I prefer to bide here meantime."

"But . . . why? And where is your son?"

"Colm is left at our lodgings. He mislikes large gatherings. As to why I wait here, the last who enters ranks highest. I do not give place to this archbishop. Nor yet to Fergus. In this, or other matter."

"Ah—I see. We do not greatly consider such formalities here. But . . . perhaps you are wise. I shall wait here with you. I cannot think that the others will be long. It will be Affrica—she has little notion of time."

So they stood, Olaf shrugging and lesser folk staring, as the musicians played.

A stir behind them heralded the arrival of Affrica, on her father's arm, followed by a youngish man, heavily-built and sullen-looking, whom Ragnhilde murmured was Ronald, son to the King of Dublin. At the entry of the Queen all must stand, save Olaf himself.

She was handsomely clad—if that word would apply to a pearl-seeded gown which left so much of her unclad—but nothing would make her person or face handsome, although she possessed a sort of urgent magnetism. Fergus was richly-dressed and smiling—although when his glance reached Somerled the smile faded for the moment.

Affrica smirked at him, however, and as still he waited and she and her father passed, spoke briefly.

"The mighty Somerled—who wearies of a night!" She had not forgotten.

He inclined his head but his eyes sought Fergus's. "Daughter and father of a like . . . flavour!" he said.

They swept on.

The Archbishop was not far behind. Thurstan was a frail, elderly man of quite noble appearance but thin, and with a somewhat sour expression. He did not so much as glance at Somerled. He was followed by another prelate of a very different aspect, bullet-headed, close-cropped, with an underhung jaw and beady eyes—Raoul, the Norman Bishop of Durham.

As these moved in towards their places, Somerled bowed to Ragnhilde and offered her his arm. Together they paced in the wake of the churchmen. So, in the end, the King of Argyll was in fact the last to reach his seat, between Olaf and his daughter. The rest of his party were disposed at a special table over on the left. All sat, after Thurstan pronounced a brief Latin grace.

It became evident, as the meal proceeded, that this was to be no occasion for significant discussion of affairs. Olaf was genial, but applied himself to the business of eating and drinking, putting away an extraordinary amount for so diminutive a person. On Olaf's other side, Thurstan merely toyed with his food and had nothing to say to anyone. On Ragnhilde's left, Fergus sat, and certainly made no more attempt than did Somerled to engage in mutual converse.

The latter made no complaint. He had Ragnhilde to talk to, the provender was good and plentiful if fairly plain, and no confrontation appeared likely to develop meantime.

"Your son," Ragnhilde said presently. "How old is he?"

"Fourteen years," he told her. "I was wed young. At sixteen. To the MacMahon's daughter. Bridget was

201

younger still, only fifteen. The matter was arranged by our fathers—a convenience, just! She died at the birth of Gillecolm."

"How . . . pitiful! Grievous. All wrong!"

"Wrong, yes. Mistaken, fated from the first—or so my father decided. The child was . . . not right. Lacking in some degree. My father saw it all as a curse on our house. He had lost his lands, then his wife, my mother—who was his strength—then this. He was a weak man—kindly but weak."

"So you had to be otherwise? Strong—a fighter?" she commented.

"I grew up being told that fate was against our line. That he, and so the rest of us, were next to damned. Why, I could not discover. I was not told. I did not believe it, could not accept it. So . . ."

"So you proved that you were right and your father wrong! Somerled the Mighty. But you left your son behind!"

"I could not do otherwise. I had Argyll and the Isles to conquer. The Norsemen to defeat and drive out. No task to take a child on."

"No. And now? What of Gillecolm?"

"I do not know. I must come to terms with him, with his disability. He clings to me, much needs me always. I find it difficult. But I am coming closer to him, understanding him better. We shall find a way."

"He is gentle, and a little fearful, I think. But there is spirit there also. I see his father in him, somewhere, as well as . . . the rest."

"You do?" He grasped her arm. "You do, in truth?"

"Yes. I perceive a kind of strength. Beneath it all. You will be proud of your son, yet."

He gazed at her, realised that he was still holding her elbow, and releasing her, applied himself to his venison.

The banquet was succeeded by the usual entertainment, bear-dancing, juggling, wrestling and the like, scarcely calculated to appeal to senior churchmen. Olaf himself soon fell asleep; and since none might leave before their royal host, and Affrica was much preoccupied tonight with the Prince Ronald of Dublin, Ragnhilde presently rose and went to waken her father, indicating the restless prelates.

Olaf was nothing loth to depart for his bed, and with some relief Thurstan, Raoul and Wimund got to their feet, the signal for other, lesser clerics to do likewise, in a partial exodus.

With the top table now reduced as to numbers, and restraint rapidly vanishing, Somerled found Fergus's fleering gaze upon him.

"I had not thought to see you here, Islesman, at such a gathering," he announced. "Have you become a belated supporter of Holy Church? I believed that you still prayed before standing-stones, the rising sun, and the like? Has your friend David converted you?" That was slurred over somewhat, the Earl obviously drink-taken.

"I pray as best I may—especially for patience!" he was answered shortly.

"You say so? *I* say that patience is apt to be the refuge of the weakling! Myself, I leave patience to others."

Somerled did not answer. He certainly did not want to be involved in trouble with the Queen's father, here in Olaf's hall. He turned to Ragnhilde.

But Fergus persisted. "Your father, now—he was a patient man. And lost all. Take heed lest you go the same way, Islesman. I recollect how this patience held you back, you and yours, at yonder Cowton Moor in England! To my hurt."

Somerled's fist clenched. "You misremember, my lord," he said.

"Not so. You retired, man, after the first assault. You pulled your Islesmen back. Then stood by . . ."

The younger man's chair scraped on the floor as he rose abruptly. "I shall not bandy insults with you, sir, at another man's table!" he got out. "I bid you a good night." He made a sketchy bow in the direction of Affrica, and turned, to find Ragnhilde standing also. She took his arm, and together they left the hall.

"I am sorry," she said, low-voiced. "That man is hateful! That you should have to suffer this in my father's house! Perhaps, perhaps I should not have urged you to come?"

"Fergus and I mislike each other. And he is all but drunk."

"Yes. But it was unforgiveable. You must also mislike Man and all to do with it."

"Not all," he said, and patted the hand on his arm. "By no means all! Think no more of it. Wherever Fergus and I met, there would be words, I fear. But . . . where are you taking me? Our lodging is the other way . . .?"

"I told you that I would seek to find you better quarters. For yourself. The castle is full to overflowing. But I have found a chamber that will serve."

"There was no need . . ."

She brought him to a building of no great size, somewhat isolated from the others, and took him in and up the stairway, passing an open doorway wherein a young woman dipped them a curtsy. On the upper floor, she opened a door and ushered him into a smallish bedchamber, simply furnished but comfortable and smelling, by no means unpleasantly, of woman—as indeed did the rest of the building.

"It is small for a man, let alone for a king!" she said. "But it is better than where you were. It is Berthe's room, my attendant. That was Berthe, below. She will share my chamber, meantime."

"No, no. There is no need for this. I thank you—but I shall do very well where I was. I am used to less comfort of a night, in ship and on the march . . ."

"But not in *this* house! All is arranged." She paused. "Your ship-woman? Shall I have her brought here? Is the bed sufficiently large?" That was levelly said.

"H'mm—no! Not so. I sleep alone. Cathula is, is an excellent shipmaster. As good as any man . . ."

"It would be a pity to, to deprive you."

"I assure you—no! You must not think . . ."

"No? Very well. Then there is the boy. Will this small place here serve for him?" She showed him what was little more than a wall-closet just across the passage from his chamber. It was heaped with sheepskins and blankets. "It is no more than a garderobe, and he is a tall lad . . .?"

"Yes, yes—he will do very well there. A deal better than on the ship. You are kind, thoughtful. I shall go fetch Colm."

Downstairs, she paused at the door where the young woman Berthe waited. "I bid you goodnight, King Somerled. This is my chamber."

"Ah. So near. That is . . . pleasing. My friends call me Sorley. I would hope that you might do so."

"You count me your friend?"

"I would count you more than that, lady."

She looked at him thoughtfully, in the dim light. "Then sleep well, Sorley," she said, and left him there.

In excellent spirits, considering how he had felt so recently in the hall, he went for Gillecolm.

*   *   *

The new abbey of Rushen, built in memory of Olaf's former queen, Ragnhilde's mother—who no doubt seemed the more dear in contrast with the new one—was sited some distance inland, at Ballasalla, on higher ground amongst low rolling hills. A large company assembled there, at noon, many more than the church would hold. Fortunately the weather was kind, and something of the atmosphere of a fair prevailed amongst the crowds thronging the greensward between the monastic buildings, which were not quite finished yet, and the church, with singing, even dancing, and chapmen and hucksters selling their wares. The principals mustered in the refectory, to make procession to the church behind a choir of singing boys. Apart from the boys, it was noticeable that the holiday atmosphere was much less evident within than without.

Even though Olaf was not greatly concerned with ceremonial and precedence, some order had to be arranged for the procession, posing the usual problems. The archbishop and two bishops, of course, led the way, followed by the other clergy in all their finery. Olaf himself came next, with Affrica and Ragnhilde immediately behind—his legitimate son, Godfrey, was still in Norway, more or less a hostage, apparently. The question was, who next? Was it to be the King of Argyll or the present queen's father, neither of whom were desirous of walking together? The matter was solved, after a fashion, by putting Prince Ronald between them, so that they walked three-abreast. Then followed Olaf's three illegitimate sons—who carefully avoided meeting Somerled's eye—then the mass of the Manx nobles and chiefs, who presumably sorted out their own precedence.

So they marched, with varying expressions, behind the sweetly-singing choristers, through the admiring crowds, to the church. At least here there was no precedence problem about seating, since there were no seats. The clergy filled the chancel and the rest filled the nave, little order being possible, save that Olaf and his party were at the front.

When the singing stopped and the shuffling and talk was approximately stilled, Thurstan was commendably brief. In a surprisingly strong voice considering his frail appearance, he announced that, in devotion to Holy Church, out of a pious mind and in memory of the former Queen Ingebiorg, the most admirable King of Man had endowed and built this house, to the glory of God and the furtherance of His work on this island, in all time coming. He then launched into Latin, presumably a prayer but which, being beyond the comprehension of the majority present, quite quickly became so for the clergy also, owing to the growing murmur and chatter in the nave—to the glares of Bishops Raoul and Wimund. This over, Thurstan sketched the Sign of the Cross and muttered a few words over a large bowl of water on the altar, and turning, peremptorily summoned a waiting priest forward, to take the bowl, this individual at the same time handing the archbishop a spoon with a longish handle.

Thus equipped, the pair of them started off on a perambulation of the church, commencing at the altar itself, moving to each side of the chancel, down to the font, the crossing, the transepts, and splashing water from the bowl, with the spoon, in liberal fashion on the stonework, whilst the choir gave voice again and a monkish acolyte followed them round with a piece of chalk, to mark crosses where the water had struck.

This finished, back at the altar, the priest with the bowl was signed to kneel; and dipping a finger into what remained of the water, Thurstan anointed him also, on the brow, declaring that he, Ivo, was hereby ordained and inducted Lord Abbot of this newly-consecrated abbey, and all within its discipline, with the full power, authority and anathemas of Holy Church to bind and to loose, to save and to condemn. Amen. Arise, Ivo, Abbot of Rushen.

The new abbot then took up the bowl once more and with the choristers forming up again, to lead the way, the clergy paced down through the thronged nave and out into the sunshine, to the cheers of the waiting multitude. There Thurstan proceeded around the exterior of the building, spooning more water at specific points, the main west doorway, the east gable buttresses, the chapter-house entry and so on, again all being marked with the chalk for the masons hereafter to carve consecration-crosses thereon.

Back at the decorative west doorway, the Abbot Ivo announced that Mass would be celebrated by the Lord Bishop of Durham at the newly-consecrated altar—but it was noticeable that only a limited number of the former congregation trooped inside after the churchmen, Somerled and his people amongst the abstainers, the word being that only the senior clergy themselves would partake.

The women also remained outside, and Somerled found his way to Ragnhilde's side, where she talked with a distinctly stiff Cathula MacIan, who had young Gillecolm by the arm.

"Thus far we survive—without being swept away in a flood of holy water!" he commented. "What now?"

"I fear, my lord King, that your testing is yet to come," Ragnhilde said. "There is to be refreshment in the refectory. I should think that it will be there that this of the Isles bishopric is announced, since nothing has been said hitherto."

"And your father's attitude to this? He has said nothing of it to me."

"No. Nor will he, I think. He is not happy, but has been persuaded. He does not wish to offend King David. Nor yourself, indeed. But he fears others more."

"So he will side with Thurstan, who acts for Stephen?"

"And for the Pope and the Roman Church," she added.

They moved across to the refectory, through the holiday crowd.

The celebratory Mass must have been distinctly modified, for there was only a short interval before Olaf and the prelates arrived and were led to the laden tables, the new Abbot Ivo acting as host now. He was another Norman, d'Avranches by name, and related to the Earl of Chester.

There was little formality here and Somerled shared a table with his own Argyll folk, served by the monkish brethren.

Presently the abbot rose. "Sire. My lords spiritual and temporal," he announced, ignoring the ladies. "My lord Archbishop has a matter of great moment to pronounce upon. It is my very great privilege that he has chosen to declare it here, in our new abbey. It concerns us all, in some measure, and represents, I am sure, a further step in the working out of the purposes of Almighty God. My lord Archbishop."

Thurstan made his announcement sitting. "There has long been a grievous failure in the rule of Holy Church in these kingdoms," he said, in a level, almost matter-of-fact voice very different from the sonorous tones he had used in church. "The Scotland of King David is now within the fold of Christ's shepherd and vicar-on-earth, His Holiness of Rome—however unworthy that monarch. As has long been the realm of England, with Wales, and of course this kingdom of Man, like much of Ireland. Only the one area remains in spiritual twilight, lacking the care and oversight of the Holy See and its servants, of whom I am the humble representative in this the North. That area is the Hebrides and Western Isles, your neighbour. This failure it has now been decided to amend. A new diocese of Holy Church has been created, the Bishopric of the Isles, Sudreys and Nordreys, which, reaching up to the Orcades, will complete the embrace of the true faith in these northern regions of Christendom. As first Bishop thereof I have appointed your own good father-in-God, Bishop Wimund of Man, who will meantime care for both sees, as Bishop of Man and the Isles. His task will be a heavy one, but of great opportunity in God's service. I commend him to the prayers and thankfulness of all here."

Amidst the pious acclamation of the clergy and the murmur and throat-clearing of less dedicated folk, Wimund rose.

"My lord Archbishop," he said briefly, "I am much honoured and exercised by the trust you have put in me in this matter and will, with God's help, do all in my power to ensure that the true light of the Gospel will shine more brightly in these remote isles and northern seaboard." He sat down.

The Bishop of Durham stood—but Somerled spoke first, even though, like Thurstan, he did not stand.

"Olaf Godfreysson, as guest in this your kingdom, I, Somerled of Argyll and the Isles, would ask whether you knew of what these Romish churchmen proposed? And if so, why I was not informed and consulted before any such announcement was made?"

There was a stunned silence for a few moments, and then outraged murmuring from the clerics.

Olaf, looking unhappy, blinked and took a gulp of wine from his chalice. "Friend Somerled," he said, "this matter was privy until the Lord Archbishop chose to divulge it. No concern of mine. Nor, would I have thought, was it any concern of *yours*, since you are King of Argyll, not of the Isles. Is that not so?"

"I had not thought, friend, to have to explain my position to such as yourself—even if these others are ignorant. Which I misdoubt! My kingdom of Argyll includes much of the isles—Mull, Islay, Jura, Rhum, Eigg, Lismore and many others. Moreover, my longships control the rest! Ewan MacSween has borne the title of King of the Isles, yes, with my consent. But Ewan is a dying man—which is no doubt why these clerks have chosen this moment to attempt their folly and device, before he dies and I become King of the Isles in his room, in name as well as in fact. For that has long been agreed between us. I made call on Ewan, on his death-bed, as I came here to Man, and he confirmed all. He may indeed be dead by now, for he was far gone—in which case I am already King of the Isles. If not, I am *Lord* of the Isles. Can any deny it?"

Olaf flapped his hands, shook his head and looked anxiously at Thurstan.

But it was the bullet-headed, bull-necked Raoul of Durham who spoke, and gratingly. "Lord Somerled, whatever your title, this matter is no concern of yours. It is entirely a matter for Holy Church. Of which, I understand, you are no true member, being of the heretical Columban faith. Holy Church may create sees and bishoprics where she will. Indeed she has the Christian duty to do so."

"But not in the realm of another monarch, Sir Priest. Without his permission."

"You are not monarch of the Isles, my lord. Nor even Ewan MacSween. Both are but sub-kings—Regulus."

"Ha—so that is it! As, then, is King Olaf here, all sub-kings of the realm of Scotland. Do you, Archbishop Thurstan, have King David's agreement and permission to officiate *here* today? As certainly you do not have his permission to create a diocese of the Isles, part of the realm of Scotland."

Raoul was beginning to answer, pugnacious jaw out-thrust, when Thurstan twitched his magnificent cope. Frowning darkly he sat down.

"Young man," the Archbishop said sternly, "You may be very effective with sword and battleaxe, but in matters of religion and church-governance you would be wise to heed those better informed. I am Metropolitan of the North, with spiritual jurisdiction over all lands and territories wherein no other Metropolitan has function. I may ordain bishops where I will."

"But not in an independent realm which has not granted you leave to do so, old man. Has King David agreed to this?"

"King David is not to be considered. He has proved to be an enemy of Holy Church. He fought against God's own Body at Northallerton—as did you, I am told. He has made himself excommunicate . . ."

"An enemy of the Church—he who has founded the abbeys of Jedburgh, Kelshaugh, Melrose, the Holy Rood and many another? You rave, Sir Priest—you rave! As to this of appointing bishops of your Romish Church, is there a single bishop of Scotland appointed by you or your predecessors? All have been nominated by the Kings of Scots and appointed directly by the Pope in Rome. This is but a base ruse, a device, to seek to claim a false overlordship over part of Scotland, at the behest of your master the usurper Stephen of Blois, Count of Boulogne. No religion in it. Dare you deny it, Clerk?"

Thurstan all but choked, raising a quivering hand to point at Somerled, wordless.

Bishop Raoul was more vocal. "King Olaf—how dares

this cut-throat Islesman speak so to a prince of Holy Church! It is intolerable! He must withdraw. Withdraw, I say—his allegations and slanders. Or better, his person, from this sacred building."

"I withdraw what I have said only if the Archbishop withdraws this false and insolent bishopric. Not otherwise."

In the uproar, Olaf beat with his chalice on the table-top. "King Somerled! My lords! This is too much! Restrain yourselves, of a mercy! In my presence. And of my queen and daughter. If there is disagreement, let us discuss it calmly. All can be resolved, I swear."

"It can and shall be," Somerled nodded. "By making an end of this folly and deceit of a bishopric in my Isles. In name—as it will be in fact! For I tell all here, I will not have it. Any attempt to send a single Romish Priest into my territories will be met by my longships. We have our own good Columban priests, from Iona. You, Wimund, take heed. Sail a keel into the Hebridean Sea, as Bishop of my Isles, and you will not sail out again! Come as my guest, as Bishop of Man, and you are welcome. Can I say fairer?"

"Safer not to come at all, whatever!" Saor MacNeil added, to vigorous acclaim from the Argyll table.

Thurstan had recovered his voice, even though it trembled a little. "This is sacrilege! Infamous sacrilege. Not to be borne. To threaten Holy Church with force! Hear me, young man, in your rash and heretical pride. In God's cause, Mother Church too can call upon the sword, the sword of righteousness. And when she does so, let him beware who provokes it! Your barbarous petty kingdom will drown in a welter of blood greater than that with which you carved it out!"

"You threaten *me*, old man, Somerled of the Isles, with priestly swords and clerkly arks? Know you what you say? Have you ever *seen* the Hebrides? Ever fought one longship, let alone hundreds? Ever even tried to land on a defended beach? You will require more than bread and wine shamefully hoisted on a mast, to gain even a foothold on the smallest isle of my kingdom!"

"Hold your ranting tongue, upstart, heretic!" Raoul bellowed, all Norman baron now, episcopal dignity forgotten. "Little you know what you so arrogantly challenge.

It is the might of England that you will face. King Stephen will answer the call of the Church. As will others. You will be swept into your precious Western Sea, with all your piratical crew . . .!"

"With what, sirrah? Oar-boats and fishercraft and merchanters? Stephen has no war-fleet. Where are the longships and galleys to challenge mine? Do you, in your ignorance, think that the Isles can be taken by a land army? Even if they could, think you King David would permit you to march through his Scotland?"

"You are not the only one with ships-of-war, barbarian! King Olaf has many. The King of Dublin not a few. The Earl of Orkney, even you cannot deny, has sufficient to more than match your own."

"All these know better than to challenge the Islesmen in their own Isles, with the King of Scots watching! Eh, Olaf Godfreysson? I am David's ally and vassal, you will mind, and have his protection. And this is David's quarrel also. I answered *his* call; he will answer mine. And have you forgot the Norsemen, still in Skye and the Long Island? How think you they would welcome churchmen and Englishry into the Hebrides? Even if Dublin and Orkney would—which I doubt."

"The pirate Norsemen will not oppose their own kin. They are almost all from Orkney. And Orkney can call on the King of Norway . . ."

"But Orkney will not! The last thing that Earl Ronald Kali would wish is for King Ingi Cripple to come sailing into his waters. Always the Orkneymen are concerned to keep Norway at a decent distance. Nor has Ronald any interest in this seaboard. They say he sets his eyes on Jerusalem! He would be thought a saint . . .!"

"Ha—tell him otherwise, Olaf." That was Fergus, making his first intervention. "Tell this arrogant Islesman of Ronald Kali's interest!"

Olaf, frowning, shook his head. "On another occasion, my lord. Not now."

"Why not? The sooner he learns, the sooner he will recognise that his fool's bladder is pierced! For Ronald of Orkney, as he knows full well, can launch three longships for every one of his!"

"That is so. But this is scarcely the occasion. In this bicker. My daughter's presence . . ."

"Then *I* shall tell it—since it much concerns this issue," Fergus exclaimed. "King Olaf, my own goodson, intends to marry his daughter, the Princess Ragnhilde, to Earl Ronald of Orkney. A firm alliance between Man and the power of the Orcades. It will . . ." The rest was lost in the tumult of outcry and clamour.

Somerled was part-way to his feet, appalled, when gazing across to where Ragnhilde sat, with Affrica, he saw the shock, bewilderment and horror of her expression and realised that this was as much as a surprise and blow to her as to himself. He resumed his seat as the young woman rose from hers.

Ragnhilde did not speak. Set-faced and looking at none of them, she turned and hastened from the refectory.

A silence descended upon the company, broken only by a tinkle of laughter from the Queen. Olaf frowned on her, looked as though he was going to hurry out after his daughter, then thought better of it.

Raoul spoke. "An excellent provision, we must all agree. Such alliance must make it clear, even to this intemperate Islesman, that his vaunted reliance on his ships of war will not save him. The combined fleets of Orkney and Man must much outnumber his own, without counting that of Dublin. King Stephen's armies will not lack for transport."

"Stephen's armies will require more than transport!" Somerled said grimly. "You clerks know nothing of warfare at sea and in the islands, or you would not speak as you do. Troops have got to *land* from ships, and landing-places are few and often dangerous. All would be defended, to the end. And if one isle was taken, there would be another and another and another to assail. Held by men who *knew* such warfare. I tell you, you know not what you say. King Olaf is no warrior, but even he, I swear, knows that talk of conquering the Isles, in borrowed ships, against my power, is folly. Tell them so, Olaf Godfreysson."

That man said nothing, seeming as though he scarcely heard, his eyes on the door through which his daughter had disappeared.

Somerled himself would have wished to leave and go in

213

search of the young woman, but recognised that this would look odd and serve no purpose for either of them. But at least he did not have to sit there indefinitely being harried and browbeaten. As Fergus began to speak again, he slammed down his hand.

"Enough!" he cried. "Further talk is profitless. You now know my mind. Any attempt to impose this bishopric on the Isles will be met with the drawn sword. Any invasion of my kingdom will be fought island by island. And King David will be apprised forthwith of what has been proposed here. You, Fergus of Galloway, now one of his earls, take heed! And you, Olaf Godfreysson, one of his vassals, likewise! Now, sir—may we make an end here?"

Amidst contrary shouts, abuse and threats, Olaf stood. Clearly he was glad enough to be finished with this confrontation, meantime at any rate, anxious to be off after his daughter.

Somerled and his party rose and stamped out of the building, waiting for none.

CHAPTER 12

That evening, having been informed that there would be another banquet in the main hall of Rushen Castle, and having returned a message that he and his preferred to eat in private this night, Somerled removed himself from his friends and went to his own borrowed chamber. After a while, he descended the stairs again, to knock at the door of Ragnhilde's apartment. He guessed that she, likewise, would not be dining in the hall.

From beyond the door, the girl Berthe's voice sounded. "The princess is indisposed. She does not wish to be disturbed."

"I regret that. I would not wish to intrude," he called. "But I would esteem a word with her, for I intend to leave early in the morning. This is Somerled."

There was a pause and then the door was thrown open, and by Ragnhilde herself.

"I did not know that it was you," she said. "Do not leave so soon, I beg of you. I . . . I need help."

"There is nothing for me here, now. All has been said. Too much! I should be off."

"No. All has not been said. *I* have said nothing, as yet! Come." She took his arm and drew him into the room, shutting the door again.

It was a handsome chamber, amply furnished, with a great bed and a small, tapestries on the walls and white bearskin rugs on the floor. Berthe discreetly went to busy herself in a garderobe closet attached.

"You did not know? Of this of the marriage?" he put to her.

"Think you that I would know and not tell you?" she demanded. If he had expected a stricken woman, distraught, possibly in tears, he did not find it. She was clear-eyed, unbowed, determined. "I will not wed this man—I *will* not!

215

I am not to be married off like some chattel, to a man I have never seen. It is beyond belief that my father should do this. Without a word to me. He is weak, yes—but kindly. It is shameful, not to be borne. He has been forced to it. That Fergus and Bishop Raoul, between them. It is their doing—with Affrica. I know it."

"Perhaps, yes. But how will you gainsay him? If he is determined on it, and has committed himself."

"I shall find a way, some way. I will not be bought and sold, like, like some cattle-beast!"

The thought of this graceful and spirited young woman likening herself to a cattle-beast was such as to draw a brief smile from the man, even though he was feeling far from amused. Seeing it, she flared up, in marked contrast to her normal calm assurance.

"You laugh! You do not believe me! You think that I am but a weak, foolish girl? I tell you that I will not be used so."

"No, no. Yes. To be sure. I rejoice at it. I do, indeed. More than, more than . . . I can say. But, if your father insists, it will be difficult."

"Difficult, no doubt—but not impossible. If he can be persuaded against his own daughter, he must be persuaded again, otherwise."

"You know him better than I do. I wish you well."

"How well do you wish me, King Sorley?"

He searched her eager features. "More than I can say, woman," he told her, again, deep-voiced. "For when I heard what your father said, back there, I all but cried out. Cried that it could not be, must not be! That I would not permit it. In my folly, I all but shouted it out, there before them all."

"You did . . .?"

"Aye, Ragnhilde, I did indeed. You see, I could not bear the thought of you given to another. God help me, I wanted you, want you, for myself! Ever since the day when first I saw you, I have wanted you, dreamed of you, longed for you—aye, needed you. I, I . . ."

"You mean this, Sorley? In truth. You are not cozening a foolish woman?"

"Mean it, lass? I mean it more than I have ever meant anything. Why do you think I came to Man, again? Not because of this of the bishopric. I could have fought that from Argyll. But because *you* asked me to come. I told you. Because I would see you again. Because I hoped that, some-how . . ."

He got no further just then. She launched herself bodily upon him, into his arms, part-laughing, part-sobbing, in gasping incoherence.

"Oh, Sorley, Sorley!" she cried. "My dear, my heart! I, too . . . oh, my love! I, too! Hold me—oh, hold me fast. I . . ."

His lips first closed then presently opened hers and their breathless, stumbling words gave place to a true and basic eloquence which had nothing to do with speech, a com-munion of lips and hands and persons which left little unsaid and promised more, much more.

In time Ragnhilde remembered Berthe, and after some tentative adjustments managed to insert a finger between her lips and his, and nodded towards the open garderobe. Reluctantly he relinquished her and drew a little way apart but still held her by the arms.

She recovered speech first. "How good, good! Oh, I am glad. Why did you not tell me, before. I hoped and hoped, but could not be sure."

"I have had little opportunity, girl! I had to, to feel my way. I dared not be too bold, at first, lest I offend. I could not tell how you felt. You were kind, gracious, but . . ."

"Am I so fearsome? Somerled the Mighty did not dare! Are all the tales false? But—save us, my dear, what does it matter now? Now that we both know. That we are for each other. We *are*, Sorley—we are for each other? Always?"

"Always," he assured, and kissed her again.

"Then we must make plans," she declared. "We shall have to act quickly."

He nodded. "Yes. I will speak with your father in the morning. Delay our sailing."

"But that will serve nothing, Sorley. He will not heed you. These others have persuaded him."

"You yourself said that he must then be persuaded otherwise."

"Only actions will persuade him. I meant that I would go, run away, leave Man. And still I shall do so. With you,

217

my dear. You must take me off with you. In your ship. When you sail."

He stared at her, mind racing.

"That is it. You will go early, as you planned. I will make my way to the haven secretly. None will know. Berthe will come with me. That is what we must do. In the morning."

He wagged his head. "But—lassie! That may not be the best way. Would not serve us to best advantage. It would get you away, yes—but not to your good repute. Nor to mine. We must do better than that . . ."

She had drawn back. "You do not want me on your ship? You are not so eager? Repute! You shrink from it . . .?"

"No! It is not that. On my soul, Ragnhilde, the thought of you, gone away with me, together, makes me all but lose my wits! But . . . not quite, my dear. We must *use* our wits, not lose them! See you, girl, I want you, want you for my wife, my queen. Not my, my paramour! As do you, I swear. But this has to be done decently. I am a king, now, and you a princess. We cannot run off like any pirate Norseman and his woman! We require your father's agreement . . ."

"He will not give it. How can he, having made his announcement? He has thrown in his lot with England and the churchmen."

"I am not so ill a match for his daughter—King of Argyll and the Isles. Is that so much poorer than the Earl of Orkney?"

"No, foolish one—it is not that. It is this of alliances and statecraft. He is committed to Thurstan and Stephen and Fergus and this Raoul. The Orkney fleet is necessary to them. No doubt they threatened him with English invasion here if he did not aid them. And Papal anathema, perhaps— for he is much concerned for his immortal soul these days. You must see it. He will not heed you."

"I could threaten too. Threaten to assail Man . . ." He paused, as another thought struck him. "This running off, Ragnhilde, without your father's consent, could cause much trouble. For us, but for others also. It could, indeed, bring on war. Nothing would be more likely to bring the Orkney fleet down upon the Isles, or the Manx fleet up, than for me to run off with the Earl Ronald's promised bride. He would have to do something—insulted before all."

"Then—you will yield me up? For fear . . .?"

"No, woman—no! But somehow we must get Olaf's agreement. If Olaf consents, Orkney's quarrel would not be with *me*. You must see it, my dear. There must be much that I can offer your father, in exchange. For he will not truly desire war, I think. Any more than do I. I have done much fighting, and do not shrink from it. But to force large war upon my kingdom, against the combined fleets, with England eager to take the pickings . . ."

"Oh, I do not want war, either. Over me! But what can we do? I do not see you changing my father's mind, Sorley—with these others here to threaten him."

"If I could bring King David into this . . ."

"There is no time for that. They will have me shipped off to Orkney."

"That must not be, no. I will think of something, lass—I must. Give me a little time to consider it all. My wits are awhirl at the thought of your love for me. I cannot think clearly of anything else. So wonderful . . .!"

That threw them into each others' arms again and constructive thought into further retreat. But presently she pushed him from her.

"Go then, my love—go now. And try to think. Leave me—I but distract you. Let it suffice for tonight that we have found each other. I . . . I need to be alone also. Lest I act . . . unseemly! Go—and perhaps the morning light will show us a way for our love . . ."

Loth as he was to leave her, he kissed her and went.

He went back to his party's quarters in a strange mixture of elation and desperation. He told them there merely that they would not be leaving first thing in the morning, as planned, that he had to have a further interview with Olaf. Then he took Gillecolm back to their lodging in the princess's building and saw him into his couch in the garde-robe.

He went back in his own chamber, the boy asleep, and very much aware that it was directly above that of Ragnhilde and that he was in fact separated from his new-found love by no more than a score of feet. He was undressing and seeking to put such thoughts firmly from his mind, to concentrate on their dire problem, when there was a light tapping on his door.

He went to open, and found Ragnhilde herself standing there. She put a finger to her lips and gestured towards Gillecolm's wall-closet, and then slipped past him into his bedchamber, closing the door quietly behind her.

He gazed at her, as well he might. She was a sight to fire the masculinity of any man. Dressed in some sort of bedrobe trimmed with fur, although it was not wantonly open and revealing, nevertheless the division between her breasts was plainly to be seen where the material gaped a little, and as she moved into the room, the white of a bare leg gleamed briefly. Clearly she was wearing little or nothing beneath the robe. Her red-gold hair hung loose to her shoulders.

At his fireside she turned to him, and her face was flushed, her eyes seeking his urgently for reaction, both determination and apprehension evident in them.

"Sorley—hear me!" she got out, breathlessly. "Before you judge! This is not . . . as it seems. I assure you, not as it seems!"

"It seems to me—very—shall we say—acceptable!" he said, having trouble with his own voice.

"No! Not that. Oh, my dear—hear me. This is a device. I am not shameless, as I must seem. I confess that I could be—but, no. I came here thus, of a purpose." She huddled herself more tightly in her robe. "Not the purpose you think. But to aid our, our cause."

He opened his mouth to say the obvious, then closed it again and moved over to her. "Tell me, then," he said.

"Yes. This, if you will agree to it, may serve us well. What we require. I can think of no other. If I am found here in your room, Sorley, thus. By my father. And others. Then I am compromised. It will be assumed . . .! You see? I will be esteemed . . . fallen! He cannot offer me to this Orkney earl, then. You—he will wish only for you to wed me. Is it not so?"

"Lord . . .!" he breathed.

"Oh, my love—you understand? It will oblige him to change. Hurt your repute also, I fear—but men are different in these matters. I think that it will bring us together, as

220

nothing else will." She gulped a little at the sound of that. "I mean . . . otherwise!"

Firmly he clasped his hands behind his back, to prevent them from reaching out to take her, so utterly and compellingly desirable was she. "Yes. It could . . . suffice. You are strong, Ragnhilde—as I must be! How is it to be achieved?"

"Thank God that you see it! Berthe is to act the betrayer. She will go tell my father. That I am with you here. Tell Affrica also. That woman hates me, and will see me humbled if she can! I am to beat on this floor, if she is to go. We can hear, below, movement in this chamber. Then . . . we wait."

"You believe that it will serve? That they will come?"

"I know my father—or thought that I did, until today! Shall I beat on the floor?"

He nodded—and had to turn away, for when she stopped to thump on the floorboards, her robe sagged open, wider, and he could see that she was naked beneath.

There was silence for a little. Then she spoke to his back, where he stood at the window.

"You do not think the less of me for this, Sorley?" Anxiety was evident in her voice.

"No. Never that. I esteem you the more. It is myself that I disesteem. I can scarcely keep my hands off you, woman!"

"That I can understand. For, I myself . . .!" She swallowed, audibly. "But we must restrain ourselves, my dear. We must start aright, together—whatever the, the appearances. That hereafter we can . . . respect ourselves. Is it not so?"

"Yes. Oh, yes. But it is damnably difficult. I am no saint, lass. A man of hot passions and temper. As you will find out, I fear. How long will they be?"

"Some time, I think. My father will be in his bed. Affrica—who knows? Perhaps she is drinking with the Earl Fergus. Perhaps in the Prince of Dublin's bed! She is wanton. It may take Berthe time to bring them here."

"Will Affrica then be so disapproving at the sight of you here? Since she herself . . .?"

"She will be moved with spleen, with delight! Not with offence. She has always mocked me as milk-livered, lily-pure, no true woman but a timorous halfling. Because I would not act towards men as she does. Now she will rejoice. To show my father that I am no better than she. And she will tell it to all!"

"And you accept all this? For me!"

"I would that it did not have to be this way—but yes." She paused. "Do not stand over there, Sorley. Come, sit here beside me." And she patted the bed.

"Sakes—think you that it will be easier so?"

"We shall help each other. See—I shall wrap this blanket round me. Is that better? More to your taste?"

"Saints of mercy—my *taste*, girl! My taste would be to, to . . . och, lassie—you do not know the sort of man you are taking to you!"

"I think that I do," she said quietly. "Strong, too. Stronger than I am. I could only be doing with a strong man." She patted the bed beside her.

He went and sat but did not touch her.

She reached a hand out from the blanket, to grip his arm. "Our time will come," she assured.

"Time!" he all but groaned. "This, of waiting . . ."

"Time will aid us too, impatient one. You will see. For there is much to be resolved, beyond tonight, is there not? What of your shipmistress? The fair Cathula?"

"Umm." He looked at her now, and quickly, temperature dropping sharply—as was no doubt intended. "Cathula MacIan will keep her own place."

"No doubt. But what *is* her place, Sorley? She is your mistress, is she not?"

"Yes," he admitted. "Or she was. I have needed someone. But she is my friend also."

"To be sure. And therefore the more dangerous to a wife! I warn you, King Somerled—I will not share you with her, or other!"

"No. You need not fear . . ."

"No? She is a strong woman, that one, and with much appetite, I think. And some allure. She will not give you up easily. I have seen how she looks at you. And at me!"

"She will keep her place," he repeated. "She masters my dragon-ship, sits at my councils, makes a good companion. These will continue. But the other—no."

"You say so now. She may say otherwise. And she is no light girl to droop when you frown."

"She will do as I say. She will remain my friend—that is all. You will be my wife, my queen and my love."

"Love, yes. You do not love her?"

"No. Not love—never love. I like her, admire her, but . . ."

"And enjoy her!"

"That also, yes. But . . . there will be no need for that hereafter."

"Although you have not tried me yet! But I will hold you to that, Sorley MacFergus."

"You need not fear, I say . . ."

"I do not fear. I am a king's daughter and do not fear that I can hold my own with such as Cathula MacIan. It is you that I warn." But she smiled as she said it. "Do you still want me?"

Tight-lipped he nodded.

"Then we shall do very well, I think. I . . ." She stopped. "Listen! Did you hear? Yes—they come! Sooner than I thought. Oh, Sorley—this will be bad. I, I . . . you must help me!" For a moment or two she seemed almost to give way to panic; then, as he put an arm around her, he felt her steady and straighten up. "Now . . .!"

Voices sounded clearly outside; and then without any knocking, the door of their chamber was thrown violently open. Framed therein were Olaf, a cloak over his night attire, Affrica, Ronald of Dublin and, shrinking behind, the girl Berthe. They stared in.

Somerled sprang to his feet, in wrath and embarrassment—and did not have to adopt either emotion for the occasion. Half-undressed as he was, he undoubtedly looked the part of guilty lover disturbed.

"What is this!" he exclaimed. "How dare you! Fore God, here is an outrage . . .!"

But it is to be doubted whether any heard him. They were gazing past him, with varying expressions of shock, astonishment and frankest prurience. Olaf raised a trembling finger to point.

Somerled turned momentarily. Ragnhilde had also started up from the bed—and in doing so had managed to let her blanket fall to the floor and at the same time allowed the top folds of her robe to drop. She had caught it at the waist and was hastily stooping to retrieve the blanket. But meantime all her upper parts were completely bare—and a most delectably improper sight she made as she leaned forward, one arm reaching out, full and shapely breasts free, white shoulders gleaming under the cascade of her hair, her face upturned in agitation towards the intruders.

"Look at her!" Affrica all but screeched. "Bitch! Hellcat! Harlot! See the virtuous Ragnhilde now!"

Somerled did not require to act any role. He strode to the bedside, snatched up another blanket and draped it over her, straightening her up. He kept an arm round her protectively. With the other, he pointed.

"Go!" he commanded. "Leave us. Leave us, I say!"

Olaf found his tongue. "Hilde! Hilde!" he quivered. "My child! Dear God—Hilde!" There was hurt and bewilderment more than wrath in that.

"Father!" Ragnhilde got out. "Father—I love him!" That was no mummery either.

"Love him! Love—hear her!" Affrica cried. "He came but yesterday. She loves him, she says! Somerled the Mighty! Lusts after him, *I* say . . ."

"Silence!" Olaf exclaimed, with some access of strength. "Hilde—how could you do this? How shame yourself? And me? I would not have believed . . ."

"The more fool you then, old dotard!" his wife burst out, working herself into a sort of frenzy. "Why think you she brought him to this her house? Put him above her own chamber? Away from his own people. I tell you, she is no better than a trull!"

"Enough, woman—enough, do you hear! Begone—begone, I say." Olaf pointed back whence they had come, an imperious gesture, odd in so small a man so weirdly garbed. "And you, Hilde—cover yourself. Aye, and go to your own chamber. No—not there. Go to *my* chamber." He turned to Berthe. "Girl—take the princess to my house. Forthwith. As for you, sir," he swung back on Somerled, "I will deal with you in the morning. Aye, in the morning."

The younger man inclined his head, unspeaking.

Ragnhilde hitched her robe and blanket securely around her, shook her hair free, and touched Somerled.

"Goodnight, my love," she said quietly. "I am not sorry—regret nothing. I . . ."

Her father snatched at her and hurried her away.

Somerled closed the door behind them—then opened it again and went to look into his son's closet. The boy had slept soundly through all. Back in his own room, the man went to stare out of the window into the summer dusk, seeing nothing.

*   *   *

It was late in the forenoon before the expected summons to Olaf's apartments came. Somerled went in some apprehension, not out of fear of an angry father but in anxiety as to the outcome of Ragnhilde's device. He had not been convinced of its efficacy last night; he was less so in the morning light.

He found Olaf alone, in an anteroom off his bedchamber. There was no sign of wife nor daughter. The two men eyed each other in silence for a little, two sub-kings of such very different character, calibre and appearance.

"This is a hard matter," Olaf said, at length. "Unhappy. Ill to deal with. I am much troubled. I am greatly fond of my daughter."

"As am I, sir."

"You?" The small man frowned. "How can you say that? After last night. You have abused her. Abused my house and hospitality also. Have you no shame?"

"No." That was simple as it was blunt.

The older man searched his face. "You put me to much difficulty. As well as make ruin of her name. She is promised to Ronald of Orkney. Now . . .!"

"I think that she was not promised to Orkney for long! She knew nothing of it. Was it not all hatched up between you and these churchmen? None so long ago? I swear that the Earl Ronald will get over his disappointment as swiftly!"

"What do you mean?"

Somerled reckoned that perhaps he might be going too fast. "The news will reach Orkney, no doubt. I suppose, however, that Ronald may forgive the . . . indiscretion?"

"God's Death, man—do you think that I can send her to Orkney now? After this? All this castle, and town no doubt, are ringing with the shame of it already. All Man by nightfall. It will reach Orkney, yes. Can I offer Ronald my daughter, soiled by another man? He seeks a wife to bear him sons. Not *your* son!"

Somerled's heart leapt. Was it going to work, then?

"There may be no such," he said, carefully—and not liking the sound of it.

"Damn you—do not trifle with me, Somerled MacFergus! This is no time for light cozening. What are you going to do?"

"Me? I . . . ah . . . I do not know."

"You do not? Then I do, man! *You* will marry her, not Ronald! Do you hear? That is what you will do. You have made your bed—you will lie in it!"

"Ah," Somerled said, seeking to keep his voice level.

"No ahs or doubts. I insist. I will not have my daughter misused, and then abandoned. Marry she will, and quickly. You have ruined what I had planned as well as her good name. Now you will make good the ill done—or some of it."

He cleared his throat. "Do Ragnhilde's wishes not enter into it?"

"She, she is reconciled to it. She will do as she is told. This time. But . . . it must be done discreetly. With care."

"Indeed?"

"Yes. It is difficult. The Archbishop, these bishops. This will not please them. They will be much disquieted, disappointed. When they hear."

"They have not heard yet, then?"

"I hope not, I have given straightest command that they be not told. They go tomorrow."

"Must you please these churchmen?"

"I must, yes. Holy Church is . . . pressing. But it is Stephen also. He desires this of Orkney."

"Do not tell me that Stephen of England concerns himself with the marriage of your daughter to the Earl Ronald!"

"He desires that Orkney adheres to his cause. He requires Orkney's fleet. This of the marriage is to aid in the alliance."

"Devised by the Norman Raoul, for a wager!"

Olaf brushed that aside. "It is important, therefore, that the bishops do not hear of this, meantime. Once they are gone . . ."

"I see it. But once they, and Stephen, learn of it—what then?"

The older man took small strutting strides back and forth. "If you, Somerled, would agree to this of the bishopric of the Isles, there would be no need for the Orkney fleet. And therefore for the marriage."

"Ah! So that is it! But no, my friend—no Romish bishopric. Marriage, if you will. But no creeping into Scotland by that door!"

"It would save much trouble. No need for this alliance."

"Whose alliance? Yours or Stephen's? Has it not come to you, Olaf Godfreysson, that instead of alliance with Orkney, you will now have alliance with *me*? Also with many long-ships. And closer at hand. Forby, David of Scotland like-wise. Return to your due allegiance to David, with myself as your goodson, and you may snap your fingers at Stephen and his bishops."

The other rubbed at his wispy, greying beard. "But Holy Church . . .?" he said. "The Pope . . .?"

"The Pope is far away. And with much else on his mind, I vow! And his anathemas, or Thurstan's will break no bones, on Man! Whereas David, with my fleet, is very near-at-hand. Could break bones a-many!"

"I must think on this, man . . ." Olaf took another turn of his chamber. "But, the marriage. This must be done cir-cumspectly. You must leave today, as you said. Sail off in your ships for a day or two. Sail round Man, if you will. Then, when the bishops are gone, tomorrow, return. To wed. Quietly and in some haste. You have it?"

"What of Wimund?"

"He returns to York with Thurstan, meantime."

"And Fergus?"

"They sail in his ship. He brought them from Galloway and will take them back."

"And Ragnhilde? She will be here when I return? She will not, perhaps, be on her way to Orkney? Or else-where?"

"A plague on you, no! I tell you, she is of no use to Orkney now. *You* she must wed. And at the soonest. I am not waiting for months, for you to come back, when she begins to show! She will be here, and awaiting you."

"Very well. I shall sail this day. Not round your Man, but for Scotland. The Solway. I go tell David of my, my bliss! Seek his blessing! and inform him that Olaf of Man is still his loyal vassal! You would wish me to do that? Give me four days and I shall be back. For my bride!"

The small man looked at him, varying expressions chasing each other across his cherubic features. Then he nodded. "So be it," he said. "Four days . . ."

★   ★   ★

As it transpired it was only three days before Somerled returned to Man, for when he had reached Eskmouth on Solway it was to learn that King David was meantime far from Rook's Burgh, gone to endow a new abbey, or priory, at Urquhart in Moray. So he had sent the Abbot of Glendochart, Dermot Maguire and Cathula MacIan—deeming the last to be more conveniently absent from any nuptial celebrations, in the circumstances—on a mission to the High King, to inform him of the situation and of the threat posed by Stephen and Thurstan and suggesting their joint action to deal with any developments; but adding that he, Somerled, believed that Olaf could be kept approximately loyal if David made a show of strength along the West March, and especially in the Solway area—for instance by taking suitable measures to discipline Fergus of Galloway. The three envoys must find their own way back to Argyll by land.

Back at Rushen, although they found no wedding-fever—except perhaps on the bride's part, well disguised—preparations were well in hand. However unsuitable for so distinguished a couple, in the fortunate absence of Bishop Wimund, and not wishing to involve the new Abbot, the wedding ceremony would be performed by Wilfrith, the same lowly parish priest at St. Michael's Haven who had conducted the Isles party to the castle on their first visit. This was to have been two days hence, but Olaf appeared to be only too pleased to put it all forward a day, seemingly for some reason anxious to get it all over at the earliest possible. Neither of the principals made the least objection.

They did not manage to see each other alone and could make only restrained and conventional converse in the presence of others; but their glances and surreptitious arm-squeezings and the like were eloquent enough of mutual congratulation and a sort of unholy glee. Such manifestations had to be most heedfully brief and hidden, for Ragnhilde was supposed to be in a state of shame and contrition, necessary before approaching God's altar for His blessing on their premature union—and presumably the same ought to apply to the bridegroom. It was as well that Affrica kept herself at a distance, indeed largely out-of-sight, no doubt in general disapproval. She still had Ronald of Dublin for company; and it dawned on Somerled that it was probably on this account that Olaf was in such haste to get the wedding over and the guilty pair forth of Man; for once Ronald left the island, either to Ireland or to Galloway, the cat would be very certainly out of the bag.

So, the next day, not in Rushen Abbey but in the small private chapel of the castle, in a simple, short and almost hurried ceremony, they exchanged their vows and were declared man and wife, in the sight of Almighty God and the presence of a remarkably small congregation as witnesses, more actually from Argyll than from Man itself, Saor MacNeil acting as groomsman and Olaf presenting his daughter in distinct embarrassment, Affrica absenting herself. It was a humble, not to say hole-in-corner nuptials for Somerled the Mighty of Argyll and the Isles and the Princess of Man; but neither found cause for complaint. Indeed it was the happiest occasion of Somerled's life; and from her flushed loveliness and the shine in her eyes, Ragnhilde was nowise despondent.

Feasting thereafter being considered unsuitable, only a comparatively small company sat down to a bridal repast, with no speech-making—although Olaf did eventually drink to the future well-being of his daughter, if not of his new goodson. All, in fact, seemed equally eager for a move to be made and the entire affair rounded off and tidied up. In the end Olaf and Ragnhilde did display some emotion at their leave-taking, clutching each other wordlessly for a few moments. For the rest it was mere formality, and not noticeably formal at that. Affrica was still elsewhere.

And then, in great relief, the Argyll party were on their way, on borrowed horses, to St. Michael's Haven, the newly-weds hardly able to believe that they were in fact man and wife for all time coming. They raced their mounts almost as though subconsciously they feared that they might yet be pursued and dragged back and all somehow undone.

There was no delay at the haven and as the dragon-ship and its escorts pulled out towards the open sea, bride and groom embraced each other, on the high stern platform, clinging.

"At last!" Somerled exclaimed. "My dear—what a bridal for you! What a mockery for my beloved."

"Not so," she declared. "It suffices. It all sufficed, did it not?"

"Sufficed, yes. *You* saw to that, lassie. You ensured it all. By your . . . device. I have wed a puissant and potent woman, I fear! I think that I will forget it at my peril! I am warned."

"I am glad that you perceive it! Somerled the Mighty would not wish to wed a mouse?"

He kissed her—and realised that Gillecolm was standing there beside them, watching. Also Saor, grinning—indeed, most of the ship's company, all most interested. Frowning, he turned her round, to gaze back at the receding land.

"I fear, also, that we are not alone, cannot be alone, on this ship. I am sorry. There is not even a private corner which we could make a bridal-chamber. This is a ship-of-war . . ."

"Care not—we can wait a little longer. Besides, you already . . . know my body, Sorley!" That was little more than a whisper. "You have held me close, as good as naked! Is there not . . . the less hurry, my lord?"

"By the Powers, there is!" He swung round on Saor—in Cathula's absence acting ship-master. "You, man—cease your gawping, and get this ship back to Argyll faster than any ship has moved before! Do you hear me? Beat these lazy oarsmen, if need be—or be beaten yourself!"

230

His foster-brother hooted his mirth, made the rudest of gestures and turned towards the ranked rowing-benches. "You hear? You hear, oafs? Sorley MacFergus would be back to bed it at Ardtornish. In company! Row you, row!"

Smiling, Ragnhilde held out a hand to Gillecolm.

CHAPTER 13

Somerled stretched his arms pleasurably, revelling in the sun warming his body, for the water had been cold—even though Ragnhilde did not appear to find it so. Women did not seem to feel the chill as men did, why he knew not.

He extricated a fly which had got entangled in the damp hairs of his chest, and leaned back to watch his wife at her splashing in the loch, a gratifying picture in every way on a golden day of late September, amongst the low, green, cattle-strewn hills of Islay. Without being a strong swimmer, she loved the water, and on this benison of a day, after a week of wind and rain, nothing would do but that he must postpone his intended sail across to Colonsay, where still another castle was being built in his chain of strongholds for the security of his island kingdom, and go swimming with her. He had not grumbled overmuch.

He felt a little guilty that they had not brought Gillecolm with them, who liked swimming also. But Ragnhilde, although no prude, drew the line at appearing naked in front of the boy, and hated to enter the water in clinging, encumbering draperies. She and Colm got on very well together, indeed next to his father she was the lad's favourite company—though this could hold its embarrassments. Anyway, he could go swimming at any time.

They had rowed here, to the other end of Loch Finlaggan from the castle-isle, over half-a-mile away, for privacy. Somerled, contemplating the energetic beauty flaunting before him, was likewise contemplating the possibility of showing suitable masculine appreciation of such beauty and energy, deliciously wet and cool from the water as it would be, and was consequently glancing around him for a convenient spot a little more private still, when alternative movement caught the corner of his eye. He cursed in irritation.

Another small boat was being sculled towards them, from the direction of the castle. It might not be actually making for them, of course—but the chances were that it was, for there was nothing at this southern end of the loch to bring strangers, save the remains of a stone-circle; and his castle people knew what he was at.

He considered calling a warning to his wife but decided against it. Splashing as she was she probably would not hear him; besides she might prefer to remain part-covered in the water whilst the oarsman was sent about his business, whatever that was.

As the boat drew nearer, something about the posture of the rower suggested that it was in fact a woman; and in a few moments he was able to recognise that it was Cathula MacIan. Frowning, he wondered. Cathula had been left behind at Ardtornish when they had come for a few days to Islay. She and Ragnhilde made less than comfortable company. They did not actually openly disagree; indeed they were almost excessively polite to each other. But there was mutual resentment, however queenly gracious the one and elaborately respectful the other. This island of Islay, chiefest of the Sudreys, was the favourite location which Ragnhilde thus far had discovered in her husband's territories, more gentle, open and fertile than most of the rugged if grand West Highland scene, wild-flower decked and wild-geese haunted—and Cathula knew it. He would have expected her to keep her distance.

She did not, but rowed directly for their position, passing within a score of yards of the swimmer without making any sign. Beaching the light craft, little more than a coracle, she stepped out, with a gleam of long white legs, and came striding up over the grass to the reclining man.

He lay still, unforthcoming. He did not attempt to cover his nakedness; but he acknowledged to himself that she was very good-looking, and knew an alternative and shameful stirring at his loins.

"Greetings, my lord," she said formally. "I come . . . less than eagerly."

"Ah. But you come, nevertheless!"

"Yes. There is news which you should have. I have

233

brought it on, myself, believing that you would wish me to do so."

At the direction and veiled mockery of her glance, he belatedly reached for some clothing to part-hide himself. "Well, woman, well?" That was rougher than was intended.

"That priest, Wilfrith, from Man. He who married you. He came to Ardtornish. Seeking you." She spoke with an unaccustomed jerkiness.

He sat up. "The Romish priest from St. Michael's Haven? *He* came? All the way to Argyll? What does he want?"

"What he may want, I know not. Some comfort and shelter from you, perhaps—for he is dismissed from his church at St. Michael's. For wedding you! By the Bishop Wimund, when he returned and discovered it. But it is the tidings he carried which bring me here, strange tidings . . ."

She paused and turned. Ragnhilde had waded ashore and was walking up towards them unhurriedly, wringing the water out of her long red-gold hair as she came.

Cathula stared, as well she might. The younger woman, so calmly assured and candid in her approach, was gaze-worthy to a degree, slender but shapely, splendidly proportioned and unblemished, full but firm breasted, her bodyhair darker than that of her head, carrying herself with a quiet confidence such as could defy criticism but did not. She smiled, moderately cordial.

"Highness," the other acknowledged a little huskily.

"You have not come swimming?" That was kindly asked.

"No. No, lady. I act messenger, whatever."

"Well, then—what did this priest say?" Somerled asked, but scarcely urgently, admiring these two women. "The priest who wed us, Hilde. He has come to Ardtornish. From Man."

"Not from Man—from Galloway," Cathula said. "He was dismissed from Man. He tells a strange tale. He swears that it is true—even though it sounds scarcely to be believed . . ."

"Wilfrith dismissed!" Ragnhilde interrupted. "From Man? From his church? My father would never do that."

"Not by King Olaf—by Bishop Wimund. When he returned from York. For marrying you. Before he himself left Man again. It is all hardly to be credited. This Wimund—is

234

he crazed, think you? You, Queen, know him." Her glance at Ragnhilde who stood at ease allowing the sun to dry her, was this time not at her body.

"Wimund is no friend of mine. A stiff and ambitious prelate. More concerned with power and position than with religion, I would say. But I do not know him closely—few do, I would think."

"Ambitious for power? That could be . . ."

"Lord!" Somerled exclaimed. "What is this? Out with it, Cathula! What are these tidings that you talk around like some old wife?"

She shrugged. "Wilfrith says that Wimund has declared himself to be lawful son to Angus, the dead Earl of Moray, he who was killed in the battle. And so rightful heir to the Scottish throne! Before David . . ."

"God in Heaven!" The man rose to his feet in a single lithe movement, nudity forgotten quite. "Wimund! Angus of Moray? Son to Angus? You are in your right mind, woman?"

"I am, yes. As to this Wilfrith, he appears to have sound wits. He swears that it is true. Not that Wimund *is* this, but that he claims it. He has left Man and is gone to Galloway. Or to Cumbria, I know not which. There to pursue his cause."

"But . . . how can this be? It makes no sense, from start to finish. Sheerest folly! How can he expect any to believe him? Sakes—my own sister is wed to Angus's brother! Would *I* not have known if Angus had a son? And his age. How could he be? To be sure, Angus was a deal older than Malcolm. But he could scarcely have had a son of that bishop's age."

"Wimund is younger than he seems," Ragnhilde said. "A strange man. My father always wondered as to his birth, his breeding. He never spoke of it, to my knowledge. But, to have been made bishop so early, he must have been highly bred?"

"But that would make no more sense than the rest. Angus did not belong to the Romish Church but to our own. Why should his son be made a Romish bishop? And not in Scotland, that is certain."

"I do not know. All we knew was that he came to Man

from Furness Abbey, in Cumbria. Sent by Archbishop Thurstan, no doubt. Cumbria was attached to Scotland, was it not? Part of the old Strathclyde?"

"Aye—but Cumbria was never held by Angus of Moray's line. The Lord William of Allerdale, King Duncan's son . . ."

"Is it not all a ruse?" Cathula asked. "A trick to give excuse for the Archbishop and King Stephen to take a hand? When you refused to have their bishopric of the Isles. There need be no truth in it . . ."

"Yes. Yes, that could be it. Angus's mother was King Lulach's daughter, the last of the ancient line of our kings. Malcolm Canmore slew Lulach, as he slew MacBeth, and took the throne. David's father. That is why Angus rebelled, and Malcolm too. Angus is dead and Malcolm a prisoner with David. So, if a son of Angus could be found . . .! Yes that could be Stephen's game. To foment more rebellion, and then to move in. For England to seem to support the rebels, but in fact to take over Scotland. *That* makes sense. But—why Wimund? A bishop?"

"Perhaps to gain support from churchmen in Scotland? More likely, to win the Pope of Rome's backing. As in this of the Isles bishopric. The one with the other. These are cunning men . ."

"Why wait until now? Wimund could have made his claim long ago."

"Because it is *their* need—the English. When you refused to have this bishop they required other excuse for a move into Scotland. This would serve. This Wimund may believe that he *is* the Earl of Moray's son, but might never have made aught of it. But now it will serve Stephen's needs."

"That could be, yes. Wimund has left Man for Galloway, you say? So Fergus is in it, also. I sent warning to David to deal with Fergus—as you know. But it seems he is too busy endowing abbeys! David should look more to his defences and the safety of his realm and less to church-building! He nurtures a snake in Fergus."

"What will you do, Sorley?" Ragnhilde was putting on her clothes now.

"Do? What can I do? Up here. Why did this clerk Wilfrith come to me with this? It is David's concern."

"He told me that he knew none in Scotland, save only you," Cathula said. "He is only a poor priest—who would heed him? You he wed. He has no charge now, no support. Because of you and your marriage. No doubt he hopes that you will succour him, show him some favour and employment."

"If he was a Columban monk . . ."

"*I* am no Columban," Ragnhilde pointed out. "He could act chaplain for me—and serve you also in clerkly duties. Do not tell me that the King of Argyll and the Isles could not use a clerk? We owe him something, do we not?"

"True. We shall see." Somerled too began to dress. "I shall have to send further word to David. Where he may be, I know not. What else I can do I know not either."

"You have ships and men," Cathula declared. "You could sail south. As a gesture and warning, if no more. Off the Galloway shore. And further, off Cumbria and the English coasts. To give them pause. Let them see that *some* in Scotland are ready, and concerned with more than abbey-founding!"

"M'mm."

"Besides, is it not time that Somerled the Mighty showed some might? How long is it since you drew a sword? Your fighting-men grow fat and slack, your longships gather barnacles in a score of havens, your oarsmen's hands soften. But . . . if you are too lovesick with chambering and bedding, you could always send Saor MacNeil to act leader!"

As hot rebuke surged to the man's lips, Ragnhilde gripped his arm.

"It might be a wise move," she said, easily. "However ill-put. Serve David and yourself both. And my father also, perhaps. For your fleet between Man and Cumbria would warn him not to let himself be persuaded to join in this folly of Wimund. They will try to bring Man in, you may be sure. I could sail with you and call upon him. It is three months—and hereafter I may not be in fit state for sea-going for some time, I think."

It was Cathula's turn to catch her breath and glance involuntarily down at the Queen's belly—as she was meant to do. To be sure there had been no sign of any thickening there, as yet. She did not comment.

Somerled looked from one to the other. "Time we returned to the castle," he decided. "We shall think on this . . ."

*　　　*　　　*

It was odd, perhaps, that quite the greatest fleet that Somerled had ever assembled, a couple of weeks later, should sail down through the Sudreys and into the Irish Sea, with no real warlike intent—at least on the part of its commander. It comprised fully one-hundred-and-twenty ships, not all of them of the first order admittedly but making a brave show, and with sufficient fully-manned longships and galleys to ensure that, should hostilities eventuate, they would be able to give a good account of themselves.

Although now mid-October and the weather blustery, conditions in the Hebridean Sea were still not so bad that exercises and manoeuvres were out-of-the-question; and as they sailed southwards, Somerled took the opportunity to engage in a number of sham-fights, feints and trials in the handling and best disposal of large numbers of vessels in various situations, good for all concerned and, he admitted to himself, overdue.

They encountered no opposition, seeing only fishing-craft and the occasional longship, Norse almost certainly—but these naturally gave the fleet a wide berth and disappeared from the scene as quickly as possible.

Once beyond the Mull of Kintyre they turned eastwards towards North Galloway, to proceed down that coast, fairly close-inshore so that there would be no question as to their being seen and reported. Then, round the jutting Mull of Galloway, they entered the wide Firth of Solway.

Here they could not risk going near the land, so shallow and sand-bound was this firth; but at least they could move in to show themselves at selected points where there was deeper water and where, consequently, were havens and centres of population, at Monreith, Whithorn, Cruggleton and off the Dee estuary at Kirk Cuthbert's Bay. The Earl Fergus had houses or castles at all of these, and so would be likely to get the message.

No craft came out to investigate, much less to challenge them.

After lying-to for a couple of days off the Dee estuary, performing more exercises, most there hoping that Fergus or other would venture out to try conclusions, they moved on almost due eastwards now, making for the Cumbrian shore. This northern portion was almost as shallow as on the Galloway side, and they had to content themselves with making another demonstration fairly far-out, off Silloth, which was the closest they might venture to Carlisle, the Cumbrian capital—still to no effect. It was only when they were off Ellenfoot, where there was a deep-water harbour, and Somerled was about to give the order to increase speed and head south-westwards for Man, that there was some reaction. Out from the haven's bay there came four war-galleys. As they drew nearer their sails could be seen to be painted with the lion emblem of Galloway.

"So the stalwart Fergus ventures out at last!" Saor exclaimed. "What to attempt, think you? It cannot be to fight—four against so many."

"If it is to parley, or treat, he will be the more dangerous," Cathula declared. "I would sooner trust a Norseman's word, even, than that one's!"

"I need no warnings as to Fergus," Somerled returned shortly.

"Why does the first one fly a different beast?" young Gillecolm asked, pointing, where he stood beside the Queen. "Four lions and one other. A boar, is it?" The youth's eyes might lack lustre but they were sufficiently sharp-sighted.

"Eh . . .?"

"He is right," Ragnhilde said. "That leading ship flies a banner. Of a blue boar on white, I think. That is the device of Scotland's royal house, is it not?"

"Lord—do not say that this Wimund is impudent enough to use David's own banner . . .!"

The galleys drew close enough to Somerled's great dragon-ship to hail—while around them closed the Argyll longships in menacing array.

"Who are you who dares flaunt this might of shipping off my lord King's coasts?" came a voice from the craft with the banner. "Are you Norse? Or Manx? Or Irish?"

"None of these," Somerled shouted back. "Who are you, to ask?"

"I am the High Constable of Scotland. Hugo de Morville. I demand answer, in the name of King David."

"David! De Morville!" Somerled exclaimed. "What is this? It cannot be Fergus, despite the lions. Unless . . ."

"Unless it is trickery," Cathula said. "That Fergus is capable of it."

"A bold man to pit four vessels against this fleet, even in deceit." Somerled raised his voice. "What does David's Constable in Fergus of Galloway's galleys?"

"Surrendered," came back the brief answer. "Who asks?"

"Somerled of Argyll, man. Do you not know my emblem?"

There was a pause. Then the voice sounded again. "King Somerled I know. Are you still the High King's man?"

"I am my own man, and David's friend! Where is the High King?"

"In Caer Luel. In fullest strength."

So that was it. David was not so preoccupied with abbey-founding, after all. He had heeded the warnings. "I shall come speak with him," Somerled shouted. "Is there space in yonder bay for my ships?"

"I know not. Come and discover it."

Somerled ordered one of his longships to speed shore-wards to inspect Ellenfoot Bay. Then he had Cathula steer the dragon-ship close to the foremost galley. He was able to recognise Sir Hugo, whom he had found, in the past, to be one of the more civil of David's proud Normans. Standing on the galley's high poop beside him, he identified the Earl Cospatrick of Dunbar. No trickery here.

"Well met. Come aboard my ship, my lords," he called. "I have not seen you since the sorry business on Tees-side. Northallerton."

Expertly the dragon-ship was laid alongside the galley, and the Norman knight and Celtic earl jumped across, to be presented to Ragnhilde and to greet Saor, Conn, Dermot and Cathula, and be offered wine. They were polite but wary.

"David has come south, then? And not before time," Somerled commented. "I sent him warnings three months back."

"But not of this impostor, this Wimund," Cospatrick said.

"No, that is new. But the same Wimund who was in the bishopric plot. A clerkly snake! But, Fergus?"

"The Earl Fergus is now at Caer Luel, with the High King."

"With David? That rogue? He is a greater snake than Wimund, a treacherous dog! Is David fool enough to have him close?"

"He is powerful and master of a troublesome, unruly province. Forby, married now to the late King Henry's daughter, Henry who was David's friend." Cospatrick pointed out.

"His Grace is over-merciful," de Morville observed. "But we shall be watching that man. We came to Galloway with a great force, and he yielded without battle. Better if he had fought, perhaps. Now he is as good as hostage—like your own kinsman, Malcolm, sir! So many snakes!"

"M'mm. And Wimund? Where is he?"

"He has fled south. Into the Cumbrian mountains, they say. That is why we are at this Caer Luel. Parties are out, probing for him."

"He will be making for York, to his master, Thurstan. Or else to Stephen. It is all another plot, by these two."

"He will not reach Stephen, at least. Stephen of Blois, the usurper, is a prisoner."

"What . . . ?"

"The Empress Maud has come, at last. Henry's daughter. To take her throne. She landed at Portsmouth. Stephen has been misruling, persecuting. So many of the nobles abandoned him and flocked to Maud. There was a battle, at Lincoln, and she won. Stephen was captured."

"Save us—so the threat is by with! It is all over?"

"We want this Wimund . . ."

The longship returned, to declare that there was sufficient room for all the Argyll fleet, packed close, in the shelter of Ellenfoot Bay. The dragon-ship led the way in.

Part of the Scots army proved to be camped around the

little town. Apparently David had taken this threat seriously, at least, and had marched with almost twenty-thousand men, much too many to billet and quarter in and around Caer Luel itself. So the force was meantime scattered over a quite wide area. Towns were few in North Cumbria.

There was horseflesh in plenty. It was more than twenty miles to Caer Luel; but it seemed that they would not have to go that far to see King David, for he was spending much of the waiting period at Holm Cultram, an abbey he had founded, in conjunction with his son Henry, only a year or two earlier, and which was now nearing completion. It appeared that he had planted this monastery here in Cumbria for political as well as pious reasons—David was like that—Henry being titular Prince of Strathclyde, and Cumbria being part of that ancient sub-kingdom. So Somerled's party had only a few miles to ride.

They found David actually helping the monkish builders to select the best roof timbers from a great pile of cut wood. He greeted Somerled with much surprise and obvious pleasure—with gratification also when he heard that it was the Argyll fleet which had been demonstrating in the Solway, and that it had done so, unbidden, against this Stephen-Thurstan-Wimund project.

"I think that this trouble is now all but overpast," he declared. "You have heard that Stephen is captured by my niece, the Empress? And I am told that Archbishop Thurstan is fallen sick. And he is an old man. But I am more happy than I can say, my friend, that you should have done this, made this sally. Indeed, that you are still actively on my side."

"Why, Sire? Would you have expected otherwise? I swore allegiance, did I not? And offered my friendship with it—which is the greater matter."

"True. And I much value both. But I had heard that you had wed Olaf of Man's daughter—and he, it seems, has turned against me, thrown in his lot with Stephen. This Wimund is his bishop . . ."

"I married his daughter, yes. She is here, with me. Yonder, with my party. But I was much against this traffic with Thurstan and Stephen. As was she. We sought to dissuade him. But they threatened him. With force but also

242

with the anathemas of your Church. He is weak but not evil, I think. Unlike his new wife's father, Fergus!"

"Ah yes, Fergus. I have Fergus with me at Caer Luel. A man to watch. I have netted Fergus and clipped his wings. I think! But must use him still, over Galloway. Ruling a realm is no simple task, friend Somerled. You believe then that Olaf is in truth not my enemy? Only weak and constrained by those who are?"

"I do, yes. His kingdom is very vulnerable, and his sons are of no help to him in it. His daughter, now, was otherwise. Ragnhilde did all that she could to have him fight against Thurstan's threats. Come, Sire, and let me present her to you . . ."

Presently they all rode on to Caer Luel.

David persuaded Somerled to stay with him there for a few days. As well as building Holm Cultram Abbey he was busy turning Caer Luel itself into a fortress, so that it could serve as his base and watch-tower over both Galloway and North Cumbria. David's son and heir, the sickly Henry, Prince of Strathclyde, was both Earl of Cumbria, by appointment of his father, and Earl of Northumbria as inherited from his mother. Stephen had forfeited him from both, claiming that they were English territories; and now David was seeking to reimpose his hold over them, in case the Empress, even though his late sister's daughter, should think to follow Stephen's policy in this respect. Somerled, himself concerned with castle-building to enhance the security of his Hebridean kingdom, was glad to avail himself of this opportunity to study the advanced fortification works and engineering skill of David's Normans, the most renowned castle-builders in Christendom, David pleased to demonstrate and guide.

It made a pleasant interlude, although Somerled could not leave his fleet for long in cramped idleness at Ellenfoot. Ragnhilde got on well with David, not difficult of course; and young Gillecolm and Prince Henry seemed to find satisfaction in each other's company, their handicaps, however different, perhaps constituting a bond.

On the third day a courier from the south brought news—Archbishop Thurstan had died at York. It is to be feared that there was no mourning, at any rate in Scotland, only relief and a sort of wonder that so old and frail a man should have been so preoccupied with plotting and power right up to his latter end.

The very next day there were more tidings, from not so far south, from Furness in South Cumbria. Bishop Wimund had been found there and apprehended by local nobles. They awaited King David's instructions as to the impostor's fate. Being a bishop they had not slain him out-of-hand meantime, being content with emasculating him and putting out his eyes. They trusted that this would commend itself to the High King.

David grieved over the savagery of his vassals, however thankful that the entire upset was now at an end. He sent orders that Wimund was to be no further maltreated, delivered to Furness Abbey and put in the care of the abbot there as a perpetual resident.

So all was more or less satisfactorily settled and there was nothing to detain the royal visitors at Caer Luel; the various building activities there, and at Holm Cultram, must go on without the monarch's supervision. It was perhaps typical of David mac Malcolm, however, that he felt it necessary to give thanks to God in suitable fashion, for all this bringing low of his enemies with minimum effort on his own part; so he decided that another abbey was the answer. This plethora of abbey-founding, to be sure, had its very practical side. David was involved in the cherished project of dividing up Scotland into a diocesan and parish system, not only for religious advancement but for the better administration and governance of his realm, and the consequent limiting of the powers of his barons and chiefs in local affairs. But this enormous and ambitious task required vast numbers of priests to take over and staff the hundreds of parishes. Hence the need for seminaries and training centres, carefully placed all over the kingdom—the abbeys. David was very much a practical as well as a practising Christian, as he demonstrated to Somerled, seeking to convince that rather more secular and strategic administrator to go and do like-wise. Demonstrated in more than persuasive words, too— for his immediate thanksgiving, he decided, would take the form of furthering God's good cause, as well as improving civilisation, in Galloway. They would build a new abbey at a desirable spot somewhere near Fergus's main town of Kirk Cuthbert's Town on the Dee; also restore the defunct priory of Whithorn or Candida Casa, of ancient fame—both at the expense of the Earl Fergus. What could be more apt and suitable? They would go prospecting for a site for the former, and thereafter repair to Rook's Burgh for Yuletide.

David sought to induce Somerled and Ragnhilde to remain with him, over Yule, if possible. But Somerled pointed out that he had a great fleet to captain and that he wanted to get all back safely to his Hebridean havens before winter storms set in, especially in view of his wife's condition.

So they said their farewells and parted, in enhanced mutual esteem.

CHAPTER 14

The cuckoos were calling again, with their haunting promise of summer to come, and summer in the most hauntingly beautiful place in God's creation this side of Paradise, the Sea of the Hebrides. In the narrow waters where the birlinn sailed in the early June sunshine, with only occasional dipping of the oars to aid the helmsman, the birds' gently reiterated antiphon came drifting across the mere quarter-mile of coloured water from the wooded Kintyre shore, where tender young greens of every hue complemented the aquamarine, amethyst, azure and cobalt-blue of the sea over shallows of gleaming white cockle-shell sand.

Somerled himself steered, lazily watchful, while at his side on the stern platform Ragnhilde stretched at ease on a couch of deerskins, the wicker basket containing the precious, gurgling Dougal close by, a picture of domestic bliss. The oarsmen, a mere score of them on this smaller vessel, stripped to their kilts, murmured to each other, as relaxed as their betters; while, supposedly more watchful, the two escorting longships hung back a good half-mile behind.

It was a holiday indeed, celebratory and to be enjoyed, although with an objective, Ragnhilde's reward and treat. She had quite fallen in love with this lovely and varied seaboard, its prospects and vistas, its character and colours; and when, after a none-too-easy labour, she had brought forth a fine and wholly normal son some five weeks previously, this had been her request to her relieved and delighted husband, to go sailing quietly in no haste through that complex labyrinth of land and water which made up Argyll and the Sudreys, when she and the child were fit for it, wheresoever the spirit moved her. Somerled was only too happy to agree; but being the man he was, had tacked on a suggestion of his own, namely that in their wayfaring they should look for a suitable and convenient site for a modest abbey. Such would please David, he pointed out—without actually emphasising that it would also enhance his own style and renown, serve as a thank-offering for this excellent son, and in due course provide a dignified resting-place for what, it was to be hoped, would be a long line of illustrious Lords of the Isles. If Olaf and Ronald of Orkney, not to mention the deplorable Fergus and even that Constable, de Morville, could build abbeys, in David's wake, so could Somerled of Argyll. Ragnhilde smiled her own thoughts.

So, with June opening fair, they had sailed from Islay eastwards, round Jura and Scarba to view at a discreet distance the noted whirlpool of Corryvreckan, then on to the isles of Luing, Shuna and Seil, before turning southwards down the Sound to the secret sea-lochs of Knapdale, Sween and Mhuirich and Caolisport, Stornoway and Tarbert; and on to the gem of Gigha before skirting the long west coast of Kintyre, to turn the Mull and circle Arran of the mountains; then up through the Kyles of Bute to the Cowal lochs of Striven and Riddon and lengthy Fyne. Now they were heading down the eastern coast of sixty-miles-long Kintyre again, through the Sound of Kilbrannan, with the towering hills of Arran to leeward. Already it was calculated they had covered some five-hundred delectable miles in eight days, and after leaving Kintyre, if Ragnhilde was still so inclined, they would beat north for Colonsay, Mull, Iona, Tiree, Coll, Eigg, Rhum and the rest. Somerled, although he did not admit it, was sometimes all but overwhelmed by the extensiveness and distances and far-flung ramifications of his island kingdom, especially by the problems of its defence.

They had inspected many possible sites for his abbey and noted three or four as distinctly possible. Ragnhilde, actually, would have plumped for somewhere on Islay itself; but Somerled had the strategic aspects in mind. He was concerned to place this establishment where it would do most good, attract most credit to his name and fame, and be safest from attack. He felt that it had to be sited on the mainland, for even on a large island like Islay few would ever see or hear of it save the islanders themselves. Also it would be the more endangered by Norse raiders. Many parts of mainland Argyll, to be sure, were more remote and inaccessible than the islands; these were ruled out. He kept coming back to the fact that this Kintyre was possibly the most likely of all, for extending as it did almost as far south as North Galloway and within sight of David's Ayrshire coasts, it certainly would not pass unnoticed; and at the same time, for the same reasons, it was unlikely that the Vikings would venture much into these all but enclosed waters of the Firth of Clyde. Again, this east coast of Kintyre was notably sheltered from the prevailing westerly winds off the ocean, and fertile—hence the notable growth of trees, especially oak and ash, valuable for building. Here his monks could plant and harvest their crops and orchards in almost ideal conditions—to the increase of their wealth, and his. Moreover, there were many fair natural harbours. Lastly, this, with Cowal nearby, had come to Argyll only comparatively recently, in his deal with the late Ewan MacSween; and some concrete evidence of his possession would be no bad development. So, coasting down the Kilbrannan Sound, however lazy-seeming, he was keeping his eyes open.

So was Gillecolm. The birlinn boasted a small, high bows-platform for a lookout, and the boy had adopted this stance as his own throughout the voyage, from which he could survey the scenery and where he had proved quite useful frequently in watching out for reefs and shoals just below the surface, a constant hazard when they were, as today, skirting close inshore. Somerled suspected too, that he had chosen this position to get as far away from his infant half-brother as possible, of whom he was a little jealous.

Gillecolm it was who first spotted the dun on the cliff-top of the long headland in front, so well hidden and disguised amongst outcropping rock as to be scarcely noticeable. Somerled sat up at the boy's call. These ancient ruinous Pictish duns, forts, were often valuable pointers to important features, for their Pictish forebears had been expert in their use of the land and its contours and resources. These duns were always placed in the best strategic sites of any area, usually had a hinterland nearby of fertile land for the growing of crops, and if on the coast, were fairly sure to have a landing-place, boat-strand or natural harbour conveniently close. In this search for the best abbey-site, such duns had frequently proved to be the best indicators.

Here this major headland projected almost a mile out from the rest of the coastline in a sort of southwards-turning horn, rugged and broken—so broken indeed that the dun turned out to be actually set on a detached islet, like a segment of the cliff severed from the rest, highly inaccessible—which set Somerled, at least, wondering. Why place a fort in such a difficult position unless there was something particularly worth guarding near-at-hand? But of which there was as yet no sign. He steered closer.

There was no access possible from the sea, that became clear. So the approach must have been from behind, from landward, by some sort of no doubt removable bridge, now gone. Which implied something behind and beyond calling for this protection, and worth going to the trouble of building this most awkwardly-placed fortification on the seemingly uninhabited coast.

They circled the sharp point of this steep islet, really only a dun-crowned stack, and discovered that the entire horn of headland was in fact a curving screen to hide a large and unexpected bay almost a mile deep and a similar distance across. None of Somerled's present company knew this coast well nor could suggest an identity for the place. Yet it was very much a major feature. And at the head of the bay was much level land, open and green, some of it obviously cultivated and with a sizeable community of cabins with a hallhouse.

Somerled turned his birlinn in towards this.

It did not take many minutes before they could see folk fleeing away inland from the township, towards backing woodland, driving off such cattle as were sufficiently nearby. This reaction the travellers had experienced before, of course, with strange ships bearing down apt to mean Norse raiders—although they would have expected this Kintyre east coast to be free of such. Somerled's rule had banished major Viking attacks and occupation, but hit-and-run raids from the Outer Hebrides and Skye and further north still took place.

They landed and found it to be a pleasant place indeed, south-facing and sheltered from all the winds that blew. A wide gentle valley with a stream that was almost a river probed into the low wooded hills behind. Strips of oats grew and there were fruit-trees, whilst cattle and sheep dotted the surrounding slopes. Blue woodsmoke curled up from many of the houses, but no occupants issued therefrom.

Somerled made for the larger hallhouse but found it empty like the rest, although poultry clucked around its open doorway. He sent some of his men to enter the flanking woodland, to shout aloud that all was well, that it was King Somerled their lord come visiting, and that no harm would come to any.

Eventually a group of people appeared, led by a tall old man, all still wary. The sight of Ragnhilde with a baby in her arms seemed to reassure them however, and Somerled was at pains to proclaim his identity and goodwill.

The old man proved to be MacKay of Carradail, this being his community of that name, which Somerled had heard of vaguely. He hastened to offer simple hospitality and explained their alarm. This entire coast had been visited and terrorised by four raiding Norse longships only a month previously, with much slaughter, rapine and pillage.

Somerled expressed his distress and concern at this and promised that he would try to learn who were the culprits and to take appropriate steps—however little consolation this might bring to the victims. Ragnhilde asked much about the district and its surroundings, obviously taken with the place; and presently she was suggesting that this was as good a site as any they had seen for their abbey, with fertile land and excellent pasture, much wood and a river, a sheltered haven and people to support the monks and aid in the building. Her husband agreed with all that but had his doubts nevertheless. He felt that it was all just too open and vulnerable. Perhaps the word of this recent Viking raid affected his judgement—although, to be sure, that could happen anywhere. He declared that he would prefer somewhere less wide open from the sea. An abbey built in this river-mouth would be all too obvious to raiders sailing the Sound, and might well draw the Norsemen. And yet this Kintyre east coast was ideal, from other aspects. He asked old MacKay if he knew of other fertile, sheltered but more secure and secret places where a religious house might be established and its community flourish in peace?

The other spread his hands. Where was safe from the heathenish devils, he asked? Nothing was sacred nor secure. But there *was* a place not far away, he mentioned, a patrimony of his own, which certainly had escaped hitherto, being hidden from the Sound although quite close to the shore. It was called Saddail, another five miles down the coast, where the Saghadail Water reached the sea and where his second son lairded it. Because of the twistings of the river and wooded bluffs at the mouth, the little community of Saddail was not visible from seaward or any indication of settlement evident. Yet half-a-mile inland its valley opened out fairly and there was much good land.

Thanking their host for his hospitality and help and promising vengeance, if possible, on the Norsemen, they took their leave.

Having been directed to it, Saddail was easily found—although it would almost certainly have been missed otherwise. A small headland, also crowned by a dun, hid another south-facing bay, but this one much less wide and deep than Carradail's. That a river entered here was not obvious, owing to the configuration of the land, wooded hillocks masking it effectively. The birlinn leading, when the ships probed their way in, Somerled found that, round the first bend, although it became too shallow for navigation, there was a sort of basin to hold their vessels, already quite out-of-sight of the Sound. Three or four small fishing-craft were beached here, but no cabins or houses.

Disembarking, he took a small party inland by a wide track which followed the bends of the brawling stream through woodland, amongst more slopes and bluffs. Then, in a bare half-mile, the trees thinned and a pleasant green vale opened before them, a placid, gentle place in the afternoon sunlight, more than a mile of it at a guess, by half that in width before the low wooded hills began to close in again. A little township with a single larger house nestled at the foot of this, with a mill, barns, cattle-pens and fruit-trees beyond, a scene of peace and well-being. Ragnhilde exclaimed with pleasure at the sight.

So small a party did not arouse undue alarm and there was no hurried flight from the township although neither was there more than a very cautious welcome. On enquiry, Donald MacKay proved to be away hunting, but his young wife, infant in arms, received them somewhat abashed although she was soon put at ease by Ragnhilde, with baby-talk.

A few questions put and a quick survey decided Somerled that they were unlikely to find a better place for their abbey. He even selected a possible site, back from the river on a sort of low platform of land above an incoming burn, amidst tall old trees. Here nothing would do but that he must pace out dimensions for church and main monastic building, basing his measurements on what he had inspected at Olaf's Rushen and David's Holm Cultram, only a little doubtful over the thought that these, and all others that he had seen, were Romish establishments whereas his own would be a Columban one—and the Celtic Church did not go in for these great stone abbeys, contenting itself with modest timber-and-turf hutments and cabin-like sanctuaries within palisaded ramparts, which they called cashels, even though these were usually in the care of abbots. However, there was no real reason which he knew of why the Columbans should *not* have a handsome stone edifice, to the glory of God—and to be sure, of its founder—and he, Somerled, could lead the way, as in other matters. He already could visualise the Abbey of Saddail, dedicated perhaps to Saint Brendan, after whom the nearby Sound was called, rising majestically out of this grove of trees in the quiet valley, the noble, indeed royal resting-place of a long line of Kings of Argyll and Lords of the Isles to come, the serried tombs of his successors a place of pilgrimage. It was all a most excellent conception, he pointed out more than once.

They stayed the night at Saddail, informing a less than enthusiastic Donald MacKay, when he returned, of the honour being done him and his little community. The abbey would much advantage him, it was pointed out, providing additional wealth, amenities and prestige, as well as occupation for his people. And, to be sure, worshipping facilities.

252

In the morning they sailed on southwards, to round the Mull of Kintyre.

* * *

Once again it was young Gillecolm who drew attention to the situation, pointing away northwards, from his roost in the bows. Smoke, he called, much smoke, far in front. There was a change in the weather, the sun gone, and they were sailing up towards the Sound of Jura in fine style before a freshening southerly wind, the rowers able to rest on their oars. It looked as though it might rain.

Sure enough, now that they looked, there was billowing grey-brown smoke rising, some miles ahead—which would have been more evident in sunlight and clear skies. It seemed to come from within the mouth of the Sound, which must mean that the fire was on the Isle of Gigha or its satellite, Cara.

As they drew closer it became obvious that the smoke emanated not from one but from several fires, the breeze soon rolling it into a single great cloud; and that it was on Gigha, that picturesque and pleasant green place which had attracted Ragnhilde on their way south. Fires of such size and number were, to say the least, unusual, especially at this time of the year. Somerled grew concerned.

Gigha was a comparatively small member of the Inner Hebridean archipelago, only some seven miles long by a mile or so in breadth; but fertile and quite populous, situated a couple of miles off the Kintyre west coast and sheltered somewhat from the ocean winds by the bulk of Islay some fifteen miles to the west. Its havens and landing-places, like most of its housing, were almost all on its east, and up that side the birlinn led. When they drew near enough the first fire to recognise that it was a burning cot-house, their fears were confirmed.

"Raiders!" Somerled exclaimed. "Accursed raiders again! Dear God—are we back to that! Who dares? In *my* isles!"

"The same Norsemen who raided Carradail?" Ragnhilde wondered.

"It could be, yes. MacKay said four ships—although they could have been only part of a larger force."

About one-third of the way up the east coast was the main

bay of Gigha, and the harbour and township, called Ardminish. It was apparent that the greatest volume of smoke was rising from thereabouts.

Somerled was in a quandary. What to do? He was in no state for engaging any large number of raiders, not equipped for fighting and accompanied by his wife and baby. He had the two escorting longships behind, but they were not manned for war, with only their rowers and crewmen, some one-hundred-and-twenty in all. In the birlinn he had some forty more. And he had none of his veteran leaders with him on this holiday cruise. The Norse longships, manned for raiding, would carry up to one-hundred-and-fifty on each vessel. So the probability was that they would be outnumbered four to one. And surprise could be ruled out, their approach almost certain to have been observed.

As they rounded the islet which formed the south horn of the Ardminish bay, sure enough, there lay four Norse longships at the head of the bay, with most of the township behind in smoking ruin.

"I should have built a castle here," Somerled exclaimed. "But I cannot have one on every island. There are scores, hundreds. Those ships are guarded. And we can see men moving around the township, watching us for a certainty. We cannot move in and try to capture or destroy those ships. Yet I cannot just sail away . . ."

"Can you not get help?" Ragnhilde asked.

"How can I? The west coast of Kintyre is little populated, open to the ocean. The nearest haven of Islay is fifteen miles away. To go there, raise a sufficient force from parts of the island, and win back here would take all day. By which time these would be gone, belike. Yet there is nowhere nearer. Castle Sween is even further. And I doubt if I could find sufficient men and craft there."

"Can you parley with them? Tell them who you are and that you will follow and destroy them unless they stop savaging this poor place . . .?"

"What heed would they pay? And seeing me little protected, they would probably rejoice to slay me—whatever they might do to you! No—that is not the way . . ." He was only part attending to her, the rest of his mind active, considering, recollecting the conformation of this island, assessing. It was some advantage that they had been here only a few days before and, with Ragnhilde so taken with Gigha, they had spent most of a day on the island exploring it. So he could visualise the features of the place.

She saw the calculating look in his eyes. "You plan something, Sorley? What?"

"I do not know. I wonder . . .? It is but a notion. But it might just serve. At least to distract them, drive them away . . ." He paused, to point. "See, men hurrying down to the ships. We could have done nothing there. They may row out, to challenge us . . ."

"Will you wait for them?"

"No. Not with you and the child and Gillecolm aboard, by God! That is not the way."

"What, then . . .?"

"We flee!" he answered grimly. "Or seem to." Having slowed almost to a standstill, in the mouth of the bay, his escorts had come up with him. He raised his voice to shout to them, and to point, northwards.

"Follow me. All speed. Seem to flee. Close inshore. Keep near." And to his own oarsmen and crew. "Quickly. Your fastest. Off with us, as though we take flight . . ."

So off the three Argyll craft raced, oars flashing and spray drifting on the breeze, up the broken and indented east coast of Gigha in seemingly craven haste. Soon Ardminish Bay was hidden behind. Although Somerled watched, no Norse ships issued therefrom to give chase.

They had some four miles to go to the northern tip of Gigha, and for most of the way they would be hidden by the cliffs and low hills of this more rocky and much higher end of the island. For the same reason, it was little occupied and given over to moorland and rough pasture, so that there was little at this northern sector to attract raiders and no fires smoked here—which was as Somerled had guessed. At the narrow northernmost headland, still close inshore, he swung the birlinn round in a tight curve, ordering the sail to be lowered—for now they were heading southwards into the wind. Close behind, the two longships did likewise, all oar-work now. Unless the Norse had sent someone up to the top of Creag Bhan, the highest hill of the island, it was highly unlikely that they could have seen them for the last miles, or observed this latest manoeuvre. They rowed on down the western coast.

After passing a hammer-shaped penisula, they came to a wide shallow bay, over a mile across and littered with reefs and skerries. They skirted it cautiously. Now they were rowing through acrid smoke-clouds blown northwards— but this would help to hide them. At the far end of this bay there was a kind of indented lagoon, reasonably clear of reefs, with Creag Bhan rearing lumpishly behind. Into this Somerled steered, Gillecolm watching for rocks. In here the ships would lie hidden, he hoped, certainly there seemed to be no house in sight when the billowing smoke cleared occasionally.

He summoned on to the birlinn the two other ship-masters—one of whom happened to be the Manus O'Ryan who had greeted him on the Isle of Rhum and who had remained with him since—and the steersmen likewise, the nearest to leaders he could raise. He told them his plan. He would land here, with as many men as he could take, leaving only the absolute minimum aboard to handle the ships, with only a few oars used. The Norsemen, who it was hoped would assume that they had fled the scene, would almost certainly disperse again in bands to continue their looting and burning sport; and it would be his endeavour to stalk them, unobserved, and to pick them off group by group, if possible. The ships would remain here meantime, in case the attempt was unsuccessful and they had to retire and be taken off quickly. If all seemed to be going reasonably well, then he would send a signal, and the ships should sail back round to the east side of the island, to lie off Ardminish Bay again, and so add to the concern and alarm of the Norsemen, who would not know that they were almost empty and would be apt to assume that there were at least two forces attacking them. They were not to seek to come ashore at Ardminish unless signalled by himself to do so. And, of course, Queen Ragnhilde's and the child's safety were to be ensured at all costs.

Ragnhilde protested at this, declaring that she was not to be treated as helpless and a mere impediment. She was, after all, the daughter of a long line of Vikings. She would take charge of the ships.

256

Gillecolm pleaded to be allowed to go with his father but Somerled would have none of it. This would be a desperate venture and no occasion for beginners to learn the trade of war. Besides, his part was to look after the Queen.

The parting was tense.

With some one-hundred-and-ten men, Somerled splashed ashore and started to climb inland, making for Creag Bhan. He reckoned that the hill was one sure place where the invaders would be unlikely to frequent; and it ought to provide the necessary viewpoint above the worst of the smoke, even though it was no mountain, no more than a few hundred feet in height. There were no houses nor farmeries to be seen on these north and west slopes.

Although his crewmen were scarcely enthusiastic climbers they made it to the ridge near the summit in fairly good time, with only a mile to cover. Leaving the company below the skyline, Somerled took Manus O'Ryan up to the ridge with him, to peer over. There was a thin film of smoke even here, but not sufficient to blanket-out all prospects.

The scene which met their gaze was grim, however anticipated. At least a dozen isolated homesteads were burning, down there, apart from the larger conflagration which was Ardminish township, between the hill and the east coast, two comparatively near, on the lower hill-slopes. A little to the south a herd of cattle was being rounded up. And further over, nearer Ardminish, there appeared to be some sort of gathering, although what was going on was unclear, owing to distance and smoke.

The two men strained their stinging eyes, trying to make out which burnings were new, or at least which were still occupying the attentions of the raiders, and which were now left to burn out. It was hard to tell, in all the obscurity. But when a sudden burst of flame and new, blacker smoke arose from a point a little further to the north, not half-a-mile away, there could be no doubts.

"We start there!" Somerled decided, and hurried back to his people.

Instructions were minimal, consisting mainly of the command to follow him and to keep quiet. He led the way, partly downhill at first and curving round to the north, to cross the ridge much lower down, in thicker smoke now.

This grew worse as they proceeded, setting men cursing beneath their breaths. But however unpleasant, it was of course greatly to their advantage, giving them all the cover they required, difficult although it made direction-finding. When Somerled judged that they had gone far enough, he turned due southwards again. Eyes streaming, men sought to cover their faces as best they could.

Tripping and stumbling, they advanced. The orange-red murky glow of flame through smoke guided them. They soon could hear men's shouting and women's screams ahead. At least they were not too late, here. When they were within one hundred yards or so of the conflagration Somerled halted his men, formed them into something like a crescent and, himself at the centre, waved them forward. Swords, axes and dirks in hand, they surged silently on.

It was, of course, utter and complete surprise. Out of the rolling brown smoke-clouds they burst upon the scene of terror, providing a new dimension thereof. The timber-and-thatch buildings of what had been a fair-sized farmery were all alight; and a little south of the centre, out of the smoke, about a score of Norsemen were busy. Some were in process of hanging three men on an improvised gallows; others were raping four women, one old, one only a girl, but all naked; still others abusing cowering children; some merely gulping down liquor. They were all too much engaged to perceive the Argyll men before it was too late to put up any effective resistance. In yelling, bloody astonishment, they died, one and all, none being allowed to escape to warn their compatriots.

It was all over in a minute or two, almost too easy.

Although Somerled had every sympathy with the victims, he did not permit the delay which would have resulted from helping them further. Anyway, they were all probably too shocked to respond. Leaving them with their slain attackers and burning premises, he rounded up his men for the next assault. Clear of this conflagration it was not difficult to perceive how they should proceed. The colour and density of the various smokes was a simple guide. When it was black and thick but shot with flame the fires were newly lit and so apt still to be occupying the attention of the invaders. Brown represented somewhat earlier burning and might now be abandoned. Blue, thinning smoke could be left alone.

Somerled's further strategy was self-evident. It was to try to keep always within the cover of the denser smoke, however much back-tracking and circling this called for, so as always to approach the scattered, burning homesteads from the north; and to try to ensure that while they were attacking one group, another would not be likely to spot them at it and so be warned—this last being more difficult. They were aided, of course, by the crofts and farmeries being, by their nature, seldom close together, each sitting in its own small territory, and so could be approached individually and carefully.

The second one produced a mere dozen or so Vikings; but was too late to save the lives of the occupants, a man, two women and a child. The third was better, a larger place which had attracted a larger group of raiders, who were still at their grievous sport with the owners. There were over thirty Norsemen here when the bodies came to be counted, but assailed without warning by one-hundred-and-ten they had no least chance.

They reached the east coast thereafter and Somerled sent a couple of men climbing back to signal to his ships from the top of Creag Bhan, before turning inland south-westwards again.

They were less successful at their next place, owing to a sudden veering of the wind which blew the smoke off to one side, revealing the attack when still some distance off, so that this time the Argyll men had to do some fighting. Even so, vastly outnumbering the enemy, they fairly quickly beat down a distracted and unready opposition. But unfortunately two or three Vikings made good their escape, bolting off southwards, to be lost in the smoke.

Somerled now had to reconsider. These would warn their colleagues and surprise could no longer be assumed. Admittedly there still would be much confusion amongst the Norse as to the situation; the comprehensive smoke would ensure that, numbers would not be known, nor as to what had happened to the others—nor, even, who were the attackers. Also, at first at any rate, these escapers might well get no further than the nearest group of their compatriots.

He was not forgetting that gathering which he had seen from the hilltop. Whether this was still going on they had no means of knowing, for even without the smoke they would not see the place from this low-lying position, for it had been in hollow ground near Ardminish. If the fugitives ran there, as they might, then the results could be more serious, warning a larger concentration of the enemy than at any single farmstead. He had no idea what proportion of the total had been assembled there, but assuming that some four hundred had come ashore from the four ships and that this gathering represented the leadership, there could well be up to one-third involved—perhaps more than his own numbers. Warned, and coming to look for him, they could be dangerous.

He decided to change tactics and go seek a major confrontation whilst surprise was still on his side—however risky. He consulted O'Ryan, and together they came to the conclusion that the assembly had been just inland of the little peninsula which formed the northern horn of Ardminish Bay, north-east of the burning township by about half-a-mile—which would make sense, to be out of the worst of its smoke but still in the most populous part of the island. How best, then, to seek to approach that area unseen? They decided that back along the actual shoreline would be best, for although there was least smoke there, the natural drop of the land surface to the beach produced the usual bank, no cliffs or high dunes in this instance but enough of a rise to offer some cover from sight from inland.

So they turned back for the beach, however doubtful O'Ryan was as to the wisdom of it. They reached the rockbound shore at another small, low headland, and in the blue haze could just make out the larger peninsula which was their landmark, with its offshore islet, about half-a-mile to the south. There was no sign, as yet, of Norsemen.

Keeping as close under the bank as possible, and necessarily strung-out, they made their difficult way round the broken, curving, stony coastline, which was scarcely a bay. They attained the root of the peninsula without incident, and leaving the men there, hidden, Somerled and O'Ryan moved up to the higher ground. They found, nearby, the ramparts of another Pictish fort which offered both cover

260

and a vantage-point. Creeping thither, they prospected the area from behind the grass-grown mounds.

They had no difficulty in perceiving the situation. They were approximately right in their direction. The hollow ground they had seen lay some three hundred yards ahead to their left, and still was thronged with men. But what had been a gathering now was scarcely that but a feasting. There were fires here too, but not from burning buildings and thatch, cooking-fires, many of them, with great sides and haunches of beef being roasted on spits, with cauldrons steaming. Men stood and lay about, many men, everywhere. Clearly no alarm had reached this company as yet.

Also clear was what the earlier gathering had been about. Fully a score of white bodies hung from an erection of poles normally used for drying fishing-nets—white splashed with red, that is, for all these bodies hung upside down, by the feet, and were headless. From another rail, just discernible nearby, hung the heads, by the hair.

"I feared something of the sort—God's curse on them!" Somerled said. "How many Norse, would you say?"

"Over one hundred, to be sure."

"I would think half that again. This will be the main body, the leaders. And they do not expect us—not yet!"

Carefully they surveyed the scene and the lie of the land, assessing, visualising their attack.

"Two parties," Somerled decided. "You take forty. Round to the south yonder. When you can get no nearer without being seen, make a display, a flourish. Come on, shouting. Then, when they are distracted, I will fling in the seventy, from here. Confuse them. Two attacks will seem greater numbers. Unready, they will not have time to form any real defence. You have it?"

"Yes, then. You will have to give me time, to get there. Unseen."

"To be sure. Come, then . . ."

Back with the men, Somerled told them the situation and plan and divided them into the two unequal-sized groupings. O'Ryan's party would have to continue along the beach for some distance before they could take advantage of more broken ground and whin-bushes, to get into a suitable position. They hurried off.

Somerled took the main body up to the dun, some of the way having to be crawled on hands and knees. They had plenty of time. The ramparts gave ample cover thereafter. They crouched, waiting.

Even the best-laid plans can go agley, however. They were still waiting when there was a development not anticipated, an alarm—but not O'Ryan's. Two Norsemen came running down to the feasting-area from the west in obvious urgency. It was too far to hear what they shouted but their gesticulations and pointings were sufficiently eloquent. Somerled cursed. Clearly they were announcing the attacks inland, however belatedly.

So surprise was gone. What, then? To assail them at once, before they formed up and became a fighting body? But O'Ryan would know nothing of this and there would be confusion. His seventy might well be overwhelmed before the others could join in, and all lost.

Watching the stir of alarm amongst the enemy and biting his lip in momentary indecision, another thought occurred to Somerled. This new situation might hold advantage as well as the opposite. All the pointings westward would certainly give the Norse leaders the impression that there was a force, possibly a large one, in that direction, and none so far away. When two more forces erupted on either side of them here, would the effect not be the more shattering? Surrounded. Outnumbered. Dire danger. It might serve him none so ill . . .

He was so considering when O'Ryan's party made their appearance. He and his men saw them first, about five hundred yards away, for the Norse tended to be looking in the other direction, north and westwards, or huddled in discussion. But the shouts and bellowings, sufficiently threatening, swiftly swung them round. Yelling, brandishing axes and swords, the forty came on at the run.

Somerled gave them time to get fairly close to the agitated enemy as they rushed for their arms, difficult as it was to restrain his own men. Then leaping up, and crying his Argyll slogan, he led his seventy down.

It was not much of a fight, in the end. Unprepared, relaxed and drink-taken, assailed on two sides, the Norse defence was on the whole scrappy, unco-ordinated. Some

262

fought well but most were really beaten before they began. No doubt, fears of another force to the north, as reported, had its effect. And another unplanned aspect may well have had an influence. Somerled attacked from the north-east, O'Ryan from the south-east, the threat of further trouble was to the north and west; which left only the south and south-west open, and thither lay Ardminish and the ships. Longships were always both the Norse strength and their weakness, representing safety as well as power. They were never happy far from their vessels.

So, as the attack developed, the tendency was to give ground in the one free direction, towards the ships. And as the struggle went against them, the tendency became a drift, and the drift before long a frank retiral. And then, as glances tended to turn over shoulders towards Ardminish Bay and the four waiting craft, there round the north head-land came the three Argyll ships.

It was the last straw. The raiders broke off piecemeal and fled.

Somerled made a pretence of pursuit, but it was only that. There would be men left aboard the enemy craft and these would be likely to come ashore to the aid of colleagues if they saw them hard-pressed—but would be apt to stay on their ships if they saw only the others hurrying back. Let them go, then. There was still much work to be done in dealing with the remaining invader parties. Somerled blew his horn for a recall.

It was a strange situation. At a guess, adding the numbers disposed of here to those already slain, his own party were still likely to be outnumbered two to one. But they held the initiative, and the remaining enemy would not know their numbers, nor even, in the main, of their existence probably. For himself, it was difficult for Somerled to know what to do next. Just to go back into the general smoke, looking for further groups to surprise was scarcely a prospect to attract his now tired and sated men—and they were at the wrong side of the conflagrations here. Moreover, he was beginning to become worried about his own ships. If these four Norse vessels were to sail out and attack them, practically un-manned as they were, there could be disaster. Ragnhilde—would she perceive the danger and draw off?

He decided, after all, to hurry on after their fleeing foes, to Ardminish. At least it would keep up the pressure, perhaps prevent them from essaying any attack on the Argyll ships. It would enable himself to see what went on; indeed, there would almost certainly be fishing-boats on the Ardminish boat-strand, one of which he might be able to send out with instructions for Ragnhilde. He would have to leave the other Norse parties inland meantime.

Belatedly leading his men on southwards, anxious again, breasting an intervening small ridge, he obtained a good view over the bay, less than half-a-mile off. What he saw gave him pause. There was much activity about the four longships, the fled Norsemen already there. But something about the activity was odd, not what he would have looked for. Then he realised—they were transferring all the men to only two of the ships, leaving the others empty. It made sense, of course. With the crewmen who had been left aboard and the survivors from the attack, they could fairly fully man two; and the other two would be left for the remaining pirates if they could reach them. He might well have done the same.

So—with only two longships and the odour of defeat on them, would they be apt to attack the three Argyll ships out there? Probably not—unless they themselves were assailed. And, unmanned as they were, Ragnhilde would never order that. Somerled felt distinctly better.

Hurrying on towards the smoking township, they watched the two Norse vessels head out to sea—and thankfully Somerled saw that they made directly for the southern horn of the bay, at speed. The Argyll ships were still lying off the north horn. Quickly the enemy rounded the point and disappeared from sight.

"We are richer by two longships!" Somerled told his people. "Come, let us take them."

The ruined, reeking township was abandoned save for some poultry which had eluded the raiders. Bodies lay scattered, however. First things first, Somerled waded out to the longships. They found all more or less in order aboard, everything just hastily left. Surprised, they found something else left behind—a man, so completely drunk as

264

to be incapable of movement. O'Ryan had his dirk out to despatch him when restrained by Somerled.

"Wait," he said. "He can tell us who these devils are, where they come from. Pour water over him. Get him to talk . . ."

Ragnhilde, not knowing what the position was, still kept her position at the mouth of the bay. Leaving O'Ryan to deal with the inebriate, Somerled had the other longship rowed out to his own vessels, standing in the prow to wave and demonstrate who came, afraid that his wife might sheer off. She did not, however, and there was a relieved and distinctly emotional reunion.

Explaining the situation, Somerled was at the same time considering what to do now. The remaining invaders had to be dealt with and this sad, ravaged island to be given what attention they could. He ordered the four ships into the anchorage beside the other, where he found that O'Ryan had managed to get some information out of the drunk man, before hanging him. It seemed that these Norsemen were from Skye, under one Ketil Left Hand, a lieutenant of the same Thorkell Svensson who had been sent about his business from Ardtornish those years ago. Grimly Somerled nodded. Further education for Thorkell was, it seemed, in order.

It was difficult to instil keenness and enthusiasm into his men for the work which still remained to be done here—even in himself. But they could not just sail away. Leaving the shipping at anchor, strongly guarded, he set some men to gathering up the bodies of the dead islanders, making a heap of the Norse slain, and dousing what fires persisted. Then he and O'Ryan each took a party of about forty and set off to try to locate the remainder of the raiders.

Somerled's own company, taking the higher ground, were examining a savaged croft not far from the township when, warned by the wailing cries of women, they hid, to perceive presently a group of Norsemen materialising out of the smoke-haze dragging by the hair some dishevelled female captives. Pounced out upon and dealt with in bloody and merciless expedition, the women were delivered in a state of terror greater than ever. Somerled sent them on to Ardminish, where Ragnhilde would look after them. They counted fifteen Norsemen dead here, at least all were dead when they moved on.

They surveyed two more harried homesteads but discovered only corpses and saw no more invaders. By this time they were fairly high on the slopes of Creag Bhan again, and Somerled decided to climb to the summit ridge to gain a prospect of the overall position, if he could, from that lofty viewpoint. And up there, as he scanned the scene and saw no new fires, one of his men drew his attention to the other, west, side of the island. There, very near where their own three ships had waited earlier, the two longships which had fled from Ardminish were to be seen lying close. Clearly they were taking aboard some of their people from this north end. As they watched, they could see another small party working its way down to the beach to be evacuated.

So that was it. This Ketil Left Hand was not quite such a craven as he had seemed. He had not entirely deserted his friends, merely sailed round Gigha to collect such of them as he could. Well, Somerled assessed, there was nothing that he could do about it. No point in trying to interfere, at this stage, even if there was time to muster his men for any assault. The probability that the enemy, when they had taken off as many men as they could, would attempt any further hostilities, was remote.

They waited, then, on the hilltop, for a while longer, and presently saw the two Norse ships cast off and pull out from the land, and head off south-westwards as for the open sea. They watched until the pair were mere specks on the horizon. Any Norsemen left on Gigha, now, would be dead Norsemen.

Satisfied, they returned to Ardminish and their own ships. Now, to do what they could for the surviving islanders. They would stay that night, possibly another night also, to assist, bury the dead and seek to help in the tasks of salvage and some reconstruction. And Somerled would arrange for further aid and for compensation hereafter—and promised vengeance.

Ragnhilde went to work as hard as any.

CHAPTER 15

Somerled's intended punitive expedition to Skye had to be delayed for quite some time, for war on a major scale broke out in these northern areas, complicated war in which he was not involved but which constituted a threat to peace in Argyll and the Isles. It all started in Ireland, where King Ronald of Dublin, the same who had been visiting Man when prince, shortly before succeeding to his father's throne, was slain by one Ottar, grandson of a former king there. Thanks to the way in which all these Norse kinglets had links with one another and with the ruling house of Norway itself, this brought in that power, as well as setting much of Ireland in a blaze and involving Orkney and even Iceland also, some for, some against Ottar. So the Hebridean seaboard being geographically in the middle of the turmoil, it behoved Somerled to be very much on his guard, with his forces mobilised, in case he was unwillingly drawn in by having to protect his domains; for some of the combatants were apt to be tempted to do a little private raiding during lulls in hostilities. It was no occasion for a venture such as he had planned, especially as King Stephen was now at loose again and had driven the Empress out of England meantime, and might well decide to take a hand in the present upset, being the man he was—in which case David could scarcely remain unconcerned.

In the midst of all this, Ragnhilde bore another child, a daughter whom they named Anna.

It was almost two years later before Ottar was himself slain by the late Ronald's brothers, and peace of a sort returned to this part of Christendom. Somerled was all in favour of peace; but he had this business to transact before he could really embrace it.

He had heard of Thorkell Svensson's doings from time to time, and little good of them. Thorkell had made himself master of all Skye, or at least the coasts thereof, either driving out or absorbing other Norse raiding groups and bloodily subduing the local folk, making his main base at Loch Dunvegan, to the north-west of that great island, and from there terrorising far and wide, even to Lewis and Harris and the Outer Hebrides, and eastwards to the mainland coasts of Morar, Knoydart, Kintail, Torridon, Gairloch and northwards. Apart from the Gigha venture, by his minion Ketil Left Hand, and one or two nibblings at North Moidart, he had not turned southwards. Nevertheless, Somerled was of the opinion that there was not room on this western seaboard of Scotland for himself and Thorkell—especially as the latter had involved himself in the recent hostilities, by all accounts, and on the winning side, gaining some access of strength in the process. Better to seek to deal with him before he got any stronger. Moreover there were the savaged, ravaged lands to free from this blight, and nobody else appeared to be concerned to do so—although in theory most of it was part of David's kingdom. He would act King David's loyal vassal, then.

So, in the early summer of 1148, Somerled sailed with a score of ships. He had chosen the number carefully. There was something of a convention to be observed in such matters. A larger fleet than that was apt to signify war, real war, a threat to neighbouring and entrenched powers. The Nordreys and northern mainland seaboard, with the Outer Hebrides, was more or less accepted as within the sphere of influence of the Orkney earls—and since they were in name subject to the Norwegian throne, of the Kings of Norway also. Skye was just within that sphere, and Somerled certainly had no desire to challenge Orkney and Norway. Twenty ships would be about as many as the Lord of the Isles could be expected to take on a private venture out of his own territories without posing a threat to other great folk. Whether it would be enough to deal with Thorkell Svensson remained to be seen.

They sped up the Hebridean Sea, before a fresh south-westerly, in fine style and fairly compact formation, with some fifty-odd miles to go. Somerled's dragon-ship had a new shipmaster, none other than his own son Gillecolm, now changed from youth into young man. He was still lacking in certain mental qualities and awareness; but amongst the compensatory abilities he had developed a marked proficiency in the art of boat and ship handling, apparently largely instinctive. His father, surprised and gratified, had given him every opportunity to advance this useful talent, first his own fishing-boat, then control of the family birlinn, then one of the lesser longships. But this was the first occasion for him to be actually mastering the dragon-ship itself, and Somerled would nowise have risked it had he not been present himself on the stern platform, with his watchful eye. In fact, Gillecolm was there largely at Cathula MacIan's own pleading. She had been responsible for much of the youth's expertise, taking a close interest in his development when she perceived his aptitude. And when, perforce, she had to give up the vessel's direction, for sufficiently compelling reasons, he was her nominee as successor. So now Cathula was left behind at Ardtornish with her new-born son—for a year or so before she had been wed to Saor MacNeil, a peculiar marriage which neither pretended was any love-match but which had its own advantages and suitabilities, as well as conveniences, for two very tough and redoubtable characters—and was in fact working out well, within its limits. None doubted that Cathula's heart was truly Somerled's; but since he was now unattainable this arrangement had to serve. Saor's attitude tended towards wary admiration, very good for that head-strong and normally disrespectful individual.

With the Isle of Muck to starboard and Eigg and Rhum ahead and the blue mountains of Skye just appearing like jagged teeth on the northern horizon, Somerled sent Saor ahead, with his own and one other longship, to try to discover the situation on and around Skye. The rest of the fleet would meantime hide in Loch Scresort where they were unlikely to be discovered, for Rhum was little more than a cluster of mountain-tops and but scantily inhabited. They would wait there until Saor returned, spending the night in its shelter.

Although passing the island often, Somerled had not been back here, to land, since that day when he found his father ill at Kinlochscresort and he had all but come to blows with Malcolm MacEth. So much had happened since then.

He told some of it all to Gillecolm, but could not assess whether his son was really interested or taking it in, although he seemed to listen dutifully, even gratefully—but the look in those strange eyes was far away, as so often when he was not actually engaged in some chosen activity.

They had longer to wait than anticipated; indeed Somerled, becoming concerned, was considering sending out another vessel or two to try to learn what had happened when, just after noon the next day, Saor's two ships came into Loch Scresort, and from the south, oddly.

The news they brought was complicated, good and not so good. Saor, after a preliminary discreet survey of the southern Skye coasts, without perceiving anything significant, had put into the great isle-dotted Loch Bracadale, midway up the west coast, where his craft could skulk inconspicuously behind any of the many islets. They had seen no sign of Norsemen there, and in the evening dusk had landed at Ullinish, a small township on the Skye mainland, hidden behind the island of Wiay. There, after with difficulty convincing the local people, MacAskills and MacFingons, that they intended them no harm, they learned much of the current situation on Skye. Although Loch Bracadale was a good score of sea miles south of Loch Dunvegan, from its most northerly inlet, called Loch Vatten, it was only four miles over the hills to Dunvegan itself—so the Ullinish folk were all too well aware of what went on at Thorkell Svensson's base. Indeed, normally there were three or four longships stationed in Loch Bracadale itself, not at Ullinish but at Harlosh to the north; but these were away meantime, hosting as the Norse term was. Thorkell was, in fact, off on the first major raiding expedition of the summer season, it was believed to Barra and the Uists, with over a dozen ships.

Somerled naturally received this news with mixed feelings.

But there was more. Slipping out of Loch Bracadale again at first light, Saor had proceeded northwards, hugging the dangerous coast, to try to discover what numbers of Norsemen had been left behind at Dunvegan, and if possible when Thorkell might be expected to return. They had not so discovered, for off Loch Pooltiel, just short of Dunvegan

Head, they had been surprised by three Norse vessels emerging from that loch to challenge them. Saor indicated, typically, that he could have dealt with these three without any difficulty but that the stramash might have attracted the attention of others and so spread alarm. So—in Somerled's interests, he pointed out—he had turned tail, greatly as this was against his own inclinations. Pursued, so as not to give away the presence of the Argyll fleet at Rhum, he had headed off south-westwards as though making for Canna or even Tiree, and eventually shaken them off. It had all taken time. . .

Somerled's mind was busy, his commendation less than enthusiastic. He questioned his foster-brother as to the features of land and water in the Bracadale area, and this of Loch Pooltiel. He knew Loch Dunvegan, but only slightly.

What was it to be, then, Saor demanded? Follow Thorkell to the Outer Hebrides? Attack Dunvegan without the main Norse force—which would leave Thorkell still as much of a menace as ever? Or postpone the venture?

Certainly not postpone, Somerled declared. No, it was attack, and here in Skye. Hunting for the enemy at Barra or the Uists would be a doubtful strategy and risk giving Thorkell warning. The aim should be to capture his bases here, but allow escapers to get away to inform Thorkell and so, hopefully, bring him back with his force and so to defeat and punish him on his own ground.

Saor agreed that this would be the ideal proceeding. But *would* Thorkell come back, when he heard that a great force was waiting for him? After all, it was not territory that these Norse were interested in, but pickings, rape, slaughter. They had found Skye a convenient base, yes. But rather than face a superior enemy in possession of Skye, would they not rather sail off elsewhere and choose some other base? There was plenty of land, to the north, or even in the outer isles themselves.

Somerled nodded but pointed out that if Thorkell did not know that it was a large force that awaited him, thought that it was only a minor attack, say half-a-dozen ships, would he not return then, in his wrath? The strategy, then, was to send the tell-tale escapers hurrying westwards with false tidings. Use only a few vessels at this stage, with the

majority kept in reserve, out of sight. The problem was—
how many men and ships had Thorkell left behind? Saor
had seen three, at this Pooltiel. But he had not seen into
Loch Dunvegan itself. There might be more there, probably
were. What was the sort of minimum force which would be
needed to deal with these?

Nobody could help Somerled there. He went striding up
and down the Kinlochscresort beach, alone, to think the
thing out.

He came back presently, mind made up. Thorkell was
said to have more than twelve ships with him—if this was
an accurate account. He was a powerful Viking, but no
prince, and so was not likely to be able to muster much
more than a score of vessels at the most. Which would mean
that he could not have left behind more than seven or eight,
if that. There might, indeed, be little more than the three
already seen.

So here was the plan. They would sail tonight, no more
than six ships—but these each carrying more than the usual
number of men, leaving the other fourteen craft hidden
here. In the darkness they would make for Loch Bracadale
and disembark many of the men there, to cross the hills to
Dunvegan. Then the six ships would sail on northwards,
round to Loch Dunvegan, to make a joint attack by sea and
land—but allowing escapers. Then they would do some
burning, as at Moidart, to help the effect—and wait. Conn
Ironhand would remain in charge here at Rhum, with look-
outs posted on the mountain-tops. When they saw the
Norse ships returning, they would make smoke signals—it
would look merely as though Rhum also was being
harried—and this would warn them on Skye. Conn would
then be ready to sail out, behind Thorkell's fleet, to aid in
their defeat. Was it understood? Could any improve on it?

Even Saor could find no fault with that. The thing was
accepted.

They waited until dusk, then, which was later than they
would have liked, in the northern early summer, and transferred some hundreds of men from the ships to be left
behind. They had set out with almost two thousand, and
now Somerled took almost half of them, without leaving
the rest actually undermanned. Heavily-laden, the chosen

five followed the dragon-ship eastwards along Loch Scresort, to turn northwards into the wan, murky relics of the sunset.

Time was vitally important now, for even this half-dark would not last much more than five hours. They had at least twenty miles to go to the mouth of Loch Bracadale, and once within that loch they would have to go very slowly, to avoid in the darkness all the islets and reefs with which it was strewn. Somerled wanted to be able to look into Loch Dunvegan by sunrise, if possible—which would demand hard going. So it was all hands to the oars, the gongs beating fast on the night air, a strange, urgent, yet eerie sound, phosphorescent spray flying. They had plenty of rowers admittedly and fortunately fresh wind persisted from the south-west.

They were off Loch Bracadale in two hours—although it was difficult to identify features in the gloom, especially with the loch-mouth over four miles wide. However there was the island of Wiay, a mile long and rising quite high, almost central, and this they could hardly miss.

Threading their way thereafter through the innumerable skerries and tidal rocks within the irregularly-shaped loch, which was really a vast bay with inlets, the ships had to creep cautiously, heading north by east now with almost four miles of these difficult waters to cover to reach the head of the shallow, narrow arm called Loch Vatten. Here indeed they made a false move in the mirk, groping their way into a side inlet thereof and quickly finding themselves in trouble in weed-hung constriction, and having to back out again, Somerled fretting at the delay. But eventually they accepted that they were at the head of this Vatten, for they could get no further, and dogs barking over on higher ground to their right indicated dwellings, presumably the small township of that name.

Here the four hundred extra men were put ashore, with Saor to command. They were to climb north-westwards over the rising ground, by a sort of modest pass, and down to salt-water again at the southern head of Loch Dunvegan, some four miles. In the dark, and over difficult country, this would take them a couple of hours—but anyway it would require longer for the ships to sail round the coast. The men were to wait in hiding just short of Kilmuir, as the main Dunvegan township was called, until the flotilla actually came into the mouth of that loch and Somerled signalled the advance from the dragon-ship.

So the six vessels had to crawl their way back through the islets again, out of Bracadale. By the time that they were into the open sea, Somerled reckoned that they had less than an hour till dawn, and sixteen or seventeen sea-miles to cover to Dunvegan Head. Most evidently they were going to be later than intended with their assault, however hard he made the oarsmen work.

The coast here, cliff-bound and barren with the seas spouting whitely, took a major dog's-leg bend at the blunt headland of Moonen; and it was whilst approaching this, still fully seven miles short of Dunvegan Head itself, that they began to see the paling of the sky to the east, behind the black loom of high land.

Disappointing timing as this was, it did produce a certain advantage, in that just beyond Moonen was the quite small inlet of Loch Pooltiel, only a mile or so deep. And by the time that they passed the entrance to this it was sufficiently light to see in—and clearly there were no ships moored there, only some fishing-boats drawn up below a scattering of cabins. This was to the good.

Dunvegan Head now towered before them, with enormous cliffs rearing to lofty hills close to the coast. Rounding the clenched fist of this, Loch Dunvegan opened, slanting back south-eastwards.

It proved to be much deeper than Somerled had recollected, five or six miles of it, at least, nearly a couple of miles wide, open at first but with a shallow, islet-dotted head. It was too far to see what shipping there might be up there amongst the islets—and certainly too far for Saor to be able to see any signals from himself. Nothing for it but to turn in and sail up-loch, risky as this could be.

They had to go a long way, probably four miles, before they could see details ahead—which worried Somerled, although there was no sign of any opposition. The islets in front were all low, fortunately, mere holms of rock and grass, so that they did not hide too greatly features behind. Two items stood out boldly—a circular Pictish broch, a beehive-shaped refuge-tower, on a bluff to the left; and right ahead on a steep knoll, the ramparts of an ancient fort, obviously the dun of the name Dunvegan. Around this were the typical sail-cloth awnings of the Norsemen, ten or twelve of them apparently.

They did not perceive the ships, however, until they were level with the ruined broch, and then it was only masts which they saw, rising from behind one of the larger islets, the most southerly, five masts hitherto almost indistinguishable against the background of stone and whin-bushes. Five, only five—better by far than it might have been.

Somerled gave orders for the signal-flag to be hoisted to the dragon-ship's masthead. They could see no sign of Saor's men but surely they would be in position long ere this?

They were. The flag had not been up for long before the flood of men appeared, pouring over a lip of ground a little way behind the fort and awnings. They disappeared again almost as quickly, for clearly there was a dip in the land behind the dun. The tide of men did not reappear—so it was to be assumed that they were in contact with the enemy there, out of sight.

Somerled debated with himself what to do. Should he land some of the ships' crews to Saor's aid? This was what he had intended, but with only five enemy craft involved apparently, would help be required? The Norsemen would have seen the Argyll vessels long ere this, surely, early in the morning as it was, and therefore would be expecting attack from the sea. They could not number many more than Saor had, if that—and would be taken by surprise over the landward assault. The chances were, then, that they would be very much on the defensive, and be apt to make a break for their longships. In which case, it would be wiser and more effective to wait for them out here, afloat?

He held his ships about a quarter-of-a-mile from the island behind which the five masts showed, though somewhat doubtful. It was difficult, not being able to see what went on ashore.

For what seemed a very long time there was no visible development at all, and Somerled was about to send in one ship to learn what was happening, when Gillecolm noticed movement. Not of men but of those slender sticks of masts.

Three of them had begun to move, only three. They were edging southwards. Uncertain what this might mean, Somerled still delayed.

In a minute or two, three longships came into view at the south end of the islet, sails still furled. They were moving only slowly, clearly with very few oars manned. The impression given was of scanty survivors very limpingly fleeing the scene. Somerled ignored the urgings of his son and others to dash forward to take them. Two questions struck him. If so few had escaped, why take three ships? Would it not have been more effective to use one vessel, all oars fully manned? Secondly, heading southwards like that would seem the less likely direction to take. There were no more islets to dodge amongst that way, whereas there were a dozen and more to the north. Moreover, as far as they could see this course could only lead them into the long southernmost arm of the loch, a dead-end, unless they turned sharply westwards round the islet, directly towards the Argyll ships—which they showed no sign of doing.

As he watched, a notion came to Somerled. This did not make sense—therefore it could be only a decoy. Intended to lure him into that arm of the loch, after the escapers. And then? Why—the two other hidden ships would bolt out *northwards*, their route open, and so get away. It could be that.

Gillecolm's impatience was only enhanced when at last the figures of men reappeared on the scene, on rising ground to the south of the fort area. They were over half-a-mile away but it was apparent that they were wearing kilts— Saor's people. Apparent too that they were trying to convey a message, waving plaids and pointing, pointing northwards. Somerled took it that they were confirming his own assessment, wanting him to know that the true escape attempt would be to the north and that these three going south was a device. Well, he required some to escape, to tell Thorkell, didn't he? These Norsemen were playing his game for him. He moved now, leading his ships in towards the three false escapers now entering the long southern arm of Loch Dunvegan. Saor's men visibly grew the more urgent, no doubt in frustration.

Somerled was not concerned with them, however. He

was watching those two remaining masts. In a short while indeed he would be in a position to see behind the islet, to observe what went on. He did not have to wait that long. He saw the masts beginning to move, and northwards—and then he noted that, unlike the three, these had hoisted sails—for of course they had the benefit of the southerly breeze. It was all as he had calculated. He gave them a minute or two to win a lead and then, for the looks of the thing, detached two of his own craft to turn back to pretend to try to head them off—but on no account to catch them.

He ordered Maguire onwards with his three remaining vessels, after the first trio—which they would no doubt find abandoned, in due course, up in the loch's narrows—and himself turned the dragon-ship in, to make a landfall where the five had lain behind the islet.

There, presently, he met his foster-brother, well content with the morning's work.

Saor had perceived the developing situation and now made no criticism, for once. His own activities had been successful, his four hundred achieving near-surprise of the Norse camp. He reckoned that there were less than three hundred of the enemy altogether, and the struggle in the hollow behind the dun had been little more than a token resistance, with their main concern undoubtedly the Argyll ships behind. Not a great many of the Vikings had been slain before the rest broke and bolted over the ridge for their own vessels. He had not realised the significance of their escaping ruse at first.

Dermot Maguire was soon back, declaring that he had come up with the three longships about a mile up the inlet, where it shallowed, deserted by the skeleton crews who had decamped inland amongst the low wooded hills, probably no more than fifty men altogether. He had not attempted any pursuit; these would be no danger.

Look-outs on the dun reported that the two escaping vessels were now well out towards the open sea, at speed, and the supposed pursuers had turned back.

So far so good. The question now was how long until, hopefully, they might expect Thorkell Svensson back? The Uists, North and South, and Barra, at the south end of the outer isles chain, lay variously between twenty-five miles and forty-five miles to the west and south-west. It would take those two ships some five hours, tacking, to get to all but North Uist, against a south-westerly wind. Then they would have to find Thorkell, who could be anywhere in a very large area. And Thorkell would have to reassemble his raiding bands—which might take some considerable time if they were spread over the island-chain. So they could take it that Thorkell could not be expected back at Dunvegan in less than, say, fifteen hours at the earliest, more probably somewhat later. Which would bring them to at least midnight. First light next morning, then.

Meantime they had much to do.

*   *   *

Sunrise saw most of them in place and Somerled's dispositions made, as far as was possible. Assuming that all went as foreseen—and Thorkell did make a return—today's engagement would be in two distinct actions; and the first would be the more difficult almost certainly. With only one-third of his total force, he had to cope with the Norsemen until Conn and the rest came up. They would be much outnumbered and so must employ delaying tactics. This would have to be a sea-battle, for best use of his resources, and should preferably be fought within the confines of Loch Dunvegan itself. So he had disposed his ships—nine now, with the captured three, and plenty of men to man them—as best he could. The main loch was between four and five miles long by about one-and-a-half broad, and fairly regular, with no deep bays or inlets until its islet-dotted head. So there was not a great deal of choice as to strategic manoeuvre. There were two small islands right at the mouth however, the Lampays, close to the eastern horn. Somerled had stationed himself, in his dragon-ship, and two other vessels, in the narrow channel behind these, with the rest of his ships hidden amongst the islets at the head. From here he would be in a position to move out for an over-all view of the scene; could seek to block the loch-mouth if there should be any break-back on the enemy's part before Conn's fleet appeared; and would be well placed to take charge of his main force when it did arrive. Saor commanded at the loch-head.

The wind had dropped overnight and day dawned quiet and grey—save for the glow of fires landwards, although these were fading now and the pall of smoke thinning, for they had made merely a token burning, to be visible on the night sky from the outer islands. The local people had been, as usual, only moderately enthusiastic over their delivery, cowed and apprehensive, as well they might be. The women who, as ever, had been found at the Norse encampment, were resigned, apathetic.

So the Argyll men waited as the light grew stronger. Somerled had lookouts posted on the highest point of his islands, which was not very lofty.

The hours passed, and these failed to make any signal.

By mid-forenoon Somerled was growing concerned. Would Thorkell fail them, after all? Would he perhaps decide to write off Skye and stay in the Outer Hebrides? Surely not, with these generally considered to be the preserve of the Orkney pirates.

It was nearly noon before the look-outs sent their first signal—sails in sight to the west. Half-an-hour later they were able to sign down the numbers of the ships approaching—seventeen. This would be Thorkell.

The mood of waiting changed dramatically now. None required to have pointed out to them the initial dangers for Somerled's people, in especial those on the three craft out here at the loch-mouth. If they should be spotted early on, hiding there, then their chances of survival were not great—although they might just make their escape out to the open sea. Somerled sent a man up to warn the look-outs to lie very low on the skyline.

Presently signals indicated that the leading ships of the fleet were entering the loch. There was no indication that Conn's force was in sight.

The worst danger would be when the incoming craft were well into the loch, and if any of their crews looked back—and, of course, the oarsmen did face the stern; if they were to raise their eyes half-right, then there could be the possibility of catching sight of the three hiding vessels. Somerled had his rowers with oars poised, ready to pull off the moment he gave the order, seawards.

But there was no need. The loch-mouth was wide, well

over a mile, and when the Norse ships came into view they were far over to the other, western, side, and so at a poor angle for seeing in behind the Lampays. Moreover they were all very evidently concerned only with what was in front, driving in in tremendous style in a positive curtain of spray from lashing oars—which could not but restrict rearwards vision. They were in notably close order, too, not strung out in file, making a most impressive naval phalanx. Thorkell Svensson was clearly intent on major vengeance.

Still no signal, from the look-outs, of Conn's coming.

Somerled waited until the Norse ships were fully halfway up the loch and then gave the command to move. They pulled out north-about round the island and into the open loch-mouth, leaving the look-outs on their height—for because of the towering Dunvegan Head there was no prospect westwards from sea-level. They drew out into mid-loch, well apart, to be the more evident.

At first there was no obvious reaction and Somerled wondered whether to sail in up-loch some way, to draw attention to themselves—for the sake of Saor and the others on the six vessels hiding amongst the loch-head islets, who must by now be feeling distinctly alarmed at the dimensions and determined aspect of the Norse threat. But then there was some apparent development, a change in the compact enemy formation, which presently was seen to be six longships breaking off, to turn in a wide arc and to head back northwards.

Six to three—better than seventeen to three, at least. And this would considerably aid Saor. Somerled signalled for his two escorts to close in again on the dragon-ship, for mutual support. They would make as difficult a hedgehog as possible for those six to dispose of.

They were awaiting the onslaught in close order when Gillecolm's strange but very keen eyes once more proved their worth. Reaching for his father's arm, he pointed. Their two look-outs back on the highest Lampay had abandoned their hiding posture. At about a mile's distance they were difficult to see clearly but apparently they were dancing about and waving something, perhaps clothing or a whin branch. Whatever they were at, there could be only one reason for their excitement—Conn's fleet must be in sight from there, and not too far off, to account for the urgency.

This assumption caused Somerled to change his tactics abruptly. No sense in engaging in a desperate fight against odds if this was unnecessary. There would be plenty of fighting hereafter. He ordered his three ships to turn and head seawards—but not too fast to discourage the Norsemen and cause them to turn back.

They had over a mile northwards to go before they could see seawards of Dunvegan Head—by which time the pursuers were less than half-a-mile behind and coming on hard. Then, as Somerled was beginning to doubt whether he had rightly interpreted his look-outs' signs, with the sea westwards still open, empty, shouts turned his head to leeward. There, close in under the soaring cliffs, came Conn Ironhand and his fleet, hugging the coast, and not a mile away, having been almost too good at keeping themselves out of sight of the Norsemen. With an explosive exclamation of thankfulness, Somerled's mind switched to the task of coping to best advantage with a dramatically altered situation.

He restrained the impulse to turn in towards the oncoming Conn, but in fact ordered increased speed and continued to head off westwards. If Conn swung over to join him on this course it might not spoil anything. The prime necessity was to entice those six Viking ships further out, so that Conn could drive across behind them and cut them off.

Conn could have no inkling of these circumstances, of course; but with the Vikings behind so close now, it should very quickly become apparent what was happening.

For a few tense minutes the situation seemed to remain unaltered, all three groups continuing on as though unaware of developments. Then Conn's fleet could be seen to be dividing. Four vessels swung out further north-westwards, towards Somerled's trio, the other ten heading straight on, north-eastwards.

"Thank God—he has his wits about him!" Somerled exclaimed, "He has seen them and guessed aright."

It took a little while for the Norsemen to perceive their danger, in the eagerness of their pursuit. When they did, there was swift, all but frenzied, reaction. With a mighty splashing of oars the six ships started to wheel directly round, to make a dash back whence they had come.

Somerled's three promptly did the same.

Now, suddenly, it became a race indeed, Conn's ten to close the gap of the loch-mouth, the Norse to get through first, Somerled and the other four to catch up. Fortunately for the Argyll force the enemy had come just too far out of the loch to be able to get back in time.

When this became apparent and the Norsemen saw that they were going to clash with the ten, in desperation they turned again. Somerled's ships were only a few hundred yards from them.

It was a dramatic moment, the six and three face to face at close range. Somerled, for one, did not hesitate. Straight at the group of Norsemen he drove the dragon-ship.

It was, of course, a question of nerve—and the Norse were already to some extent unnerved, seeking escape. Someone had to take avoiding action—and it was not the dragon-ship. At the last moment two of the enemy vessels veered away left and right, to avoid a crash.

Somerled made swift assessment, and grabbing the steering-oar from Gillecolm, swung hard over, to starboard, shouting to his rowers. Those on that side promptly raised their long dripping oars high—they were well-trained in this manoeuvre—and the leeward men pulled the more strongly. Down on the right-hand Norse the dragon-ship smashed—and before the enemy rowers could be warned to raise their oars.

It was bloody havoc. The bows of the larger ship sheered down the side of its victim like an axe through brushwood, the long oars snapping and splintering, tossing, spearing and mangling their handlers in indescribable butchery. In mere moments that fine ship was a reeling, reeking shambles of screaming men, yawing round helplessly.

As the dragon-ship scraped viciously past, Somerled, grim-faced, ordered his starboard oars to be lowered again, and pulled his vessel round in the tightest of turns. Ignoring the temporarily crippled craft, he drove on for the nearest Norseman, which was in circling battle now with one of the Argyll escorts. Preoccupied with this, its shipmaster delayed too long in drawing off and saving his oars. Down on this vessel's starboard side the dragon-ship bored—and although the impact was less terrible here, and the carnage less—for the stern facing oarsmen could see the menace bearing down on them and some raised oars in consequence, unordered—much damage was done and the longship meantime spun round out of control.

Shouting and signalling to the escort's master to deal with this, Somerled swept on.

But now the four detached craft from Conn's fleet were coming up, and with the ten behind swinging in on them, the remaining Norsemen wisely decided that the odds were altogether too great, broke off and headed desperately for the open sea. The second escort managed to corner the last one between itself and the oncoming four, and seeing its position as hopeless, this craft yielded tamely. But the other three looked like making good their escape.

Somerled, seeing his ships swinging off in pursuit, banged on Gillecolm's great gong urgently, to draw attention, and went on banging, signing to all to give up the chase and close in on him. He was worried about Saor and Maguire.

Leaving his escorts to cope with and put skeleton crews on the three disabled enemy ships, he rowed to meet Conn.

*   *   *

It was, by any standards, an impressive array of ships which drove up Loch Dunvegan, no fewer than twenty now—for to Somerled's three and Conn's fourteen were added the three captured craft, although these were scarcely in fighting trim, with their surviving crewmen working reduced oars under threat from their captors. They would make a daunting sight for Thorkell and his people at the loch-head—whose ships would now number only eleven.

The question was, how many of Saor's six survived?

Even as they drew fairly close to the maze of islets, it was difficult to perceive and assess what went on there. Ships and masts could be seen shifting and straggling amongst the holms and skerries, but there was no distinguishing who was what, nor any pattern discernible. There would *be* no pattern, to be sure, Saor's obvious tactics being to double and dodge and hide, avoiding actual conflict as far as possible until reinforcements came up. How successful he had been remained to be seen—but at least there was still much movement in process, which would imply that the situation was still fluid.

In the circumstance, Somerled came to the conclusion that an attitude of confident superiority was called for meantime, instead of plunging head-long into more action—since he certainly had no ambitions to get involved in all that dodging and scurrying amongst the islets. There was that low headland jutting out on the east side, on which the ruined broch sat, a fairly modest feature in itself but narrowing the loch there considerably; which was no doubt why the broch was sited there. At this point the loch was little more than half-a-mile wide, and barely a mile from its head. If he could block that . . .?

Even twenty ships solidly take up nothing like half-a-mile of water, of course; but ranked in a single line, each could be near enough to its neighbours to ensure that no approaching vessel could win through without a struggle. Somerled so ordered.

In took a little while for any reaction to become apparent ahead. But gradually it was evident that centrally amongst those islets ships were coming together, concentrating. Sails were of no use to any in these close waters, so that it was not possible to identify them from the painted symbols thereon, whether Norse raven or Argyll galley. But since the assembling group was soon larger than six, these were obviously the enemy.

Thorkell seemed to be at a loss as to what to do. At least, the Norse concentration remained more or less stationary behind a central scatter of low holms. Other vessels appeared here and there, now, on the move, presumably Saor's. Two of these, presently, came dashing out from the extreme eastern corner of the maze, not far from the broch-headland itself, towards the waiting line. As they drew close, one proved to be Dermot Maguire's ship.

He came straight to the dragon-ship, to shout that the fleet had been the devil's own time in arriving, that they had been hunted like deer, that one of their vessels was stranded on a reef, that another had been captured, by the Norse. He did not know where Saor was.

Somerled directed him, and the other newcomer, to take

place in the line. Then he signalled the entire array to move slowly forward.

He reckoned that, although the loch widened again a little, they could move a quarter-mile closer to the enemy, and with the two extra craft could still block the channel effectively.

The aspect of creeping menace, twenty-two ships, must have been alarming for the waiting foe—of whom there appeared to be only ten in the group.

Then another longship appeared scurrying out of the north-eastern corner, and quickly identified itself as Saor's own. Somerled was much relieved to see his foster-brother safe, but cut short the shouted exchange. He ordered Saor to take the dragon-ship's place in the centre of the line, and he himself moved on, closer to the enemy, alone.

As he saw it, Thorkell had only two options now. He could come out and fight, outnumbered more than two-to-one; or else he could beach his ships and flee inland, or try to put up a fight at the fort. He believed that the Vikings would choose the first, cherishing their ships as they did. In these close waters it would be a dire struggle, but some of the ten might possibly make good their escape. His present approach was to challenge them to attempt just that.

He ventured to within half-a-mile of the enemy behind their screen of skerries, hoping to coax them out—for the dragon-ship, larger than the others, could be taken to contain the opposing leader. He was not taking any very great risks, however, for with half-as-many oars again as the general run of longships, he could probably out-row any attack.

His move did achieve a reaction—but not what he had looked for. One Norse craft detached itself from the rest and came rowing slowly round the reefs towards him.

So Thorkell thought to parley—unusual choice for a Viking? And yet, of course, once before this one had come parleying, to Ardtornish.

The Norseman advanced only so far beyond the islets, fairly evidently seeking to ensure that he could scuttle back to cover if need be. Somerled moved forward to within hailing distance.

He took the initiative. "Is that Thorkell Svensson, the pirate?" he shouted. "I, Somerled, ask it."

"I am Thorkell, yes," came back. "What do you here, far from Argyll?"

"I come for *you*, Thorkell! I warned you, that day, to keep away from my territories. Yet your barbarians savaged my Gigha. Now, you pay."

"That was mistaken, Somerled. Ketil Left Hand made mistake . . ."

"Mistake, yes. *I* make no mistakes, ravager, wrecker! Nor will you, again. This is the end, Thorkell."

There was a pause. "We need not fight," came across the water, at length.

It was Somerled's turn to ponder.

"We can come to terms," Thorkell shouted, further.

"Terms? What terms can *you* offer, man? I hold you in the palm of my hand."

"Many men will die, if we fight. *Your* men."

"Many have already died. Women and children also. At your hands."

"There need be no more, King Somerled. If I leave here. These isles."

"Nor if you are dead!"

"I will not die easily, I promise! And kill you first, if I may! So consider."

"I hear nothing to consider."

"If I give you all Skye, at no cost? For always. Is that nothing?"

"It is not yours to give." But Somerled paused again. "You *would* come back. As you came back to Argyll, to Gigha."

"No. I swear it. I will not come back. Nor any of mine."

"You are not eager to fight, Thorkell!"

"You outnumber me. My men are weary with much rowing. Is it agreed? A bargain?"

"Not so fast! You have ten ships remaining. I could sink them all. Or I might take six. Leave you four. To take you away. Out of my Hebrides. Outer as well as these. To Ireland. Or Orkney. Or Iceland. Or back to your Norway. Or to Hell itself! But never again the isles. How say you to that, pirate?"

In only moments the reply came back. "Accept."

It was as easy as that. Thorkell Svensson, surly now,

agreed to go back to his ships, decant all his men into four of them, and sail off, leaving the rest—on Somerled's sworn oath that they would not be molested as they departed.

The vessels each turned back to their own groups.

So presently four much-overladen enemy longships came rowing out from behind the islets, in file, to thread through the narrow gap in the Argyll line which the dragon-ship left open between itself and Saor's craft. Men jeered and cheered and fists were shaken—but no physical obstacle was offered as the Norsemen headed northwards for the open sea.

Later, the victors found the six abandoned ships, oars missing but otherwise in fair order, run aground on the holms. More important, they found their own three missing craft, two also aground and one drifting abandoned, but the crews ashore and more or less unhurt.

Thus, with scarcely the loss of a man, Somerled MacFergus became Lord of Skye and all its appendages, a huge addition to his domains. More important perhaps, the Norse presence on this entire seaboard was eliminated. As vital could be the proof to all it might concern that Somerled was still the Mighty—in case there had been any doubts.

He set out to explore his new territories.

PART THREE

CHAPTER 16

The dragon-ship was sailing south again, in fine weather, alone, with no single escort, so safe these years had become the Hebridean Sea, thanks to Somerled's rule and dominance. The Norsemen kept their distance, Stephen was tamed and David's Scotland was comparatively law-abiding. It was midsummer, the year was 1153, and the family were on their way to inspect progress at Saddail in Kintyre.

This business of abbey-building Somerled had found more difficult than he had foreseen. Although he had collected a number of stone-masons for his castle-building programme, now more or less complete, none of these had any experience in the elaborations and special skills of erecting abbeys and great churches; and he was determined that this monument to his kingdom and line should be no humble edifice but worthy of comparison with the shrines King David was putting up in such numbers, even though smaller. And of course there was no native tradition of fine stone buildings in the Highlands and Islands, where the Celtic Church had other ideas. So work had been held up time and again over these years. But fairly recently he had acquired a new monkish mason, who had been completing work on a chapter-house at Rushen Abbey on Man; and now, with summer upon them again, Somerled was taking his family on what was something of a holiday, to see how the work went and to plan further developments.

He had become very much a family man these last years, and gladly so. Ragnhilde's fertility was as notable as her other excellences. She had presented him with two more sons, Ranald and Angus, to add to Dougal, and of course Anna, everyone's pet. They were all aboard the dragon-ship, which in consequence presently much belied its name and style, seemingly more nursery-ship than leader of a war-fleet dreaded in all the Western Ocean, whatever its tough oarsmen thought—although its captain at least had no objections, for Gillecolm doted on the children. Now in his later twenties, and a big strapping young man physically, and an excellent shipmaster, in many ways he was still a child himself and clearly would be always. Somerled no longer felt embarrassed and uncomfortable with him, with three other fine and normal sons; indeed he had developed a real affection for his peculiar first-born. Ragnhilde had loved him from the first.

They had left Islay at sun-up, Finlaggan Castle there become their summertime home, and not rushing it, before noon were closing the Mull of long Kintyre, notorious for its difficult seas and tide-races. In consequence, Gillecolm was using the off-shore island of Sanda as breakwater as they made their broadside-on turn against the great Atlantic swell, when they came, as it were, face-to-face with a fairly large fishing-boat using the same tactics but in the other direction. There was nothing unusual about this, save that normally such craft would hastily and prudently keep their distance from all war-vessels; whereas this one, after a minute or two, actually turned to head towards them. Men in fact could be seen waving, as though urgently.

As they drew near, a young man richly-dressed, it appeared, and no fisherman, could be seen as principal waver. It was Gillecolm's keen eyes, or perhaps some instinct, which identified him.

"Donald!" he cried. "It is Donald."

Somerled certainly would not have known his nephew, now a slender handsome figure, for it was over ten years since he had seen him, then a mere youth. But Gillecolm was sure—and the waver certainly seemed eager enough to join them. No doubt he recognised the great galley-device painted on the dragon-ship's sail and the personal standard of the Lord of the Isles.

As the great and small craft came together, the young man shouted. "My lord! My lord Somerled—it is I! Donald—Donald MacEth. Well met, Uncle—well met!"

When they had aided him aboard and dismissed the hired fishing-boat with suitable payment, amidst incoherent greetings, with Gillecolm all but weeping with joy, introductions

292

to Ragnhilde and the children, it transpired that Donald was in fact on his way to see Somerled and this fortuitous encounter the more fortunate—for haste was essential it seemed, with every day vital. This came out in something of a gabble. He was afraid that he might be pursued.

"Pursued?" Somerled exclaimed. "You mean that you are in flight? That you have left your father and mother, at David's court? Fled?"

"Yes—it was necessary. They are in danger, great danger. We all were. I had to come to you. Nowhere else we could turn . . ."

"But why? What danger? Malcolm—he has not been plotting again? Against David?"

"No, no—not that. David is dead. Did you not know?"

"Dead? David the King! Oh, no—not that! The good David . . ."

"He died weeks ago. In late May. At Caer Luel. He is now buried at Dunfermline. And all is now changed. We are in much danger . . ."

"David! He was my friend. Gone—dear Lord, David gone! How? How did he die?"

"He had been failing. Ever since his son Henry died, last year. He seemed to lose all taste for living. He ate little, spent his days brooding and in prayer. While his Normans grasped the power. Now they have the young King and his two brothers in their hands, David's grandsons, and all is lost. Malcolm, now King, is but sixteen years, and weak, feeble."

"All changed indeed, to my sorrow. But not all lost, lad. You say that your father is in danger? Even your mother?"

"The Normans have always hated him. They would have had him slain, long ago. David and he became friends—they were uncle and nephew—and the Normans resented it. Now, they have the power, with the young King their puppet. They can do as they will."

"Your father is one of the Seven Earls of Scotland, one of the *Ri* who appoint the King, grandson of Malcolm the Third and Margaret. They would not dare to harm him now, after all these years, and insult the people of Scotland?"

"The Frenchmen care nothing for that. They have him,

and my mother, in close confinement now. There was talk of slaying him. We decided that I should escape from Rook's Burgh and come to you for help."

Somerled stared at him, mind busy.

"What can you do?" Ragnhilde asked unhappily.

"I must think. This changes all. My oath of fealty was to David—him only. I am no longer bound by it. I must do something. I cannot leave my sister and her husband to their fate at the hands of their enemies. I never loved these Normans—nor they me. Hugo de Morville was the best of them, the Constable. What of him, Donald?"

"He is our friend, I think. But only he. The Marischal, the Steward, Bruce, Comyn, Baliol, Soulis, Lindsay and the rest, are against us."

"What do you want my husband to do?" Ragnhilde demanded.

"I do not know, lady," the young man admitted. "But something. He is strong, powerful. All the North would heed him. Most of the other earls, weak crew as they are. Something is possible, surely. Who else can we turn to?"

"I shall think on it," Somerled said. "We go to Saddail, where my new abbey is a-building. There I shall decide . . ."

*   *   *

Somerled's initial action, with speed essential, could only be in the nature of representations, threat and ultimatum inferred. He would send urgent message to the new young King of Scots, Malcolm the Fourth, declaring that he was no longer vassal to the Scots crown, since his allegiance had been personal to David; demanding good and fair treatment for his good-brother and sister, the Earl and Countess of Ross; requiring assurances of their welfare; and if these were not forthcoming promptly, promising that he would use armed force, rouse the North, indeed all Celtic Scotland, against the alien power presently surrounding the throne—although he would pray God that this would not be necessary. He would also approach his goodsire, Olaf of Man, for similar action.

The problem was, of course, who to send to deliver this message? To a monarch, it could not be any humble courier but somebody substantial. But with the urgency of the situation there was no time to send back to Islay or Ardtornish or elsewhere in his far-flung domains for suitable personages—in which he was notably weak anyway. The only people he had brought along on this trip, other than the family, were Farquhar MacFerdoch, Abbot of Glendochart, and the Romish priest from Man, Wilfrith, who now acted as his secretary and Ragnhilde's chaplain—brought because they could be helpful with the abbey-building. Farquhar was no true cleric, of course, only a hereditary abbot of the Columban Church, a secular figure, custodian of the staff, bell and altar of St. Fillan. But he had the title and was a chieftain in his own right, and Somerled had appointed him nominally responsible for much of the abbey project. The priest Wilfrith was really of more use in this, to be sure, knowing more about real abbeys, having been trained in one.

Somerled had little choice, then, but to send Farquhar MacFerdoch to the Scottish court as his emissary. He could send Wilfrith too; as a true Roman cleric he could, as it were, speak the language the Normans understood—Ragnhilde suggesting that he call himself Prior of Saddail for the occasion, as sounding better. Somerled toyed with the idea of sending back Donald with them, but recognised that he might well be seized and held as valuable hostage—after all he was in the direct line of the old royal house.

So the pair of very reluctant envoys were primed with instructions for their mission, with half-a-dozen of MacKay of Saddail's men as escort, and sent off in the dragon-ship for Eskmouth on Solway, from whence they would make their way to Rook's Burgh. They were promised that a longship would be sent to pick them up again in perhaps one week's time, so that the dragon-ship could return here as required.

None pretended that it would be a pleasant embassage.

All this cast something of a shadow over their Saddail stay, but for the children's sake they made the best of it. Donald was impatient that they should be wasting precious time on stone-masonry and the like when his parents were in dire danger, but admitted that he did not know what better they could be doing in the interim. They had to wait for reaction from Rook's Burgh before they could decide on any further moves. Anyway, they had to await the dragon-ship's return.

Their abbey had progressed far enough, however slowly, to begin to be quite impressive, the cruciform church building furthest ahead naturally and the cloister-garth and monastic outworks little more than foundations as yet. Impressive for its site and situation, that is, rising out of the Highland wilderness, for compared with the great Lowland abbeys it was hardly that. The church, with its double rows of octagonal pillars partially decorated with intricate Celtic carving of interlacing design, and mythical animals, after the fashion of the renowned high crosses, had not yet reached wallhead and roof-level, and was one-hundred-and-thirty-six feet long by twenty-four wide, the transept measuring seventy-eight feet, the narrowness of it all emphasising the length and height. There had been an argument about the level of the chancel flooring, Wilfrith wanting it raised two or three steps above nave and transept, Somerled and Farquhar contending that there was no tradition in the Columban Church of the clergy being raised higher than the other worshippers; however the priest pointed out that the increased elevation also assisted visibility by the congregation of what went on at the altar, and a compromise was reached of raising by one step. The cloister-garth had to be on the south side, on account of availability of level land on the platform site, the cloisters themselves being modest in size, fifty-eight feet square, with the abbey-well enclosed. Their monk-mason, a lay brother of the Cistercian Order from Wales, named Idris, had a team of only eight local men to assist him. Somerled offered more but was told that further untrained hands would be of little value. Skilled stone-carvers were what was required, for the decorative work. It was too soon for the woodworkers, although many would be required eventually.

The visitors were duly gratified, if a little disappointed at the apparent slowness of progress. They tried to help where they could but found their efforts little appreciated by the dedicated workers, and were quite prepared to call a halt when, on the third day, the dragon-ship returned. The fact was that the adults at least had their thoughts preoccupied elsewhere. They did not long delay their embarkation thereafter, to head back for Islay.

At Gigha, where a couple of longships were now permanently stationed, they called in, and sent one of these to collect Farquhar and Wilfrith at Eskmouth on Solway.

When they got back to Finlaggan on Islay, however, it was to find news awaiting them which had the effect of pushing rather from the forefront of their minds—Somerled's and Ragnhilde's, if not Donald's—the problem of Malcolm MacEth and his wife. Messengers had arrived from Man. Olaf Morsel was dead, assassinated. A force of Norse-Irish from troubled Dublin, led by the three sons of Olaf's late brother, Harald the Blind, had descended on Man, demanding half the kingdom; and when they were opposed, laid waste the countryside, and, gaining the presence of their uncle, at Rushen, stabbed him to death, actually cutting off his head. Their father, admittedly, was called The Blind, and sometimes worse than that, because he had been emasculated and his eyes put out by Olaf's other brother Logmann many years before, after a rebellion. These young men were now in control of the island, Ragnhilde's unsavoury half-brothers having apparently put up little or no resistance.

Ragnhilde was appalled, Somerled less so, but much perturbed. He had long recognised that Man was a danger-spot, a weak kingdom positively asking to be taken over by the unscrupulous and power-hungry, Norse or English. Olaf had managed to sit on its uneasy throne for nearly fifty years, but Somerled had long feared that it was only a question of time—and a now practically bed-ridden monarch was temptation compounded. Grievous as this was for Ragnhilde, and for Man, it was also of course a serious matter for Somerled's kingdom and lordship. Man, neighbouring realm, in wrong hands would be a constant threat. And its rulers, in the past, had from time to time called themselves Kings of the Hebrides, however nominal such claim, even though Olaf himself had never voiced any such ambition. But these aggressive Norse-Irish new-comers might look northwards. Here was a new and potent danger.

Ragnhilde's legitimate brother Godfrey should now be

lawful King of Man. But he was very much an unknown quantity, having spent most of his adult life at the court of Norway, as a semi-hostage—and was presumably in Norway still. What his reaction would be remained to be seen.

Ragnhilde's own was predictable. Of spirited Norse blood herself, she urgently demanded immediate vengeance on her father's slayers, Somerled to descend on Man with his whole power. Her husband temporised and demurred, however sympathetic. He could not do that—at least, not at this stage. This was not just some Norse pirate raid. It would mean war, full war—and possibly with Dublin also. And at a time when he might well be in trouble with the Scots Normans. They must see how her brother took this—the new King. Aid him, perhaps. What would he be apt to do? What sort of a man was he?

Ragnhilde admitted that she scarcely knew her only lawful brother. He had gone to Norway whilst she was little more than a child. She thought of him as more Norwegian than Manx. But at least he was friendly with the Norwegian King and could look for help there—if not from his sister's husband!

They must wait a little, Somerled insisted. Wait to see what transpired, in Man, in Scotland, in Norway. Only a fool would rush in, at this stage. It was too late to save her father.

They waited. In a few days the emissaries returned from Rook's Burgh, thankful to be safely back in Argyll. They were both much shaken. Farquhar declared that Scotland was a different place from heretofore, the difference scarcely to be believed. With King David's good but firm hand removed and little more than a child to succeed him, it was every man for himself, with the Normans everywhere grasping for power, lands, offices. No man's property or position—or women—was safe. They had not so much as seen the young King, the Normans about the court keeping him and his brothers hidden. They had had to give Somerled's message to the High Steward, the Marischal, the Lord Chamberlain and the High Constable, the men who now ruled Scotland—all English-born Normans. Only the last, de Morville, had been so much as civil to them.

298

They had even feared for their freedom and return to Eskmouth.

The kernel of their report was that they had obtained no assurances as to the continued well-being of the Earl and Countess of Ross. They had not even been permitted to see them. But the High Constable had assured them that they were in good health and although under sterner restraint than in the late King's time, lived in fair comfort—he, as Constable, was responsible for them. Clearly they were not to be freed, and the visitors were left in no doubt that should there be any rising in the North, led by Donald or Somerled or other supporters of the alternative royal line, Malcolm MacEth would be the first casualty. As for Somerled of the Isles himself, let him watch his step, and Donald MacEth with him; the days of David's long-sufferance were over and Norman-style rule had a longer and stronger arm—and an iron fist at the end of it.

This account brought fury from Donald, predictably, more restrained reaction from Somerled, who had anticipated little else. Indeed uncle sought to soothe nephew somewhat by pointing out that despite the arrogant threats, the object of their mission had probably been achieved, meantime. Evidently his father and mother were still to be held, but now mainly as hostages for the peaceable behaviour of the North and West. And it went without saying that dead hostages were of no use to anyone. So at least it was now probable that the Earl Malcolm and his wife were safe enough from physical harm, however grievous the restrictions on their freedom. But, after all, they had been restricted for years now, anyway.

Needless to say, this did little to satisfy Donald—or Somerled himself if the truth be told. The former wanted action—but did not see what could be done without endangering his parents—the latter perceived that any action would be premature, dangerous in the circumstances, and must be postponed. But it was postponement rather than rejection, he emphasised. Rulers must be prepared to play a waiting game—as Donald would find out if he aspired one day to be King of Scots.

So they waited. But young men, lacking major responsibilities, and footloose, usually find it harder to be patient than their elders, and presently Donald MacEth announced that he was for the mainland North, going to visit his father's earldom of Ross, to test out opinion, also Morayland, Mar, Buchan and the rest of the Celtic North, to discover the willingness and preparedness there for armed uprising against the Normans. His uncle warned against any premature overt move which could put the Earl Malcolm at risk, but otherwise was glad enough to see his nephew go. His was an unsettling presence and tended to distract Somerled's preoccupation with the most immediate danger, Man.

*   *   *

That uneasy summer passed, with rumours in plenty but no actualities to affect Argyll and the Isles. There were stories of dire happenings on Man; that Orkney was preparing to take a hand in the Manx situation; that Godfrey Olafsson was on his way; that the Norse-Irish were mustering—to what end was uncertain. On the Scottish front, the Normans were not letting the grass grow under their mailed feet either, making three different expeditions against Fergus of Galloway—whom, as a Celtic earl and nearest to their power-base, they presumably deemed a danger. Fergus it seemed had finally been cornered and now, rather than execution had allegedly chosen to become a lay-brother at the Abbey of the Holy Rood at Edinburgh, a curious fate for that individual. Clearly he was one more hostage.

This last rumour, if true—and it sounded sufficiently circumstantial—was ominous, as indicating not only the Normans' effectiveness in bringing Fergus to book but their military predilections. Actual warfare had always been a last resort with David. Now things were to be different, obviously. Somerled took note.

It was late September before any positive development of the Manx situation was revealed, when news was brought to Islay from the further-out Isle of Tiree that a great fleet of no fewer than forty-eight ships had been seen sailing southwards, nearly all bearing the spread-winged-raven device of the Earls of Orkney but the leading vessels also flying the unmistakable emblem of Man. There could be little doubt as to what this meant. Godfrey Olafsson was on his way to recover his kingdom, and had won the support of Ronald of Orkney, if not the King of Norway, to do so.

Ragnhilde was delighted but Somerled less so. It would have been courteous, he pointed out, for a large armed force to inform him before passing through his narrow seas; if they did not wish to do so, they could have taken the slightly longer and more exposed route in the open ocean beyond the Outer Isles. And that Godfrey had not asked for the help of his sister's husband in such venture was perhaps significant?

Thereafter, Somerled made it his business to learn what transpired on Man. He had not very long to wait, in this instance. The Kintyre, Galloway and Manx fishermen were always in constant touch, and great purveyors of news. Godfrey and his Orkney allies apparently had recovered the island kingdom speedily and with no great difficulty, the people rising to aid them against their oppressors. He had captured his three cousins and executed them after first putting out their eyes. He now sat secure on the throne of his fathers.

This all seemed, on the face of it, satisfactory and a resolving of one of the problems and dangers which concerned Somerled. He sent Farquhar MacFerdoch and Sir Malcolm MacGregor to congratulate his brother-in-law— and of course Ragnhilde sent her sisterly greetings. But there were no corresponding civilities on Godfrey's part; indeed the two emissaries had only a very cool reception.

On the other front, there appeared to be a lull. There were stirrings all over the North, with word of Donald being well received. Galloway seethed, the defeat and removal of its earl evidently by no means subduing that difficult and unruly province. The Normans appeared to be biding their time for the moment, with winter coming and the campaigning season past.

Somerled and his family packed up at Islay to return to winter-quarters at Ardtornish in Morvern, only a little easier in their minds.

CHAPTER 17

Ease of mind scarcely prevailed at Ardtornish in the following months, despite winter's usual inactivity; less so when they moved back to Islay with the swallows' return and the cuckoos calling. The news from Man was consistently alarming. Godfrey—he was already being called Godfrey the Black, and not for the colour of his hair or complexion—was proving to be a very different ruler from his father, moody, harsh, oppressive. Stories of savagery and tyranny were constantly reaching the neighbouring island kingdom.

Ragnhilde was much grieved. Her husband was still more so when informed that Godfrey had been heard to refer to himself as King of Man and the Hebrides—that old folly. Somerled was further angered but equally mystified when later he learned that the wretched business of the bishopric of the Isles had been taken up anew by Godfrey. He had thought, with Wimund's fall, that nonsense had been disposed of—especially as Godfrey's links were with Norway and Orkney, not with Stephen's England and the archbishopric of York. Yet the word was that Godfrey had made especial confirmation to Furness Abbey in Cumbria—where Wimund had come from, and died—of the right to nominate *his* Bishop of the Hebrides, and that chapter had actually chosen someone called Reginald for the see. The authority for this peculiar claim and development, out of Cumbria, was not explained; but it was suspiciously like part of a move on the part of Godfrey to try for power in the Hebrides. When, a month or so later, a messenger from Moray told them, amongst other tidings, that Pope Anastasius the Fourth had appointed a new Archbishop of Nidaros, in Norway, as Metropolitan of all the North, including Norway, Sweden, Denmark, Orkney, Iceland, Greenland and the Hebrides, the thing became clearer. This was not York using Man for its ambitions, as before, but Norway stealing a march on England and York, in getting round an anti-English Pope. That the Hebrides should be included in this Papal pronouncement seemed to imply that it had all been arranged between Godfrey and the Norwegian king before ever the former started out on his venture, the price of Norwegian and Orkney support.

Somerled perceived that he was going to be forced to do something about Ragnhilde's brother, unhappy situation as this was.

His thoughts in that direction were complicated however by other tidings brought by the courier from Moray, which included a message from Donald himself. It seemed that that young man was taking up a much more positive attitude than had been contemplated when he left Islay. For one thing, he was calling himself Earl of Moray as successor to his late uncle, Angus. He appeared now to be discounting the danger to his captive parents, as mere threats, arguing that the more immediate the menace in the North, the less likely the Normans were to liquidate their valuable hostages. He was getting support from all over Ross and Moray for a campaign to unseat the youthful King Malcolm and place either his father or himself on the Scots throne. Resenting the Norman grasp of power and alarmed at their military attacks on Galloway, the remaining five earls—that is Fife, Strathearn, Angus, Mar and Buchan, who with Moray and Ross made up the traditional *Ri*, the Celtic Seven Earls of Scotland who appointed the High King—had agreed in principle to rise in the MacEth cause. This was *only* in principle so far, and it was important to turn it into positive action, mobilisation. Undoubtedly the best way to achieve this would be for one powerful force to be seen to make a move as threat to the Normans, to show that all were not cowed by the example of Galloway. Only his Uncle Somerled was in any position to do this with little danger of reprisal, at this stage, having a fleet and large numbers of men available. Moreover he was brother to the imprisoned Countess. Donald was not asking for actual war—only for a muster and token invasion of the mainland, to encourage the other earls and to serve warning on the Normans.

Somerled's initial reaction was to dismiss this plea out-of-hand, as a young man's headstrong folly. But on second thoughts it occurred to him that such gesture might serve him well enough, in the other regard. To have any army mustered and a fleet gathered was possibly just what was required to give *Godfrey* pause in any dreams of taking over the Hebrides with Orkney or Norwegian help. This way he could demonstrate his preparedness and strength, in both directions, Manx and Scots, without actually declaring out-right war. If he was to descend in force on some southerly part of mainland Argyll where he would be seen to be poised equally well for an assault on Lowland Scotland or the Isle of Man—or even to go to the help of rebellious Galloway—then much good might come of it, Donald and his earls be suitably encouraged, Godfrey discouraged and the Normans given warning that any hurt to Earl Malcolm and his wife could precipitate war on three flanks, west, north and south-west. Yet in itself the move could be disclaimed as any provocation, if need be, since it would be still contained within his own kingdom of Argyll.

The more he thought on it, the better this seemed. The messengers accordingly went out all over Argyll and the Isles, to muster—not full mobilisation but sufficient to produce a major force.

All July, then, the west was mustering, from Skye down to Kintyre, from Tiree and Coll to Appin and Lochaber, for the show of strength—in no great hurry, for the longer it took the more certain the news of it reaching the desired quarters. Shipping assembled in the Sound of Mull from every port and haven on a thousand miles of seaboard. Also provisioning went on, on a large scale, for this host would have to be fed, in idleness, for some considerable time probably, certainly not living off the land where they were going, to the hurt of their own people. Somerled foresaw it all as something in the nature of a holiday for large numbers of men—and therefore to be planned very carefully if it was not to get out-of-hand. He had seen sufficient of what idle soldiery could do on David's invasion of England prior to the Battle of the Standard. Womenfolk, indeed, were to be taken along—to spare the local females somewhat—the first time Somerled had permitted camp-followers, however respectable.

So, at the beginning of August they sailed from Ardtornish, a huge fleet of almost one hundred vessels, the greatest concentration of shipping these parts had ever seen, to head southwards down the Firth of Lorne. Admittedly quite a large proportion were not longships, nor fighting-ships at all, but transports and cargo-carriers and scows bearing cattle and meal. But it made a brave display, led by the two dragon-ships—for Saor, Chamberlain of Argyll, now had his own, thanks to Thorkell Svensson, with Cathula acting his shipmaster once more. Ragnhilde and her children were there, and many other families. They were bound for Arran.

Once again they coasted down Nether Lorne, Knapdale and long Kintyre, to round the Mull and enter the wide Firth of Clyde. They turned north thereafter, for a short distance, to the southern end of the Isle of Arran.

Somerled had selected Arran with some care. It was not the mainland, as Donald desired, but it was in clear view of the Ayr and Renfrew coasts of Lowland Scotland, a mere dozen miles off. So the fleet's presence could not pass un-noticed. On the other hand, it was an island and so could not be approached and assailed by surprise. It was a large island, a score of miles long by ten wide, and so could bear this 'invasion' better than a smaller area, and next to the Mull of Kintyre itself, a barren and inhospitable place, it was the nearest to Man of all his domains. Also, this southern end was only a short distance across the Kilbrannan Sound from Saddail and the abbey.

They made a landfall at Kiscadale on the great bay between the headlands of Largybeg and Pennycross and set up a vast sailcloth encampment, after the Norse fashion, stretching along the sandy shore. Somerled had brought altogether about six thousand people, so that much organisation and settlement was called for; yet all must be prepared to re-embark at short notice. He hastened to reassure the island community and to gain their co-operation. He set up watching-posts at strategic points and made adequate commissariat arrangements. Then they settled down to wait, relying on the local fishermen to ensure that the word and threat of their presence was carried to all whom it might concern.

The waiting was not in idleness—Somerled saw to that. Indeed he contrived it all as fully and as carefully as any of his military campaigns, well aware of the problems and dangers of slackness. Feeding in itself was a major pre-occupation, of course, and many men always involved in hunting and fishing especially, as well as in more humdrum foraging. Arran was mountainous, and rich in deer and game, its rivers in trout and salmon—although sea-fishing produced the major supply. To help compensate for their large-scale presence, numbers of men were allocated to local chieftains and lairds to help in building work, wood-cutting, peat-digging and harvesting activities. Games and sports and competitions were devised, almost daily, and enter-tainments for the evenings. The time passed, with only minor problems.

Somerled and his family, with some of their closer associates, spent much time at Saddail.

The local Arran fishermen were useful in gathering as well as disseminating news, being enjoined to learn all they could from their mainland and Manx counterparts. In due course, tidings were forthcoming, some interesting. There were the expected reports, on the effects of this concen-tration of shipping and men at Arran, on various quarters, states of emergency promptly developing in the Steward's lands of Ayr and Renfrew especially, the Bishop's burgh of Glasgow in much alarm and all the Clyde basin aroused. On Man presently they learned that King Godfrey had assembled his fleet at St. Michael's Haven and was standing by. The Galloway folk were more restive than ever, always eager for trouble; and there were rumours of great move-ments of men in the North. All this was satisfactory and to be anticipated. But other news reached them, less expected. First of all, there was what almost amounted to a famine in mainland Scotland, touched off by an animal pestilence which had struck down huge numbers of cattle, draught oxen, horses and sheep, in the vital breeding months and so affected not only the beef and mutton supply but gravely interfered with the tilling of the soil and was now reflected in a disastrous harvest. This had not crossed the Firth to

Arran, fortunately, but it was seriously upsetting life in Scotland as a whole.

Then came word that the Earl Duncan of Fife had died. This was of importance, for Fife of course was the senior of the Seven Earls, and Duncan the leader on whom Donald most relied to stir up the others. This was bound to affect and delay Donald's plans.

Lastly came the news that King Stephen had died in England—and this was highly relevant to the present position in Scotland. For he had been much tamed these last years—but now was to be succeeded by Henry, Duke of Normandy, the Empress's son. Maud herself had died some years earlier, and her agreement with Stephen was that he should have her throne for his lifetime only, but thereafter her son would wear the English crown as Henry the Second. And this Henry was known to be a spirited, hot-tempered and ambitious young man—just the sort of king Scotland feared on the English throne. The Scots Normans were bound to be considerably perturbed and to start looking south—for although all English-born, David's importations from his long years as a hostage with Henry the First, they had carved power and possessions for themselves in Scotland and were as much against English domination as were the indigenous Scots.

Altogether, then, it looked as though there was unlikely to be any major trouble for Somerled and the Isles for some time to come, the Normans being preoccupied, famine prevailing and Donald's cause for the moment almost certainly held up.

With the autumn gales imminent, therefore, Somerled ordered a return home. Most of his people left Arran quite reluctantly, the general verdict being that it had all been a pleasant interlude. Whether it had been unnecessary, in the circumstances, abortive even, was impossible to tell; but it certainly had done no harm and would serve to warn all that Argyll and the Isles were not to be trifled with. And it had probably had a restraining effect on Godfrey the Black.

CHAPTER 18

Somerled's assessment proved to be accurate, and so far as Argyll and the Isles were concerned there was a fairly prolonged period of peace, or at least absence of immediate threat, two years in fact, the rest of 1154, all 1155 and much of 1156, good years for the MacFergus family, with the children developing apace—Dougal now in his sixteenth year, Anna in her fifteenth, Ranald thirteen and the youngest, Angus, eight. They were a great joy to their parents and to Gillecolm, who made himself almost their slave, his need to serve as great as his need for personal affection. It was strange how Dougal already seemed the elder of the two, a quietly reliable youth with a capacity for taking pains. Anna was going to be a beauty, dark, unlike her mother and father, vivacious and attractive, an outgoing personality. As indeed was Ranald, although his was a boisterous irrepressible nature which was going to take a deal of disciplining. Whereas young Angus was as yet diffident, sensitive, but with a streak of obstinacy which seemed at odds with the rest of him. None had the least taint of Gillecolm's trouble, happily. All treated the eldest of the family rather like a beloved dog—except when he was acting shipmaster, when they accorded him entire respect.

The summer of 1156 was over, uneventful save in domestic matters, and the royal family of the Isles had moved back to Ardtornish for the winter when, one day in October, a single strange longship came down the Sound of Mull, its sail painted with the three-legged emblem of Man. It brought a visitor to see Ragnhilde, and to a lesser extent Somerled, a fierce-looking character, pure Viking in appearance, of middle years, great down-turning moustaches and a hot eye, by name Thorfinn Ottarsson, called Oak-Hewer, one of the foremost of the Manx chieftains.

Despite his looks, Ragnhilde greeted him warmly, even

embracing him. "How good to see you, Thor, after so long," she exclaimed. "A joy!" To Somerled, she said, "You have heard me speak of Thorfinn Ottarsson, Sorley—one of the oldest of my friends. As a girl he often aided me when I needed aid, did Prince Thorfinn." Apparently he was entitled to that honorific, since he was a son of Ottar, one of the Norse Kings of Dublin..

"Prince Thorfinn's name is known to me," Somerled agreed. "Did you not lead the van of Godfrey's host at the victory of Cortcelis, last year?"

"I did so—although Godfrey has forgotten that!" the other said. "As he has forgotten much else, a curse on him!" Recollecting that he spoke in front of Godfrey's sister, he spread great hands. "I am sorry, Hilde—Queen Ragnhilde. But he is become a sore affliction, is Godfrey Olafsson. A man possessed of the Devil, I think! He is making his name hated in Man."

She shook her head unhappily. "It is sad, grievous. Why he should behave so, I do not know. But then, I scarcely know him. I thought that he was for fighting foreign wars, now? This of Dublin . . .?"

"Aye—what came of the Dublin venture?" Somerled asked. "We heard that he had gone to make himself King of Dublin. And won a great victory, at this Cortcelis. We were . . . relieved that he concerned himself with Ireland not threatening my Isles. Yet he has come back to Man, leaving Dublin . . .?"

"He won the victory, yes—or *I*, and others, won it for him! But then he learned that it was not only Muirchertach, High King of Ireland, whom he had to beat but the Norse kings, of Meath and Leinster and Munster and the rest. These, some kin of my own, misliked Olaf Morsel's son coming to take *their* Dublin. So they warned him off. He was not strong enough to fight them all, and Muirchertach. So he came home to Man. And now inflicts his spleen upon his own people."

"Why? What ails him . . .?" Ragnhilde wondered.

"He wants all for himself. He covets every man's lands and wealth and power. He has already dispossessed many—myself with the rest. I tell you . . ."

"*You*? Godfrey has dispossessed you, Thor?"

"That is why I am here. To speak for others, as well as myself. *Godfrey* must be dispossessed of his throne. Before Man itself bleeds to death, God help us!"

They stared at him.

"It has to be. This cannot go on. Everywhere there is talk of revolt, of sending to the new English King Henry for aid to unseat Godfrey. He is a fighter, is young Henry—but if he comes to Man, he will stay. Man will become but an English province."

"*That* must not be!" Somerled said grimly. "On my doorstep!"

"No. But Scotland is of no use, a boy-king in the hands of Normans who care nothing for Man. And who fear attack from their North. And Orkney and Norway are Godfrey's friends. It has to be you, King Somerled."

That man looked at his wife.

Following that glance, Thorfinn turned on Ragnhilde. "You, Queen, must see it? If you have any love for the Manx land and people. Godfrey must go, and Man have a new king on Olaf's throne. And there is only one, lawfully-born, whom Man would accept. Olaf's brother Harald had those three sons who slew your father. Godfrey slew them all. Olaf had no other lawful issue, but Godfrey and yourself. And you have sons. Man needs your eldest son, for king."

She gulped. "Dougal? Oh, no!"

"Who else? Godfrey must go, all are agreed. If King Somerled does not aid us, it will have to be England. And an end to Man's independence."

"What of the Norse-Irish? Will they not help?"

"They are at constant war with the true Irish— Muirchertach, the High King and his lesser kings. You know that. Muirchertach smarts from his defeat at Cortcelis and the death there of his brother. The Norse kinglets will not leave all, to come to Man." Thorfinn turned to Somerled. "*You* must see it, my lord King?"

"Aye. I see it. But this requires thought, much thought."

"Think you then, my lord. And you, Hilde. For Man's very life is at stake."

Later, in their own bedchamber, Somerled and Ragnhilde thought indeed, and talked late into the night. And as their talk developed it became Somerled seeking to persuade his wife that what Thorfinn proposed was right, wise, even inevitable. For Man, for their son, for Argyll and the Isles. They just could not afford to have a tyrant, who called himself also King of the Hebrides, threatening from the neighbouring island kingdom—and still less could they contemplate the English sitting in Man, a still greater threat. Godfrey was unmarried, so Dougal, his nephew, was already lawful heir to his throne—they could not shut their eyes to that. And Man deserved a better monarch than Godfrey the Black.

Ragnhilde perceived all this but could not get over the horror of her husband and son going to war against her brother, her young Dougal a mere pawn in this game of power.

They eventually slept, with the matter still unresolved.

The very next day a new aspect of it all opened before them when, unheralded, Donald MacEth, now being styled Earl of Moray, arrived at Ardtornish. He came as eager for action as was Thorfinn Oak-Hewer—Somerled's action. The time was ripe, he declared, over-ripe. They must strike, and strike soon, or all might be lost for good. Henry of England, the new man, was showing his claws.

Almost wearily for him, Somerled sighed and listened.

Henry Fitz-Empress, as he was being called, was wasting no time. He had been on Stephen's throne a bare two years but already he was making a grasp for the overlordship of Scotland. He had begun by restoring the Honour and earldom of Huntingdon, in England, to young King Malcolm, forfeited by Stephen; and when this was accepted, summoned Malcolm to come south and to do him homage for it, as vassal.

"But—even this young Malcolm will not do that, surely?" Somerled exclaimed. "His Normans—they would not allow it."

"The word is that they will. This late famine and the bad harvests have hit Scotland sorely—as I know to my cost. Food and wool and wealth are in short supply. And this Honour of Huntingdon is one of the richest plums in all England—whence David gained all the gold to build his many abbeys, through his wife, the Countess thereof. Manors in no less than eleven English shires. The revenues of Huntingdon could set Norman Scotland up again—and Henry knows it. A rich bait for his trap."

"The Normans will not fail to see that."

"They are English-born, all. What care they for vassalage? Perhaps they think that they can play Henry at his own game, later? The word is that King Malcolm the Maiden will go make his fealty, next summer. And I want Scotland's throne before that! For my father—or for myself."

"M'mmm."

"You must see that it is now, or never? Once Malcolm has done his fealty, admitted English overlordship—for Huntingdon, only, certainly, but Henry will claim him a vassal-king—then we would have England to fight, as well as the Scots Normans. If Scotland's independence is to be saved, Malcolm must be unseated. And quickly."

"Lord—you sound like Thorfinn Oak-Hewer! So much independence to be saved—and by *me*, it seems!"

"Thorfinn . . .?"

Somerled explained the Manx situation.

His nephew frowned. "This is more important than the Isle of Man!"

"For you, perhaps—not for me. And for Dougal."

"What is proposed? By this Thorfinn?"

"That I take a hand. Aid him to unseat Godfrey the Black and put your cousin Dougal on his throne."

"When?"

"So soon as may be. So soon as I can muster the men. And the fleet."

"And you will do it?"

"I have not yet decided. But it seems . . . necessary."

Donald paced the floor. "You could do both," he declared, after a pause.

"What do you mean—both?"

"Save both causes, Uncle. Both require that you muster men and then sail south."

"So . . .?"

"You aided me before, with your expedition to Arran. I could not take full advantage of it then, owing to the death of Duncan of Fife. And the pestilence in Scotland. But it cost you little, I think, and no blood was shed. You could do it again. Differently. See you—I have had to change my plans. My five earls are timorous. The new Fife, Constantine, is only a youth and no leader. I have to rely on Strathearn to lead—and he is a cautious man. He will not rise to strike the first blow. Even with my men of Moray and Ross in arms, he needs the first blow to be struck elsewhere . . ."

"And you want me to strike it for your waverers—*me*!"

"No. At least . . . not that, Uncle. It is Galloway that is to strike it. Already they are in revolt there. I am to go to Galloway and to lead them in a united assault on Lowland Scotland. Your aid in this I wanted. But even if you only sailed your fleet down off the Ayr and Galloway coasts, it would serve. Serve to draw off the Normans. Then the earls would strike from the North. And you could sail on to Man . . ."

"Another gesture! That would serve your purpose?"

"It would greatly help! If it was timed aright. My aim is to allow the northern earls to win over Forth into the Lowlands with little opposition. Always the crossing of Forth at Stirling is the great hazard to any assault from the North. Even a few can hold up a mighty army there. Strathearn much fears this. If you could show a great fleet off Ayr and Galloway, and I lead a Galloway host northwards at the same time, the Normans will be forced to turn their whole strength in that direction. Then the earls will move their forces down and across Forth to assail the Norman rear. You need not land one man, Uncle—so long as you are there, and seen by all to be there."

"And when would this be?"

"Best when they would least expect it—in the winter. It is October now. It will take time to muster and arrange all—in the North, in Galloway and here. Yuletide, then—they will not look for war at Yule."

"That is a bad time for sailing these seas. There could be storms."

"Do not tell me that Somerled the Mighty is afraid of putting to sea in winter! Besides, it would help you at Man, would it not? Godfrey would not expect assault then."

Somerled pondered. "We shall have to see what Thorfinn says . . ."

The Norseman raised no objections, sufficiently thankful

313

that an invasion of Man was in fact contemplated. His only concern was that the Argyll fleet, hanging about off the Galloway coast for long enough to serve Donald's requirements, would almost certainly be reported to Godfrey and give him time to organise a defence. To which Donald countered that, if Godfrey was so well informed, he would know well of the Galloway rising and would surely assume, as would the Normans, that Somerled was concerned with that, not any invasion of Man—which seemed reasonable.

So the thing was agreed, even though Ragnhilde remained unhappy.

Yuletide it would be, when few would look for armed ventures. Meantime, there was a great deal to be done.

*   *   *

The great fleet sailed from the Sound of Mull on the Eve of St. John the Evangelist. It was slightly smaller in numbers than that which had gone to Arran two years before, eighty ships as against over one hundred; but there were no transports nor cargo-carriers here, all longships, the largest concentration of war vessels Somerled had ever assembled. And filled with fighting-men, to a strength of over five thousand, no women and children on this occasion. Despite the weather, a thin cold rain and fitful wind from the north-west, they set off in fine style and high spirits—even though Ragnhilde, for one, saw them go with strained face and bitten lip, her first-born off to war.

There was one longship which did not sail with the fleet, and that was the Manx vessel which had brought Thorfinn to Ardtornish. For, one morning in early December, unaccountably it was no longer at the moorings it had occupied since its arrival in the bay below the castle. Thorfinn was mystified, as were such of his companions as were in the castle. One proved to be missing, however, Paul Snake-Tongue, a considerable Manx chieftain. He, and the ship, never reappeared—so it looked very much as though this character had decided to live up to his by-name and had reckoned to buy his way back into Godfrey's favour by returning to Man with the information of what was being prepared in Argyll. This did perturb Somerled and Thorfinn; but cancelling the venture was not to be thought of at this late stage of mustering, and with Donald already departed for Galloway. So surprise for the invasion of Man was presumably no longer likely.

Only the leadership was much worried over this.

With winds behind them they made good time down the coast, sufficiently so to be able to be able to lie-to for the night at Gigha, where the men were able to go ashore and stretch their legs and gain such shelter and comfort as they could. By next evening they were off the same Arran bay where they had moored two years before, and where Somerled sought information from the fishermen as to the latest news from the mainland. He was told that there was considerable excitement in Lowland Scotland, with varying rumours about the rising in Galloway, but general agreement that the Gallowegians were this time doing more than merely driving out Normans locally but actually on the march northwards out of their own province. Everywhere, it seemed, forces were being raised to move to check them.

The following day the fleet moved directly across the firth to the Ayrshire coast, to Irvine Bay, where they could lie offshore with some protection from the northerly winds under the lee of Ardrossan Head. Here they waited for most of the day, to allow their presence to be reported. This was the High Steward's territory and it undoubtedly would not be long before he was apprised of their arrival—if he was not already on the march against the Galloway men. They did not go ashore.

As light began to fade they moved on southwards, to Turnberry, where there was another jutting headland which would give shelter from the fresh winds and seas. They could land here without causing much upset, for Turnberry was a property of Fergus of Galloway, in fact the seat of his son Gilbert. However, Gilbert, now acting Earl of Galloway in lieu of his immured father, proved to be away, with most of his men, involved in the rising, and there were no problems.

The next day followed the same pattern, with a demonstration off the coast at Ballantrae and a landing for the night in the mouth of Glen App. The weather had brightened and the wind swung into the east, but even so conditions scarcely enjoyable for idling along exposed shores. Men grumbled and discipline was difficult to maintain in so large a host. Somerled and his lieutenants were kept busy, if nobody else was.

After Glen App they moved on, in mixed rain-storms and watery sunshine, round Corsewell Point, the jutting northern horn of the Rhinns of Galloway peninsula, and so into the Solway Firth, where presently it was more sheltered. It seemed pointless now to continue with their flag-showing activities with only the Galloway folk themselves to observe them, so Somerled led the way directly eastwards to the Dee estuary and Kirk Cuthbert's Bay, where was Kirk Cuthbert's Town, the principal seat of the earldom. And there they were received distinctly coolly by Gilbert of Carrick himself, who promptly berated Somerled for coming too late. If he had brought his host a week earlier, all might have been saved. As it was, there had been a disastrous battle with the Normans at Whithorn and the foreigners' armour and archers and heavy cavalry had prevailed. The Galloway force were defeated—if only for the moment—and the present campaign lost. If only the Islesmen had come when they were needed instead of lurking about the coast . . .

Somerled pointed out, with what patience he could muster, that he had done all that had been arranged with the Earl Donald, his nephew, and at the time specified. He had not agreed to take part in any actual fighting on land. He was sorry—but no blame rested on himself, as Donald must admit. Where was Donald now?

God alone knew that, the Earl Gilbert declared—possibly he was dead. The Normans had captured him at Whithorn.

This grievous news changed all, of course, and made a folly of all their recent moves and demonstrations. The MacEths were consistently unfortunate, it seemed. There was nothing that Somerled could do here now, for his nephew, his sister or her husband. He would be about his own business, now—Man.

None were sorry to turn their backs on accursed Galloway, to sail westwards

*   *   *

Now able to bend his whole mind upon the situation ahead, Somerled recognised that, on this occasion, he had

316

indeed given hostages to fortune. If Paul Snake-Tongue had warned Godfrey of the planned attack, as seemed probable, then all this lingering off the Scots coast by so large a fleet would most surely have been reported on Man, and so given Godfrey ample time to prepare his defence. Surprise, both in the long and short terms, could now be ruled out.

But Somerled was a born strategist, and the head-on-clash methods of warfare anathema to him. If he could not use surprise in project or in timing, he might still achieve it in sundry details and tactics. Certain factors were basic. He should endeavour to fight at sea, rather than on land where the local enemy would have the advantage of knowledge of the terrain and availability of reinforcement. So, since presumably Godfrey would not fail to recognise this, it would be a question of enticing the Manx fleet out to sea. How many ships Godfrey might have available it was not easy to compute. Olaf had had a large number, little as he used them—as any island kingdom must. One of Somerled's worries was that Godfrey would have had time to send to Orkney for aid, since it was now a full month since the man Paul's defection. So they might well be faced by a larger fleet than his own, and tough fighters. Somehow, then, as well as drawing the enemy out, they must try to split up his numbers.

Consulting Thorfinn and Saor, Somerled evolved the following strategy. It could be taken that Godfrey's main force would be concentrated at the south end of Man, where were Rushen, the best anchorages and the greatest population. Saor, therefore, should take half the Isles fleet and sail openly to the *north* end of Man, round the Point of Ayre, and threaten the north-west coast of the island—indeed probably make a landing and set a few places alight. Enough to give the impression that this was the major assault—especially as Thorfinn's lands lay at the north end. It was probable that Godfrey would have no exact information as to their full numbers, and forty longships would seem a sufficiently impressive fleet. It was to be hoped that the enemy would therefore send a substantial proportion of their ships up the west side of Man to deal with this. Somerled and the rest of his force would remain out-of-sight of land meanwhile, with only a couple of longships out as scouts, to observe if possible. Then move in towards the southern end of the island to seek and coax out the remainder of the Manx fleet. If *all* the enemy ships had sailed off northwards, then Somerled would land, set Rushen afire and all else necessary to draw back the Manx shipping—and be back out at sea waiting to receive them. Whereupon Saor would sail south, after them, to attack from the rear.

The success of such a plan would depend upon good information and communications between their two divisions—which meant some very fast-moving longships to spy and shuttle to and fro. Happily they could produce these, with double crews of oarsmen. Timing also would be vital; and since confusion of the enemy was a necessary condition, dusk, even darkness, would be an advantage. A naval battle at night was almost unheard-of—therefore let them make it so. Darkness would handicap them also, of course, but less so if they had planned and prepared for it. They would need daylight to lure the enemy north-westwards and then south again, so that timing would have to be such that the main engagement in the south started as light began to fade. The island was thirty miles long and it lay about thirty miles off the Galloway coast—so careful calculations were essential.

If the others were somewhat doubtful about this most complex strategy, Somerled was not. This was the man in his element. He ordered the fleet to sail only slowly and to follow a more westerly course than otherwise necessary, in case they were observed and reported on by Manx fishing-craft.

Nightfall saw them about fifteen miles due north of the Point of Ayre on Man. The weather was not calm but not stormy either. Somerled had the fleet heave-to and ordered torch-making on all ships, using pitch and tarred-rope and canvas such as the longships carried for running repairs. Then some practice with manoeuvring with torches lit fore and aft on each vessel. This was all distinctly confusing and confused, admittedly, and took a great deal of time and patience before lessons were learned and some effective operating and signalling achieved. But they had a long winter's night to fill in and this at least kept all busy and alert.

At dawn, the two divisions separated, Saor to sail south by west, directly for the Point of Ayre, and the others south by east on a course to keep well out-of-sight of the Manx east coast. Each sent out the fast-rowing longships ahead as scouts.

Somerled's forty had some fifty miles to go and aimed to do it in five hours, which should be about right for timing. They were to heave-to level with the southern tip of Man but just out-of-sight from the land. This around mid-day, awaiting their scouts' report. It was an unpleasant day of drizzle and poor visibility—which was, on balance, in their favour.

A rendezvous in open sea in poor weather is always difficult and Somerled had to wait, fretting, for over an hour beyond the agreed time before one of the scout-ships found them, coming lashing up in showering spray. Its shipmaster declared that he had looked for them farther south. He informed that a large fleet had indeed left St. Michael's Haven over two hours earlier and sailed off westwards. It was difficult to say how many ships— naturally he had had to keep miles away—but he would think that there were fully fifty sail. How many that might leave at St. Michael's he had no means of knowing, hidden as that anchorage was. His companion-scout was trailing after the Manx ships and would try to report developments.

On business bent now, Somerled gave the orders to proceed for St. Michael's Haven at their fastest.

They reached the almost landlocked bay in an hour, with only another hour of daylight left. Their approach revealed no sign of enemy shipping—but of course most angles of approach allowed no view into the bay itself. When they did round the corner of the obstructing island however, and could see in behind, it was to count some twenty longships still in the bay.

There was no debate nor hesitation now. Straight in the forty Isles ships rowed, in tight formation, gongs beating, oars flashing. Speed was essential here. All the Manx ships appeared to be at moorings, none looking immediately ready for sea or fully manned. Almost certainly most crews would be ashore. Somerled saw that, with any luck, he should be able to swoop down on these moored craft and either destroy or capture them almost without any real fighting—if he could reach them before the crews could be gathered and got back aboard. They had a bare half-mile to go.

In fact, the assault on those vessels was a complete success and almost bloodless. There proved to be men on board some of them, but nothing like full crews, and these mostly put up a mere token resistance; outnumbered six or eight to one, and unready for battle, they usually dived overboard and struggled ashore after a gesture at defence.

On the land, large numbers of men were gathering and staring, uncertain what to do.

Somerled himself had to make up his mind as to what next. This cheap victory was welcome, but he did not delude himself that the real test was not still to come. It was no part of his intention to battle with the Manx people if he could help it, much less to sack the island kingdom, whatever some of his folk might like to do. On the other hand he wanted to draw back Godfrey's main fleet, and the only way to do this was to light sufficient fires at this south end to make it plain to Godfrey, sailing north, that his base was in dire trouble. Which meant a landing, resistance and fighting presumably, for which he had little time.

Seeing that the score or so of Manx ships were theirs for the taking, he shouted orders that his spare crewmen should board and man these, or such as were approximately ready for sea. Half of the rest of his men to follow him ashore.

So the Isles longships were driven shorewards and their prows run up on the beach, the men pouring over the sides with swords drawn and axes at the ready, yelling their challenge. The Manxmen, who seemed to be more or less leaderless, made no concerted attempt to oppose them, but retired hurriedly amongst the huddled houses of the quite large town of Rushen. Somerled with difficulty restrained his men from following them. Once they got caught up in those houses and lanes, they could be grievously delayed and hopelessly broken up as a force. This was not what they had come to Rushen to achieve. Leaving some to guard their rear and to counter any unlikely attempt on the shipping, the rest would come with him up to the higher ground to the west of the town, where they would find some cothouses, barns, haystacks and the like to burn and be visible from a long way off.

This part of the programme in fact presented no difficulties. The fire-raising party were not pursued. Up on a shoulder of hill above the town and castle there were three farmeries well-placed for their purpose. Somerled, whilst sympathising with the innocent occupants there, had no compunction about setting alight their barns, cattle-sheds and hay stores, although he spared their houses. This was war. These multiple fires on the high ground, as dark fell, would light up the night sky with a red glow which would be seen from one end of Man to the other. If it did not bring Godfrey back southwards, at speed, nothing would.

With the conflagration well established, they hurried back to the ships, for time was now of the essence. There appeared to have been no trouble at town or shore, both sides warily keeping their distance. Dermot Maguire, in command there, informed that one of the Manxmen wounded in the take-over of the captured ships declared that Godfrey the Black had been sent a fleet of thirty Orkney longships.

It was almost dark now, except for the ruddy glare of the fires, and Somerled ordered a quick return to the ships and no delay about setting sail. He wanted to be out of that bay just as soon as possible.

Getting through the narrows at St. Michael's Isle was not easy in the darkness, but the danger of collision was so evident that no crews required to be warned. Somerled was concerned for the competence of the newly-acquired craft and their scratch complements; but longships were all built approximately to the same design and should not present many problems.

Out on the open sea it seemed less dark, with the water to some extent reflecting the flames inland. The fleet, now almost sixty strong, could spread itself more—but not too much, advisedly. Most vessels could see half-a-dozen or so others but no more.

The dragon-ship led the way westwards, to round the off-shore isle of the Calf of Man at the south-western tip of the main island, and then turn northwards. He kept about two miles out from the land, his desire being to lie seawards of the returning fleet—if return it did—with it to some

321

extent silhouetted against the glow of the fires whereas they themselves would remain unseen against the western sky. The problem was, of course, how far west to go, how close to the shore Godfrey would sail, how much room they must give him and still be sure of seeing him. If the fires did not bring him back, as indicating his base invaded, then all this was wasted effort, and Saor was in trouble. But if he came, he would be in a hurry and apt to cut corners, might take his fleet through between the Calf and his mainland, but not so close to the shore as to endanger his ships on reefs and skerries. Somerled sent Conn and half-a-dozen ships to sail up and down as near land as they thought practical, whilst he and the others lay seawards, westwards, just near enough to be able to distinguish them. The refulgence in the sky to the east was a major help.

Another concern was that that glow would not last. Fires eventually died down, and already the glare had lessened perceptibly. If the enemy long delayed the chances of seeing them could be lessened seriously.

That was a problem which they did not have to solve, at any rate. It was Gillecolm, still sharper-eyed than most, who suddenly exclaimed, "How many ships has Conn Ironhand? How many?"

"I told him to take six. Why?"

"I see more. Nine. No, ten. See—there! Another one . . ."

"Lord!" his father cried. "You are right, by all the saints!"

"More—all sailing south!" That was Dougal, also on the dragon-ship stern-platform.

"Yes. It must be the first of the enemy. A plague on it—if we attack these the rest will be warned."

"Conn will see that. He will deal with them . . ."

"More!" Gillecolm shouted, pointing northwards. "See—more sails."

"Aye—here they come. Too many for Conn. Godfrey likely will be in a leading ship. Nothing for it but to attack now." Somerled raised his horn and blew loud and long. Everywhere around the wailing was taken up. Gillecolm began to beat the dragon-ship's gong, slowly at first but quickening. Other gongs commenced to sound. Oars dipped and splashed. The Isles fleet moved eastwards, gathering speed.

When the Manx ships became aware of them was hard to discern. Indeed everything was hard to discern, nothing certain. As they drew nearer Conn's flotilla could just see, by the confused huddle of ships, that they were engaged, which their own and which enemy ships impossible to tell. Somerled blew the succession of short sharp blasts on the horn, which was the agreed signal for a change of course to leeward—and all but rammed two of his own vessels tardy about obeying. Cursing he ploughed northwards, as he heard other horns repeating the signal.

Almost at once they found themselves in the path of one of the oncoming Manx vessels. Yells of alarm greeted them, but that was all. Taken wholly by surprise, the enemy craft tried to swing off; but against a deliberate assault it was for the moment helpless. The dragon-ship swung the same way and its rearing prow made contact and sheared viciously down the other's side, cutting through oars and oarsmen like twigs on a bough. In only moments they left the screaming ruin behind, for the next Isles ship to deal with, and steered straight for the next enemy vessel which was looming up ahead.

This craft presumably had not seen just what had happened in front of it, for it came on, and only sought to take avoiding action at the last moment, too late to be spared the same fate as its predecessor—the advantage, for the attacker, of an action in darkness. But the disadvantages were quickly demonstrated also, for pressing on and leaving this one temporarily crippled, Somerled realised that he was now faced by three ships more or less in line abreast and very close. With only seconds to make up his mind, he chose to tackle the centre one, in the hope that this, if it sought to veer away as the others had done to avoid collision, might itself collide with one or other of its neighbours.

But these three had been close enough to see approximately what had happened to the ship in front and were able to react fairly effectively. The two outer vessels swung away left and right, and the centre one had time to have its rowers raise their oars high, out of danger, before the dragon-ship bore down on it, and so avoided disaster. The two vessels swept past each other only a few feet apart.

And now there were other enemy craft ahead. But the

two flanking ships of this trio had obviously perceived the situation and were pulling round to close in on their attacker from either side, whilst the central craft was seeking to back-water and turn also. The ships in front would not know exactly what went on but would be able to see that there was trouble ahead, and come on alerted.

Somerled realised that he was, in fact, practically surrounded now. Looking back, none of his own ships were close enough to be distinguishable as such. For the moment he was alone amongst at least six enemy, who would perceive a dragon-ship as most certainly not one of their own fleet. He drove on at the nearest, hoping to run it down.

He was only partially successful in this, the other getting most of its oars up, in time. He sought to ram it head-on, instead, and the two ships ground together with an impact which shook both, unseating rowers and toppling men who were unprepared.

Somerled's people, who naturally were more ready for this than the others, and in greater numbers likewise, promptly poured over the side and into the enemy vessel, yelling, swords and axes slashing. From the voices, the other was an Orkneyman.

Gillecolm handled the dragon-ship with expertise and Somerled had brief opportunity to gaze around him. Two other craft were bearing down on them, apparently intent on close attack, and more were circling nearby. A quick count showed no fewer than eight ships—whether any were his own it was impossible to tell. He had to make a swift decision. To remain side-by-side with this Orkneyman could be disastrous, with all these others able to move in and board him. Shouting to Farquhar MacFerdoch, the Abbot, who was leading his own boarding-party, to cope on the enemy ship as best he could, Somerled beat his sword against Gillecolm's gong, to galvanise his oarsmen into swiftest action. The dragon-ship pulled away from the other, just in time.

With two ships converging upon him, Somerled required both room for manoeuvre and time for decision. Fortunately he controlled much greater oar-power, and therefore speed, than any ordinary longship. He was able to make good his escape, therefore, from the immediate dangerous situation, whilst remaining in the more general danger.

He was still surrounded by vessels, seen and of course more unseen. He could distinguish a dozen or more now. The trouble was to know which was which. Almost reluctantly he gave orders for the torches to be lit.

The lighting-up of the dragon-ship was to be the signal for all the others of his fleet to light theirs. Which, to be sure, would work both ways, identifying themselves but also singling them out as the enemy to the Manxmen. It would reveal their numbers as well as their positions—although he had sought to confuse in this respect by arranging for some craft to light two torches and some only one. The dragon-ship, which would be identifiable anyway by its size, lit two. The twenty captured ships would have no torches—which would admittedly confuse more than the enemy.

The pitch and tow of the torches blazed up quickly and in only a few moments other lights began to prick the darkness, near and far—no doubt all the other shipmasters had been eagerly awaiting the chance to distinguish between friend and foe.

At least it revealed three of his own ships amongst the dozen or so around him, which was a help. Two of these were close together and Somerled told Gillecolm to make for them, fast. There was one of his Manx pursuers close at hand and in the way, but on the dragon-ship wheeling round almost upon it, this vessel hurriedly changed course and swung away. No doubt its master now perceived its full size, thanks to the torches, and decided on discretion.

They reached the two Isles ships, and were glad to see the third one heading to close with them also. So now they made a tight little group of four, able to act in concert, giving mutual support and protection. Singling out the nearest pair of unlighted vessels, Somerled led his group into swift attack.

They managed to separate one of the Manxmen from its neighbour, cornered it amongst them and ran it down before others could come to its aid. Somerled put a boarding-party on to it and sent torch-bearers after them to set it alight, whilst his three companions circled closely to keep off others.

In the ruddy light of the flames, the unequal fight was soon over, with the enemy's burning sail coming crashing down on friend and foe alike. When he saw that much of the craft was alight, with most of its oars fuelling the blaze, Somerled beat his gong to recall the boarders, and leaving the dying ship, went to the aid of one of his own, assailed now by two of the enemy.

That, then, became the pattern of much of what followed, at least as far as Somerled's group was concerned—and, he hoped, with the rest of his fleet, for these were the tactics he had taught and practised. In the face of a surprised and disorganised foe they were, on the whole, very successful. Some of the Manxmen and Orkneymen perceived their lesson in time and formed similar little groups, but many did not, and paid the price. It was not all one way, of course, for they were dealing with experienced and courageous fighters. The Isles fleet suffered its casualties. But from the first the enemy was at multiple disadvantage. They had been hastening back to Rushen, strung out in no sort of order, and no doubt with the leadership well in front. They were taken by surprise and in darkness, and could have no idea as to the strength of the assault. The fires at their base area must weaken resolve, drawing men towards homes and families at risk—and they must also be aware of Saor's fleet somewhere behind them. All this was as Somerled had planned it.

Undoubtedly many of the Manxmen cut and ran. But sufficient stayed to fight, and make Somerled realise that there must have been far more than any mere fifty ships, as their scout had suggested. Either he had been hopelessly out in his observation or else Godfrey had been reinforced, possibly by another flotilla from somewhere up the west coast of Man, Fishwick or Peel.

To offer any coherent or even summarised account of that scattered, confused and prolonged battle would be quite impossible, even Somerled's own part in it. Nor could it be stated that there was any overall victory or defeat. By the very nature of it all, there could be nothing clear-cut nor decisive, since neither side could know how many of the other there were, what state the rest were in, whether indeed fighting was still going on elsewhere at any given time. A large-scale night sea-fight was something new, and the combatants had to learn as they fought—if it was not too late to learn—and how many chose not to fight-at all no-one knew.

A further complication was the weather. The wind freshened and swung round to the south-west as the night advanced, and the seas steepened, so that more and more attention had to be paid to seamanship and coping with conditions, less to fighting. Also the new airt of the wind and seas had the effect of gradually dispersing the struggling ships and setting them northwards. As time went on and men grew ever more weary, so less and less battle was fought. With supplies of torches running out and the fires on land dying down, it became difficult, once more, to distinguish friend from foe.

Almost inevitably, then, the engagement more or less fizzled out in the small hours of the morning rather than came to any recognisable conclusion. Somerled was aware of the process for some considerable time before he finally admitted that the battle was over. They had not found an enemy to engage for the best part of an hour.

It became a time for wound-licking. On the dragon-ship there was little damage to the vessel but considerable casualties amongst her complement, the various boarding-parties having suffered fairly heavily. Few were dead but many were wounded, some severely. Somerled himself had a grazed brow, where his great horned helmet had been knocked off by a glancing axe-blow, the pain of it only becoming evident now that the fighting was over. His companion longships—only two of them now, one having disappeared—were in worse case, having both sustained structural damage, stove-in timbers, splintered oars and the like. Blood was everywhere.

There was time to spare now for first-aid and clearing up, for little could be done about reassembling the fleet and discovering losses before daylight. Even their present position was uncertain.

When at length the grey dawn broke over the snarling whitecapped waters, it was to reveal much that was un-expected. They were nearer to land than they had thought, no more than a mile off a savage, cliff-girt shore. Also evidently further north than they had realised. Ships were scattered near and far—and one, no great distance off, was another dragon-ship, Saor's obviously; so the northern half of the fleet must have joined the battle without Somerled being aware of it. Many of the vessels looked to be mere drifting hulks, some abandoned, dismasted or burnt-out. Many others could be seen piled up along the rocks and skerries of the shore-line. How many were their own and how many enemy was not evident. It all made a sorry sight in the bleak morning light.

The two dragon-ships quickly pulled together and held a brief shouted exchange. Saor said that he and his had been in time to take part in the tail-end of the fighting, although he had found it hard to find who to fight. Probably it was their arrival which had hastened the end. He knew nothing about reinforcements for Godfrey and had not been involved in any real battle further north.

Somerled perceived that his ship and its companions were amongst the farthest north of the scattered fleet. He ordered a move southwards, followed by Saor and the others. As they went, vessels moved in to join them, some obviously limping and damaged and with reduced oar-power—but they left a lot of hulks behind, most of them probably Manxmen although it was hard to tell at any distance.

Somerled was grimly counting. By sun-up, and down near the southern corner of Man again, he added up to fifty-eight ships accompanying him, in various stages of impairment and dilapidation. He had started out with eighty, plus the twenty captured at St. Michael's Haven—so there were over forty missing. It made a daunting thought. Some might yet appear, some might be salvaged, a proportion of their crews surviving. But by any standards it was a dire and costly victory—if victory it could be called.

Apart from the abandoned hulks there appeared to be no sign of Godfrey's fleet. Presumably therefore the survivors had scuttled for Rushen and the shelter of its haven.

Somerled had not come all this way and at such cost to leave matters thus indeterminate, even though his depleted force was in no state for further battle meantime. He summoned Conn MacMahon, told him to take three other ships, to go back looking for stragglers, to aid any semi-crippled vessels and salvage what he could, as well as collecting survivors and wounded. The other fifty-four ships he ordered to follow him to St. Michael's Haven.

Slowly and lacking *élan* the Isles fleet headed eastwards. They would still look a formidable force from a distance but that would be something of a misapprehension. Somerled hoped, however, that he could still make use of this appearance.

But when they had rounded the jutting tip of Langness, the south-eastern headland of Man, and approached St. Michael's Isle and the hidden entrance to its bay, it was to discover what Somerled had half-expected. The narrow channel between island and mainland was tight blocked by Manx shipping, longships lying side-by-side and in rows. There would be no entry there, no amount of boarding and battling on so narrow a front would force this bottleneck. It looked grievously like stalemate.

A dragon-ship was very evident in the middle of the front of the barrier—Godfrey's, for a wager. There lay any hope of extracting some gain from this ill-starred venture.

Somerled called to Saor to take charge of the fleet and to hold it there, about half-a-mile from the enemy. He was going forward to talk to Godfrey.

So, spurring on his tired oarsmen to make a special effort in dash and style, the Isles flagship surged forward in a cloud of spray, banners streaming, a fine, challenging sight. Still, silent, the ranked Manx ships waited.

At less then two hundred yards from the centre of that line, Gillecolm had his rowers pull up, back-water and slew broadside-on, in expert fashion. His father cupped his hands, to shout.

"Ha—Godfrey Olafsson, are you there? I am Somerled. I am sorry that I missed you last night. We could have settled our differences decently, as honest men should. No doubt you sought me also? It was difficult in the dark."

There was no reply to this sally for moments, and then a voice came thinly across the water. "I, Godfrey, speak. What do you here, Islesman? What do you want?"

"Much, good-brother—much. We have a deal to settle, you and I. We can do it by the honest method of another trial of strength—if you will come out and meet me. Either your ship and mine, or your fleet and mine. Or we can make a compact, a bargain. Yours is the choice."

"I have nothing to bargain over, with you, upstart!"

"I think you have. And that is no way to name your sister's husband!"

"What do you want with me?"

"Ah—that is better. I want peace between us, Godfrey. I want no more threats from you. I want no more talk of you being King of the Hebrides. Whilst you remain without lawful offspring, I want your sister's son, Dougal here, named heir to the throne of Man—as is his right. Aye—and I want an end to your oppressions on Man, your persecutions of your own folk and my friends here. You make a bad king, Godfrey—and bad kings as neighbours endanger others."

There was silence from the enemy line.

"How say you, then?" Somerled called. "Is it to be peace? A compact? Or more battle?"

"You rave! You are mad!" That came less than distinctly, as though choked over.

"You shall learn if I rave, man! I hold you and your kingdom in my hand. If you will not come out and fight, I can land anywhere on this island and take it. Your people hate you—they will not fight for you. And Orkney is far away."

Again silence. Somerled's throat was getting sore with shouting. He turned to Thorfinn Oak-Hewer to make his contribution.

"Godfrey Olafsson—I, Thorfinn Ottarsson, speak. He whom you unlawfully dispossessed. Along with others. You have heard King Somerled. Now hear me. I fought for you, in Ireland, gained you much. Yet you turned on me, and the others, when we came home. You laid your father's kingdom waste. Now you pay!"

Another voice sounded from the Manx dragon-ship. "King Godfrey does not speak with rebels."

"Then he is a fool as well as all else! For he will have a lot of rebels. How many of that fleet will fight for him, now? How many prepared to die for a tyrant?"

There was no answer.

330

"I tell you," Thorfinn went on, "if you come out of there, we will beat you, as we beat you last night. If we land, few on Man will fight for you. We shall win and you, Godfrey, will die. That is a promise! We have here Dougal mac Somerled MacFergus, your sister Ragnhilde's son. Him we will make King of Man in your place—and Man will welcome it. None here love you. Deny that if you can."

After a pause, it was Godfrey's thinner voice again. "What do you want?"

"Ah—that is better! We want an end to your rule and tyranny. We want . . ."

Somerled gripped the other's arm, to silence him, and spoke instead.

"We want peace between our realms, as it was in King Olaf's day, good-brother. We require your sworn oath upon it. But since we do not altogether trust your oath, we shall have surety for it. We shall take half of Man, half of your kingdom. Since the Lord Thorfinn's lands, and others you have stolen, are in the north of the island, we shall take that end. And hold it. Until we are assured that you have mended your ways."

"You cannot do any such thing . . ."

"We can, and shall. The north is loyal to its lords whom you have dispossessed. We shall take it over and hold it as a dirk at your throat! To ensure that you keep your word. You remain King of Man—meantime. But if you invade the north, if you continue to persecute your folk, if you call yourself King of the Hebrides again or seek my kingdom's hurt, then I come back. To make Dougal, your nephew, King of Man. Is it understood?"

There was no acknowledgement of that from across the water, with an interval on both sides. Even to Somerled how to push the matter forward was not very apparent at this stage. This shouted exchange had its limitations, but he had no wish to risk closer contact with Godfrey meantime. His men and ships behind him badly required a spell of rest and recovery, whatever he had just threatened. None had slept for longer than he could recollect. This was no occasion to try to draw up treaty terms.

It was Thorfinn who achieved some practical advancement. He raised his strong voice. "We take the north,

Godfrey—you hear? As surety. A line from Maughold Point on the east, across the island by Snaefell and thence down to Knocksharry on the west. Some of that land is my own. North of that your writ will no longer run. South it may still do so—but only so long as you keep clean hands. You have it? From Maughold to Knocksharry. Or else you lose all *now*, and your life with it. Choose!"

"For how long?" That came back without any undue delay. It seemed as though the stipulating of actual places and boundaries had brought Godfrey to the point of decision. Thorfinn and Somerled exchanged glances.

"For sufficiently long to be sure of you!" the latter called. "A year? Perhaps two. We shall see."

"I will get all back thereafter? My full kingdom?"

"If you keep the peace, yes."

"I have your oath on it, Somerled? Before all these as witness? You will not name this son of yours king here if I agree to this?"

"You have my word. A score of months and we shall see." In a year-and-a-half Dougal would be eighteen and his own man.

"Very well. For peace and the kingdom's sake, I accept. That line—from Maughold to Knocksharry. No more. No raiding or threatening. No interference south of that. No seeking to raise my people here against me. And you will return to your Argyll?"

"All that—although I shall leave ships and men with the Lord Thorfinn. For his comfort. In the north. And he can send to me, in one day, I remind you!"

"Yes. Be it so, then."

"I shall send you papers, for signing and sealing. That all may be done in good and lawful fashion. Is all understood?"

"Yes."

"Then I bid you a good day, good-brother. Shall I give the Queen Ragnhilde your greetings?"

There was no response to that. Grinning, Somerled turned to Gillecolm and signed to him to take them back to the waiting fleet.

It was a victory, of a sort, after all.

They sailed north to Ramsey, the nearest sheltered haven to Thorfinn's lands, and in the bay there the fleet lay for a few days, for much-needed rest, repairs and tending of the wounded. Somerled wrote out two copies of an agreement, signed one and sent them south in a longship to Rushen, getting Godfrey's signed copy back in due course. Conn turned up, with no fewer than seventeen damaged craft and some hundreds of survivors of the battle. Leaving these ships for repair and also a score or so of others for Thorfinn's support, under Dermot Maguire's command, in mid-January Somerled re-embarked and set sail for home.

Young Dougal at least was vastly relieved that he was not left behind as nominal King of Man.

CHAPTER 19

Ragnhilde and her husband eyed each other in the little boat rocking on Loch Finlaggan of Islay, as Somerled rested on his oars. The cuckoos were calling hauntingly from the lochside alders, answering each other across the water. The couple were alone, and deliberately, as so seldom these days, with the children left behind at the castle. For once they were not listening to the cuckoos nor consciously joying in the Hebridean summer.

"She is so young," Ragnhilde said, not for the first time. "Still no more than a child in truth. It is too soon."

"She is fifteen. Almost as old as you were when first we met. When first we began our loving of each other, Hilde."

"That was different. My life had been very much other than Anna's. I had lost my mother early, was reared in a broken household, had to look after my ailing father, take decisions. Anna has had none of that. She is too much of a child to be facing marriage."

"This is scarcely marriage, only betrothal. And only God knows whether it would ever in fact come to marriage, with the situation as it is, whether he will indeed live to marry."

"But that is the very reason for this betrothal, is it not? To save Donald? Or a large part of it."

"Yes. But it may not serve. His position is not good. Many of the Normans would have him dead. If his father cannot pacify the North I would not give much for Donald's life. And now, with the King gone, the Normans rule Scotland."

"Poor Donald! I grieve for him, yes. But—Anna! It is unfair for *her* to pay the price."

"Anna has always liked Donald. They are good friends. And she will have to marry, one day."

"You sound as though you *approve* of this! Do you?"

"No-o-o. But . . ."

"I believe that it is because Donald's wife just conceivably might one day be Queen of Scotland that you favour this, Sorley!"

"I do not favour it, lass. I but grope for a right judgement. There is so much at stake here. This *could* be a good marriage, and I must seek to do what I can for my sister and her son. The position in Scotland also means much to me . . ."

They eyed each other in doubt and perplexity—which was something fairly unusual with that couple.

The courier from Moray had reached Islay the previous evening, from Malcolm, Earl of Ross, bearing a strange message and plea. Malcolm was released at last, after all the years of captivity, not exactly a free man but on parole, his wife and son still prisoners at Rook's Burgh. He had been sent north, even confirmed in his earldom of Ross for the occasion, with the task of convincing the northern earls and chiefs that they should be reconciled with the present royal house, withdraw their profitless opposition and come into King Malcolm's peace. It seemed that the young King of Scots was to leave his country for a while—was already gone, presumably. He was known greatly to admire the dashing King Henry the Second of England, and that monarch had persuaded the younger man to go south to Chester to do homage to him for the English earldom of Huntingdon, to receive knighthood at Henry's hand, and then to accompany the English army on an expedition to France to assert Henry's authority over Aquitaine, which he had gained title to by marriage. This extraordinary programme for a King of Scots seemed to have been accepted without major reluctance or suspicion by the younger monarch. But he—or at least his Norman advisers—had concern that there should be no renewal of revolt by the Celtic earls during his absence. So Malcolm of Ross, as the representer of the ancient royal house, was temporarily released and sent north to counsel peace and moderation—but his son and wife remained as hostages.

It was this hostage situation which appeared to worry Earl Malcolm, on two counts. One was that he was not finding the northerners easy to convert and convince; and he had been warned that a failure of his mission would have unfortunate consequences for Donald and his mother. The other was that a powerful faction of the Norman lords at court wanted to execute Donald out-of-hand, for treason and rebellion—himself also, perhaps—as the best way of ensuring that there were none of the old royal line left to challenge the present incumbent. If this faction gained the ascendancy over the more moderate lords during the High King's prolonged absence, as was distinctly possible, then Donald's life would be in grave danger.

In this situation the Earl Malcolm turned to his brother-in-law for help. The Normans did fear Somerled, with his ability to land from his fleet an army anywhere he chose around the Scots coastline. Why the Kings of Scots had never built or assembled a navy of their own was a mystery, but there it was. Somerled's fleet was a perpetual threat. So some indication that the King of Argyll and the Isles was much concerned over the present situation of his sister and nephew would be most valuable. The Earl Malcolm urged that his good-brother would announce the betrothal of his daughter Anna to her cousin Donald, Earl of Moray, forthwith. This would serve warning on the Normans that Donald was not to be endangered and also strengthen Malcolm's hand in the North. Moreover it would be an excellent match in every way, giving Somerled a permanent lever against the present Scots crown.

This, then, was the situation confronting Anna's parents in their boat.

"Surely there is some other gesture you could make to show that you are concerned for Donald's fate?" Ragnhilde said. "Why must it be a marriage?"

"I *could* sail another fleet along the Scots coast, as threat. But if I do this once more, without making a landing and striking a blow, I will lose all credit and effect. And I have not the strength, nor the wish, for all-out war."

"No—not that, never that. But you could send a message to these Normans. Telling of your concern for your sister and nephew."

"That would be taken as the surest sign of weakness. When Somerled of the Isles starts writing letters instead of drawing sword, then all will say that he is not the man he was. No, this of a marriage—or a betrothal, at the least—has much to commend it. Not only towards the Normans and Scotland. But towards your brother Godfrey."

"Godfrey? What could it serve there?"

"It would warn him that I am strengthening my power. By an alliance with the Celtic forces of Northern Scotland, of old Alba. See you—at present I am but an island kingdom, alone. I have lost all touch with Fermanagh and Ulster. A move to ally myself with the old Alba, the Scots North, where the Normans and the house of Canmore have no power, must greatly strengthen my influence. Good-brother and then wife's father to the alternative High Kings of Scots."

"But what is that to Godfrey?"

"Do you not see it? Godfrey's strength is not in himself and his unhappy Man. It lies in his friendship with the King of Norway. And with the Norse Orkney sea-power. That is always a threat to me. The Outer Isles, Lewis, Harris and the rest, are in their hands now—and should be in mine. Now—where is there any threat to *Orkney*? Only in the Scots North. Orkney dominates the Celtic earldoms of Caithness and Sutherland—and the other earls hate that. There is always war simmering between them. Ally myself to the northern earls in some fashion and Orkney must take heed. And be less eager to send aid to Godfrey."

"You have thought it all out, I see! All considered."

"I have long wondered how to warn off the Orkneymen—and the Norse raiders they shelter. Without going to war. Now here is a way which might serve, at little cost. And warn Godfrey. For he is not mending his ways. He oppresses and threatens still. Thorfinn much fears more trouble, as you know . . ."

"At little cost, you say! To you! What of Anna? Do you not think of her?"

"My dear—I do think of Anna. I love the lassie. But she will marry someone, one day. Who? Have you thought of any husband for her? Suitable for our daughter? She knows and is fond of her cousin. And *we* know him, for a man of good nature and life. We like him also. I think our Anna might be none so ill-disposed to this match."

"How can you say that? You do not know. Nor could

she. She may have girlish dreams—but marriage, to a fifteen-year-old, is but rosy fancies . . ."

"*Betrothal* at fifteen, not marriage, lass. It could be years before they are wed—if ever. Donald is a prisoner, and like to remain one. This is to save his life, perchance, not to release him. It may not save him, but it is worth the trial. And it will serve us well enough in other ways, I say."

"So you are becoming set on it, Somerled? Marry our daughter, our own flesh-and-blood, for the sake of statecraft! As you would have used Dougal, over Man. Aye—and as my father would have wed me to the Earl of Orkney!"

He wagged his head at her. "My love—this is not like you! Is marriage so ill a state? Have *we* found it so? Anna may find it none so grievous . . ."

"We were in love. And took notable steps to prevent marriage being forced upon me. Can you deny that?"

"No, nor would wish to. The cases are entirely different."

"We are both king's daughters, having marriages forced upon us."

"Well—shall we make a compact on it, my dear? Announce the betrothal—but inform Malcolm and Donald privily that Anna is too young for marriage meantime. And that, when she is older, if she strongly wishes not to marry Donald, she must not be held to it. How that?"

"M'mmm. That is better, yes . . ."

"Indeed, that may suit Donald also, who knows? This may all be only his father's notion, not his own. He may come to desire another woman. If he survives!"

"True. Very well—let it be that way. So long as it is well understood, by Anna as well as by Donald and Malcolm . . ."

They rowed back to the castle-isle.

Later, when together they revealed and explained the situation to their daughter, Anna surprised them by being enraptured with the entire idea, even clapped her hands in spontaneous reaction. She thought that Donald was wonderful, she announced. So darkly handsome and attractive. There was no-one she would like better to marry. And one day, if he had his rights, he would be High King of Scots and she would be his Queen. Did they call her High Queen? It was all most splendid. Poor Donald!

Her parents actually found themselves playing the project down somewhat. It was all girlish romance, of course, unconnected with reality, giving Anna a fine glow of excitement and glamour. Also suddenly giving her a welcome sense of importance for once above her brothers.

Gillecolm, who had always loved Donald, was scarcely less delighted; and even his half-brothers were happy about it, these sort of dramatics appealing to the youthful fancy.

Ragnhilde's doubts remained, but all the others sent the courier back to Morayland with a fair show of enthusiasm.

CHAPTER 20

Somerled stamped the stern-platform of his dragon-ship, angry. That he should be heading southwards again with another large fleet, for Man, only twenty months after the previous expedition, was deplorable. There were a great many urgent affairs which he would have preferred to be about; indeed he had had to cancel at short notice an important gathering of Skye chiefs, in favour of this Manx business, and Skye was presenting him with problems. Also, because of the suddenness of this call, he had had to come away with a much lesser force than last time—fifty-three ships and only some three thousand men—September, the Highland harvest month, being the worst time of the year for taking men on military ventures. The entire affair was a major nuisance and Godfrey a plague. Yet he had to be dealt with, and swiftly, if Somerled's kingdom was not to be seriously menaced.

Godfrey, of course, had been misbehaving throughout most of the agreed eighteen-month interval. Thorfinn Ottarsson's reports and complaints had started within a comparatively short time of Somerled's departure from Man. At first they had been fairly minor infringements of the terms laid down; but they had grown worse, with interference in the northern half of the island, raids over the declared boundary and boasts that Godfrey would soon be in possession of all again. Somerled had held his hand, in the hope that his wretched brother-in-law would not push matters too far, although Thorfinn was pressing for another descent on Man, the dethroning of Godfrey and the proclamation of Dougal as king. Dougal was now eighteen, but with no enthusiasm for ruling Man.

Now the situation had reached crisis point and could no longer be shelved. Two developments had forced Somerled's hand. The most serious was an urgent message from Thorfinn that he had it on good authority from an informant at the court of Rushen that Godfrey had decided to switch loyalties or allegiance from Norway to England, that apparently feeling that King Eystein was too far away, he was about to offer his vassalage to Henry the Second, in return for the latter's support for him as King of the Hebrides. The second development was the assassination of Earl Ronald of Orkney, Ragnhilde's erstwhile prospective husband. He had been away on a Crusade, a sufficiently odd activity for a Viking jarl—which had resulted in his new by-name of The Holy—during which time Orkney had been ruled for him by Harald Matadsson. He was not long home when he was murdered and Harald had assumed the earldom. Now Harald was no holy man, and known to be in favour of Orkney breaking its ties with the Norwegian crown—and he was a close friend of Godfrey Olafsson.

So the position looked suddenly grim to Somerled. Henry Plantagenet of England was a thrusting, dominant individual and he possessed a large navy. If this situation was allowed to develop further, and Godfrey became a puppet of Henry, then the Isles kingdom was direly threatened, with menace from both south and north, great fleets in a position to menace it. There was only one brighter gleam in this suddenly murky prospect. The weak and rather pathetic King Malcolm of Scots was now returned from his adventure in France with King Henry, having taken part in the Battle of Toulouse and been duly knighted thereafter. Despite this, however, he had fallen out-of-favour with Henry, although he had ceded all Scotland's rights in Cumbria and Northumbria to England in return for the Huntingdon earldom's revenues. Presumably this was not enough for the Plantagenet, who would no doubt covet the illusory paramountcy over Scotland so desired by his predecessors. Indeed, almost the first thing Henry had done on his return from France was to order the enlarging, strengthening and garrisoning of the great Northumbrian castle of Wark, just over Tweed and a clear threat to Malcolm's Rook's Burgh, only nine miles off. In the circumstances Malcolm the Maiden, as he was now known, and his Normans, might well be looking for allies, to help contain Henry; and

Somerled would be an obvious choice, with so limited a field. So there could be improvement on that flank.

But none of this made unnecessary the taking of swift action against Godfrey. This time, despite the smaller fleet, it must be once-and-for-all, no more warnings and treaties.

Sailing thus in September, there could be no hiding the approach of the Isles armada, with insufficient hours of darkness, so Godfrey would have warning. But at least he would have no time to send to Orkney or even Dublin for aid.

Somerled might well be outnumbered by the Manx fleet, so was contemplating disembarkation and warfare on land. Thorfinn had said that he could raise four thousand men from the northern parts of the island. The ships would still be used, of course, to threaten Godfrey from the sea, but with much reduced complements.

They had left Islay with the dawn and, with a favourable breeze, by late afternoon were within sight of the North Manx coast, still with over three hours of daylight ahead. Somerled had to decide whether to sail straight on openly and land his troops, so offering the enemy full information as to numbers of ships and men and some indication of strategy; or else to wait well offshore until nightfall and so make the landing under cover of darkness—which would give them the cover but also allow Godfrey more time to make defensive arrangements, assuming that word of the fleet's coming would have been relayed by fishermen.

In the event, no such difficult decision was called for. They were sailing southwards about fifteen miles off the east coast, and still not level with Ramsey where the landing was to be made, when coming up from the south to meet them they sighted another great fleet. Surprised, they could have little doubt but that this was Godfrey come out to challenge them—which must mean not only that he had been timeously informed but that he was reasonably confident of being victorious—which in turn would seem to imply that he believed that he had superiority in numbers and strength. It looked, then, as though his brother-in-law was not relying on any mere fishermen's sightings but on much more detailed information—which indicated a spy or traitor in Somerled's camp, presumably on Islay.

But this was no time for dwelling on that. Now it looked like battle, and a swift decision on tactics. Soon they could count over eighty ships ahead, accounting for Godfrey's confidence. Presumably he had gained aid, either from England or the Norse-Irish. This, then, was going to be a struggle indeed.

Quickly Somerled made up his mind. He hailed Saor and his other commanders alongside his dragon-ship and shouted his designs and orders. They would divide into five flotillas of nine ships each, and fight in those formations. He had long admired the Norman cavalry tactics of tight arrow-head groupings, and believed that this could be translated to sea-warfare in certain conditions. Each of these nine-ship groups would act as a unit individually, but always with a concern for supporting others. They would each form up in the shape of a spear- or arrow-head, as close to each other as was practical for the oarsmen, the leader at the apex, and seek to retain that formation throughout, although individual ships would take turns in the most exposed and vulnerable positions. Protecting each other and backing-up their leader, they would be very difficult to assail and break-up. They would try to act as six flotillas but one fleet, concerned with an over-all strategy. It would admittedly make great demands on their seamanship and on the abilities and judgement of the leaders.

There was something like chaos for a short time after the gist of all this was announced and commanders sought and found each their eight satellites and marshalled them into position, amongst much confused shouting and manoeuvring. However, with Somerled and Saor in their dragon-ships acting rather like sheep-dogs, the tangle was sorted out fairly expeditiously. Then the five flotillas were ordered to form a line, abreast, each about five hundred yards apart, with the two dragon-ships and the remaining craft comprising a smaller wedge in the centre. The resultant front therefore extended over a mile-and-a-half. Whether it looked more impressive and formidable than did a solid mass of shipping was a matter of judgement.

The enemy had, of course, drawn considerably nearer. At first they displayed no evident reaction to their opponents'

343

dispersal. Then they began to spread out—and Somerled nodded to himself in satisfaction.

Soon the oncoming fleet formed an extended front considerably longer than that of the Isles, but not in any groups. So the two armadas drew together.

As they came close it could be seen that while most of the enemy vessels bore the Manx emblem, a number had the Plantagenet leopards painted on their sails. So the story about an English connection was true.

The eventual clash was head-on and dramatic, neither side wavering nor swerving aside further than was necessary to avoid the shearing-off of oars. But despite the dramatics and flourish of that first encounter, there was little damage done on one side or the other, all driving past each other and on in brave style but little actual contact, primarily concerned for their rowers. But if this might seem feeble, something of a failure in tactics, it was not so—not on Somerled's part, at any rate. For in those few minutes the situation was transformed. As they emerged and proceeded onwards, the Manx fleet, from being a unity, a coherent front under central control, was abruptly chopped up into seven or eight portions of varying strengths, as it were fragmented.

What happened then was salutary. The Isles groups knew more or less exactly what to do, each behind its leader; whereas the enemy was now scattered, each ship practically on its own or at least without either central or immediate leadership for the moment. As a result, there was hesitation, indecision, no over-all strategy. And such was required, and at once.

For the Isles flotillas acted in concert, swinging round, some right, some left, in as tight turns as was possible for groups of nine, and went driving back upon the opposition ships in their ones and twos and clusters. And these, of course, were immediately at a grave disadvantage, however effective they might be as individual units. They lacked direction, any unified plan of action to deal with this strange attack, and although they much outnumbered their adversaries, by the nature of the move the ships actually borne down upon by the Islesmen were outnumbered one, two, three or four to nine. Moreover, those in clusters were apt to get in each other's way in trying to take avoiding action or in swinging round to face the assault from behind.

This time the oar-shearing process was not to be evaded by not a few of the enemy. Some were rammed by the flotilla-leaders with their knife-edged prows, and blazing torches were tossed into others. There was no attempt at boarding, however, for that would have broken up the arrow-head formations. The Isles flotillas swept on and round again.

That second phase had hit the Manxmen hard. No fewer than eleven ships lay at least temporarily crippled, two actually sinking from stove-in timbers. And what was almost more important, the remainder of the enemy fleet was more scattered and far-flung than ever.

Somerled recognised that they could not expect to repeat this manoeuvre so successfully with the surprise of it gone. But whilst the consternation, alarm and lack of effective central control lasted, they might risk another attempt—indeed his commanders were obviously intent on doing that without any signal from him. The groups swung back, admittedly more raggedly than before, and went thrashing down on new targets.

This attack was only a little less effective, nine enemy vessels being left wallowing helplessly.

Somerled beat and beat on his gong, and other commanders took it up. This was the signal for individual action, individual flotillas, that is, not ships. The arrow-head tactics had proved even more successful than he could have hoped, so far, with a score of the enemy out-of-action, their fleet strewn far and wide and their morale almost certainly badly affected.

Now it was wolves-amongst-sheep tactics, with the flotillas dashing off in all directions after the far-flung Manx vessels. Somerled's own group went seeking the only dragon-ship amongst the enemy, presumably Godfrey's, with a small cluster round it, which had so far avoided contact.

The enemy were now in a strange situation. There were still more of them than of their tormentors but they were in no position to bring their superiority in numbers to bear. Not only was there no direction from Godfrey, nor any means of conveying it, but clearly no general and accepted method of coping with the revolutionary Isles strategy was developing. Some shipmasters evidently saw their best chances in huddling together in groups large or small, others in keeping their distance and acting alone. But whichever way they chose, the basic concept was most obviously the same, defensive, avoiding defeat by the Islesmen's extra-ordinary aggressive onslaughts. Which, of course, was in itself next to an admission of defeat.

In fact, Somerled's commanders much preferred the huddled and grouping reaction, since this gave them more worthwhile targets, something to smash into and which could not so readily dodge and twist away as could indi-vidual ships.

So the great harrying started, a savage, merciless business of charging and smashing and wheeling and boring in again, desperately wearing on the Isles oarsmen, although they were apt to be sustained by success and victory. This became less applicable as time went on, not only because of the rowers growing ever wearier but because the enemy learned not to stand and fight, or at least try to do so, in groups. More and more it became a matter of individual craft darting and swerving away from those dire wedges of destruc-tion—and this applied equally to Godfrey's dragon-ship which Somerled's group tried consistently to bring to battle.

The situation, indeed, became less and less satisfactory for the attackers, and Somerled was seriously considering whether he could somehow contrive to change strategy so as to try to drive the enemy towards the land where they might be able to pen them up against the shoreline and give them no room for this dodging and circling, thereafter to revert to the wedges. He was debating how to do this when Gillecolm grabbed his father's arm and pointed, pointed with three jabs of his finger, grinning. After a moment or two, Somerled saw what his strange son had perceived. Three enemy craft, not together, were not exactly hull-down but very far away, two heading in a northerly direction and one easterly, not dodging nor circling. It could only be flight. These were off, had had enough. And once that started . . .

Clearly, in a little, Gillecolm was not the only one to notice this defection; some of the enemy were perceiving it also. The young man, crowing, was able to point again and again. Others here and there were following suit and breaking off the profitless encounter. The complaint was becoming infectious.

But now Somerled was ignoring his son's gleeful indications. For it became evident that Godfrey's dragon-ship itself had been smitten by the need to be elsewhere. It was drawing away from its neighbours and, having half-as-many oars again as they had, was able to do so quite quickly. It began to distance itself, eastwards.

Somerled, frowning, signalled to Saor to take over command of their wedge, and ordered Gillecolm to speed off after Godfrey's vessel.

But now the effect of all the dashing and smashing and wheeling became apparent in Somerled's crew. They could by no means match the speed of Godfrey's oarsmen, who had had nothing like such strenuous demands made upon them hitherto. It did not take long for Somerled to perceive that he had no chance of overhauling the other dragon-ship. The only thing that he could do, he decided, was to try to head off the other vessel from making any southerly turn in its easterly course, as it would have to do if it was making for any of King Henry's ports. By maintaining a course well to the south of the other, that ought to be effective.

Whether indeed Godfrey had intended to make for England, or was merely fleeing in the direction most open and available, was not to be known. But fairly soon he reacted on Somerled's course by swinging away northwards. As the Islesman followed suit, the Manxman maintained the new course, and steadily drew ahead. Presently, going fast, the other was miles away and still heading north. That satisfied Somerled. Godfrey could go lick his wounds in Orkney or Norway—not England. He turned his own ship back, south-westwards.

By the time that he got back to the former battle area, it was to find it all over. Godfrey's flight had clearly been the last straw and it had become a case of general exodus. Like Somerled's own crew, the other Isles rowers were all too weary to engage in any purposeful chasing of the departing

Manxmen. Only his own fleet and the many crippled enemy vessels remained on the darkening scene.

It had been an extraordinary and unprecedented victory and at the most insignificant cost to the Islesmen. They had, of course, suffered a few damaged ships, crushed prows and splintered timbers, but had not actually lost a single craft. Casualties amongst the men were minimal, although exhaustion prevailed. A new dimension in sea-warfare had been introduced.

Somerled ordered an unhurried move to Ramsey Bay as night fell.

*   *   *

By and large, Man welcomed the Islesmen. The North was already conditioned by Thorfinn and his friends to accept them as deliverers; and the South had suffered so much at Godfrey's hands as to hail his departure with relief and be prepared to see any successor as a possible improvement. Ragnhilde had been well-loved on the island, and her son was received with fairly general goodwill. Godfrey's minions and supporters quietly absented themselves, although angry islanders captured some and made them pay for their sins; and there was considerable sacking and burning of the houses and lands of such folk, as was inevitable after a period of tyranny and oppression. Ragnhilde's illegitimate half-brothers had disappeared, but their properties suffered. Many of the defeated Manx longships turned up in remote havens around the island and were left abandoned by their discreet crews.

On Thorfinn's urging, no time was lost in proclaiming Dougal mac Somerled MacFergus as King of Man before a hastily-summoned and distinctly reduced Manx High Council at Rushen Castle. Dougal was still not enthusiastic but went through the motions; and thereafter, with his father and Thorfinn, made a tour of the island, showing himself and receiving fealties. All this took nearly three weeks—by which time word reached Man, via the Outer Hebrides, that Godfrey Olafsson had gone to Orkney but sailed on soon thereafter for Norway, whence he had come.

With this news, Somerled decided that he could risk a return to his own kingdom and Ragnhilde. Dougal, who

348

would have liked to accompany him, leaving Thorfinn and the Council to govern Man in his name, at least until he was a little older, was persuaded to stay on a while longer—for Somerled was anxious that it should not appear as though he himself had taken over Man as an appendage of his island empire, with his son as a mere puppet. He took pains to emphasise that his only concern with Man, apart from his wife's son's inherited interest, was that it should remain a good neighbour and not become a base to be used against his own kingdom, by any.

He sailed for Islay in mid–October, Gillecolm electing to remain with his half-brother meantime.

CHAPTER 21

Ragnhilde loved Saddail. Her favourite home in her husband's wide-scattered domains was undoubtedly Finlaggan of Islay, that fair green island in the sapphire sea; but in autumn, as now, Saddail was even more lovely. This was because Islay, like most of the isles, lacked the rich woodlands of the mainland, and at this season the colours at Saddail were breathtaking, the crimsons and golds and russets against the dark green of the pines, all glowing against the backcloth of the browning purple of heather, a vivid tapestry which never failed to enchant. On this occasion, however, she could have wished that there was a little more colour on the man-made scene—as there would have been on Man or anywhere else where the Romish Church prevailed. The Islesmen's Celtic Church no doubt had many virtues, but it certainly lacked colour and flourish. Its abbots and priests and serving-brothers all looked alike in either sober black or plain off-white girdled habits, lacking even a relieving stole or scapular, much less the glorious copes, chasubles, dalmatics and other vestments of the Roman clergy. For such an inauguration as this, surely, they could have risen to something a little more joyful and celebratory. As it was, her own chaplain Wilfrith provided all the clerical colour to the scene, and though active at the moment, he was officially only a mere spectator. The laymen, to be sure, were in their multi-hued best, in tartans and plaiding and dyed leather and furs, Somerled himself magnificent in cloth-of-gold doublet and kilt, instead of the usual saffron, under a polar-bearskin half-cloak lined with scarlet silk—although Dougal was quite the most resplendent of all, and made deliberately so as King of Man, even though normally he cared not how he dressed. Gillecolm, Ranald and Angus were notably fine for the occasion—as indeed were Anna and herself for that matter, and Cathula too—for this surely was a great and memorable day, the consecration and opening for worship of the first true abbey of the Columban Church, other than Iona itself, even to be built in Scotland. So-called abbeys or cashels, monastic steadings under abbots, or earthen ramparts and beehive-shaped cells and hutments, were common-place of course; but a towering stone minster and shrine, with cloisters and oratories and all the rest, after the Romish fashion, was something new in Highland Scotland. Which made it a pity, in Ragnhilde's estimation, that the officiating clergy could not have found something better then drab, stained and tattered habits to celebrate in.

Not that she disapproved of the visitors from Iona them-selves—on the contrary. Abbot Augustine was a saintly old man but with a twinkle in his eye—actually reminding her of St. Malachy O'Moore, which was scarcely surprising since that odd character had been a Celtic abbot before he became a Roman prelate. Augustine was not, in fact, titular Abbot of Iona and Primate of the Columban Church but, as it were, only sub-Abbot in charge, the true head of the Church being domiciled in Ireland, at Derry Abbey, where the Columban hierarchy had taken refuge long ago, from the Viking raiders, and never come back to Iona, sacked so many times; although Somerled was trying hard to get the present man, Flaithbertach, to return, with assurances that he now had the pirates well under control. Along with Augustine had come, for this ceremony, Dubhsith, the Iona lector, a genial barrel of a man, and MacForcellach, chief of the Keledi, the Friends of God, the special priestly order within the Church, a surprisingly young man for such position, silent but with a piercing glance. With a group of lesser clerics, a cheerfully unpretentious lot, they stood out only by reason of their drab clothing.

It was rather amusing, really, in that since none of these had had any experience in opening new abbeys, it had fallen to the Romish Wilfrith, ably assisted by Somerled, to advise and organise the affair. They were presently assembled in the refectory, not yet quite completed but decked in foliage and greenery for the day, to process from there around the establishment to the great church itself, behind a troop of fiddlers—at which Wilfrith raised his eyebrows. He was, of course, basing his attempts at organisation on his experience of the consecration of Rushen Abbey on Man—and finding gentle resistance from the Columbans, who obviously had a deep suspicion of ritual and display. Without Somerled's support the thing would have been done with no more ceremonial than one of their ordinary brief baptismal services. At least, unlike the Romans, the Celtic clergy had nothing against women taking full part in whatever was done, and Ragnhilde and Anna were lined up to process with the rest.

At last Wilfrith was as satisfied as he was likely to be, and they moved off. Saor MacNeil, as Chamberlain of Argyll, led the way, bearing aloft the great galley banner of the Isles and looking notably pleased with himself. Then came the eight fiddlers, playing with much *élan*. That they rendered what amounted to a quick-step, of spirit and verve good enough to dance to, no doubt emphasised the holy joy of the occasion, but it did have the effect of sending the company along at a pace which few sacred processions can have equalled, and which forced old Abbot Augustine into a sort of tottering run, his pastoral staff waving about alarmingly, the rest of the clergy hurrying after. Somerled, with Ragnhilde on his arm, strode out as though to urgent war, the Queen having to kilt up her skirts. Dougal followed on with skipping Anna, then Gillecolm with Cathula, then Ranald and Angus grinning widely, Conn Ironhand muttering about his old bones and Dermot Maguire deliberately refusing to be hurried, the long tail of chieftains and captains thereafter inevitably getting left behind, losing their places and becoming something of a rabble. All this to the cheers of the delighted crewmen, soldiery and watching local populace.

Thus they wound round the monastic buildings, completed and otherwise, through the grove of tall old trees carefully retained, through the new-planted orchard and apiary, to reach the handsome, lofty, cruciform church in almost less time then it takes to tell, Wilfrith panting along in the rear, profoundly shocked.

The fiddlers finished with a splendid flourish, approximately in unison, and there was silence save for puffing breathing. It was now time for Augustine to take charge but meantime that saintly character was in no state to do more than lean on his crozier and gasp.

Perceiving this, Somerled called on the musicians to give them another offering whilst they waited, and after something of a false start they launched into *Cuchullin's Wedding March*, a lively air productive of much toe-tapping and beating time. Clearly the instrumentalists believed that joyful occasions should be celebrated joyfully.

When this was finished, Augustine was sufficiently recovered to turn and take the handsome carved bronze bell-shrine from the lector, Dubhsith, and extract the battered old rectangular bell therefrom, to wave it to and fro, with a hollow clanging, notably deep-sounding for something so small. This was St. Moluag's Bell, from Lismore, the second-most-holy in the land, St. Columba's own bell presently being with his other relics in Ireland. Thereafter the old man raised his crozier and led the way round the outside of the building, tapping at the masonry here and there and murmuring a few words each time, in a quite conversational tone, as it were wishing it well. He had quite refused, although courteously, Wilfrith's direction about sprinkling holy water, declaring that such was for baptising human souls into the Body of Christ, not for spilling on lumpen stone. Back round at the main arched and carved western doorway, splendid with Celtic beasts and interlacing, he beat on the great oaken doors with his useful staff; but when they were flung open by someone inside, he did not go in but turned to face the throng. There, hand uplifted, he uttered a prayer for the good and proper worship of God ever to take place here, and Christ's teachings to be expounded worthily to receptive ears, with the saints' guidance and comfort on all who came with humble minds, especially that of blessed St. Marnock—for this was St. Marnock's Day, 25th October—and ending with a benediction on those present. Thereafter he stood smiling beatifically at them, obviously finished. He did not actually enter the church. The Columban clerics conducted most of their services and worship in the open air, weather accepted as part of God's providence, using their small and humble buildings mainly to house portable altars, fonts, communion-elements, chalices, patens, spoons and the like. Augustine was gently reminding all not to have too much concern with the towering monuments of man's self-glorification—with perhaps a special glance at Somerled.

Ceremonial being thus suddenly at an end, most others thereafter went into the church to admire, wonder and exclaim, of course—but the lesson was not entirely lost on them.

Later, however, as they enjoyed a celebratory feast in the refectory, a very different note was struck. Abbot Augustine was displaying another side to his character, that of the born storyteller, entertaining all by recounting the story of St. Marnock, how as a small boy in Ireland he was present at the splendid reception given to St. Columba on his one and only return to his native land from Scotland, in the year 585, at Clonmacnois, and was so carried away by his wonderment and admiration for the holy man that he actually crept in under the hangings of the tent-like canopy being carried over the saint in procession, and there clutched on to the tail of Columba's cloak; duly uncovered and upbraided by all but the saint himself, he was told to put out his tongue—and then all were informed that the lad would indeed grow up under his shadow and become a noted fellow-worker for Christ and that this tongue they all saw would be gifted by God with especial eloquence. So it was meet that on this St. Marnock's Day this new abbey should be dedicated to his name, especially as he had laboured abundantly in these very parts all those years ago, as witnessed by his island of Inchmarnock off Bute, less than twenty miles away, and the cells of Kilmarnock in Cowal and in Ayrshire.

They had got thus far when there was an interruption. A courier, who had obviously travelled far and fast, was shown in and brought to Somerled. He came from distant Ross, from the Earl Malcolm thereof, with an urgent message. The five Celtic earls, under Fertech of Strathearn, hitherto so reluctant to take up arms, had now suddenly and much against Malcolm's advice, risen in revolt against the High King, on the grounds that he had betrayed them, and Scotland, by absenting himself from the country for so long and paying fealty to the King of England. They were marching south with the armies of the North—but not that of Ross. Malcolm was sure that this was folly, at the present juncture, with no hope of success. Moreover he, Malcolm, was only released on parole and the High King held his wife and son as hostage for his good behaviour. Strathearn and the others would almost certainly appeal to Somerled for aid, if they had not already done so; and he urged him strongly not to give it, instead to send them word that they should give up this ill-timed project.

This was the first that Somerled had heard of the earls' surprising move and he required no persuading not to become involved. He was getting a little tired of being used by the men of the North in their consistently ineffective ploys, and always without any return service or advantage to himself, or even thanks. He would send the courier back to his brother-in-law, assuring him of his non-intervention on this occasion.

The Saddail Abbey celebration continued.

*   *   *

On their return northwards to winter at Ardtornish, Somerled received a request indeed, not to join the Five Earls in war but the High King in peace. This surprising development was intimated by the arrival of an envoy from Malcolm the Maiden, Gregory Bishop of Dunkeld, no less, chosen no doubt as one of the few Gaelic-speaking prelates of the Roman Church, most of whom now were Normans. He brought the good wishes of the monarch for King Somerled and an invitation to join him and his court at Perth for the Yuletide festivities.

This unlooked-for courtesy naturally called for some explanation on the part of the Bishop—although Somerled had anticipated that King Malcolm might well be looking for allies in the present state of threat from Henry of England, his erstwhile friend. Master Gregory amplified. The High King had answered the unexpected danger of the northern earls' revolt in forthright fashion, marching promptly against them and summoning all loyal men to rally to his standard at Perth. He had been rather swifter to act than were most of the said loyal subjects, with the result that before any large numbers had assembled, he had been in fact besieged in the walled city of Perth by the said rebellious earls. However, this crisis brought about a speeding-up of the loyalist muster and a major host came to the relief of the besieged monarch, in the face of which the earls discreetly withdrew north-eastwards. In due course, King Malcolm followed them, with a large army now, into the earldoms of Angus, Mar and Buchan, laying waste these lands and placing Norman governors therein, to teach the folk the cost of revolt, the earls fleeing ever further north. The High King was now back at Perth, supervising the assertion of the royal authority in the more southerly earldoms of Strathearn and Lennox. He intended to remain there over Yule. Hence the invitation to Somerled.

That man did not take long to decide on his course. He would go to Perth. If the young King wanted now to be friends, at least on the surface, that was surely to his own advantage. For he himself could do with allies. The Celtic North was obviously a spent force. Godfrey was still at large, and might possibly succeed in obtaining aid from Norway, Orkney or even England, just conceivably all three—in which case Somerled would be glad indeed of Scottish support. And there was his sister and nephew at Rook's Burgh to think of. He would go, but in style, as one king to another, or rather two, for he would take Dougal also, as helping to establish him as accepted King of Man. Ragnhilde also, and Anna as Donald's betrothed, all in the interests of due recognition. And, of course, a goodly train of armed men.

So, at the end of November they set out, on a fairly leisurely progress, by ship first to his new castle of Dunstaffnage, built on the site of the famed Pictish fort at the mouth of Loch Etive in Lorne, where Somerled had had horses collected for them, a great many of the short-legged, sturdy Highland ponies and garrons. From there they rode, a long cavalcade, eastwards along Etive-side and through the mighty Pass of Brander below towering Cruachan, to the foot of Loch Awe, where they stayed for the first night at the hallhouse of Sir Malcolm MacGregor of Glenorchy, who was to accompany them onwards to Perth.

The next day they had to cross the high spine of the land by the long, bare and lofty gut of Glen Lochy and over the summit of Mamlorn into Breadalbane; and so down to Tyndrum, where there was a Columban cashel to provide modest comfort for the ladies. There was snow on the high tops already but fortunately none on the drove-road which they were following, the route by which the great West Highland cattle-herds were driven each year to the low-country markets. This would be their longest and toughest day, over the passes. Thereafter it was comparatively easy, a mere few miles through forested country now to Glen Dochart, where Abbot Farquhar MacFerdoch made them welcome at his house before likewise joining their company.

Easy stages up Dochart and down Glen Ogle and along Loch Earnside into Strathearn, took them into a cowering land, however fair, which had so recently felt the royal—or Norman—wrath. They came to Perth in four more days.

St. John's Town of Perth was a semi-walled town, set on the south bank of the Tay, here a broad and noble river. The place, although notable as a religious centre, with many monasteries and churches, was now as an armed camp, of course. Somerled's cavalcade was challenged a mile off, but discreetly, for it made an impressive sight, obviously not to be provoked lightly. Messengers were sent on ahead to announce their arrival.

At the west gate of the town proper they were met by a group of Norman knights, clearly sent hurriedly to welcome and escort the King and Queen of Argyll and the Isles to the High King's presence. These were more respectful than had been those who greeted Somerled at Rook's Burgh on his first visit to the High King, David, all those years ago.

David's grandson received them civilly but without warmth, obviously surprised to see Ragnhilde. But then reputedly he was not a warm young man in many respects, and uninterested in women. Pale, slightly-built, unimpressive, Malcolm the Fourth was a strange representative of one of the oldest lines of warrior-kings in Christendom. By-named the Maiden, meaning virgin, because of his determinedly unmarried state, there were nevertheless stories about his secret habits which were scarcely maidenly. Somerled did not like the look of him—a more different character from his own would probably have been hard to find. But he also was civil, courteous, careful to give no more and no less than one monarch should give to another. Dougal too, as King of Man, heedfully took the same attitude. Ragnhilde was reserved. There appeared to be very few women about this court—Malcolm of course was still more or less on campaign.

Malcolm mac Henry mac David was, it transpired, a man of as little subtlety and finesse as he was of grace, and that very night at table, with Somerled seated on his right and Ragnhilde on his left, without preamble he plunged into business.

"You, sir, were friend to my grandsire David—his vassal, I am told. I hope that I can call you mine also?"

"Ah—yes and no, my lord King. Friend, yes; vassal, no."

"But, I am told . . .?"

"I gave him my oath of fealty, my lord, as High King of Scots, gave it of my choice, not of duty. *Because* he was my friend."

"But . . . fealty and vassalage, King Somerled, are they not the same?"

"No, sir, they are not. The *Ri*, or lesser kings of Scotland, are not vassals of the High King but his appointers and councillors. You would not name the Earls of Fife, Strathearn, Moray, Mar and the rest your vassals, I think?"

"They are rebels, sir, rebels! In shameful revolt against me. But I have drawn their teeth."

"Perhaps, sir. But they are not and never were your vassals. The *Ri* of the *Ard Righ*. I chose to be of a like accord with my friend King David."

Malcolm scratched his hairless chin uncertainly. He had been wholly reared and educated, if that was the word, by Normans and neither knew nor cared much about his ancient Celtic inheritance—which was why his earls were in rebellion against him. He changed his stance.

"If not my vassal I would wish you to be my friend, Lord Somerled."

"Ah, that is different. Friendship is . . . admirable." That was carefully said.

"Yes." The other hesitated. "I could be a good friend to you," he declared.

"That would be gratifying, my lord King. And what would I have to do to earn such . . . felicity?"

"*Act* my friend—that is all."

"Would I do otherwise, lacking cause? Forby, you must

have a fair sufficiency of friends, have you not? All these Norman lords and bishops. Not to speak of the puissant King Henry of England."

Malcolm frowned and plucked at his sleeve. "Henry is no true friend. He threatens me."

"You say so? But he is your companion-in-arms, is he not? You went to his wars. He knighted you. Returned to you your earldom of Huntingdon?"

"At a price. He claims paramountcy over me and my realm, now. Summons me, *me*, High King of Scots, to Caer Luel to do homage to him. And claims all Cumbria and Northumbria as his."

"That is an old story, to be sure. You have already done homage to him, have you not?"

"That was only for my English earldom of Huntingdon. For nothing in Scotland."

"Nevertheless it was unwise, I think. It gives Henry excuse to say that you are in vassalage to him . . ."

"For an English earldom only—which was mine by inheritance. My grandmother's."

"Even so. Vassalage, I say, is to be eschewed!"

The other looked sour and turned away. There was Ragnhilde on his other side, hitherto ignored. Finding nothing to say to her, Malcolm looked beyond her to Dougal, more to his taste presumably. But Dougal was in animated converse with Prince William, the High King's brother. Perforce he had to turn back to Somerled.

"Henry means war, I think," he blurted out. "He builds up and strengthens the great castle of Wark, over Tweed from my Rook's Burgh. Raises many men in Northumbria. He delights in war."

"And you desire my aid against him?"

The younger man cleared his throat. "Yes—it would be an act of friendship, sir."

"It would indeed, since I have no quarrel with Henry Plantagenet."

"If he won Scotland, you would have!" That was the first touch of spirit displayed.

"Perhaps. But I believe that I can defend my own kingdom. If I were to squander my strength aiding you, sir King, I might be the less able."

"No, no—I do not ask you to do great battle, King Somerled. It is but your ships . . ."

"Ah!"

"Yes, your ships, your fleet. With that of Man. Off the Cumbrian coast. A threat to Henry's flank. He would not dare strike into Scotland, with such a threat. Although he has many English ships, they are wide-scattered. He has no war-fleet to match your longships and galleys."

"I see. So my longships, and my son's, are to save you, and Scotland, from invasion?"

"It would much help."

"No doubt, sir. But at much cost to me, and Man, and little to you, I think!"

Ragnhilde put in a word, from the other side. "My lord Malcolm will, I am sure, have much to offer you in exchange—beyond merely his valuable friendship, husband."

"That is to be expected, yes," Somerled agreed gravely. There was a pause.

"I will do what I can," Malcolm said, at length.

"That is good." Conversationally, the older man went on. "You have my sister and my nephew held prisoners in your castle of Rook's Burgh, for one matter!"

"Not prisoners, no. Not that. Guests, rather. Living at my charges. In fair comfort . . ."

"Confined in your castle these long years, my lord King."

"Donald—he was in revolt against me."

"Because you held his father and mother hostage."

"I have pardoned the Earl Malcolm. Restored to him his earldom of Ross. Even now he acts in my name in Morayland. Dwells in the Priory of Urquhart there . . ."

"With you holding his wife and son as hostage, so that he does *your* will. I do not name that pardon and restoration, sir."

"He might have joined these other rebellious earls, otherwise."

"Perhaps. But if your policy towards your ancient Celtic realm was, I say, wise and proper, none of these would be in revolt and you would have no need of hostages." Somerled shrugged. "Whatever your policies, King Malcolm, I could not consider bringing my fleet to your aid, much less friendship, whilst you hold my sister and nephew close."

360

The other spread his narrow, womanlike hands and looked almost longingly over to where his senior Norman nobles sat watching, the Chancellor, High Steward, High Constable, Chamberlain, Knight Marischal and the rest.

"I shall consider the matter," he said, at length.

"Do that, my lord. Also there is the matter of Arran and Bute. Although they are mine, your Steward's people continue to trouble these islands. They raid there, steal cattle, take women, even demand rents. This must stop."

"I know naught of that, King Somerled. But will speak with Walter Stewart!"

"Yes. I have driven the Norsemen out of my isles. I hope that I do not have to do the same with the Scots!"

There was silence for a little, as they ate and drank. It was Somerled who resumed.

"You say that Henry Plantagenet has summoned you to do fealty at Caer Luel. When, my lord?"

"At Eastertide. When he is to be in the North."

"And what will you do?"

"Nothing. I shall not go."

"M'mmm. I think that would be a pity."

"Why? you would not have me to agree to this?"

"No. But go, to *disagree*. In strength. Muster a great host. March south. Leave your host just north of Caer Luel. Go meet Henry. Then, when he talks of fealty, tell him . . . otherwise. He will perceive the message very clearly, I'll warrant. Much more surely than if you merely stayed away. Especially if you had come to an arrangement with me, whereby my fleet, and Man's also perhaps, lay offshore in Solway at the same time."

"You . . . you would do that, then?"

"If my reasonable requirements were met, I would consider it, yes."

"I like that—yes, I like that. I shall speak with my lords . . ."

"Speak this also with them, then, my lord King. Change your policy towards the Celtic North, to all your Celtic heritage. You have the most ancient throne in Christendom, a Celtic throne. Yet you, the *Ard Righ*, have all your *Ri* against you, your lesser kings who should be your shield and strong support. They cannot all be mistaken, nor traitors. Seek their goodwill then, not their enmity. Heed not only your Normans. Bind the North to your side by showing favour, not drawn steel. Show concern for your Celtic people, not scorn. Learn their customs. Even learn something of their language. You are Malcolm the Fourth. Your forebears Malcolm First and Second could speak none other than the Gaelic. Only Malcolm Third, Canmore, learned the Saxon and Norman tongues—to his cost! Do this, and you need fear no stab-in-the-back when you outface Henry. Indeed you might have a Celtic host to add to your army facing Caer Luel."

Malcolm was staring at him in next to astonishment; indeed Somerled himself found a certain surprise at his own sudden fervour and eloquence. He had not come prepared to say quite all that. He found Ragnhilde eyeing him interestedly too.

The young High King wiped his mouth with the back of his hand. "We shall talk more of this," he said, uncertainly. "Now we shall have the dancing bears from Muscovy." And he signed for the entertainers to come on.

In their chamber of the Blackfriars Monastery that night, Ragnhilde remarked on her husband's unexpected advice-giving to Malcolm the Maiden, venturing her opinion that he was scarcely worth it all.

"Perhaps not. But he is almost as a child," Somerled told her. "I felt that he required some other advising than these Normans give him. I confess that I cannot greatly like him, but for his grandsire David's sake, I spoke as I did. Whether he will heed me, who can tell . . .?"

In the days that followed it seemed that Malcolm was at least prepared to listen to Somerled's advice, although actually heeding it would be another matter, for he carefully did not commit himself. But he sought out the older man's company much more frequently than was required in mere hostlike hospitality towards an important guest, asking many questions and initiating discussions. This clearly was contrary to the wishes of most of his Norman advisers. They coined the name of Somerled-sit-by-the-King for the visitor, and did not seek to hide their disapproval—save only for Hugo de Morville, the High Constable, now an ageing and obviously ailing man. He had ever been the most courteous and moderate of David's importations.

The Yuletide celebrations, although prolonged, were less elaborate and extravagant, in this semi-military court, than they would have been in normal circumstances; and since the Celtic peoples made more of Yule than did the Normans and Saxons, retaining much of the pre-Christian and sun-worship ceremonies and festivities concerned with the winter solstice, the New Year, the mistletoe, log and evergreen traditions, Somerled suggested that here was an excellent opportunity for the High King to go out and demonstrate some interest in his Celtic subjects, to observe and take part in some of the activities of the good folk of Perth and its surroundings. Without any real enthusiasm Malcolm allowed himself to be escorted to a number of the celebrations and thereby countered, to some extent, the sullen hostility of the local people to their monarch—for Perth, of course, was situated in the Gowrie area of Strathearn and since Fertech, Earl of Strathearn had been the moving spirit in the recent rebellion, Malcolm's reprisals on this province and earldom had been the most harsh.

Peacemaker was something of a new role for Somerled the Mighty, but he reckoned that Malcolm was a young man who could be led, essentially weak but not without possibilities. And the results might benefit himself and his Isles kingdom as well as the Scots people and monarchy.

Twelfth Night over, and the weather worsening and growing ever more cold, it was decided that a move should be made before snows closed the Mamlorn passes. Besides, the Argyll contingent had all had quite enough of Malcolm and his Normans. But although real friendship remained no nearer attainment than when they had arrived, at least Somerled left with the promise that his sister and Donald would be released and that there would be no more raiding of Arran and Bute. In return, he would demonstrate with the combined fleets of the Isles and Man off the Cumbrian coast next Easter—but he did not commit himself to land a single man.

He assessed his visit to St. John's Town of Perth as having been worthwhile. Ragnhilde was not so sure.

CHAPTER 22

Iona, the small jewel of the Hebrides, basked in the summer sun, and if there was a spot more fair on such a day in all his colourful and far-flung domains, Somerled did not know of it; the gleaming white sands, the lichened rocks and skerries, the greens and amethyst and azure of the water, the multi-hued seaweeds, the fertile, verdant cultivation rigs and cattle-dotted pastures, the scattered whitewashed cot-houses and the splendid high crosses, brown-stone and carved, of the saints and kings, all must delight the eye of even the least perceptive of observers. Only the shattered, fire-blackened and ravaged shell of the abbey itself affronted, although there had been many partial patchings and repairs from time to time; but only temporarily, superficially, the scars not to be hid. The Norsemen had not been back now for many a long year, but the centuries of fear were not to be overcome quickly; and the Columban Church was scarcely in good and confident heart.

It was this state of affairs which had finally brought Somerled to Iona, this fine June. He had long felt guilty over the situation. This was the heart and centre of Scotland's ancient Celtic Church, from whence all the land had been Christianised by Columba and his Brethren—and it lay in the midst of Somerled's kingdom of Argyll and the Isles. He had endowed and erected his fine new abbey of Saddail, in Kintyre, but he had done nothing about this vital shrine of the faith. Last year had been the twenty-first anniversary of their marriage, and Somerled and Ragnhilde had decided that something must be done about Iona. So here they were.

They sat out in the forenoon sunshine, actually on the stepped plinth of St. Martin's Cross, from which the Street of the Dead, a causeway of stone, led to the Relig Oran, the burial-place of the kings. Forty-eight Scots kings, no less, were reputed to lie there, Malcolm's ancestors in the main, along with seven Kings of Norway and four from Ireland. Nearby was the later chapel, built by Margaret, queen and saint, David's mother, it was thought as something of a plea for forgiveness from the Celtic Church which she had so sternly brought low, in favour of her Romish one—now also damaged by the Vikings.

"Flaithbertach must be persuaded to return here," Somerled declared, not for the first time. "Until he comes, nothing here will prosper as it should. You, Abbot Augustine, do very well, none would say otherwise. You bear the burden nobly. But you are not the Co-Arb, head of the Columban Church, whose place this is. Flaithbertach is that, for better or worse. And so long as he remains in exile, Columba's successor, his Church and faith will not flourish."

"We have sought his return from Ireland many times, my son," the Abbot assured. "But he does not come. We cannot make him come."

"Why should he refuse? It is safe now. Since I took over the Isles no Viking raider has come to Iona, nor will. Peace prevails here now. There is no reason why he, and all the precious Columban relics, should remain at Derry. They, and he, belong here. They were only taken to Ireland for safety from the Norsemen."

"I do not think that it is all of Flaithbertach's wishing, my lord King," Dubhsith the lector put in. "It is said that the High King of Ireland, Muirchertach O'Lachlan, is against him returning. Why, I do not know . . ."

"Then Muirchertach must be told otherwise. The Irish Celtic Church is sister-church to our own. But only that. They have no authority over the Columban Church. Muirchertach, and Flaithbertach also, must be told so."

"Perhaps if you were to build up this abbey again, as you did Saddail, this Flaithbertach might be coaxed to come and see it," Ragnhilde suggested. "And once here, he might be prevailed upon to stay."

"Would you not require the Co-Arb's permission to rebuild the abbey?" Augustine asked. "It would be a great and godly act of faith, my son—but you would require the authority of the Church, I think."

"That may be so. Then we shall seek to achieve both these purposes. We shall send to Flaithbertach at Derry, asking him to return, and gaining his authority to rebuild the abbey. Aye, and if necessary, deal with King Muirchertach too. An embassage from myself. *You* shall go, Abbot Augustine. And friend Dubhsith with you. I shall send you in one of my ships, with an escort . . ."

"But—my lord King! No, no—not me, I pray you!" the Abbot exclaimed. "I am too old for such travel . . ."

"Nonsense, man! My ship will carry you from door to door. The Abbey of Derry is on Lough Foyle, a sea-loch. It has to be you, to speak of Iona with Flaithbertach. Saor MacNeil, my chamberlain of Argyll, will accompany you, to speak with the High King, if necessary. It will be a pleasure for you, just. To see Columba's old abbey of Derry . . ."

"Visitors!" a voice said, behind them. Gillecolm, ever keen-eyed, was pointing. "A galley and a longship."

They all turned to look. A couple of vessels were beating up the narrow sound between Iona and great Mull, obviously making for the sheltered landing-place at St. Ronan's Bay. The longship's sail bore Somerled's own device. The other craft flew a large banner.

"Can you see what banner is that?" Somerled demanded.

"It is red and white. A white lion, on red."

"Ha—that is Ross! Now, what? Could it be my good sister . . .?"

It was not the Countess of Ross who landed from the galley, under Conn MacMahon's escort, but her husband the Earl Malcolm. And he came grim-faced.

The brothers-in-law had not seen each other for years. Malcolm was looking a deal older—no doubt Somerled was also, but not to the same extent, for he remained very fit, active and vigorous for his fifty-odd years. They eyed each other uncertainly, Malcolm perhaps a little uneasy over his welcome, Somerled fearing trouble, for the earl never seemed to be the bearer of good news.

"You are alone, Malcolm?" the latter asked, after greetings. "Bethoc—she is not with you? Nor Donald?"

"I left Bethoc at Urquhart. She is less than well. Captivity has told on her—as on us all. And Donald is prisoner again. In Stirling Castle this time, not in Rook's Burgh. In worse state, God damn them!"

"But—he was to be freed, pardoned. They both were."

"Aye—but only to be retaken. No doubt my wife also would have been held again, but she came straight north to me in Moray. Donald lingered in the south, foolishly, and was seized."

"In Heaven's name—why? I bargained for his liberty."

"Your bargain was but a poor one, then! To bargain with the Normans is a profitless folly!"

"I did not bargain with the Normans. I bargained with the High King of Scots."

"It is not different. He is a weak fool and is wholly in their hands."

Somerled clenched his fists.

"There is more than that—a deal more. Malcolm has given his sister Ada in marriage to Florence, Count of Holland. And for dowry has given the earldom of Ross— *my* earldom!"

The other stared. "Lord—that cannot be true! He could not do that. Give away your earldom—one of the ancient Celtic lesser kingdoms of Scotland. To the Hollander."

"He has done it. He has declared it forfeit to the crown, and myself with it; and vested it in his sister, as marriage portion. Now he drives out all the chiefs and lairds and landed men of Mar and Moray and Ross, replacing them with Normans and Flemings."

"Is the man run crazy-mad?"

"They say that he is determined to break the North. Or his Normans are. To pull down all the Celtic earldoms. And so starts with mine."

"This is beyond all belief! What has come over him? When I spoke with him two Yules back nothing was said of this. We were in agreement. I was to aid him against Henry of England, as indeed I did, the next Easter, when I sailed my ships to the Cumbrian coast . . ."

"Henry! He has come to terms with Henry—is now in Henry's pocket, in fact. He has sworn to be his man. Has renounced all Scotland's claims to Cumbria and Northumbria . . ."

"But why? Why?"

"I know not. He had a secret meeting with Henry early this year. This damnable treachery is the result."

"You are sure of all this, Malcolm? It is not mere tales and hearsay?"

"It is all true. And here is more truth for you, Somerled. Henry Plantagenet has received your wife's brother, Godfrey the Black, at his court, after some treachery in Norway. Received him with honour, making much of him. Hails him as King of Man, and *his* vassal. Has even had made for him a costly suit-of-armour—horse-armour also. And a charger to carry him. He has promised to aid Godfrey to recover Man—and Malcolm has agreed to aid in this."

"Precious Soul of God!"

The Iona project was distinctly overshadowed after that. The clerical deputation was still to go to Ireland to try to coax back Abbot Flaithbertach. But Saor MacNeil's remit was much widened. He was to approach the High King Muirchertach, and such lesser kings and leaders as he could contact, to warn them that the warlike Henry Plantagenet was becoming dangerous indeed to the Celtic polity. If he could contemplate taking over Scotland and Man, Ireland also would not be beyond his ambitions, that was scarcely to be doubted. It behoved the Celtic peoples to unite against the threat. In the event of war, major war, could Somerled of the Isles rely on aid from Ireland? He would need it, against England and Scotland both.

Back at Islay a few days later he found a courier awaiting him from Malcolm, King of Scots. The letter he bore was brief and to the point, wishing him well but requiring Somerled of Argyll and the Isles to resign all his lands, territories and titles to himself, as High King, preparatory to having them all re-issued in vassalage and fealty. This forthwith and by order, on pain of direst penalties.

CHAPTER 23

Undoubtedly it was by far the greatest fleet ever to sail out of the Sea of the Hebrides and into the Firth of Clyde. Somerled could not restrain a surge of pride and even emotion as he counted no fewer than one-hundred-and-sixty vessels, longships and galleys, as Gillecolm held the dragon-ship steady against tide and currents whilst they all turned the mighty thrusting headland of the Mull of Kintyre and into the more sheltered waters of the firth. The great majority were his own, of course, but there were over thirty from Man and almost as many from Ireland. And there was no subterfuge nor pretence here, all the ships were packed with fighting-men, a vast army of nearly twenty thousand. All would be required no doubt—but it made a heartening sight for the only man who could have assembled such a force out of the Celtic lands.

As, safely past the dangerous cape, the armada headed eastwards to pass the southern tip of Arran, Somerled's vessel swept on again with clanging gong and flashing oars, to put itself at the head once more. There were three other dragon-ships there now, besides Saor's, one flying the banner of Dougal, King of Man, one that of Ranald, Lord of Moidart, his brother, the third that of the MacMahon, Conn's chief from Fermanagh, in command of the Irish contingent. He was Somerled's first wife's brother and uncle to Gillecolm.

In fine style they turned north round Arran and beat up firth, to pass between the Isle of Bute and the Cumbraes. All eyes tended to be on the mainland coast on their right, only some three miles off, the Stewartry of Renfrew and Cunninghame, the territory of Walter the High Steward, foremost of the Normans in Scotland, which must be their first target. But not yet, unfortunately.

Dumbarton was the present destination, where the firth

took its dog's-leg bend eastwards and suddenly narrowed, Dumbarton with its great rock crowned by the ancient Pictish fort, capital of Strathclyde. Here there was a fine sheltered anchorage, fit to take their huge fleet; and here Somerled had arranged a rendezvous with the Earl Malcolm and an army to be raised by the northern earls. The place was on the wrong side of the firth for their purposes, but that could not be helped.

Dumbarton received them only doubtfully, very naturally, most of the folk fleeing from their homes into the hilly lands behind the town. Somerled gave strict orders however that since this was to be their base there was to be no trouble, no harassment of the population. There was no sign of the earls' army as yet. This day, the Eve of St. Blane, and the next, had been agreed for the rendezvous.

They waited three days for the northern force, Somerled fretting—for of course their arrival at Dumbarton was all too obvious from the other, Renfrew, shore and all this delay would be giving time for a defensive host to muster and position itself. The High Steward's main castle was at Renfrew town itself, some ten miles up Clyde. Somerled's scouting parties informed him that there was much activity thereabouts, men assembling all the time, marching, training.

When, a few weeks before, Somerled had heard that King Malcolm Maiden was lying dangerously ill at Doncaster in Yorkshire, where he had gone at King Henry's imperious command to deliver his younger brother David as hostage for Scotland's good conduct, he had decided that this was the time to venture all in an attempt to bring Scotland under better government and to make an end of the Norman— and now English—control. The ruling party would be in some confusion, with the King away and said to be like to die, and with so many of the nobles and their sons gone with him—for Henry had demanded not only the Prince David as hostage but the sons and heirs of most of the Norman-Scots nobility also, for good measure; presumably he did not trust his new vassals, and with reason. So if ever there was to be a major assault on mainland Scotland, to put Malcolm of Ross or his son Donald on the throne of their forefathers, this was the time. It had all taken a while to mount, of course, with men and shipping to be brought from far and near, and weeks had passed, inevitably. King Malcolm might be dead by now—or recovered and possibly even back in Scotland; Somerled had had no recent news. But every day's delay now could have serious consequences and this waiting for the northern earls was galling.

On that third day, Somerled decided that he could wait no longer. He would commence the necessarily protracted business of ferrying his army across Clyde, and hope that the missing reinforcements would arrive during the process. The firth was a mere mile wide at this point, and it was a temptation just to carry his people over this short distance and land them on the opposite shore at Langbank where there was a boat-strand which they could see. But Somerled decided that, although this would greatly simplify the ferrying, it might well be inadvisable. The land on the south side of Clyde was fairly flat, fertile tilth and pasture for many miles, open and ideal ground for cavalry tactics, And, of course, heavy, armoured cavalry was the Norman speciality, with archery, in warfare; whereas Somerled's host, brought by ship, was without horses. It might be foolish, therefore, to offer the enemy a possible battlefield conditioned in their favour. Somerled could choose to land where he would. Up near Renfrew town itself the terrain was different, still flat but marshy, broken up by the Black and White Cart rivers which entered Clyde there, and their tributary burns and ditches, with actual islands formed— which indeed was why the Steward's castle was built there, on one of the islands, a strong defensive position which could not be assailed readily. Somerled had no intention of attacking Renfrew Castle itself, but if he could lure the Steward's people into fighting in the surrounding marshland, their advantage in cavalry would be negatived and their heavily-armoured knights likewise.

His scouts were sent prospecting, from fishing-boats, and informed him that there was a variety of fairly suitable sites to make a landing in the area west of Renfrew town; so, that third day, Somerled took to a small local boat and went up-river, to decide for himself. He had little difficulty in selecting the best place for his purposes, with a large army to land, especially in darkness, as he planned. The area was between Erskine and the larger of the mud-and-sand islands, which the fishermen called Newshot, about a couple of miles west of Renfrew Castle. There was here a reasonably firm strand for the landings, almost a mile of it, and level, wet-looking land behind, only roughly drained by stanks and ditches. Although unpleasant for fighting in, it would at least be less hard on Somerled's lightly-armed fighting-men than on armoured knights.

So, as the dusk settled on the land, the move from Dumbarton began. It had to be very carefully carried out, for the Clyde narrowed notably after about six more miles, and negotiating the remaining three or so in darkness would demand skill and caution, for the navigable channel was very restricted and fringed with mud-banks on which the longships could all too easily run aground. In these conditions the minimum number of ships was indicated, since they could not risk two sailing abreast, also the most skilful shipmasters, with local fishermen as pilots. So each vessel used had to be loaded with the maximum number of men, and to be rowed well spaced-out. The same ships would return for further loads.

Somerled went with the first batch. It was a fairly dark night, threatening rain—which was good for their secrecy but bad for navigation, making the selected landing-places difficult to locate, with landmarks non-existent. However, with almost a mile to choose from, with positions of varying suitability, the landings were effected, not without some confusion but with no disasters. At least there was no opposition. Leaving his lieutenants to supervise further disembarkation, he took Saor to go probing inland, rousing protesting curlews and peewits, to prospect for camping sites on firm ground.

After much circling, back-tracking and ploutering through mire and bog, stampeding shadowy splattering cattle, they found a slightly elevated area around a farmery which one of the local guides named as Bargarran. They were fortunate in having the co-operation of many local fishermen—but of course these were Celtic folk also, with no love for the Normans.

So a line was plotted out through and around the pools and runnels and mires, from the landing-place to this chosen area, and thereafter the long and trying process of leading the gathering army from one to the other commenced, this whilst the selected longships ferried back and forth from Dumbarton with fresh loads.

By grey dawn the task was almost completed and by sunrise a vast encampment spread itself over the Bargarran pastures and meadows, seething like a cluster of ant-hills, busy, colourful, all banners, tartans and glinting steel—and all in plainest view of the town and castle of Renfrew, a mere two miles away, where another army was assembling, although not quite so evidently, in the built-up area. Up and down the Clyde, meantime, the entire Isles fleet sailed and rowed in a mighty show of naval strength.

Somerled waited, now—indeed he slept in his sail-cloth tent.

They waited, not so much for the missing Celtic earls, who still had not appeared, as for reasons of tactics. Somerled's immediate purpose was to engage and defeat any mainland army which might oppose him—and which here, presumably, would be under the command of the High Steward himself, on his own doorstep. He had scores to settle with Walter fitz Alan. He was not at present concerned with winning territory or capturing towns and castles. And undoubtedly if he could coax the enemy into these marshes and muddy flats, he was much more likely to defeat them than on higher and firmer ground—and if by any chance he lost the fight and failed in his efforts, his ships were waiting there to evacuate his people. Admittedly the Steward would be able to perceive all this also, and therefore be reluctant to commit his troops and heavy chivalry to such an unrewarding battle-ground; but Somerled was confident that he would, eventually, relying on his conviction that the proud Norman would not be able to resist the challenge there so blatantly under his very nose, of what he would no doubt describe as a barbarian rabble come to sit in his private lordship below the windows of his castle. It would be very hard for a great lord and commander to remain inactive in these circumstances, before his own army and townsfolk, especially such arrogant conquerors as the Norman leadership, assured of their own military superiority. The Steward would not be able to wait for very long,

Somerled calculated—whereas *he* could wait, now, more or less indefinitely, expecting his reinforcements. Feeding his great host would be his major problem, but these lush meadows and pastures were strewn with cattle, and already much of the Bargarran stock was roasting on spits over the camp-fires.

So Somerled waited, and slept.

Gillecolm wakened him in the early afternoon. A deputation was approaching from the direction of Renfrew, under a white flag and the gold, blue and white banner of the Steward.

It was not Walter fitz Alan himself who came but a party of young Norman knights in splendid armour and heraldic bearings, finely mounted—although they had to dismount and clankingly lead their beasts before they could win through the soft ground to where Somerled awaited them, which much spoiled the impression. There also proved to be a couple of clerics with the group, in rich robes.

Their spokesman introduced himself as Raoul de Carteret, principal esquire to Walter, High Steward of Scotland and Lord of Renfrew and Cunninghame. He also indicated that one of the clerics was Herbert, Bishop of Glasgow. The Lord High Steward had sent them to enquire who it was who came thus with so great a host of armed men to his peaceful domains, and why?

"I think that your master the Steward knows very well who has come," Somerled answered. "Who else could land a score of thousand fighting-men anywhere he chose on the Scottish coast but the King of Argyll and the Isles—with the aid of his son, the King of Man, to be sure? I do not doubt that the Steward knows why, also. I am here because King Malcolm, on the advice I would guess of the Steward and his ilk, has broken his word to me and mine, threatened me, and demanded my attendance in vassalage. I attend—but not in vassalage!"

De Carteret glanced at his companions. "Whilst not accepting such statements, my lord King Somerled, I am to ask what is your intention here? What do you want?"

"That, sir, is simply told. I am come to right a great wrong. Not only to myself and my kin but to this ancient realm of Scotland. King Malcolm, by making himself vassal to King Henry of England, has betrayed his own kingdom and nation and forfeited all right to the position of High King of Scots. I have come to put a better man, of the ancient and indeed more senior line, on the throne he has betrayed. That is all. Is it sufficient?"

There was an appalled silence. It was the Bishop who broke it.

"You . . . you speak the words of a madman—of a shameless heretic! How dare you to threaten the Lord's Anointed!"

"I dare, clerk—oh, I dare! If the Lord's Anointed betrays his people and his coronation oath, then he must needs expect more than threats."

"Watch your words, sir, I charge you—if you do not want God Almighty to strike you down where you stand! Scoffer, savage, spoiler of the innocent, enemy of Christ's Holy Church!"

"All that, Priest? I scarce recognise myself!"

"Do not think to mock me, miscreant! You vaunt yourself—but the power from on high will bring you low, that I promise you! You, who have ravaged and defiled the lands and people of my see of Glasgow."

"Defiled? I had occasion, once, if I mind aright, to punish certain ill-conditioned folk from your Glasgow who were raiding my lands of Bute and Arran. Is it that to which you refer?"

"Think not to hide your shame behind such hypocrisy, sirrah!" The elderly prelate was quivering in red-faced choler. "You, or yours, came from your outlandish islands to Glasgow, the holy burgh of St. Kentigern, and wasted its substance, assaulted its godly citizenry, sullied its sanctity and proclaimed that your heretical and barbarous faith was superior to that of the one true Holy, Catholic and Apostolic Church of Rome . . ."

"Scarcely superior, Priest, only more ancient, more in accord with the Gospels and more native to this land. After all, your Kentigern was a saint of the *Celtic* Church, was he not?"

"I charge you, do not utter that blessed name from your idolatrous lips, wretch! Or Almighty God and all His saints will assuredly punish you—this I swear! I have called upon

375

the Blessed St. Kentigern, from before the High Altar, to avenge the injury done to his beloved shrine and foundation. And he will, Somerled the Impious—he will . . .!"

De Carteret coughed. "My lord Bishop's, h'm, intervention is understandable," he said. "But we are here in the name of the High Steward. To enquire your purpose, King Somerled. And to express his concern at the large numbers of your company come landed unbidden on his soil . . ."

"Also to spy out my situation and dispositions, I think?" That was quite pleasantly added.

"M'mm. You mistake, my lord. The Steward invites you to come speak with him. So that it may be that any differences between you can be resolved in peaceable fashion . . ."

"That is . . . judicious of the Steward! But, if he wishes speech with me, why send you, sir, and this bishop, to talk? To the King of Argyll and the Isles. Why did he not come, himself? He has known me, after all, these many years."

"I . . . ah, that is not for me to say, sir. No doubt my lord had his reasons. I am but his esquire and servant . . ."

"Precisely! Should I send my cup-bearer or sagaman to speak with the High Steward? Tell him that if he comes, I shall be pleased to talk with him—but that I scarcely see talking as any answer to my purposes! And tell him that if he waits until tomorrow, he will also have the Earls of Ross, Strathearn, Fife, Angus, Mar and Buchan to talk with—to his further guidance!"

Eyebrows rose at that. "I shall tell my lord so," the Norman said thickly.

"Do that. I shall await his reply." Somerled turned away.

The deputation, less assured-seeming than when they had come, retraced their winding steps through the marshland, Bishop Herbert still muttering anathemas.

"Why tell them that the earls would be here—when they may not, a curse on them?" Saor MacNeil asked.

"To try to make the Steward attack before they come. And before he may be fully ready. Attack us here, where we have chosen the ground. The sooner we have this battle, the better for us, I think."

"Aye, perhaps. Those young Normans were peering, searching-out, spying the land and our numbers and quality, all the time that you were talking."

"I know it. That is why they were here. And why that bishop was given so long to rant. I wonder what Walter fitz Alan will do?"

"He can scarcely mount an attack before nightfall, now."

"He will not attack in the darkness, I swear. To put his heavy cavalry and armour into this soft ground at night would be folly. Above all, they must see where they are going or they will be hopelessly bogged. And his archers need light to see their targets. He will attack at first light, I think. But likely that one will try to lure and lull us into unreadiness, carelessness, first. Send some message, perhaps, to make us believe that there is no danger for the moment . . ."

Unreadiness, then, was the last thing to be looked for in the Isles host thereafter. Somerled spent the rest of that day, with no further visitors from Renfrew, prospecting every stretch and aspect of that difficult and wide-scattered watery terrain, seeking to position his forces to take advantage of every pool, ditch, mere and swamp, in mutual support and effective defence; for it must be a defensive battle, in the first instance, to lead, hopefully, to something much more aggressive. The aim was to founder this first mainland army in the bogs, to frustrate and depress it and so dispel the myth of Norman invincibility; and thereafter to strike on inland, southwards, through Cunninghame, Kyle and Carrick, but always keeping sufficiently close to the coast to remain in touch with the fleet, to eventually link up with the Celtic Galloway forces. Fergus had died three years earlier, immured in Holyrood Abbey, and the new Earl Uhtred was a very different character, who needed leading. Somerled intended to lead, there, and take advantage—for, however unruly and savage, the Gallowegians were magnificent fighters and implacable in their hatred of the Normans, impatient now with Uhtred's lack of initiative. Then, with all the South-West in his hands and the North risen again in revolt, he would turn on the South-East, the Norman base-area, it was to be hoped himself now with the reputation of invincibility. But, first, the Norman armoured military might must be shown to be vulnerable.

By nightfall, then, the Isles host was spread far and wide over those Renfrew marshes in a formation which, on the face of it, looked like no formation at all, indeed a scattered confusion and reckless squandering of strength and resources. In fact it was a most careful exploitation of the strange terrain, with every apparently isolated unit in a position to back up its neighbour or to cut off its attacker, every re-entrant in the wetlands a trap, every spine of firmer ground ripe for ambush, every flank protected. Somerled intended to swallow up the Steward and all his proud chivalry on his own doorstep. He gave Dougal his first command in the field, the left wing based on the Clyde itself, so that in the event of disaster he could retire to the shipping; Saor and the MacMahon took the right, necessarily the most hazardous and furthest from possible rescue; whilst he himself commanded the vital centre, at Bargarran. From Dougal's far left to Saor's extreme right there could have been as much as three muddy, meandering miles. From whatever direction or angle the Steward might choose to attack, he would not find an exploitable gap in that curious front.

Orders were explicit. Although attack during darkness was not anticipated there must be no reliance on that. Sentries and guards were to be posted and kept on the alert along the entire front all night, no camp-fires were to be lit, no lights shown. Direct communication with the centre was to be maintained throughout by all commanders.

It was not far off midnight when Somerled and Gillecolm finished their final tour of examination of all positions and returned to their sail-cloth tent, satisfied that nothing more could be done, meantime. They would snatch an hour or two's sleep, but first they would have a bite of oaten bannock and a mouthful of wine. Somerled called his cup-bearer, young Murdo MacIan, Cathula's nephew, who sleepily brought the refreshment, in the darkness—for the King would be the last to contravene his own orders about no lights.

However, before they were finished the youth was back, to announce that there were in fact lights showing, out in the marshland, in the general direction of Renfrew, moving lights. Somerled went to look, at the tent-door. There were indeed winking yellow lights out there, perhaps half-a-dozen of them, all fairly close together and fairly evidently moving towards Bargarran, however slowly and spasmodically.

"It seems that we may have visitors," he commented. "Their purpose at this hour, who can tell? They may be of no note or significance. Only if they are, bring them to me. I require to sleep . . ."

Gillecolm was already asleep and his father almost so when young MacIan re-entered the tent, a gleam of light behind him.

"Messengers, my lord King," he declared. "From the Normans. From this Steward, they say."

"So! Have them in, then."

Three somewhat mud-spattered individuals were ushered in, bringing a lamp with them. Two Somerled recognised from the previous afternoon visit, although de Carteret was not one of them.

"You are abroad late," Somerled greeted them. "What brings you here at this hour?"

"We have a message for you, Sir King, from the High Steward," one said. "A letter."

"Ah—the Steward chooses a strange time to send his letter. It must be important?"

"Most urgent, my lord." The speaker held out a folded and sealed paper.

Somerled, still sitting on his couch, took it and broke the seal, to spread out the paper. "Bring the lamp closer," he directed.

The man with the light, who looked like a servant, standing a little way behind the other two, came forward—and doing so, seemed to trip and stagger. Flinging out his arm to recover balance, he dropped the lamp, which overturned. The flame was extinguished. The man cursed briefly.

"Fool! Clumsy oaf!" the spokesman exclaimed. "You, page—go bring in another lamp." The glow of light from the door showed that there were more of the lamps lit out there.

MacIan turned and went out.

"What is to do?" Gillecolm, awakened no doubt by the falling lamp, asked, sleepy-voiced.

"It is a letter. From the Steward. They bring more light . . ."

Those were the last words ever spoken by Somerled MacFergus, in this life at least. The scrape of steel stilled them, as dirks were drawn. The first two visitors launched themselves upon the sitting man, daggers plunging, whilst he who had dropped the lamp flung himself on the recumbent Gillecolm. Not much light filtered into that tent but enough for expert assassins to do their work. Father and son, scale-armour laid aside for the night and clad only in their shirts, died together, hearts pierced by many accurate stabs. Only a gasp and groan or two sounded, as their faces were swiftly, efficiently muffled by cloaks.

"A good night to you, my lord King," the spokesman said, quite loudly although his voice was uneven. "Have we your leave to go?"

Out into the night the three men pushed, dirks hidden now. Young MacIan seemed to be having difficulty in persuading one of the other lamp-carriers to give up his light.

"You will not need that now, page," the spokesman declared, the only man who had uttered throughout, save for that curse from the lamp-dropper. "Your king has the message. He will now sleep. You are to escort us past the guards, on our way back . . ."

The youth, and two of the sentries, went with the deputation as far as the edge of the marshland and then turned back.

They did not notice, therefore, although others did, that oddly the visitors extinguished all their lamps almost immediately thereafter, to proceed through that miry wilderness in darkness.

*   *   *

As Somerled had predicted, the Normans attacked at first light—by which time the Isles army was in a state of complete confusion and disarray, with the word that their lord was dead borne from mouth to mouth, from unit to unit. Saor and Dougal took charge, after a fashion, but both were really more concerned with getting Somerled's and Gillecolm's bodies back to the ships, and thereafter extricating the army from its extended position, than in giving battle. There was some fighting, inevitably, but mainly as a rearguard action,

380

as the Isles host withdrew to the Clyde, none having any heart to continue with the campaign. Some casualties were sustained but not many—although the Steward and Bishop thereafter claimed it all as a great victory and God's judgement on apostates, heretics and traitors. The Normans, of course, found the terrain almost impossible to fight over, and most of the Islesmen's casualties were inflicted by the arrows of the dreaded bowmen.

With no sign of the northern earls back at Dumbarton, the great fleet turned and sailed whence it had come, sorrowing.

Young MacIan, the cup-bearer, did not sail home with the rest. The word had got swiftly round that he had failed his master and was blameworthy. His body was found, stabbed also, before the embarkation. Curiously enough the real assassins found it convenient to adopt a similar line, and it became the accepted version in mainland Scotland that Somerled and his son had been slain by their own servant, although they called him page.

HISTORICAL NOTE

Just who was responsible for the assassination of Somerled and his son has never been established; none of course suggested that either the High Steward or the Bishop of Glasgow had anything to do with it, however joyful they were at the result. The bodies were buried at Saddell Abbey, where Somerled's tomb is pointed out to this day.

The kingdom of Argyll and the Isles, although never conquered, did not long survive the death of its creator. It was divided up between Somerled's surviving sons, into three great lordships, under Dougal, Ranald and Angus who all called themselves kings but were scarcely that. Dougal, who never had much real interest in Man, took Lorn, Mull, Jura and lesser isles; and from him is descended the Clan MacDougall. Ranald got Kintyre and Islay; he it was who changed the Abbey of Saddel into a Cistercian monastery later that 12th century; it would be nice to say that the Clanranald descended from him, and it did, in fact, but took its name from a much later Ranald; however, his son, Donald of Islay, gave *his* name to the great clan of MacDonald. Angus, Somerled's third surviving son, got Bute, Arran and lands to the north, and although he no doubt left progeny, no clan, so far as I know, takes its name from him. Clan Donald it was which carried on the designation "of the Isles", and which played so vital a role in Scotland's story.

History is silent, as so often in the affairs of women, as to what happened to Ragnhilde thereafter. Probably she passed her widowhood at Finlaggan on Islay.

Her brother Godfrey the Black in due course won back Man, as Henry of England's vassal, and reigned for many years, oppressive and unpopular to the end. Malcolm, Earl of Ross, died four years after his brother-in-law, ineffective as always; and his son Donald is heard of no more, so presumably died in captivity. Other MacEths, however, although they never achieved the Scots crown, did found the Clan Mackay.

King Malcolm the Fourth did not die at Doncaster but survived till the following year, dying at the age of twenty-four, one of Scotland's most ineffective monarchs. He was succeeded by his brother William, who despite his accepted style of William the Lion, was not much more lionlike than Malcolm the Maiden, getting that by-name because he it was who adopted the Lion Rampant as the Scottish royal heraldic emblem, instead of the boar. Fortunately his grandson, Alexander the Third, was a great improvement and put Scotland back on its feet.

It is perhaps odd that their descendant today, via the Stewarts of course, should bear as subsidiary titles to Prince of Wales, that of Lord of the Isles, High Steward of Scotland and Baron Renfrew.